platinum bible of the public toilet

Sinotheory A series edited by
Carlos Rojas & Eileen Cheng-yin Chow

PLATINUM BIBLE OF THE PUBLIC TOILET

ten queer stories

edited by

Petrus Liu &
Lisa Rofel

Cui Zi'en

Duke University Press Durham & London 2024

Printed in the United States of America on acid-free paper ∞
Project Editor: Ihsan Taylor | Designed by Aimee C. Harrison
Typeset in Portrait Text and Helvetica Neue LT Std,
by Westchester Publishing Services

Library of Congress Cataloging-in-Publication Data
Names: Cui, Zien, author. | Liu, Petrus, editor, translator. | Rofel, Lisa, [date] editor, translator.
Title: Platinum bible of the public toilet : ten queer stories / Cui Zi'en ; edited by Petrus Liu and Lisa Rofel.
Other titles: Sinotheory.
Description: Durham : Duke University Press, 2024. |
Series: Sinotheory | Includes bibliographical references.
Identifiers: LCCN 2023025138 (print)
LCCN 2023025139 (ebook)
ISBN 9781478024880 (hardcover)
ISBN 9781478030065 (paperback)
ISBN 9781478059066 (ebook)
Subjects: LCSH: Chinese fiction—20th century—Translations into English. | Chinese fiction—21st century—Translations into English. | BISAC: FICTION / Short Stories (single author) | FICTION / World Literature / China / 21st Century | LCGFT: Short stories.
Classification: LCC PL2854.5.U39 A2 2024 (print) | LCC PL2854.5.U39 (ebook) | DDC 895.13/6—dc23/eng/20231103
LC record available at https://lccn.loc.gov/2023025138
LC ebook record available at https://lccn.loc.gov/2023025139

Cover art: Still from Cui Zi'en's *Refrain*, 2006. Courtesy of Cui Zi'en.

Contents

Series Editor's Introduction
vii
Carlos Rojas

Editors' Introduction
xi
Petrus Liu & **Lisa Rofel**

Preface
xxiii
Translated by **Petrus Liu**

Uncle's Elegant Life
(舅舅的人间烟火)
1
Translated by **Lisa Rofel**

Intrigue like Fireworks
(奸情如焰火)
10
Translated by **Fran Martin**

Some Admire Wisdom,
Others Do Not
(有人赞美聪慧，有人则不)
20
Translated by **Derek Hird**

Orphans of the Japanese Empire
(日本遗民)
45
Translated by
Elisabeth Lund Engebretsen

The Silent Advent of
the Age of Sexual Persuasion
(言性时代悄然莅临)
71
Translated by **Petrus Liu**

Men Men Men
Women Women Women
(男男男女女女)
82
Translated by **Yizhou Guo**

Men Are Containers
(男人是容器)
117
Translated by
Casey James Miller

Fire and Wolf Share
a Fondness for Male Beauty
(老火和老狼同好男色)
129
Translated by **Yizhou Guo**

Teacher Eats Biscuits
Thin as Parchment
(老师吃饼薄如纸)
141
Translated by **William F. Schroeder**

Platinum Bible of the Public Toilet
(公厕白金宝典)
153
Translated by **Wenqing Kang**
& **Cathryn H. Clayton**

Interview with Cui Zi'en
257
Petrus Liu & **Lisa Rofel**

Appendix:
Works by Cui Zi'en
273

Bibliography
279

Contributors
283

Place of First Publication
285

Series Editor's Introduction

Carlos Rojas

I first met Cui Zi'en twenty years ago, when I drove him from Manhattan, where New York University had just organized a mini film festival of his early work, to Cambridge, where Harvard was doing the same. This trip occurred near the beginning of Cui's cinematic career. Although he is currently best known for the provocatively queer-themed films that he began directing in the early 2000s while a professor at the Beijing Film Academy, he first attracted international attention as a queer activist in the 1990s, when he began writing prolifically as both a scholar and a creative author.

Cui's directorial debut, *Enter the Clowns* (2002), opens with a now-infamous sequence in which a young man named Xiao Bo (played by Yu Bo) is speaking to his parent (played by Cui Zi'en himself). The parent—who was originally Xiao Bo's father but has begun identifying as a woman—is on their deathbed, and after a discussion about funeral arrangements and other practical matters, the parent tells Xiao Bo that they would like for him to "see me off with your milk." After realizing that his parent is asking to perform oral sex on him, Xiao Bo briefly hesitates, but then, as a filial son, he accedes to his parent's dying wish. The remainder of the film features several linked vignettes that include two more plotlines involving trans characters, a rape and a revenge rape, several shots of a crowd praying in a cathedral, and a lengthy Christian-style confession. Viewed two decades after its initial debut, the film may strike some as simultaneously prescient and retrograde. On the one hand, the work's multifaceted exploration of trans issues engages with a topic that is much more widely accepted today than it was in the early 2000s; even when the film depicts what are arguably transphobic reactions, it does so in a nuanced manner. On the other hand, because of the #MeToo movement and other recent developments, there is now greater attention to issues of consent, and the film's two rape scenes may sit uncomfortably for many contemporary viewers. It should also be acknowledged, however, that when the novella on which the film is based was first published in China in 1997, these trans themes and rape scenes incited considerable discussion and debate.

Enter the Clowns succinctly captures many of the tensions that animate Cui's cinematic work—including a fascination with the relationships between gender and sexuality, transgression and intimacy, sexuality and religion. Even as the film anticipates some of the themes that will come to define Cui's cinematic oeuvre, it offers a poignant reminder of his long-standing commitment to fiction and scriptwriting. Not only is the film loosely based on a homonymous novella Cui published four years earlier, it also contains two notable sequences in which characters read aloud from Cui's own fictional works. In one sequence, a couple of characters, outfitted as though performing a radio broadcast, read from a script that announces the launch of a new broadcast program titled *Ladies' Lavatory Anthropology*, about an anthropological analysis of the difficulties that women in China encounter in trying to find public bathrooms. In the other sequence, Xiao Bo reads aloud a science fiction story written in the voice of an extraterrestrial angel. Each of these sequences occupies a structurally significant position within the film itself: the first reading begins at minute thirty-eight, almost precisely halfway through the seventy-seven-minute film; the second appears in the film's final shot. Together, these two readings account for six full minutes of screen time, or almost 10 percent of the film's total length. While they have not received as much public attention as some of the other aspects of the film, they are nevertheless clearly central to the film's conception, and they reflect Cui's continued commitment to fiction writing even as he was launching his career as a director.

Although most of Cui Zi'en's films are available with English subtitles, this volume is the first book-length collection of his fiction in English translation. The volume includes translations of nine stories and one novella selected by Cui himself. Readers already familiar with Cui's filmography will find most of these stories to be significantly less speculative and transgressive than his films. Rather than detailing scenarios involving extraterrestrials and quasi-incestuous encounters, most of the stories feature recollections of childhood explorations of gender and sexuality. The works are narrated in a matter-of-fact tone that underscores the inherent normality of the assorted nonheteronormative scenarios that the protagonists observe or experience.

All but one of the works are appearing here in English for the first time and were commissioned specifically for this volume.

The translation process is a useful and necessary mechanism for making Cui's fictional work available to English-language readers, and at a structural level it also reflects several of the qualities that distinguish Cui's creative output itself. For instance, just as Cui's works are characterized by a combination of intimacy and alienation, quotidianity and transgression, translation similarly involves a careful balance of domestication and foreignization. On the one hand, the process of domestication aims to minimize the visibility of the translation process and to produce a text that reads comfortably. But it does so by forcibly coupling the source and target languages and hiding the resulting linguistic violence beneath a veneer of smooth readability. On the other hand, the process of foreignization involves preserving the underlying gaps and incommensurabilities that necessarily exist between the two languages. Although the result may appear rather jarring and alienating, it affirms the independence and autonomy of each language. Many of Cui's works explore a similar set of issues with respect to both the relationships between individual characters (which are often characterized by a combination of desire and alienation) and the relationship between the works' conceptual concerns and the presumed sensibilities of Cui's viewers and readers. Thus the works are frequently characterized by a combination of veritably transgressive and utterly mundane elements, even as the transgressive aspects are simultaneously intended to help normalize a set of marginalized queer practices and subjectivities, and conversely the putatively mundane segments frequently have a startling impact by virtue of the broader context in which they appear.

There has recently been a surge of interest in Cui Zi'en's work, with the almost concurrent publication of several volumes with direct ties to *Enter the Clowns*. For instance, the title of Cui's directorial debut is also the title of a 2022 Chinese-language collection of interviews that Michael Berry conducted with Cui, and which translates as *Enter the Clowns: The Queer Cinema of Cui Zi'en*. The fictional text that Xiao Bo spends a full minute reading aloud in the film's final scene is a section of the novella *Pseudo-Science Fiction Stories* that appeared in the Guangzhou literary journal *Flower City* (*Hua cheng*) in 2000 (and in the film Xiao Bo is seen reading directly from that journal issue). The novella was subsequently published as a stand-alone book in January 2003 by a mainland Chinese press in Zhuhai, and in January 2023 a new edition of the novel was published by a press in Taiwan. Meanwhile, the fictional story that two characters spend five minutes reading aloud at the midpoint of *Enter the Clowns* was completed in 2000, and it would have been published in a volume of Cui's collected works a few years later had it not been rejected by China's censors. The story was eventually published in Chinese in 2017 in the queer Chinese magazine *Gay Spot* (*Dian*). It also lends its title to this collection of translations: *Platinum Bible of the Public Toilet*.

Editors' Introduction

Petrus Liu & Lisa Rofel

Cui Zi'en is China's most famous, some would say most controversial, queer filmmaker, writer, scholar, and human rights activist. *Platinum Bible of the Public Toilet* brings together for the first time for an English-language audience a collection of Cui's creative fiction translated from the Chinese. Today Cui's name is inextricably fused with the history of homosexuality in China. Reading Cui alongside milestones in legal and cultural changes in Chinese homosexuality—such as the 1997 "decriminalization" (repeal of Provision 160 of the 1979 Criminal Law) and the 2001 "depathologization" (revision of the Chinese Classification and Diagnostic Criteria of Mental Disorders, or CCMD-III)—Western commentators frequently depict Cui and his work as indexing the emergence of queer cultures in the postsocialist era.

These newly available senses of sexual subjectivity are captured by Cui Zi'en's literary craft. Born in 1958 in Harbin, a major city in China's northeast rust belt, Cui came of age as a young adult during this postsocialist period, at the tail end of the Cultural Revolution (1966–76) and the beginning of China's economic reforms in the 1980s. The 1990s witnessed the emergence of queer community building, especially after the signal 1995 UN Fourth World Conference on Women held in Beijing, which gathered together lesbians from all over China and the world. Public spaces, private salons, HIV/AIDS and safe-sex education, sex hotlines, and much more emerged in the late 1990s.[1] New forms of subjectivity through the expansion of desires—sexual, consumption, wealth accumulation—became a prominent project of both the state and ordinary citizens.

Cui has been at the center of these milestones in queer politics in China. Cui's contributions to this queer community building are numerous and well known: Cui is one of the first public figures to come out in China, first in the classroom at the Beijing Film Academy in 1991 (which resulted in the suspension of his teaching assignments) and then, nationally, on Hunan Satellite Television in 2000.[2] In 2001, the Beijing Queer Film Festival was founded by a group of Peking University students including Zhang Jiangnan and Yang Yang; Cui was invited to be the artistic director and guest curator of the event, which became a beacon of hope and sociality to many other queer-identified artists and activists (notably Shi Tou, Fan Popo, and Wei Xiaogang).[3] For raising public awareness of LGBTQ issues in China, Cui received the Felipa de Souza Human Rights Award from the International Gay and Lesbian Human Rights Commission (IGLHRC), based in San Francisco, in 2002.

Internationally, Cui is well known for pioneering an avant-garde style of depicting nonconforming genders and sexualities that has earned him the reputation of being the enfant terrible of contemporary Chinese cinema.[4] He consistently challenges both heteronormativity and the middle-class homonormativity that quickly emerged in postsocialist China once Chinese lesbians and gay men began debating the best way to be accepted into mainstream society and how to protect a proper gay identity from those who sully it. Cui's documentaries and independent digital videos are thematically transgressive, depicting subjects living at a critical distance from our imagination of what China is or ought to be today: heteronormative organizations of family and kinship and capitalist accumulation of wealth. *Night Scene* (2003) and *Feeding Boys, Ayaya* (2013), for example, are both concerned with the experiences of young men known as "money boys" (in English), rural-to-urban male sex workers who sell their sexual labor in an increasingly stratified society after the end of socialism had "smashed the iron rice bowl," the phrase in official pronouncements touting the withdrawal of guaranteed livelihoods. As Lisa Rofel has shown elsewhere, these films "playfully satirized normalized work lives" by depicting how society's "normalization techniques reduce and embed desire in a structured world of intensive labor extraction, one that produces a capitalist-inflected heteronormativity."[5] In another famously scandalous scene from *Enter the Clowns* (2002), the protagonist's father (played by Cui himself) unexpectedly becomes a woman. On her deathbed, Cui's character regrets that she never had a chance to breastfeed her son and demands to taste her son's own "milk" by sucking him off instead.

But perhaps what is even more defiant is Cui's visual style. Working on a low budget—without studio sound recording, without omniscient voice-over commentary, and often in an unscripted setting—Cui mobilizes the underground film as a political strategy to disrupt the connection between mainstream definitions of aesthetics and American-infused capital. He fortifies the visually displeasing qualities to challenge Chinese viewers' Soviet-conditioned, and now Hollywood-influenced, comfort zone and taste. Cui never allows his films to cohere into a relatable sentimental drama about gay men's struggles with familial expectations or unrequited love, as one often sees in feature films by Stanley Kwan or Ang Lee. Unlike films such as *Lan Yu* or *The Wedding Banquet,* which focus on the queer person's heroic efforts to overcome adversity in life and then offer the viewer the pleasure of catharsis, Cui does not write about queer people's tragic struggles with coming out, family pressures, discrimination, or difficulties with finding love. Instead of portraying Chinese gay men and women as victims of an unaccepting society, Cui breaks up his queer narrative with randomly inserted nonqueer, sometimes nonsensical, elements to prevent the film from relapsing into a work of voyeuristic pleasure or political vindication.[6] As viewers we are immersed in stories of desire as an unstable, contingent rhizome between people and bodies.

This political task informs Cui's literary as well as cinematic projects. Cui's texts build up the reader's expectations only to thwart them by undermining their own narrative logic and refusing closure. In the short story in this volume "Some Admire Wisdom, Others Do Not," for example, Cui engages storytelling at a metanarrative level, in which the narrator continually asks an unnamed listener about how he finds the dark stories of death and love the narrator feels the need to speak about. Reading the stories requires tolerance and even appreciation for ambiguity because the narratives can be jarring and full of dissonance. Cui deliberately interrupts the narrative at the very moment when it is about to cohere into a recognizable story about a queer person's life, desires, and struggles that would provide gratification or identification to the reader.

Given Cui's visibility as an underground queer filmmaker from China, it is no surprise that there is now a large body of Anglophone scholarship on Cui's films.[7] However, studies of Cui in North America often fail to mention his work in creative fiction. In China, Cui did not achieve his cultural influence through underground filmmaking alone. Cui is also a prolific essayist and fiction writer, having published in Chinese five novels, three collections of short stories, six volumes of cultural criticism essays, and a memoir.[8] Yet there is virtually no discussion of Cui as a fiction writer and an essayist in the Anglophone world. To date, only two translations of Cui's fictional works have appeared.[9] We hope *Platinum Bible of the Public Toilet* will augment the growing body of scholarship on Cui. This volume connects his visual and written works by showing their shared roots in Chinese and Western philosophy, history, and contemporary cultural politics. These stories reveal the capaciousness of Cui's creativity. Together, they demonstrate the value of understanding his creative journey in a more holistic way. This volume represents a writing style and a set of thematic concerns that are quite distinct from other works from contemporary China.

Historical Background

The transgressive creativity of Cui's work is best appreciated against the historical background of struggles and debates in China over questions of gender and sexuality from which he emerges.

The contentious and lively debates on the changing meanings and practices of gender and sexuality that have taken place since the 1980s, with China's turn away from Maoist socialism and its rising presence as a power in the global capitalist economy, have a longer genealogy in China's encounters with both Western colonial incursions in the nineteenth and twentieth centuries and Japanese occupation before and during World War II. While the former weakened China's own imperial system, the latter decimated the Chinese republic established in its wake. Orientalist justifications for these incursions focused on the oppression of Chinese women and male-male intimacies as signs of China's supposed inherent weakness that needed uplift from the presumptive superiority of Western civilization.[10] Chinese intellectuals engaged with these depictions as they grappled with building a culture and a nation that would throw off imperialism.

Reconfigurations of femininity, masculinity, and same-sex love thus became the grounds upon which alternative futures were imagined.[11] Social and political ruptures that wrecked China throughout the twentieth and early twenty-first centuries became questions that would continually resurface and reformulate dominant forms of gendered and sexual subjectivities, in dialogue with international feminism and theories of homosexuality.

In the first half of the twentieth century, Chinese elites—both men and women—argued that women had been subordinated by the feudal, Confucian family system and needed various modes of education and social transformation.[12] Radicals called for the end of the treatment of women as property, along with the end of capitalism.[13] As for masculinity and same-sex love between men, Chinese modernizers took up a range of positions as they engaged Western sexology as well as China's premodern history of same-sex relations. These spanned from praising intimacy between men as offering the possible means to a human utopia, while at the same time distancing themselves from the premodern hierarchies of same-sex relations (notably between an emperor and his male favorites and patron-actor relations via Peking opera), to pathologizing homosexuals for their social immorality and moreover for producing a weak masculinity that these modernizers interpreted as signifying the weakness of the nation.[14] Underlying these differences, however, was a shared emphasis on the importance of a modernized understanding of gender and sex in order to strengthen the nation.

The Chinese Communist Party (CCP) inherited these debates, emphasizing the socialist revolution's liberation of women through public labor and national economic development and the strengthening of men's manhood by getting them out of poverty, while also normalizing heterosexual family life and subordinating gender politics to that of class. Using the famous phrase "women hold up half the sky," the CCP encouraged women to understand themselves as equal to men and, at times, to strive to accomplish men's work, even as men remained the unquestioned standard. Many women experienced the enormous possibilities of stepping out of their former kinship strictures. Yet the socialist government also established an unequal gendered division of labor and gender hierarchy within the party.[15]

During the post-Mao reform period in the 1980s, denunciations of socialist politics in the name of "re-naturalizing" gender and sexual life infused debates about what China is and should become. A revisionist history of the socialist past among scholars and writers argued that Maoist socialism had deferred China's ability to reach modernity and that the cause of this deferral was the suppression of so-called natural humanity and the creation of unnatural passions and interests. These intellectuals portrayed postsocialist reforms, in contrast, as setting human nature free.[16] The debates about gender and sexuality were thus vociferous in the 1980s, as various writers sought to naturalize gender, on the one hand, and challenge the persistent gender inequalities under Maoist socialism, on the other. Both positions centered gender and sexuality as the ground upon which to once again reconfigure the nation and its sociopolitical and economic arrangements, this time through the invocation of what was presumed to be a universal human nature.[17] Those who invoked presumably natural genders decried women for having become too masculine during the socialist era, which was accompanied by the inability of men to find their true masculinity.[18] Those who focused on gender inequalities argued that the socialist government's feminism had been too narrow. They called for a renewal of feminist politics that was broader than the question of participation in public labor and that should include gender consciousness and analysis of other forms of oppression.[19]

Alongside these critiques is a reevaluation of the experiences of men who have sex with men. The commonsense assumption among scholars, activists, and media about the experiences of men who had sex with men during the socialist era in China is that it was a dark era of political repression for them, after which the post-Mao loosening of social controls led to the end of their punishment. However, as Wenqing Kang has argued, this "repressive hypothesis" fails to explain the complexities of China's sexual politics. Building on the research of China-based legal scholars Zhou Dan and Guo Xiaofei, Kang shows that the much-lauded decriminalization and depathologization of homosexuality in China (in 1997 and 2001, respectively) are mischaracterizations of the problem because homosexuality was never technically criminalized and medicalized in China to begin with. Instead, the Chinese state from the Qing (1644–1911) to the Republican (1911–49) and PRC (1949–present) periods has consistently denied the existence of homosexuals. For this reason, male same-sex relations were prosecuted under the name of "hooliganism" (*liumang zui*) or social disturbance but never under the category of homosexuality as such. The emergence of queer communities and identities in the postsocialist era represented both new forms of intimacy and new modes of surveillance, as postsocialist power engaged with neoliberalism and its associated privatizations.[20] This positive fostering of a wide range of desires means that a great deal of ambivalence persists about homoerotic desire and queer identities, an ambivalence whose gaps and fissures queer community building has been able to organize with and against.

Platinum Bible of the Public Toilet

The stories in this collection draw on Cui's own experiences growing up in Northeast China in a community of underground Christians. During his coming-of-age years, the northeast was China's rust belt, with growing industrialization based mainly in heavy industries such as military equipment, chemical, steel, and alloys production, as well as textile, apparel, and construction industries. Given its geographic location, bordering Russia and close to Japan, Northeast China had also long been home to a variety of international migrants and colonial settlers. In the case of settlers from Japan, for example, many remained after the Japanese empire was defeated at the end of World War II, especially if they had a Chinese spouse. "Orphans of the Japanese Empire" in this collection describes one such family. The socialist era lies in the background of these stories. Cui's goal is not to denounce that era's politics. Indeed, as Petrus Liu has emphasized elsewhere, Cui embraces what he considers to be the true spirit of Communist internationalism.[21] His goal in these stories is rather to demonstrate that much nonnormative life took place in that socialist period, underneath and around government strictures.

Anglophone readers of gay fiction from contemporary China sometimes expect to find images of individuals suffering from state persecution or Confucian familism on account of a repressed identity that corresponds to Western notions of homosexuality. But Cui's stories offer an expansive canvas of social subjects that are queer in a broader sense, including money boys, creepy uncles, voyeurs, exhibitionists, cross-dressers, and, in other stories that do not appear in this collection, outer space sex-crazed extraterrestrials and dinosaurs. Whereas Western, in particular Freudian-inflected, accounts of individual psychosexual formations and struggles tend to focus on the private bedroom, Cui chooses an entirely different scene for his stories to challenge and deconstruct the trappings of polite society: the public toilet.

For Cui, the public toilet is an institution that emphatically reveals the coded nature of gender. It is also the site where sexual and nonsexual functions and pleasures of the body are regulated and exchanged. In this location, the possibility of a queer revolution does not begin with the assertion of a preexisting individual identity. Rather, it involves the unlearning of the social shame that accompanies the most basic functions the body performs—defecation, urination, but also touching, feeling, giving, and receiving. They strip away our rigidified notions of what is socially appropriate and what is vulgar, what is supposed to be public or private, and what constitutes intimacy and community. Everything we have learned to hide about our sexuality, religion, or political beliefs finds an outlet in the toilet, where the body, stripped of its social artifice, reminds us of our common fragility and human needs regardless of differences in station, rank, and power. Hence the title of this volume.

The stories in *Platinum Bible of the Public Toilet* specifically address the gender and sexual discoveries of young boys coming of age, usually told from the perspective of an adult narrator looking back on his childhood. Like Cui's films, *Platinum Bible of the Public Toilet* subverts normative sexuality and kinship. The stories violate all kinds of social divisions—those separating normal and abnormal, proper and improper, homophobic and homoerotic desires and relations. "Teacher Eats Biscuits Thin as Parchment," for example, upends the taboo on teacher-student sexual relationships. Many of the stories describe someone becoming aware of his own homoerotic desires without putting a label on them. In these stories, Cui feels no need to have the "inverted" person justify his way of being. He just is. It is up to others to accept him or not. Nor are his stories about "identity." It is others' relationships to homoerotic desire and nonnormative gender presentation that are examined, which usually involves either some form of matter-of-fact acceptance or an enactment of queer desire that is then deflected. These stories, in other words, compose a form of queer theory that intervenes in attempts to assimilate nonnormative expressions and desires.

In "Uncle's Elegant Life," for example, a young boy first adores his effeminate uncle and then feels shame about him, only to recapture his adoration of the uncle when he becomes a young adult. In "The Silent Advent of the Age of Sexual Persuasion," the protagonist's singular obsession is with the size of his boyfriend's cock. Full of graphically detailed descriptions of the joy of being penetrated, this story apologizes for neither penis worship nor bottomhood. For the story's protagonist, this kind of erotic submission and penetrability is in fact a survival strategy, and he urges all bottoms to let go of the values of the old age of romantic persuasion, such as modesty, subtlety, and artifice, and replace them with exuberant appreciation of their partners' sexual organs. If "The Silent Advent of the Age of Sexual Persuasion" celebrates the pleasures of being penetrated and dominated, "Men Are Containers" offers an entirely different perspective by casting the receiving partner as the active agent in the process. Instead of thinking of sex as penetration, the story describes it as a form of enveloping and containment: the mouth, the anus, and other orifices of the body are given agency as the containers of men. This formulation reverses the conventional view of the penetrator as the active or "top" partner in a relationship while deconstructing the binarism of yin and yang and the logic of gender.

Many of these stories have the quality of a fable or allegory, presenting the reader with a challenge not to assess their "truth" quality but rather to engage their vision of a matter-of-fact nonnormative world. The structure of the narratives is usually about one or more persons enacting, viewing, and evaluating others' gender behaviors and sexual desires, both public and secret. "Intrigue like Fireworks," for example, tells a recursive tale of different generations of young boys surreptitiously watching illicit lovemaking. The stories together are about commitments to one's erotic attractions and passionate attachments, even in the face of numerous obstacles. It is not just the characters who are transgressive. Cui Zi'en is transgressive in how he allows the stories to unfold, without resolution in homonormative endings. He refuses to explain or explain away homoerotic desire or nonnormative gender behavior. Often the boys and young men are those who enact homoerotic desire but declaim they are not homosexual. All these subjects, however, are "queer" in that they do not simply enact cultural norms. Cui thus expands the notion of "queer" to encompass a wide range of nonnormative expressions. For Cui, "queerness rests on a capacity to recognize the distance between received categories and the diversity of erotic desires and modes of intimacy in human cultures."[22]

Predictably, Cui's transgressive storytelling puts him in tension with the Chinese state. After receiving the Felipa Human Rights Award from the United States in 2002, Cui was put under surveillance by the Chinese state. Yet Cui's writings also put him at odds with much of society at large, as well as with many LGBTQ projects that focus on middle-class acceptability within Chinese society, that is, homonationalism. In direct and indirect ways, Cui's works tell powerful stories about a China not well known to outsiders. These stories also give us a sense of how fast China has changed in the last thirty years, as well as what persists despite such changes.

Growing up as part of an underground Christian community and as a queer person during the height of China's socialist era formed a double closet. From an early age, Cui had to learn to conceal his faith from the Maoist state's suppression of religion, while keeping his nascent sexuality a secret from school bullies. In the foreword written specifically for this translation, Cui recounts a childhood memory of himself wearing the red scarf as a young Red Guard and the immense pride he felt in the moment. The significance of the anecdote lies in the chasm between his interior self and the only source of "pride" available to him at the time. Alienated from his religion and his sexuality, Cui could express himself only through the slogans and paraphernalia created by the state. Later, through his creative fiction, Cui began to rebel against the socialist script and reclaim an authentic self. For Cui, the socialist script was particularly problematic because it flattened the complex dimensions of the human subject into categories that he felt were false: workers, peasants, soldiers; women, men; Western imperialists or Communist liberators.

To resist the state-sanctioned narrative, he turned to many intellectual resources. He was an avid reader of classical Chinese literature, which he read in secret because many of these texts, still written in traditional Chinese characters, were banned after 1949 by the socialist government as representations of feudal values. In the university, Cui studied classical Chinese literature and later published an important study of the seventeenth-century Chinese writer Li Yu (*On Li Yu's Fiction*, 1989). Western postmodern fiction, especially the works of Italo Calvino, became a major inspiration for him. He immersed himself in an eclectic range of philosophical and theoretical works, from Confucianism, Buddhism, and Christian liberation theology to the poststructuralist writings of Gilles Deleuze and Jacques Derrida. Fueled by these ideas, Cui began publishing essays, short stories, and underground films depicting alternative, antiestablishment configurations of gender and sexuality.

The stories in this collection all address the gender and sexual transgressions that many young boys and men experience, including those who do not identify as homosexual or do not even know that term. It is about commitments to one's erotic attractions and passionate attachments, even in the face of numerous obstacles. Richly imaginative and deeply unsettling, Cui's stories are bound to challenge the readers' beliefs as much as they inspire them.

Notes

1 Liu, *Specter of Materialism*, ch. 5.
2 Cui spoke about his controversial experience at the film academy in M. Berry, *Choujiao dengchang*.
3 See Cui, *Queer China, "Comrade" China*; and Bao, *Queer Media*, ch. 6.
4 Wang, "Embodied Visions," 666.
5 Rofel, "Traffic in Money Boys," 446–47.
6 Liu, *Queer Marxism*, 48–58.
7 See, among others, C. Berry, "Sacred"; de Villiers, *Sexography*, ch. 4; Voci, *China on Video*; Leung, "Homosexuality and Queer Aesthetics,"; Robinson, *Independent Chinese Documentary*, ch. 4; Zhang, "Cui Zi'en's Night Scene"; Pickowicz, "From Yao Wenyuan to Cui Zi'en"; Wang, "Ruin Is Always a New Outcome"; Yue, "Mobile Intimacies"; Zhou, "Chinese Queer Images"; Spencer, "Ten Years"; Bao, *Queer Media*, ch. 3 and ch. 6; and Bao, *Queer Comrades*, ch. 5.
8 See the appendix for a full list of Cui's works.
9 Cui, "Endangered Species Rule!" (translated by Petrus Liu); and "Uncle's Elegant Life" (translated by Lisa Rofel).
10 Western commentators, observers, religious missionaries, capitalists, and political leaders who intervened in China used these justifications for their powerful efforts to dominate life in China. What makes these justifications orientalist, as well as being colonial, modern, Western, and imperialist, is their use of cultural stereotypes that negatively portray Chinese culture as the main source of why Western interventions are needed and appropriate.

11 They were, to borrow Gail Hershatter's succinct phrasing in *Women and China's Revolutions*, "flexible symbol[s] of social problems, national humiliation, and political transformation." Hershatter, *Women and China's Revolutions*, xiii.
12 As Tani Barlow has pointed out in *The Question of Women in Chinese Feminism*, they embraced social Darwinism and eugenicist Reason about the biocultural road to a healthy nation. Barlow, *Question of Women*.
13 See Liu, Karl, and Ko, *Birth of Chinese Feminism*.
14 See Kang, *Obsession*, 1.
15 See Evans, *Women and Sexuality*; and Liu, *Specter of Materialism*, ch. 5.
16 Rofel, *Desiring China*.
17 Rofel, *Desiring China*, 1–30.
18 Zhong, *Masculinity Besieged?*
19 Dai and Meng, *Fuchu lishi dibiao*; Dai, *Cinema and Desire*; Li, "Economic Reform."
20 Instead of a linear narrative, it is more accurate to view the 1997 decriminalization of homosexuality and the 2001 removal of the category of homosexuality from CCMD-III as secondary by-products of a broader effort to standardize the Chinese legal system and the medical profession in keeping with international standards. Kang, "Decriminalization and Depathologization." See also Kang, "Male Same-Sex Relations."
21 Cui, "Communist International"; Liu, *Queer Marxism*, 49.
22 Liu, *Queer Marxism*, 55.

Preface

Translated by Petrus Liu

After I was born, I cried uncontrollably every single day for no obvious reason. These episodes persisted until I started elementary school.

On the way to school, I would wear a red scarf on my neck, which was thin because I was starving. The scarf was my own red flag for the revolution, and on my chest, close to the heart, I would wear a button of Chairman Mao with a metallic sheen. The cold winds of winter in the north would whip my red scarf against my delicate face. On my forehead, I had a secret, invisible cross made with the blessings of holy water. I had a Catholic name, Peter. Nobody knew about it because I kept it hidden from the atheist dictatorship of the proletariat. I had another secret: those who liked me and those I liked were all boys. But this eventually leaked out. The bullies on the street started chasing me, calling me names, and throwing dirt at me. From that moment, I became a famous person on the road to school and acquired a distinctive nickname: fake girl.

The classroom was not that different from the church. Above the blackboard, they hung large portraits of Marx, Engels, Lenin, Stalin, and Mao. On the sidewalls, instead of the Twelve Stations of the Cross, they displayed Mao's quotations. In music classes, we learned songs of the revolution. But at home, my mother would take out her prayer book in the dark of night. Before falling asleep, my sisters and I would hear faint melodies of "He is born, the divine Child." Half asleep, half awake, I would see the handsome faces of the boys next door or from school, as if in a movie.

In second grade, all pupils received badges as lower-ranking Red Guards. I wore the badge on my left arm and started reading the copy of *Dream of the*

Red Chamber my sister brought home.[1] I read it as the final words of sorrow for women and bisexuals. I resumed my daily silent weeping.

Though pale and weak, I was always the one to be picked out to represent the elementary school at the forum of railroad construction workers. There I read the speech that our schoolteacher prepared, affirming our undying support for the revolution of the proletarian class.

In my first year in school, the Great Proletarian Cultural Revolution broke out. It came to an end when I graduated from high school.

Many years later, I still cried a lot.

The tears formed a wide river that separated me from the red years. On the Left Bank, I immersed myself in Foucault to counteract the Marx that I was fed in school textbooks. I read all of Calvino to mitigate the forces of Lu Xun from those textbooks. I simplified the Old Testament and the New Testament and only read the Gospels. I came to the conclusion that John was the previous incarnation of Derrida and Žižek. I cultivated my study of classical literature in order to forget the imperial culture that was passed down through children's primers and Mao's poetry.

The Christian Church, sent underground by the atheist state, nonetheless coincided with socialism not only in its promotion of heterosexuality but also in its creation of patriarchal/pharaonic heterosexual marriage. As a child, I felt that the partially hidden lustful gazes of the Christian and non-Christian parents sent chills down my spine, as if the apocalypse were about to arrive. I escaped by creating a chasm between myself and my family, the church, and the nation. From the left side of the barrier, I watched them expand their domain. But they never reached me. Before I reached the age for school, I had already definitively made up my mind: no family, no offspring. I would be an alien.

The tears I shed bore witness. The persecution I felt was not the result of paranoia. It was the reality.

Earth is not my home. One of the genres I write in is pseudo science fiction. There is no Hollywood-style "saving the world from an apocalypse" here. Instead, we have humans rejoicing on alien planets and criticizing the way of Earth. In this alternate space, my tears find temporary relief. For the first time in my life, I could save those tears for another occasion.

But when I return to Earth, I am still identified as a human. Every day I have to face arrogant and powerful men. All those power struggles have shrunk their penises, and God long ago rendered their breasts useless, which are now not just flat but incapable of producing milk. For them, the Marquis de Sade is more appropriate than the Gospel of John.

There are places that tears cannot wash away, and that's where other bodily fluids come in handy. The time and space for defecation is one example. In the stench of public toilets, we are accidentally gifted with an alternative method of escape and relief from our tears. This is another genre of my writing—and the origins of this book's title.

Cui Zi'en
August 7, 2019
St. Augustine, Florida

Note

1 *Dream of the Red Chamber*, or *Honglongmeng*, is a Chinese novel composed by Cao Xueqin in the eighteenth century and commonly regarded as a masterpiece of Chinese literature.

Uncle's Elegant Life 舅舅的人间烟火

Translated by Lisa Rofel

1

Ever since he was born, he had a face like a peach blossom. Even his breath carried the sweet smell of milk mingled with honey. He was the pride of my youth. The residents of Triangle City all liked to gawk at him, sidling up to him to take in his fragrance, even carrying it into their dreams. As he grew older, though, he gradually degenerated. He turned into my shame. At thirty he still had a pale face and red lips, dimples that rippled across his face, and that perfumed scent from head to foot. He walked in a delicate, effeminate manner. Only his voice carried some grit. His inverted manner was not regarded as terribly strange. As far as the simple folk of Triangle City were concerned, he was after all a native-born, native-grown male flower. Except for the tales that had long circulated about him, people got used to seeing him like that. Two reasons led me to feel so much shame that I no longer dared to go about town with him. One was that he won top prize in the town's first ever shuttlecock-kicking contest. All those who signed up to participate in the contest were female; he was the only male. Naturally his talent stood out, shining above the other "flowers." The second reason was that he finally got his wish, to enter Triangle City's textile factory. He became a male textile worker. My friends all laughed uproariously: this broke all records, it was over the top, it had no parallel. Because Jin Jinjin was the first in Triangle

First published in *Modern Culture Illustrated News* (現代文明畫報), January 2002; and in *Collected Works of Cui Zi'en* (崔子恩文学作品集), vol. 2 (Zhuhai: Zhuhai chubanshe, 2003). This translation was originally published in *NANG* magazine no. 7 (2019): 53–58.

City's history who became a "spider girl" but with the biological "mistake" of an incriminating penis.

Note: Jin Jinjin is my uncle's name. He chose it himself. The name my grandparents gave him was Jin Xin.[1] When he sang that children's song while playing Chinese jump rope, he jostled his name apart into Jinjin Jinjin. His first year in lower middle school, he decided to write Jinjin Jinjin when registering. But the female teacher in charge of the register had been raped by the Japanese, and she opposed his use of a Japanese-style name with four characters. She took out one of the characters. My uncle thought the deletion hardly made his name appealing. There were two others who started lower middle school with him; one was named Ouyang the Great and the other Chunyu the Mysterious. Both of those four-character names also fell to the teacher's slashing of the intelligible last part of the name. They became Ouyang Big and Chunyu Without.

Another note: spider girl is the ugly nickname that the group of us rascally boys gave to the textile workers. The textile factory was Triangle City's only industrial sector. It occupied a large area at the southeastern corner of town. Not a single man entered this district. The older people say that even the sparrows who fly into that area are all female. When they got off work, the women workers dispersed onto the street, letting their hair flow out behind them. Having just washed in the factory bathhouse, they would, not without a little sense of showing off, unfurl their beautiful hair from its tightly wound place beneath their caps, cutting a striking figure in the setting sun. For us little kids, with our bald heads, who did not yet appreciate the beauty of their elegant hair, their arrival, their "battle lineup," and the type of work they did bedazzled us. To liken them to spiders was the only clean thought that could run through the narrow channel of our imaginations. So we hid behind the trees and walls; those with the greatest courage would call out "one" and "two," then the others would join in and yell: "Spider girls go 'off-duty'!"[2] To this day, I still don't really know how much we insulted them.

1 Xin (鑫) is a Chinese character symbolizing prosperity, written with three characters for "jin," or gold.

2 By "off-duty" the boys insulted these women by implying they were street hookers.

2

His older sister gave birth to me when he was fifteen years old and she was twenty-five. She was working as a nurse at the Railway Clinic, and he was in his second year at Railway Middle School. She didn't have time to take care of a child but he, on the contrary, enjoyed looking after children. So when I was still in swaddling clothes I became his "special subject" outside the classroom. He was meticulous in all things and also very affectionate. To hear my mother tell it, my infancy was filled with the scents of flowers year-round. In spring, peach and pear blossoms mingled, in autumn roses with wild chrysanthemums, while winter brought the aromas of dried jasmine, which Jin Jinjin plucked from jasmine tea. Through Mother's memories and comparing my life with Baobao, who is much younger than me, I imagine the flavor of my infancy as having the scents of sweet flowers, breast milk, and foul urine, all mixed together.

My first memory has nothing to do with my mother or father. It dwells on my uncle's chest and back, fluttering there like soft wings. Uncle sometimes held me in his arms and other times carried me on his back. In the early dawn he would take me to see the sun rise, wetting my hair with the morning dew, saying things like "We are all blades of grass" or "Spring comes and autumn departs." In the evening, we faced west, standing quietly, keeping the sun company as it set, to the last ray of light. I was a mischievous child, but in those moments, I never cried or fidgeted. It was as if an extraordinary power poured into the space between the landscape and my blood.

His older sister was a careless, negligent person. Even as he gradually became a famous character in Triangle City's northwest district, she had no clue.

His fame derived first of all from the way he carried me. He imitated the female lead character from a Japanese soap opera, sewing by hand three different nappies for me, one that was orange-yellow with silver lacing along its edges, another earth red embroidered with a phoenix, and a third the color of dark-blue ink. He took turns using each one to wrap my back and behind, carrying me to go look at the irrigation canals after a heavy rain, or to the white birch forest to hear the birds sing, or even to the theater to watch an opera or see a movie. He was a tall, slender figure. When we walked along the road, sometimes the elementary school students, smaller than my uncle but bigger than me, yelled out to him: "Hey, you male Ah Xin.[3] How did you give birth to that kid?" Then another group of children laughed and retorted: "From his ass!" I glared at them and bawled. I faced that gang of unruly boys and, in a loud voice, just bawled and bawled. I was not yet versed in human affairs, but I was like a young lion cub and, making use of my preternaturally sharp senses, blurted out my menacing message. After my crying scared them away, I came out with my first word since I had entered this world: Mama. My uncle turned his head in surprise and pressed my mouth up against his left cheek.

When I started elementary school, he had graduated from high school and, while waiting for an appropriate job, whiled away the time at home. I asked him then: Why did you use a Japanese woman's style of carrying me? He replied that that fashion was both the most relaxed but also the most burdensome of any he had seen. In Triangle City, when people carry a child, they generally don't use anything to help them. They just toss the child on their backs and expect him to use his arms to hug their neck or his hands to grab onto their shoulders. If they particularly adore their child, they use their own elbows and hands to hold his legs tight. Though it makes picking them up or putting them down relatively easy, both child and adult have to work hard. Both have to pay a lot of attention to the posture of "love," which is given definition through this action. You can't relax for a moment; otherwise the child could fall off your back, getting a concussion. The Japanese style liberates the arms and hands of the one with the bundle on her back and also liberates the child, because it doesn't place life's burdens too early on him. "Mama" just needs to use some muscle. This look of carrying a heavy burden is quintessentially rural. It also lends itself to metaphor. When the baby is little, one can think of oneself as carrying a stuffed doll. When the baby becomes a child and feels big and heavy, one can see the burdens of a heavy life pressing down on one's shoulders. In any case, it provides poetic inspiration.

Uncle's math and science grades were bad. After grandpa and grandma died, his sister—my mother—couldn't stop groaning about it. The language and literature class was the only one he sailed through. All of his essays used a feminine third person as the main character: "Sitting on the horse cart, she wore a butterfly-patterned skirt. The wind coming toward her blew open the spring flower in her heart; her face was an open petal." I was his only friend. He quietly told me that each "her" was really referring to himself. His litera-

3 Ah Xin (阿信) refers to Oshin, a female character in a popular Japanese television drama in the 1980s.

ture teachers were handsome young men. Without exception, they all liked him. But the principal disliked him intensely. When there were school exercises between classes, he took every opportunity to ridicule him, either by name or anonymously, saying, "Railway Middle School has produced a great talent, someone who can knit. It's a pity that, because he can't seem to pass his math and science, he can't leave yet to show off his handiwork around the world."

Uncle first got into knitting not long after grandma died. Grandma had knitted me a sweater, but I made a slight tear at the elbow and sleeve while climbing a tree. Afraid that Mother would bawl me out, I begged Uncle for his help. He pulled out a pair of scissors and nimbly and cleanly cut off the part below the elbow. Then he rolled up a ball of yarn that was a similar color, found grandma's bamboo knitting needles that she had left, and from above the cut part of the sleeve pulled out first one loop and then another and attached them to the needle. Without any teacher, he just knew how to start knitting. The next morning, when my mother returned home from the night shift and I woke up from a dream-filled sleep, the sweater with the newly knitted sleeve was neatly folded next to my pillow. Lying on the bed with the sweater was my uncle, sleeping deeply, with a faint smile playing across his face. His cheeks were suffused with an enchanting rose red, a beauty that brightened up our humble home. At the time, I thought perhaps he was Weaving Girl, descended from the stars.[4]

Almost from that moment of the torn sleeve, Jin Jinjin's math and science grades plummeted. In contrast, my mother's, father's, and my wool sweaters, pants, gloves, scarves, ice-skating caps, and socks, each one appeared completely knitted in one night. No one bothered asking too much about where they came from. Enjoying the use of ready-made things saves a lot more energy, time, and worry than asking about the perplexing and confusing origins of them. My family chose the former path.

The school principal was a middle-aged fellow. Looking at him you could see he had some bearing, but with just a touch of coarseness. No doubt, my good-looking uncle was like all pretty people—they are not very brave. With his failing grades in math and science, he was in danger of being kicked out of school. As luck would have it, the one who really hoped to kick him out was

4 This refers to the Chinese legend of two lovers, Weaving Girl (织女) and Cowherd (牛郎), condemned to be stars who can meet only once a year.

this man, who wrinkled his brow whenever he looked at Uncle's cute dimples. Uncle, who was intelligent, thought up a very customary solution: to send gifts to him at New Year's. Hence on New Year's Eve, that imposing man found a cooking mitt decorated in red and blue. For heat prevention, the maker of the mitt even sewed a thick lining made of hemp. Three characters were sewn in red yarn on the back of the mitt: Happy New Year. The principal reacted with fury. But his wife, who had disappointed him in so many ways, seized the mitt from him, happily put it on her left hand and entered the kitchen. Before this, because he was no good in bed, she hadn't gone into the kitchen in three years.

Two other people received knitted gifts during New Year's. One was Jin Jinjin's classmate, the sports committee member Zhao Xiao'ou. He got a long, milk-white scarf. The other was his young language teacher. He got a pair of thick wool socks, the color of blue-black. The principal knew all about it. After this, he didn't think about kicking my uncle out, but he always looked at him with the whites of his eyes and talked about him behind his back, saying that when he smelled that sweet aroma emanating from Uncle's body, he got a sour taste in his mouth.

3

As soon as Uncle graduated from high school, he went to the textile factory to sign up for work. He even added some supplementary material, an essay entitled "My Ideal," in which he described his yearning to be in a world where resplendent fabric would, like streaming water, pass through his hands. Naturally, his application was rejected. The rejection was brief and to the point: the textile factory had no men's toilet, men's shower room, men's dorm, or place for men to change clothes. So Uncle got placed in the railway car shop, where his job was to carry a small hammer back and forth from the shop to the railway tracks, hammering a bit here and there. Whether the transport bureau, which inspected the shops, suffered a loss or didn't have many workers, or whether this could result in railway cars going off the tracks was anybody's guess.

Uncle, who used to exude freshness, gradually lost some of his brightness. The more he stroked the hammer, the shinier it got. He often cradled it against the front of his dirty work uniform, just like he used to carry me against his chest when I was a baby. Sometimes he stood sedately in the middle of the railway tracks, staring off into space, hugging that hammer.

He didn't even pay attention when a train was coming. "Slipping back into his old habits" led to the cultivation of eight heroes who gave up their lives to save him. They were not his young coworkers but just ordinary workers waiting at the station. As a result, his other nickname was pulled forth from the misty past. That nickname was born the same time as "the male Ah Xin." It was Mary.

In my youth, Uncle always used a sacred manner to carry me. He followed the example of the model on the right side of the door to the Catholic church, the Blessed Virgin Mary's posture in cradling the holy baby Jesus. He didn't believe in religion, but when he carried me, he liked to sing church melodies to me. He also chattered about the mothers who passed by, pointing out and criticizing them for the tilted, crooked, chaotic, dirty, "irresponsible" way they carried their children. When he kissed my cheek, he bristled with pride at carrying me in the Madonna style.

That was one of the most beguiling scenes in the not-too-distant past of Triangle City: a beautiful youth, holding a child, standing in the spring or autumn light, like a statue.

4

When Jin Jinjin cultivated the eighth hero who sacrificed his life, people finally discovered that the hammer that he cradled like a baby just didn't go with his beauty, although twelve years of fixing train cars had already turned him into a bit of a fading flower. Some asked him cautiously whether he would like to change jobs. He answered directly: only if he could enter the textile factory. To lower the compensation they had to pay on behalf of the heroes, the personnel bureaus of the railway office and the local government together broke long tradition and, leaping over systems and sectors, transferred my uncle to the dyeing workshop of the textile factory.

As soon as Jin Jinjin became a spider girl, his beauty instantly blossomed anew. He wore the only set of men's work clothes that the factory had, which they had designed and made especially for him. He walked back and forth in front of the dyeing machine, continuously smoothing out the patterned fabric, which resembled a flowing waterfall. His eyes reflected his dreamy thoughts of the handsome men who would wear the fabric with pleasure. A nun who went on an inspection tour of the factory said that she could read a paean in his eyes.

Of course, the fact that *his* beautiful dream came true did not mean the end of others' nightmares. I was already fifteen years old. My body had developed early, leading me to enter the sports academy for youths to learn basketball. After Jin Jinjin's accomplishment was revealed in the newspaper by a reporter for the *Triangle City Evening News,* I became the laughingstock of my classmates. There were two classmates who grew up and studied in the same railway district school who had long heard the tales of Ah Xin and Mary. They represented the entire town in dragging up the past: as soon as they saw me, they would simulate cradling a sacred baby or would imitate the quick, short steps of Ah Xin. It made me so angry I came to blows with them every day.

New, embellished stories also flowed incessantly. The center forward in basketball, Li Yu, said that Jin Jinjin built a straw outhouse in the back of the textile factory. A gang of middle-aged women workers knocked it over, among them Li Yu's mother. Wang Zheng, who was learning gymnastics, said that Jin Jinjin was stripped naked during lunch. The young women workers ran away in fright, not daring to look. Wang Zheng's cousin was in the group.

I stopped thinking of him as my uncle. I gave him the cold shoulder. There was no way he could continue living in my home, so he rented a small one-room home near the factory and moved out. The day he left, my mother helped him move out. When she returned, she cried, even bawling me out. That was the first time in my life she had yelled at me.

5

During my time at the youth sports academy, a rare thing happened: One time when Wang Zheng, on the boys' gymnastics team, was fooling around, the coach discovered that his balance beam and horse vaulting were better than any of the girls on the girls' team. The coach consulted closely with the team captain: Should they get him to pretend to be a member of the girls' team to participate in the city's sports competition, to take back the gold medal in those two events from another youth sports academy? The team captain was inclined to use this secret weapon but worried there was no way to cover up the "secret weapon" right there in the middle of Wang Zheng's body. In the group meeting, Li Yu suggested cutting it off. Ji Qin suggested wearing a miniskirt and bluffing it. I had a sudden inspiration and raised my hand. "My uncle is an expert in these matters. He will definitely know what to do."

Jin Jinjin did not disappoint people's expectations. He made a girl's sports outfit just for Wang Zheng. On the inside he created a place for him to store his little cock and a device for pulling it back tightly toward his ass and securing it. On the day of the meet, the troops from the textile factory were in the very front, waving a gold-colored flag. My uncle was the flag holder. The results from Group A girls' competition startled our competitors: the gold medals for the balance beam and horse vaulting were taken by Wang Zheng—renamed Wang Little Flower. They immediately sent out a scout, hoping to dig up something on her. In the adult male high jump competition, my uncle, with a flying butterfly-like move, jumped two meters, taking first place. He was the first male worker in the history of the textile factory who was also the first male sports team member and the first male winner of a gold medal.

The night of the sports event's closing ceremonies, Mama and I brought Uncle home to eat dumplings. As we walked along in the setting sun, his sister told him that she had registered his name with the television program *The Dating Game*. He looked at me with his charming eyes and gave an embarrassed laugh. Suddenly I stopped and said to him, Carry me, just like before! Mama froze and said, You are as tall as Uncle. Aren't you ashamed of making him carry you? A teardrop rolled from my left eye. I said, If you get married, then you won't be able to carry me anymore.

Uncle made a great effort to pick me up and stood quietly holding me. I smelled again that scent of flowers. But I had already grown too big. In the setting sun, it was only Uncle holding me. He could no longer display the charming posture of Mary.

Intrigue like Fireworks 奸情如焰火

Translated by Fran Martin

1

The city where I went to grad school was square; it was called Square City. The city wall and the city lake in Square City formed perfectly orderly, perfectly precise quadrangles, and the city brought together gentlemen and commoners, sages and opportunists from all the eight points of the compass and the four corners of the world. The city where I went to college was round; it was called Circle City. At the center of Circle City was an obelisk. Beneath the obelisk was a tomb, and in the tomb was the spirit of a pioneer hero who had opened up the frontier lands. The perfectly round, sturdy stone of the obelisk, like a heavy object tossed into a pool of water, raised the layered ripples of the city all round itself. The buildings and streets of Circle City extended in concentric circles toward the city's outskirts, all the way out to the biggest circle that was formed by a band of forest that ran around the whole area. In comparison to Square City, Circle City had a few more commoners and a few less gentlemen, a few less sages and a few more fools, a little more violence and a little less intrigue. In Square City and Circle City I read ten thousand volumes, solved a thousand riddles, and wrote a hundred essays. They were cities of my adulthood. I made them places very far removed from fairy tales.

My hometown was Triangle City. To boys unversed in the ways of the world, Triangle City was a fairy tale. It had a city lake and a city wall in the shape of equilateral triangles, and lining the inside and outside of the wall, two bands of forest enclosed the city. Within the city wall, time was composed of just three seasons: one season was Spring, one season was Au-

First published in *I Love Shidabo* (我爱史大勃) (Beijing: Huaxia chubanshe, 1998).

tumn, and all the remaining time was given over to pure white snow. Spring, Autumn, and Winter formed an isosceles triangle in which the enormous obtuse angle between Spring and Autumn swallowed up Summer's incipient but always unrealized arrival.

When we were about thirteen or fourteen years old, I happened to hear a piece of piano music called "The Triangle Forest." This inspired me to call a meeting of the Seven Swordsmen of the Elm Forest in order to change the old name that our city had borne for a thousand years to the more fairytale-ish Triangle City. Of the Seven Swordsmen, I was the youngest but the biggest in stature. Until then, it had always been the other six heroes who'd taken turns presiding over our meetings. This renaming of the city was the first time in my life I'd plucked up my courage and, with trembling voice, tasted the power of leadership. It was an afternoon in early Autumn. The autumn wind hadn't yet begun its soughing, and in the elm forest in the sixty-degree elbow at the southeast corner of the city the wildflowers bloomed in dappled sunlight. The Swordsmen hung upon my every word. Unnerved by this sudden attention, on completing my solemn declaration of the overthrow of the old and triumph of the new, I hurriedly passed the scepter back to the short-tempered Break o'Day.

2

We each had our own reasons for skipping school to hang out in the elm forest. For me and White Eyed Wolf, it was because schoolwork was so easy we could finish it without even trying. For Gaptooth, Little Three, and Fatty, it was because they were lazy and scallywaggish. Break o'Day had to get up at the break of day every morning to make breakfast for his mum and dad and grandpa and granny and little sister and little brother, and so by afternoon he was exhausted. As for Butterfly, he'd been tricked by White Eyed Wolf to come out and see the fireworks.

In those days, life was simple in Triangle City. No flashy newfangled gadgets had reached the town, not even television, invented earlier that century, or fireworks, invented in who knows what year, what month, what dynasty, what epoch. We knew very little of matters outside our own daily life, and as a result we lacked ambition. But White Eyed Wolf was a bit different. He loved things he didn't understand and yearned to go wandering in regions far beyond the jurisdiction of the Ministry of Railways. He often tried to trip us up with new slang terms he'd overheard. He always had to be the first to read the comics and banned books we got hold of, and routinely devoured all our snacks. His excuse was that he was the eldest, and the shortest, and had the biggest thing down there. Break o'Day and I wanted to kick the ungrateful son of a bitch out of the gang, but Butterfly would always flutter over and beg Break o'Day to keep him on because he'd promised to take us all to see the fireworks. Our complete and utter ignorance on the subject of fireworks meant that the mere mention of the word was enough to shake us to the very foundation of our young souls. Intelligence without the support of experience led me to piece together associations from the characters of the written word, associating the term with the eerie glow of the unquiet spirits of the dead among the tombs in a graveyard, or else with some unfathomable fiery disaster. White Eyed Wolf solemnly refuted my speculations and furthermore made me use my last three cents to buy him six pieces of taffy from the store. After finishing the candy, he told us he'd heard a traveler from Square City say that fireworks were really something, better than seeing the Immortals themselves. As to how one got to see them, well, he could take us. They had fireworks in Square City at the annual city festival. And before long we'd have them here, too.

White Eyed Wolf's house was an Aladdin's cave—he'd tricked us out of just about all our toys. In spite of that, his rhetorical skills still inspired half belief on our part, and total belief from Butterfly. Butterfly was one of those white-faced, ruby-lipped types, pretty as a girl. When he walked he seemed to float, and running he appeared to take dancing flight. Of all the Swordsmen he'd had the most sheltered upbringing. Whenever he caught White Eyed Wolf's enigmatic gaze, he'd follow him behind the bushes to listen to his peculiar whispered slang. Sometimes White Eyed Wolf ran out of inspiration and would just mutter random nonsense, but even that would leave Butterfly wide-eyed, listening carefully and intently mulling over every word.

Nonetheless, as it turned out, Butterfly's trust was not misplaced. Once a small hoard of glittering treasures stolen from his house had been deposited into White Eyed Wolf's hands, we finally assumed our positions and advanced toward the wasteland at the edge of the forest, on our way to experience the world of fireworks for ourselves. It was the moment just before dusk. His face streaming with anxious sweat, White Eyed Wolf summoned us one by one from our homes. The words he used were very simple: "The fireworks are on, come see!" Immediately we forgot the games we'd been playing and fell wordlessly into formation behind him, traversing streets and lanes and at last entering the elm forest, then taking a turn to the east to be met with a great expanse of colorful autumn grassland. As we neared our objective

White Eyed Wolf signaled us to advance crawling so as not to frighten the fireworks away. When he said that, I supposed that fireworks must be a kind of flame-like bird, one that gathered in flocks and, if one weren't careful, was apt to take to the skies never to be seen again.

White Eyed Wolf stopped short and gently parted the grass, raising his head slightly but careful not to let it show above the tips of the grass stalks. We followed suit, our eyes wide as saucers, and caught sight first of a bicycle lying on its side and then of a stark-naked man and woman in the process of putting on their clothes. The bicycle was very new, practically brand-new, and the gold of the setting sun made parts of it glitter with bright sparkles like you saw on a theater stage. The man's back was to us so you couldn't see his face, but he had broad shoulders, a narrow waist, and sturdy buttocks, with very well-developed muscles on his legs. The woman had a fullish figure with large, slightly drooping breasts. Her hair all disheveled, she flashed a brilliant smile in our direction, startling me half to death. She was the mum of a girl in my class, Wu Xiaomei. I'd been over to her place several times, and each time I went she'd stroke my cheeks. Her hands were very, very soft.

White Eyed Wolf made a noise like a cricket, the signal for us to retreat. With burning face and pounding heart, covered in confusion, I returned to our base in the forest without uttering a single word. Break o'Day grabbed White Eyed Wolf by the collar and demanded to know where were the fireworks. White Eyed Wolf said, "We came too late. They'd finished, they'd just finished." Sensing that Break o'Day didn't believe him, he planted himself on the ground on hands and knees with his little bum in the air, then got into an upright kneeling position behind where he'd just been crouching and moved his body back and forth, saying, "Like this, this is how they do fireworks." With a faint glimmer of half understanding, we returned dejectedly home.

3

The long Winter passed. We had lots of homework and lots of games to play, and the business of the fireworks soon became a distant memory. Then one afternoon when Spring had begun and the flowers were in bloom, we were hanging out in the elm forest when suddenly White Eyed Wolf pointed out beyond the trees and said, "Listen up, heroes. The fireworks are starting!" Following the direction where he pointed, we heard the soft rustle of bicycle tires riding over grass. All at once my throat felt hot and dry, and a cold sweat broke out on the tip of my nose.

Following the sound of the bike and the shadow of its rider, we approached the center of the grassland where the wildflowers were in full bloom. The young grass was only about as tall as a bamboo flute, forcing us to creep along with our bellies pressed to the ground like snakes. The owner of the bicycle let it drop next to the brightest patch of wildflowers, and we watched him and the woman who had been waiting there all along begin to roll around together biting at each other's mouths. They bit and chewed on and on, making me worry that they'd end up eating each other's lips right off. But objective facts proved my concerns superfluous, and soon they were desperately pulling off each other's clothes. Wu Xiaomei's mum really did get down on all fours like White Eyed Wolf had demonstrated, with her plump, white buttocks facing right toward us. And that young guy really did kneel behind her as White Eyed Wolf had shown, and began to let off fireworks that left us wide-eyed and dumbstruck. It was a truly magnificent spectacle. It took away our breath, our thoughts, and our hopes; it took away the Spring, the grassland, and the flowers; and it took away the fairytale theme that formerly defined Triangle City. In their ecstasy, I caught my own ecstatic glimpse of a fairytale scene that no author of fairy tales would ever write about.

After that we eagerly awaited the next fireworks show. Whenever any one of us whispered, "The fireworks are on," we'd hurry to pass the word to each of the others, never leaving out a single member of the gang. At the same time, we followed an unspoken agreement to keep our lips sealed to adults and other kids. I still felt that somehow fireworks had a sort of kinship with spirits or flocks of rare birds, easily scared away. I was now more eager than ever to revisit Wu Xiaomei's house. Seeing how much I'd grown, her mother hugged me, kissed my cheek, and said I'd soon be a big guy, how she wanted a tall, lean son like me. My blood would set to boiling, my face and neck blushing dark red. When she was at work or busy with housework and not touching me, I felt quite lost. My mum said her name was Lan Bao-bao and she was a renowned beauty in the Ministry of Railways. She used to be a train conductor, traveling about the countryside all day, but after she had a son and daughter she started working in a branch factory of the Railways train car division, making bread. Manual labor and an ordinary working life did nothing to dim her natural beauty. Her husband was good-looking too, only he was ten years older than her. His name was Wu Ji.

News of the romance between me and Wu Xiaomei soon spread through our class at school. With her startling girlish beauty, Wu Xiaomei refused to have anything further to do with me. I was forced to wait for the chance to run into Lan Bao-bao on the street, to have her ruffle my hair while she laughed her bell-like laugh. Evidently she had no idea that the spectacle of fireworks she made with that strapping young guy had become life's biggest attraction for us youngsters. All this took place before I changed the name of the city.

4

The third Sunday after Triangle City underwent its name change, Break o'Day was caught at home skipping school and copped a savage beating from his parents and grandparents. To cheer him up, I went to the Railways employees' club and bought a movie ticket to the night show. At the ticket office I ran into Butterfly and his dad. His dad swept me with a searching gaze, head to foot, and, apparently concluding that I wasn't some street hooligan likely to lead his precious son astray, agreed that Butterfly could come hang out with me.

We hurried toward the elm forest to give the movie ticket to Break o'Day. Back then we used to get very little pocket money, on average about one yuan a year, so buying someone a ten-cent movie ticket for a present used up a pretty considerable chunk of an annual allowance. As we were walking by the club, Butterfly leaned over and whispered in my ear: "Look, it's the fireworks guy." I looked around and saw that the traffic cop just finishing his shift on the platform at the intersection was indeed none other than Lan Bao-bao's lover. He was wearing a trim uniform with a big cap, and his face, a picture of youthful vigor, radiated with life. For some reason I had a very positive feeling toward him. I hoped that in the future I could be like him, whether letting off fireworks or on duty directing traffic. Dimly, I felt that he was my stand-in in those dates with Lan Bao-bao. But at the same time his very existence exacerbated the pain and confusion of my coming of age. There was some magnificent new substance building up within me, but it wasn't yet at the point of bursting forth. I was growing up too slowly. Between my situation and his was only a matter of inches, but it seemed as if I would never cover the distance separating us.

Butterfly bought two popsicles and each of us put one in our mouth and sucked on it. Suddenly he let out a snort of laughter and asked me, blushing, if I'd ever ejaculated while we were watching the fireworks. I was momentarily bemused, with no idea what was meant by that word "ejaculated" he'd used. He didn't explain, yet somehow even in the midst of my confusion I faintly sensed his meaning. I divined from his manner that the word must have something to do with that organ between your legs, because whenever people raised that subject in the light of day they automatically shied away from talking about it.

By the time we finished our popsicles we were nearly at the elm forest. Break o'Day was leading some of the Swordsmen in martial arts practice. He was thrilled to receive the movie ticket. I pulled him to one side and asked him what this ejaculation thing was all about. He cuffed me on the shoulder and burst into loud guffaws, then asked, "Have you really not done it?" I didn't know what to say. He said, "Oh, it feels great—like taking a piss that's been building up for about ten years." I vaguely understood.

We practiced boxing and kicks for a while until the sun moved into the west. Butterfly and White Eyed Wolf came running back from beyond the woods, Butterfly behind and White Eyed Wolf in front, a piece of pink toilet paper clutched in his hand. Everyone gathered around to look. The paper was covered in bloody splotches, with a pattern a bit like when we used to wet the bed as kids. White Eyed Wolf held it aloft and said, like a documentary voice-over, "This is a menstrual tissue. After people let off their fireworks, they use it to clean themselves up." Hearing his words and seeing the screwed-up tissue in his hands, I felt on the point of fainting.

5

Just before the last time in my youth that I saw the fireworks, the sky, the earth, and the people around me all seemed subtly changed. Once White Eyed Wolf had spread the word that the fireworks were on, he disappeared without a trace. The sky, which very seldom had any clouds in it, was piled high with fluffy white billows. It was the moment right between Spring and Autumn, when the spring flowers had faded and the autumn flowers weren't yet out, and the grass was so green it seemed black. Lying on the ground, the smell of fresh grass and earth overwhelmed your nose. Before we could get to the best viewing position, we could already hear the moans of the fireworks people, now rising now falling, one voice higher than the other. Before, what we'd enjoyed had always been silent movies. Now suddenly the silent film turned into sound film, and its effect on us became all the harder to resist. Each time I shifted slightly, there was one more squirming caterpillar wriggling around in my lower body. They frightened me so much I didn't dare move, and pressed my groin hard against the ground. Then all at once, wave after wave of a pleasure I'd never felt before soaked me through to my bones and flowed right through my mind, body, and spirit, before turning into a spurt of liquid that burst against my jocks.

I rested my forehead on the ground, closed my eyes, and let the sensation of physical weakness that spread through my body gradually congeal into a half-transparent realization: the essence of fireworks seemed to have something to do with a great joy that lay at the very root of life, and the purpose of growing up and becoming an adult was inseparable from that great joy. A momentary impulse to weep was quickly replaced by a brand-new, adult-like calm. Only half aware of it at the time, I guess I was in the midst of the transition from boy to man.

From somewhere a chill descended. I refocused on the reality before my eyes: Lan Bao-bao and the young guy were disentangling themselves from their sweaty embrace, wanting to get dressed—but they soon discovered that their clothes were nowhere to be seen. Beside them stood the awe-inspiring Wu Ji, the short-arsed White Eyed Wolf, and his elder brother with the crippled leg, the result of infantile paralysis. The two brothers held the couple's clothes bundled up in their arms.

The lovers stood up, facing directly into my line of vision. Seeing his body, I comprehended at last what White Eyed Wolf meant by "well-hung." And seeing her body, I saw what he meant by "curvy." Wu Ji raised an iron bar and went to smash it over the guy's head; he leapt out of the way. Lan Bao-bao cried, "Run! Run away, Ding Fei—get away while you can!" As she shouted she turned toward the White Eyed Wolf brothers and tried to get her clothes back from them. She had no luck. Wu Ji put out his foot to trip her, and the two brothers ran like the wind to the other side of the grassland. The crippled boy, leaping forward on one leg and steadying the other against the ground, was barely a whisker slower than his companion.

Ding Fei fled, quick as a bolt of lightning, traversing the grassland to disappear among the trees of the elm forest. As he passed by, he glimpsed me out of the corner of his eye, hiding in the long grass with my pants wet with semen. Faintly, one corner of his mouth turned up in the suggestion of a smile, like a great actor as he leaves the stage at the close of his performance. He didn't look back at his lover or mistress, who was even now rolling around on the ground, locked in a wrestle-hold with her husband, in order to let him get away.

6

The Winter Break o'Day was blessed with a baby son, I returned from Square City to my hometown to marry Wu Xiaomei. Now in her fifties, Lan Bao-bao's looks were well preserved. No longer did she cuddle and make a fuss over me. My sixty-something father-in-law was like a big brother to her, with an arm permanently about her shoulders. When they spoke together, or ate together, or walked on the street, they were the very embodiment of a respectable older couple, harmonious and loving. To my mother-in-law, the fireworks displays on the grassland had vanished as utterly as smoke, gone without a trace. In the cloudless blue of her life's sky, that young guy named Ding Fei seemed to have left not the slightest sign of his presence. After I'd made it through the minefield of my adolescence, I no longer took her as an object of sexual fantasy. The only respect in which a suspicion of her influence remained was that all the girlfriends I had in Circle City and Square City were quite similar to her in type. And in the end it was her daughter I chose, who was practically a carbon copy of her mother.

Our wedding was generous without being extravagant. My parents had long ago become friends with Xiaomei's parents, and they took care of all the celebrations. Aside from Butterfly, all the remaining four Swordsmen came along to offer their well-wishes. Butterfly was in jail, charged with the crime of Oscar Wilde.[1] White Eyed Wolf came too, very nicely turned out. He'd made a bit of money running a quite respectable restaurant near the train station. His toast to me at the wedding banquet was very simple: "The fireworks are on—come see!" The other Swordsmen joined in the cry and insisted that I repeat the words myself.

Everything was perfect after our wedding. By then I'd already seen the aerial kind of fireworks more than once in Square City, and in my opinion the scenes we saw that year hiding in the grass really did rival the sight of fireworks in the night sky. My only slight disappointment was that the intimate moments I shared with Xiaomei each night in our bedroom were merely a progression from arousal to satisfaction, and from satisfaction to renewed desire—it was really no match for the world of fireworks.

7

A decade later I had become a renowned professor of fairy tales at Triangle City University and had an eight-year-old son who was the spitting image of me. One free afternoon, I took a bus out of the university district, planning to take a stroll around the Railways district where I'd lived in my youth. We'd

1 This reference to the crime of Oscar Wilde is original to the Chinese text (罪名同作家王尔德一样) and not a cross-cultural translation.

just crossed the rail junction when I caught sight of the bread factory where my mother-in-law used to work. I got off the bus and approached the cinema that had been created from the expansion of the old Railways employees' club to see what was showing. I'd just left the billboards when I heard three boys mysteriously whispering among themselves: "The fireworks are on!" Their voices sounded very familiar, like Butterfly's or White Eyed Wolf's or my own. I started to follow them, and when they noticed me there I said, like an old pro, "The fireworks are on!" Without hesitation they took me in: a tall, thin member of their gang.

Once we'd crossed the intersection where Ding Fei used to stand on traffic duty, their pace increased. I searched for some young man like Ding Fei in the broad area covered by the widened road, thinking that would be the target the boys were following. I was out of luck: aside from a few sturdy, well-to-do looking youths, all I saw were cars large and small. But the three boys talked and laughed excitedly. One of them asked me if I was visiting from Square City. I nodded yes.

In the sixty-degree elbow at the city's southeast corner the elm forest had been cut down and replaced with Korean red pines. It was Autumn and fallen needles covered the ground between the trees, soft underfoot. I saw neither hide nor hair of anyone, but the three boys knew intuitively that preparations for the fireworks were already complete. We proceeded crawling toward the center of the grassland, guided by a few quiet whispers and the occasional low moan. My chest and belly were bursting with that special nervous excitement of youth. Parting the grass, I saw a nicely built man down on all fours with an extremely small, puny guy behind him knocking him wildly this way and that. Since the second man was so small, he was unable to kneel on the ground and had to make do by half-bending his knees. They were at it a long time, the very picture of loving harmony. Beside them lay a bicycle, a mountain bike in the new style. It was only when their bodies had separated that I saw that the man in front was Butterfly—he must have been just out of jail—and the little skinny one with the big dick was none other than White Eyed Wolf. I stood up and walked toward them. There in the autumn sunlight I gave a whistle and calmly declared, "The fireworks are on! Come see!" The three boys behind me leapt up out of the grass, yelling as they ran off, "The fireworks are over! Time to go home!"

There on the grassland, the only ones left were the former Swordsmen of the Elm Forest, wide-eyed and staring at each other.

Some Admire Wisdom, Others Do Not

有人赞美聪慧，有人则不

Translated by Derek Hird

1

If you want to delve into the official, unofficial, and anecdotal histories of Triangle City, you've got to pay attention to insignificant people and minor details. Regarding the people, keep your eye on the old folks and children. As to details, take note of subtle things, such as how high off the ground people hanged themselves and how thick the rope was. You want to investigate the twisting tornado hairstyle and severe temperament of Little Glory's grandma? Did you ever see this suicide style: both feet hanging down at anything from one centimeter above the ground to an unlimited height, a colored rope tightly bound round the neck; if a gentle wind blows, the corpse will twirl with the top of the rope above the head as its axis, like a wooden spinning top? You say you've seen it. Hangings: they involve different people of various ages, different times, means, places, and heights. But that's nitpicking; actually they're all pretty much alike in the end. I tell you, I've only seen it once, when I was six: the person twirling in space like a spinning top was Little Beauty's grandma. Well, have you ever laid eyes on the big, important people like your grandparents? You feel sad because you've never seen them, and they didn't know you're in this world, right? Even your father and mother haven't seen them as far as they can remember. You're not an orphan, but your parents were a pair of orphans who grew up in the orphanage attached to the Church of the Sacred Heart of Jesus. I'm telling you, sadly, I've never seen my grandpas either. I only know that during the turmoil of the war

First published in *Mountain Flowers* (山花), February 2000; and in *I Love Shidabo* (我爱史大勃) (Beijing: Huaxia chubanshe, 1998).

years in Triangle City my grandpa on my father's side went to graze his herd of cattle outside the town in that chaotic, war-ravaged environment. He was robbed by wild bandits and savagely beaten by some people from the Party for the glory of the motherland. He and Grandma had four boys and one girl, but one of the boys died young. At the time he died the country was already at peace, but his own frame of mind when he died was unknown. My grandpa on my mother's side was by nature simple, a slow talker and bighearted. My maternal grandma had a monopoly on forthrightness and competence, not to mention her beauty. The most glorious moment of my grandpa's entire life was smashing the ancestral memorial tablet in the lineage hall. He could be rather bumbling in matters of daily life, but when he received the silent revelation of the Holy Spirit, he scarcely hesitated before leading his wife, son, daughter, and grandchildren away from that "group sitting in darkness under the shadow of death" to follow the Lord. I haven't seen him in this mortal world, but I'm sure we'll meet up in the kingdom of heaven.

All right, now it's your turn to ask me. You ask, Little Beauty's grandma is dead; she hanged herself, right? I nod to you, and start to recollect the astonishment of my six-year-old, tufty-headed self. With that kind of death, the person doesn't go to heaven or hell: can it really be that she just floats in midair? I didn't know Little Beauty's grandma, but I managed to shed three feeble tears for her death. Little Beauty didn't cry at all; at least I didn't see her cry. She was five, and kept playing hopscotch all alone outside the courtyard. The hopscotch squares were naturally constructed with chalk lines. They covered a wide area, like the house of a big, rich family, divided into one room after another. Everybody knew Little Beauty's family was poor, with few members. But in winter she managed to wear a flowery padded jacket, and in spring a thin jacket with a smaller floral design. It was rice, of course, not sand, that filled the flowery cloth bag she used for hopscotch. I believed in the powers of the chalk's colors and the imaginary house. I knew that the chalk house, with its one room linked to another, had no doors or windows, so no one could barge in. Only Little Beauty could hop back and forth, kicking the bag from one room to another, skillfully picking it up by the tip of her foot, to drop it into another room. I was dazzled: I didn't understand how Little Beauty and her bag were not blocked by the walls. Maybe she was a chivalrous swordswoman from an ancient Chinese fairy tale who could leap onto roofs and vault over walls. The only thing missing was a pair of double-edged swords. You need to know that her face was white and frosty, definitely a cold breed of beauty. She leapt backward and forward between the rooms, completely absorbed. She knew, or acted like she knew, that the people who turned up at her home at that time, whether friend or foe, would treat her and her family like strangers because Death had lingered there. She wasn't wrong. Since her grandma was dead, I couldn't work out how she could still be alive. I walked south a long way and, when I got near home, turned around to look back north. Feeling low, I watched Little Beauty still playing hopscotch, her flowery clothes leaping in the dim evening sun. Her grandma used her last ounce of strength to hang herself, frightened or tired of life. Her grandma used life to choose death. Little Beauty was still alive, still very young. One day she would become a grandma and her granddaughter would be like her now. But it wouldn't necessarily be my grandson watching her play hopscotch, feeling moved. I might die young like my older brother.

You ask, your older brother died young? Yes, aged three. My ma said he'd just learned a few curse words. He's in heaven for sure now. He was born twelve years before me. The drums of war were sounding all around. My young father was sent to the front line specially to dress the shattered limbs of the wounded. With my brother in tow, my young mother hid in the coldest corner of Triangle City, the days passing like years. We all come from dust. So that we wouldn't return to dust, Ma delivered us early on into the arms of the Lord. After my brother was baptized, suffering hunger and cold, he rapidly reached the age of three. Then he fell ill, then he took medicine, then that ashen, innocent little face said goodbye to this world. Ma is still grieving; she says maybe it was because she was young and ignorant, and she fed him all the medicine the doctor prescribed in one dose. As someone who had come from dust, Ma felt the pain over her beloved son's premature death, like a knife twisting in her heart, which she still feels to this day, in her old age. As a Christian who had been cleansed, Ma also felt gratified by his early death: he didn't have time to be contaminated by humanity's sins, he had cast off the temptations of the devil, the profane, and the flesh, and ascended to the kingdom of heaven. The Lord said, "Suffer little children to come unto me, and forbid them not: for such is the kingdom of God." Dust returns to dust; the baptized go to heaven. Do you still think my brother died young? You hesitate, then say, Maybe not. He went to heaven early, which is altogether different from dying young.

2

You quote a sentence of Spinoza's from three centuries ago in faraway Amsterdam to judge whether I am a free man: "A free man thinks of death least of all things; his wisdom is a meditation not on death but on life." I agree with this judgment. When we sat on the cusp between youth and adulthood, I would think about the dead, whose lives were so ephemeral. Some I had met, some I only heard about from relatives and friends, some I'd hung out with, some were my best friends, and, of course, some were elder members of my family. As for their stories, I have to tell them to you one by one. Otherwise, I'll be "meditating" on them forever and will never become a free man able to contemplate life. I wish with all my heart I were like you, but I'm stuck in my memories of death. I only want you to listen to me, or ask lots of questions. So long as you listen to me, you're helping me move closer to freedom.

3

Maybe it was because Little Glory's grandma had a twisting tornado head of silver hair that his temperament was controlled by hidden wind-like forces. His mood changed like the weather, now sunny, now stormy; happy one minute, angry the next, causing the young me great confusion. Because Little Glory's ma was a friend of my ma's, I unconditionally chose him as my friend without thinking much about it. He had very big, jet-black eyes, a high-bridged nose, a small mouth, and a bit of a stern expression. He looked insightful. This was in fact so. Every time I was especially lonely and wanted to play with him, he could see right through me and knew how much I wanted to be with him. He would coldly fold his arms across his chest, cast an apparently uninterested glance toward my left ear, and rebuff me saying, "But I don't feel like playing with you right now." I felt humiliated and disappointed, and with my face flushing red hot, I asked, "Then who do you want to play with?" My underlying point was: Is there any more loyal playmate than me? At that moment he'd look me in the eye. When he looked at me, his black eyes already contained a glimmer of the wise man's cunning and the victor's secret pleasure. He'd say: "Nobody's playing with anybody, I'll play by myself." When he finished talking, he closed the thick, heavy wooden door, deliberately making a bang as he shot the bolt from inside, and in the same controlled, calm voice said: "I don't want to play with you today, come round again tomorrow." I could hardly bear the shame. In the glittering spring sunshine, I tried hard to fight back wave after wave of scorching hot tears as I quietly left Little Glory's yard. An intense bitterness, like the disaster of losing one's first love, engulfed me. I wanted to run home quickly, put my head under the covers, and weep. But I couldn't let people on the street see me cry. I walked slowly and pinned a smile on my face, as if I were a carefree, happy child. My performance was all planned out, but there wasn't a soul on the street. The afternoon shade from the trees made the sunlight even more dazzling. There were grown-ups walking and cars passing on the main road ahead. People simply didn't notice me at the T-junction and cared even less about the rejection I'd suffered. I thought, I'm such a loser, even my own best friend has rejected me.

I was six and a half then. From that time on, through my whole life I've thought of myself as pretty unattractive. I realized this too early, so after puberty every time I fell in love, it was always a one-sided passion. This also meant I almost never switched from being the active one: I was attentive to other people, I took care of other people, I adored other people. In short, I played the part of the pursuer. The frustration born of rejection and neglect, after a long time, changed into a proud self-approval: I was never passive, never pursued (as in being hunted), never stared at (as I had stared at Little Beauty's grandma after she hanged herself). I never hurt other people's feelings (like Little Glory closing the wooden door between us).

Before the Chinese New Year, I came back from my maternal grandma's home, sporting a squirrel-colored fur overcoat and a winter flying hat, looking pretty adorable. The overcoat was my sister's; it had two big pockets sewn, with exquisite workmanship, on the front at the left and the right. Its large plastic buttons looked like chestnuts just fried with sugar. When no one was looking, I'd stealthily put the top one in my mouth and taste it. Sometimes it would give off a trace of sweetness; other times it was dull and tasteless. When I gnawed at it with my little teeth, it would release a bitter taste that didn't spread or linger. Whether I was hungry or not, I would always bite or suck on it. Before winter was out, the button had clearly lost its luster and had mouselike bite marks all over it. The flying hat was American Air Force style from World War II: the inner sides of its earflaps were made of lamb's fleece, the front and surface were all soft, shiny leather, and the brim was attached to the top with two metal buttons, giving off a bright and shining look. In the photo from that time you can see that the front edge made my pitch-black pupils appear especially pure and clear. But my mother gave that photo a piercing look. My image reminded her of my father as a child.

On the soft snowy ground that showed a few weasel tracks, there was a path made by pedestrians' footprints. Little Glory stood silently beside the path, staring at me curiously, unsure if I was a stranger. We hadn't seen each other for more than half a year. He was only wearing two snowy-white fur earmuffs. His hair was long, covering the sides of his face and making his cheeks appear thin. I called out to him: "Little Glory!" His eyes shone radiantly, and he shouted to me: "Little Question!" My nickname was Questioning (Wenwen) because I had a very questioning look in my eyes from the moment I opened them.[1] That's what Ma said, and with this in mind, she chose a nickname for me that was easy to shout out. He cheerfully ran toward me. I pulled my hand out from my mother's grasp, dumbfounded and rooted to the spot. My mind was a blank until he ran in front of me, stared into my eyes, held both my hands, and said, "You can come back, nobody wants to play with me now!" Opening my mouth, I took the cold air into my lungs in large gasps, but I couldn't utter a word. Analyzing it now, I realize it was an acute psychological symptom, which could be called pent-up passion, due to feeling extremely flattered.

Of course, as I remember it, I didn't give a whit about returning home and had no time to give my sister Grandma's small present; I just gamboled along behind Little Glory, like a pet dog following its little master. We came to Medicine Spring and spun our tops on the thick ice beside the source of the spring. Little Beauty was the only girl among the other kids spinning tops there. She was wearing her padded jacket with the floral design and was absorbed in driving a copper top up a slope. She ignored everybody, and when she met up with some mischievous boys deliberately using their tops to attack hers, she just grabbed her top, went down to the bottom of the slope, and started to drive the top up the slope again. Because I was being his little servant, Little Glory's whipping style and his movements came off with a lordly air. For sure, I had lived for half a year in Circle City, which they had never been to, and naturally I had some city airs about me; they could tell without even asking. Incredibly, such a special figure as me obediently stayed by Little Glory's side, with no top of my own, humbly keeping him company. As long as he was playing happily, I was happy. I vaguely felt that Little Glory's mighty spinning and mocking look in his eyes showed some pride on account of me. He was proud because he possessed me. I felt utterly content. At the time I simply didn't care to nitpick whether he was proud of me, or proud because he had the ability to possess me.

I stayed by his side, watching him drive his silvery steel top to the "hilltop" time and again before the other children. Occasionally, he'd give me a shot, handing me the string, and letting me spin the top so it slid over the more level part of the ice. Then when we climbed the steep slope, he'd take the string in time to finish off with the most difficult and incredibly skilled moves. We never varied our game when we went to Medicine Spring; we always played

1 Wenwen (问问) means "Ask Ask."

"King of the Hill." Whenever Little Glory became king, I cheered loudly, but he just looked into the mouth of the spring, using the water as a mirror to reflect his unruffled expression. He often glanced at Little Beauty. Among all these expert top spinners, Little Beauty never joined in the competition, even though with her skill she stood out. She was always whipping her copper top up to the rocky platform while other people were down at the start. Little Glory seemed like he wanted to compete with her. But that day, after playing for just a short time, we were shooed away by a white-whiskered old man.

Medicine Spring was a place forbidden to children. In spring and autumn it was protected by a high ring of rocks impossible for us to climb up. As soon as winter arrived, the people who came to draw water would always splash some on the rocky platform, which eventually turned into a mountain of ice. For us, it seemed like the mouth of a volcano in a fairy tale, and probably all the children but timid me had already climbed up the steep icy slope to look at the flowing waters when grown-ups weren't around. One reason they made it a forbidden place was that every year one or two boys, dizzy and dazzled from looking down at the spring, fell in and were dragged by the undercurrent to the hidden palace of the Medicine God. I remember the white-whiskered old man used really vicious words when he chased us away: "My little lambs, do you all want to see the Medicine God? If you don't get out of here, I'll strip off your skin and eat your flesh!" Little Glory's mood was not affected in the least by the power of grown-ups. But my hair stood on end. He took my hand and we went home. His hand was warm and moist, but mine was icy cold.

4

You say you've already guessed it, following the logic of life and my tone of voice. Little Glory definitely died in an accident at a young age, and what's more he died precisely in the waters of "Flowing Water Hill" (your name for it). I know I've pulled you and him closer through mystery, as if I've become close to him again through telling you about him. These memories are taking me back to the old days, returning me to his side. Spilling out my memories to you pulls the past events and you closer together. In terms of time and space, this is three-dimensional: the story, telling the story, and hearing the story.

You say that stories exist for people to tell. You add that storytellers exist for the stories they tell, just like the present world exists so we can look back on the past (or, in other words, for the past to have people to look back on it). You also say we create the future so we have a chance to turn into material to be read, to be the research topic of people in the future who don't have a long enough history of their own. Or so that people in the future will remember us.

The time and space of novels are also three-dimensional. Nearly everybody is a novelist, oral or written. So it's easy for people to understand this three-dimensionality. I've just finished reading *The Woman of Rome*.[2] Moravia uses the stories of Adriana and Giacomo to bring them, him, and me into the same world, but a world impossible to name.

You know, the reality that's so hard to accept but that people just have to accept—I'm not going to tell it all in one blow. I'm in the midst of following a path toward an abyss that I've already been along but has appeared again in my memories. Like me, Moravia doesn't dare face prematurely the grievance Giacomo nurses toward the informer, nor does he dare face prematurely Adriana's defense of him. Because, rather than describe Giacomo's suicide as tragic, it's better to describe the even more tragic sense of that prostitute's defense of him: "He's a young man from a wealthy family; he's doing this because he believes in his cause, and not to make people wait in vain . . . exactly the opposite of all of you, he will lose everything because of this, and you all will gain everything from it." You say you read this book before me. In that case, I don't need to speak any more of what Giacomo did and why Adriana loved him deeply. Anyway, those kind of people and stories would never appear in Triangle City. For us, revolution and informing on people come together in every realm of society and daily life. It's our usual diet. Basically, nobody dies on account of this. Unexpected accidents or deaths from old age, from an artistic point of view, they don't have much tragic significance.

5

Before I went off to primary school in Circle City, Little Glory's grandma gave me a good dose of her fierceness. The incident happened during preschool prep classes at Triangle City's railway primary school. You grew up in Square City, so you probably never heard of "primary preparatory class." That was a special term we used in Triangle City. These classes came about

2 *The Woman of Rome* (罗马女人) (1947, Italian *La Romana*), written by Alberto Moravia, is a novel about existentialism, morality, and alienation, set in the Fascist period.

because of the huge imbalance between the number of kids my age and the pupil capacity of Triangle City's seventeen primary schools. They called the children not too far off in age from me the "surplus population," which really sounds like the "superfluous men" of Russian literature or the "lost generation" in American literature. Naturally, the concept of "surplus population" merely comes from population politics and can never be equated with loneliness, desperation, having nothing to do, rebellion, and self-banishment. More concretely, it was the large-scale production and construction in the cities which aroused enthusiasm for reproduction in my parents' generation; not because they were fonder of copulating and giving birth than the previous generation or the one after them. People are all equal. No one is more capable of being stimulated than anyone else, nor are there types of people better at childbearing than others. Some authors' logic is: we are the victims of our era. If I took their viewpoint, I would say: the prep classes eliminated two-thirds of Triangle City's good children, pushing them into the ranks of the illiterate; we are the town's victims.

Among the group of victims, Little Glory, Little Beauty, Little Mountain, Little Red, Little Fatty, Little Firm, Little Strong, Little Iron, Little Three, Little Four, and I had a narrow and lucky escape. We stood out in the prep course. Nowadays, thinking back, Little Glory's situation was a bit unusual: his grandma accompanied him all day to and from school, and when we were studying in the classroom (actually the so-called classroom was just a storehouse loaned from the factory for free), his grandma would sit outside sunning herself and recalling bygone days (I'm guessing). Little Glory was bright, but he didn't concentrate and he could be very arrogant. An incident occurred, which originated in his cleverness and my slow and simple earnestness, and naturally also included the go-between "informer," Little Four.

Our teacher was Little Red's young and beautiful mother. Her last name was Zhang. Teacher Zhang liked to test our memory by recounting one of Aesop's fables, then making us repeat it. Through the large window, Little Glory caught sight of his grandma's motionless silver tornado-style hair in the splendid spring sunshine, and then jumped up first. I sat on his right-hand side, passionately in love with him at the time. I worried for him, because while Teacher Zhang was telling the story he was nonchalantly drawing little people and planes and rockets and steamships and trains in his notebook. He retold the story: "A god created people, and deliberately gave them a short life. When winter came on, people used their wits to build houses for themselves like hardworking magpies [Little Glory's own fanciful metaphor]. One day, the weather was pretty damn cold. Tiger, Ox, and Dog all ran to people's houses to cop the warmth. The people demanded the animals each give them some more years of life, otherwise they'd chase them outside and let them freeze to death. Tiger, Ox, and Dog all agreed. So in the years given by the god, people are honest and good; in the years given by the tiger, people like to brag and spout off a lot of nothing; when they reach the years given by the ox, they get down to work; and in the years given by the dog, they blow off a lot of steam and like to kick up a row." When he had finished, he coolly and arrogantly cast a glance toward his classmates looking at him and sat down.

I was nervous; I broke out in a cold sweat. No doubt about it, he had spoken fluently and vividly. His grandma had definitely heard her grandson's fetching voice. She turned her wrinkled face, all smiles, wanting to see Little Glory, who sat in the very last row. But I felt embarrassed for him: he had casually changed a key animal. I've always liked tigers, they're the most steadfast and powerful king of kings. Horses can't be talked about in the same breath as them, let alone the teacher hadn't mentioned tigers in the story at all. I lowered my head and clamped my upper teeth on my lower lip. Beads of cold sweat rolled down my forehead, dripping onto my knees.

Unfortunately, the teacher picked on me to stand up, asking, "Did he tell the story well? Did he get it right?" Before asking me, almost the whole class had already shouted out in unison: "Well spoken! That was right!" They knew none of them was as clever as Little Glory. Even if some suspected he made mistakes, it was only a suspicion, and eventually they'd decide they themselves were wrong. Little Beauty was an exception: she usually didn't smile or speak, and Little Red's mother hardly ever asked her a question, thinking she was out of place in the class, since she was a year younger than the other students.

I stood there, bolt upright, like the most obedient and subjugated pupil under Triangle City's standardized education of that time. I was nervous, the blue veins throbbing in my temples and the sweat running down both my sides. I just stood there, my mind a blank. I could barely see what was in front of me; only the radiance of Little Beauty's big pair of eyes watching me, as she turned round in her seat in the front row, made me feel there was something real in this unreal scene. Little Glory nudged my left knee with his right elbow, whispering: "Go on! Answer the question!" This wasn't so much about urging me or reminding me; it was more the brazenness of someone expecting high words of praise. He gave me a way out, but I mistook what he meant as: "Go ahead and speak the plain truth." I heard my own voice as clear as day, then I sat down. I let out a big sigh and felt my back bathed in a cold sweat.

"Well said, but not completely right. Wang Wenwen's [that's me] comments hit the nail on the head. Liu Baohui [that's Little Glory] changed the horse in Aesop's fable into a tiger; this is a very obvious error." Mrs. Zhang pointed to several pupils one after the other: "Li Xiaohong, Zhang Yanli [Little Beauty's proper name], Wang Tiemin, and Zhang Guangsi, didn't you figure that out?"

When class was over and we left school for the day, I followed alongside Little Glory. He was already caught up with some crayons in his pocket and didn't hold it against me that I criticized rather than praised him. But at the factory's main entrance, his grandma blocked my way. Little Four was hidden behind her stiff and dried-up body, sucking up to Little Glory (by showing that he had spilled the beans) and trying to keep this from me (acting like he was an innocent bystander). Little Glory's grandma came right up in my face. With her left hand on her hip and right hand tightly clenched, she poked me repeatedly in the forehead with her extended forefinger, grilling me in that severe tone: "Who said my Little Glory didn't get it right? You? I heard loud and clear Little Red's Ma say it was a man, a tiger, a dog, and an ox. Why did you have to say it was a horse? You better tell me right now that Little Glory got it right and said it good; and that he said it just as good as Li Tie [a famous storyteller in Triangle City]! Say it! Otherwise, don't bother to play with my Little Glory anymore, and don't even think about getting close to my door again even if your ma brings you." I clenched my teeth and held back my tears. We locked in confrontation until Little Glory pushed his grandma away, whispering, "Gran, Little Question was right. I didn't pay a whit of attention to what Teacher said. If he said it was wrong then it was definitely wrong." He pushed her forward (you could say dragged her by the arm). I stayed right there; my tears just wouldn't stop.

They walked into the distance in the midday sun, along Triangle City's broad main street. I froze in my childhood stance, watching them become smaller, until they were two small moving specks, eventually disappearing. From then on, it seemed as if I never saw them again in the real, material world.

6

I lodged with my grandma in Circle City to go to primary school. My parents took turns coming to see me from Triangle City, sometimes bringing my sister. The train set off from a "triangle" and arrived at a "circle," linking me to home through a curve on a sheet of geometric graph paper. I use the word "lodge" to summarize my situation at Grandma's, not just because my parents paid her every month for my living expenses and paid all the miscellaneous fees at the Circle City First Primary School. Even more, I always felt like a stranger there. I had a definite hostility toward my grandma (although from start to finish I didn't show it). That's because she was the first person of the opposite sex in my life to touch my sex organ on purpose (at least from what I remember). In my family, no one ever showed any special interest in my sex. I felt safe, respected, and innocent living with my parents and sister. When I lived with Grandma, I became a freak with a special attachment. No doubt about it, my sixty-something grandma liked me very much. But her behavior made me uncomfortable, even making me wonder if I was clean. I had a weird way of thinking then (which has disappeared now) that the way grandparents love their grandchildren is vulgar. I vowed that when I was old, I wouldn't get close with any little kids, no matter how much I loved them. That was what I thought. Ironically, after I grew up I treated every child I saw as the most precious treasure in the world.

You laugh at my unusual way of thinking then. You say that old people and children are the most harmonious companions in the world. Many times, I've also witnessed scenes of grandparents and grandchildren happy together. But I've never experienced it myself. I don't think I'm suited to it. It's only for old people and children who comfortably enjoy sharing the sunshine of life. But I'm by nature the kind of person who prefers his own company night and day. Even though I lodged at Grandma's house, and she showered me with love and looked after my every need, I instinctively disliked the way Grandma touched me. Using this as pretext, I peeled myself away from the family happiness an old person and a child should have. I wished I'd been born an orphan, wearing worn and tattered clothes, wandering in the streets, no one caring for me, no one loving me, but all alone (a wonderful experience of freedom).

In any case, I'm not an orphan. Grandma provided me with life's necessities. I kept Triangle City, Little Glory, and even Little Beauty (we still had never talked) in my thoughts. In real life, I found a new friend. We went to school together and came home together, we read together, sometimes played the flute together, grew up together, passed the entrance exam for Square City University together, and graduated together. He was called Lei Ye; he's already dead. I've written about him in an article; I'll show you another time. Right now, I don't want to talk about him anymore. I want to talk about a friend of his, called Li Qing. When we were in junior high, he shot himself in the head and shattered his skull. But it wasn't suicide. He won't be able to descend to Dante's seventh circle of hell, the circle of violence (for mutual brutality, suicide, and blasphemy against God and nature).

7

Li Qing's father had a gun, a genuine, heavy pistol that could fire dumdum bullets. By way of introduction, Lei Ye pointed out his back in front of us on the flagstone road. This was an eye-opener: I'd never heard of anyone in Triangle City who had a real gun at home. A single bullet was as terrifying to me as an atom bomb, which had already exploded.

Li Qing stopped when he heard us shout and waited for us to catch up. He turned the side of his face to the summer sunshine; he had a pale complexion with a warm smile on his face. In my memory, he looked like neither a youth nor an adult. He seemed to have stopped aging, but I can't say for sure at what stage in life this happened. When we caught up with him, he just nodded to me, smiling, a style of greeting rare among children. But he wasn't at all reserved, just gentle. We never had closer relations than saying hello. He was in class five; I was in class six. Sometimes Lei Ye was a bit closer to him, sometimes a bit closer to me. I can come up with three reasons why he sticks in my memory so firmly and why I think of him as an important part of my life. One is that he maintained just a nodding relationship with me, which went on for seven years, never changing throughout. The second is that his gentle personality and calm demeanor presented a great contrast with the shock I felt about the "pistol"; he simply didn't seem like the son of a guy who had a gun (actually none of us had ever seen his father). The third is that a person like this, whose age was indeterminable (but he absolutely didn't resemble an old person) would unexpectedly act so childishly and play with a loaded pistol, role-playing alone in the house, pretending to be a suicidal hero at a military impasse (Xiang Yu style, perhaps[3]) or acting the part of a tragic lover (Young Werther style, perhaps[4]). Within the smooth and evasive town walls of Circle City, his pretend drama became reality. He lost his life from

3 Xiang Yu (项羽) (232–202 BCE) was a nobleman of the Chu kingdom who fought and defeated the reigning Qin dynasty, then contended with the Han kingdom for hegemony. Losing a battle to the Han, he killed himself.

4 The reference here to Werther (维特) comes from *The Sorrows of Young Werther*, a novel by Goethe about the unrequited love of a young artist.

a bullet in peacetime. He was not a great hero, nor a great lover; apart from me, people nowadays probably don't remember him at all.

The deserter in the German song "A Grave on the Plain" was "the first dead person mourned" by Canetti.[5] The deserter had been seized. He stood before his comrades. When the firing squad was about to kill him, he sang out the reason for his desertion: a song from his native place. At the end, he sang: "Farewell, my brothers, here's my chest." Immediately a shot rang out. Eventually a rose grew from the grave on the plain. Li Qing was the first dead person I grieved for. He wasn't guilty of anything in my eyes, nor did he have any faults. He merely picked up a gun, a real gun, as if he were picking up a wooden one. Unhurriedly, calmly, without fear, and without any yearning for another world, he simply pressed the trigger. "Farewell, brothers, here is my skull." He didn't make this curtain call. I'm guessing only some small white wildflowers grow on his grave.

8

My grandma was the kind of older woman who was tall and pretty and liked to keep herself very neat. Mama inherited most of her strong points but was a lot shorter. After the age of forty, Grandma didn't do any more housework. Apart from her own toilet, she just supervised the household chores; it was left to my three aunts to carry them out. They took turns working a shift, coming to cook and clean for us. Actually, I had four uncles and aunts on Mama's side. My eldest uncle fell ill and died in his youth. Eldest aunt remarried, took her two children with her, and never came back to Grandma's house. The so-called daughter-in-law who leaves to remarry is like spilt water, gone forever. After third uncle passed away (the cause of third uncle's death has always been a big secret in the Wang household; I still don't know what happened: it's like a well, hidden in the desert), third aunt kept coming to Grandma's house to be our servant just like before. She had no children, didn't remarry, and didn't go off to become a nun. She was just an ordinary believer, strictly following Christian teachings. Actually, St. Paul's disciples in the First Epistle to the Corinthians and the First Epistle to Timothy have two suggestions for widows. They can choose either one. The first is "if the widows have sons or grandsons, they should cultivate filial piety for their husbands' families, to repay a debt to the ancestors." The second is "if they

5 Elias Canetti (卡内蒂), Bulgarian-born German-language author, 1905–94.

cannot control their lust, then let them remarry, because it is better to marry than to burn up with desire." Though third aunt had no sons or grandsons, she voluntarily chose the first. But after Grandma died, I didn't hear anything more about her. I don't know if she preserved her widowhood her whole life or got involved in profane affairs. She always gave me the feeling of a life just running its course, coming and going quietly, though I'm not sure why.

Originally, Grandma's household was a large extended family. By the time I came to lodge there, Circle City's political authorities had weakened it so that Grandma now lived alone. Despite this, Grandma still lived a carefree life of luxury as before. Generally speaking, on the Lord's Day (Sunday), she went to mass in the morning (by taxi, because the church was far away); on Saturday she went to the theater (northeastern-style opera, Peking opera, drama, Western opera, dance: she loved them all without exception so long as they had a storyline); and on Friday (the sixth day of the Christian week, the day Jesus suffered), she just ate braised carp, no poultry or other meat. After I arrived, she specially took on the responsibility of washing my handkerchiefs. She arranged this work for Monday. Every Monday, thirteen tiny flags hung in her yard (I used two white handkerchiefs per day on average; when she was washing them I only carried one on my person). If I hadn't known my parents paid my living expenses every month, and if Grandma hadn't touched my body's shameful place, perhaps I'd have wept my heart out when she was near the end of her life.

Mama, who was small and dainty, attended the theater as often and as passionately as Grandma. When I was in Triangle City, she pulled me along to the theater every weekend. She and Grandma enjoyed watching fables and heartbreaking romances the most. If by chance they watched a comedy or slapstick, they led me home quickly at the end of the play and immediately drank a glass of water, saying: "What nonsense and foolishness! Just taking us for a ride! So meaningless." Of course, they were criticizing the playwright's disregard for life's full range of joys and sorrows, opportunistically catering to the low-level tastes of some in the audience (in their opinion the people who liked to watch comedies had hearts of stone). When I finished watching a tragedy with them, they wouldn't pull me by the hand but would let me follow behind them all by myself, while they were absorbed in wiping away their tears. They shed tears for the leading character. As for me, I walked along healthy in the real world, so they couldn't bring me into their preoccupation with the hero or lover (dead because of war or disease or betrayal or a broken heart). In the aftermath of the drama, I became rather ordinary. I think they even doubted whether they loved me in those moments (because they so ardently loved Jia Baoyu and Lin Daiyu,[6] Romeo, Hamlet, and the White Swan).

I just wanted to go far away, to leave this "double security" maternal structure far behind me. I ought to have become one of those children "whereabouts unknown," at least to them, just like a heroic pilot unaccounted for from a night flight, or Tolstoy, who ran away from home. I couldn't take any sudden action, but as the years went by, I eventually broke away from Grandma's shadow. Going to university in Square City seemed like a plan I had had since childhood. It was my excuse to break away from the double-duty protection of my mother and my mother's mother. Grandma passed away several years ago. I wasn't there when it happened. To hear Mama tell it, Grandma was sick for just a month and then she closed her eyes. Before the end came, Grandma changed into a clean set of underwear and clean set of clothes, but she simply had no time to make her hair look as glossy and beautiful as it normally did. When she was on the verge of death, Mama plucked up the courage to comb her hair. Only Grandma's hands had ever wound her exquisite coil before then; no one else could even imagine touching it. My poor Mama still regrets not allowing Grandma to comb her beloved hair before meeting the archangel St. Michael, the gatherer of souls.

I asked Mama if Grandma thought of me before dying. She said no but that Grandma repeatedly asked about my father. She had seen him grow from a small child into her own son-in-law. It was a real blow that I wasn't in her last thoughts. It brought me back to the physical and mental state of being a child again, a child enduring a painful injury.

9

Are you saying people die to make the living feel badly? That they die just to increase the knowledge of regret among the living? Take, for example, an old man whose children are unfilial. They completely neglect—even abuse—him when he's alive. But as soon as he dies, their tears and wails shake the air. If they hadn't seen the coffin, they wouldn't have shed any tears; if they hadn't seen the old man's corpse, they wouldn't have recognized the sins

6 Jia Baoyu and Lin Daiyu (贾宝玉, 林黛玉) are principal characters in the eighteenth-century novel *Dream of the Red Chamber*.

they'd committed against him. Soul, breath, heartbeat, and blood flow—the old man took all these out of his body, leaving them a shell to contemplate. Another example: Group after group of soldiers fall on the battlefields. Korea, Vietnam, Iraq, Iran, Bosnia-Herzegovina. Their souls leave their dead bodies en masse, causing the victors to live on, tainted with their bloodstains. Comparatively speaking, life is more frightening than death. You think death is one of God's greatest stratagems. Death doesn't let anyone know its real nature. It paints the widest and deepest backdrop to life. That is sublime wisdom. You admire it.

I feared God's wisdom for a long time. Almost every night from childhood to adulthood, I experienced that wisdom's coldness and destructive power that penetrated to my bones. When night fell and the night wind brushed my cheeks and the leaves outside the window, I felt a powerful but invisible hand seizing my soul. My soul was like a tightly squeezed rubber balloon, alternately squashed and swollen, making all the nerves in my body feel like an instrument's highest-tuned strings. But the bones, blood, skin, and flesh surrounding my nervous system slowly went loose and limp, like molten lava, or dust and sand, liable at any time to be scattered in all directions by the wind or rain.

I'm terrified of this wisdom of death. No one knows its true nature. We meet it only in thought and imagination. But when I face the reality of death, that big hand never stretches out before me. I can squeeze right up to the front row to look up at Little Beauty's grandma hanging, with my head almost touching her feet, and I don't fear Little Iron's grandpa either.

Little Iron's grandpa tried to kill himself three times. The neighbors all treated him like a ghost, avoiding him like the plague. He always sat alone under a solitary old elm tree, looking at people and objects with a glazed expression. Before I reached school age, I had a lot of time to kill. My favorite playmate was Little Glory. When he was willing, I was like his shadow. But his fickle character meant that he often behaved in a very adult way to frustrate my loyalty.

He'd lie that he wasn't in the mood to play; and he'd treat me like a clown to be insulted and laughed at when he had a crowd around him. He often hurt my young heart, but I remained his loyal friend. I accepted his privilege to be carried away on a whim, because he had the natural character of a lord, something I was totally unfamiliar with. His arrogance, coldness, and fickle temperament, and his enthusiasm and skill in mocking other people—I was perplexed and tormented but also fascinated. I tried to imitate him in front of the mirror at home, to act like a lord, one moment wildly happy, the next moment with cold, catlike eyes. But I failed utterly. I believed then that my blood's boiling and freezing points were lower than Little Glory's.

When Little Glory ignored me, I went to the old elm tree to find Little Iron's grandpa. As soon as he saw me coming, his face would break into a smile, like a deeply and intricately carved flower. He'd gather me to his chest and mumble away to me, kissing my cheeks over and over again. His body gave off a special smell, just like the moldy smell of the fallen leaves and the bark that had peeled off the trees in Triangle City's forest. At the time, I took it to be the smell of an old tree; it held an ineffable attraction for me. When I reached adulthood, I changed, and that odor turns my stomach. So my memory of Little Iron's grandpa has inevitably been infected by my point of view. I have two standpoints: me as a child, me now. The child me doesn't understand at all why he disappeared from my life. What happened that afternoon has remained a mystery to me despite thinking about it for more than ten years.

I was doing my prep course for primary school then. Little Iron and I were in the same class. When school let out a gang of us walked home together. We passed by the old elm tree and saw a small crowd gathered around there. At the center was a young guy really giving it to Little Iron's grandpa, slapping him in the face. The bystanders were dumbstruck. They just watched; not one of them stepped up and tried to stop it. Among them was a kid a little younger than us, crying. I recognized him. It was Little Winter. Little Iron usually didn't give a whit about his grandpa. But this time he charged forward like a madman to fight with the guy. I saw who it was then: Little Winter's older brother. Anger and agitation gripped him so that his whole body shook with a wild power. He quickly knocked Little Iron to the ground. Pointing at him and his grandpa, he cursed them: "Cocksuckers! Your whole family are cocksuckers!" Finished cursing, he turned round and grabbed his little brother from the crowd. Viciously slapping his buttocks, half-exposed through the slit in the back of his trousers, he yelled: "You little shit, you just let him play with you any old way!" Little Winter bawled all the way as he obediently followed his brother home.

From that moment on, I never saw Little Iron's grandpa again. Some people said he was sick and that he had gone to the hospital. Others said Little Iron's father had tied him to a chair to stop him going out. And there were those who said that Little Iron's grandma had locked him up inside (she was still alive then), afraid he'd go out to molest young boys again. When I heard adults gossiping about him, they always used the word "buggery." I asked Little Glory about it. His eyes lit up, and he said in reply, "You don't even know about this?" I lowered my head because of my own ignorance and didn't ask again. Not long after that incident, I was sent to Circle City to stay at my grandma's house. My sister secretly told me it was to keep Little Iron's grandpa from touching me. I was confused. What was so bad about him touching me?

10

The turning point in Triangle City's history can be symbolized by the disappearance of Little Glory's grandma's white tornado-style hair. According to the records, she was the last of her generation to leave this world. She not only personally dressed and laid out the body of her own son who had died from illness, but she also took Little Glory's corpse all the way to the public cemetery and prayed for him for a very long time, at the end loudly commanding the devil not to lead Little Glory into the seventh circle of hell. According to what Little Glory's younger brother said, she got enlightened by the Holy Spirit and suddenly decided to become a Christian. As soon as she came out of the heathen darkness, she was determined not to give in to the three foes (profanity, the devil, and the flesh) anymore. She couldn't read the Bible, but she was sure God would never forsake her eldest grandson. According to the handed-down manuscript "The Teachings of Jesus" (she had only heard fellow church members talk about it), she believed that God would never send people to hell (which had been specially created for the devil). God would be ashamed if His flock stayed in purgatory for a long time and even more ashamed if they entered hell. As for the devil, there was no way he could possess her grandson's soul (he was so clever, handsome, and loving). What she said got right to the point: "Judas committed suicide because he betrayed Jesus. But my grandson loved God's creations too much, and anyway the Ten Commandments don't say 'thou shalt not commit suicide.'"

Are you surprised? In your investigations of Triangle City's past, have you ever found a believer brave enough to reject a church teaching, someone who was a recent church member and who couldn't even read? You think she used her heart and soul to tell the difference between laws which come from the Lord and laws which do not? You say there exists a country, far away from Triangle City, as far away as the North Pole is from the South Pole. There is only one national motto in that country, "In God We Trust." People who have read the Gospel according to John know that Judas's betrayal was done on

Jesus's order: "What you are going to do, do quickly." In the Gospel according to Matthew, when Judas betrayed Jesus with a kiss, Jesus maintained a loving tone, saying: "Friend, do what you came for." Judas immediately repented after Jesus was sentenced to death. He returned the thirty pieces of silver, saying: "I have sinned by betraying innocent blood." His suicide by hanging was an expression of his repentance. Would Jesus condemn this kind of person to hell in a private trial? You say we should believe in God, the same as in that country. So you believe the theory Little Glory's grandma believed in: God would never let the devil take Little Glory.

Actually, that's my wish, too. I hope almighty God because of His all-encompassing love will pardon all those who committed the sin of suicide, including my favorite author Yukio Mishima, my first friend in this world, Little Glory, Little Beauty's grandma (even though I know nothing about the reason for her death), and Judas. "In God We Trust." I believe God will pardon all those who committed suicide, regardless of whether it was for worldly love, because of desperation or unbearable loneliness, for a lofty goal, or even if it was because of a selfish desire. No matter why they died, I believe for sure there was an unbearable pressure that crushed their fragile lives.

11

To be precise, the day of Little Glory's death was the same day as Little Beauty's birthday. You know, Triangle City's winters are cold and long. On Little Beauty's birthday, Little Glory bought a beautiful fresh rosebud, put it inside his clothing to keep it warm, and heading into the heavy wind and snow went straight to Little Beauty's home (still that old house, the red-brick bungalow where her grandma hanged herself in the front hall). They say he paced up and down outside her door for a long time (clearly his state of mind was rather confused) until the cold penetrated his overcoat and approached the rosebud. After knocking on the door, he immediately stepped back from under the eaves, back into the heavy snow filling the sky. I guess he was worried that standing too close would cause her to get the wrong idea. Before this, he'd get excited when he was too close to Little Beauty, putting a real strain on Little Beauty's independent and uninhibited ways. Now he stepped back into the down-like snowflakes, waiting for Little Beauty to open the door. She stood in the shadow between the door and the eaves, looking at him coldly and angrily. He pulled his arm and the flower out from his overcoat and, waving it, carefully said: "Happy . . . happy birthday!" Through the thick snow, Little Beauty saw his bright eyes full of regret and deep love. His hands were red and stiff from the cold. The flower in his hand quivered slightly. Snowflakes occasionally fell on the bud, clinging to it, then melting. She told me that she looked on this scene with a cold expression, but feelings of warmth and an obscure ache filled her heart. She didn't want to let him see her experience these emotions. She shut the door.

Holding the flower, Little Glory silently turned round, walked down the paved path between the brick houses and came to Medicine Spring in a daze. Along the rocky platform, the "ice mountain" was already towering high. He absentmindedly climbed to the top of the "mountain," but he slipped down, as if he were skillfully skating backward, then clambered back up again. After he had climbed up and slipped down several times, he set himself down at the mouth of the spring. He stared into the spring and saw the image of a handsome flower-carrying youth. The youth looked icy-cold because of the background of snowflakes and sky. His stiff fingers could barely hold the flower's stalk. Carelessly, he dropped the flower into the spring, the bud pointing down and the stalk pointing up. Either through losing his footing or chasing the flower, Little Glory limply fell forward, plunging headfirst into the spring. Little Glory abruptly slipped to the bottom of the water just like a fish, disappearing without a sound. All that remained was the flower, floating on the water, facing the occasional snowflakes falling into the spring (this is based on Little Beauty's brief account, which I have elaborated to make the memory of it into a more splendid tragedy).

After three days and three nights of heavy snow, Little Glory's grandma staggered around every nook and cranny of Triangle City searching for her beloved grandson. That head of tornado-style silver hair, seeming to meld right into the sunlight and the brightness of the snow, appeared more and more stirring. I guess anyone who saw her would be moved by the clear contrast between the whirling speed and violent power of her movements, like an all-engulfing hurricane, and their solitariness (like a ferocious lion in the wilderness). Actually, she was just desperately looking for an outcome, whether good or bad. Finally, she found the rose in the spring. The rose had already silently blossomed in the spring water, with its fronds underneath and its petals facing upward. It was even giving off faint bursts of fragrance, like water lilies in a pool.

Old grandma sat by the spring, blankly staring into the water for a while. Then she concluded that her eldest grandson had already been carried along an underground waterway to the sea. She believed that all the world's springs had hidden connections to the sea. She understood her grandson so well, almost as well as she knew her own strong will. She'd seen the flower he bought, seen how he'd covered it up before heading out into the snow and wind, never to return home. She figured he'd done everything he wanted to, ought to, and could do. Finished with everything, he could go to a different place. Not everyone who comes from dust returns to dust; she was sure her grandson would enter the kingdom of heaven. She stood up, shed two tears, and went home.

12

Little Beauty remembers that when she saw the rose in the spring, it had already started to wither. More than astonishment, she felt an instinct deep within her shaken awake at that moment. A faint pain gripped her. Then a kind of physical pain rent through her heart and womb. Before, Little Glory's hatred of her coldness, his desire to conquer her, and his actual rape of her one time had simply evoked a deeper coldness in her. All his courting over the last three years didn't have the slightest effect on her feelings. She'd never respond to his love. In her eyes, he was nothing but a playboy. Besides his fickle way of seducing then discarding girls, he had many habits she found disgusting: he liked to boss others around, played petty tricks, had superficial talents (he only knew a smattering about music, chess, painting, singing, and dancing), acted high and mighty, and paid too much attention to projecting a free and easy image. She had grown up with him and had coolheadedly kept a steady distance from him regardless of whether other people loved or spurned him. She firmly believed they lived in two totally different worlds. When he expressed his love for her with tireless enthusiasm, she thought it was all just a new game for him. She stuck to her resolve not to play this game.

She told me about these past events as she sat on a rotten branch in Triangle City's forest. It was one day when I went back to visit my parents during autumn of last year. I sat on another rotten branch opposite her, watching the autumn leaves fall and carpet the wood. We had never been close. But she knew that Little Glory and I had been close, and after we met by chance, she decided I would be the best audience for her. She said that Little Glory's death had changed her from a quiet person of few words into a person who would burst if she did not talk with people. Her gaze was still bright and her skin still smooth and slightly dark; the only change was she had shortened her hair, just like a young Vietnamese girl.

When she had seen the withered rose floating in the misty spring waters, she had felt a very, very slight life quietly moving in her womb. She had just turned twenty-one (one year younger than Little Glory and me), with no experience of sex and pregnancy. It was merely due to her innate coolheadedness that she decided to let nature take its course. She remembered some words of his. He had said that he had already started to like her that year they spun tops together. (But she did not believe that preschool children could fall in love.) He said that he had cynically destroyed his reputation (previously some teachers had favored him) by messing around with many girls and acting like a playboy, to attract her attention and also to dispel his own strong love for her. He said that her coldness to him was the biggest defeat and pain in his life (but she believed it to be her strength). He said he loved her and would do anything for her love, whether beautiful, ugly, or terrible. (In fact he had written a poem for her, raped her, and drowned himself.) All along, she did not like him. But after he died, when the rose was already losing its freshness, she felt anguish, and an indescribable, fervent love began to spread in her heart. She wanted to stop it, but she did not succeed.

You think that her love was engendered by violence and death, that all along she had had a kind of closed mentality, which tended to coldness and congealment, and which Little Glory's undisciplined passion and violence had punctured. If Little Glory's behavior had just stopped at this, then the violence would merely have had a destructive effect: Little Beauty, with her bodily wound, would have recovered her mental faculties. In fact, Little Glory followed violence with death, pushing the situation to where he could rape and die for love, giving Little Beauty no opportunity to heal the symptoms of spiritual loneliness. From your point of view, Little Beauty seems to have been ill in the first place, but it is just that nobody noticed. It was Little Glory's love, violence, and abrupt death that imperceptibly diagnosed and treated her. As a person, all of Little Glory's behavior, behavioral style, and behavioral standards were full of vitality, health, and intelligence. He acted according to their rules. You almost want to admire him, for his primitive, simple, and resourceful style of love, life, and death.

I was confused. My past image of Little Glory was as fresh, direct, and experiential as my image of Little Beauty playing hopscotch or spinning tops. The Little Glory of Little Beauty's account, encircled by several affairs (I still have not had time to tell you everything), was a figure in a story. Anyway, he and the Little Beauty of the story (even including Little Glory's grandma) were all fabrications. In my eyes, they had moved from reality into a movie. Regardless of whatever extra time I have, there is no way I can distinguish fact from fiction. A person or thing, as soon as there is no distinction between fact and fiction, possesses certain artistic qualities, such as mystery, suspense, absolute beauty, and underlying moral meaning. With regard to Little Glory and Little Beauty's story, it seems there is nothing I can do but tell you everything I heard and let you make your own judgments as you write your book.

In the end, Little Glory did not reach the ocean. When the rose petals were swirling away, he floated to the surface. According to people at the scene, he looked like he was alive, neither stiff nor bloated. His old grandma, with her gray hair hanging down, begged the priest to let him enter the sacred ground. At the funeral mass, devout old grandma and nonbeliever Little Beauty read from the scriptures together. They did not cry: grandma because she had faith that Jesus would save Little Glory's soul, and Little Beauty because she was carrying his baby. She feared that crying would harm the fetus.

Little Beauty's tears rolled down her face as she sat on the rotten branch in Triangle City's forest. When she strongly resisted Little Glory's love (now she believed that Little Glory had indeed loved her), Cupid still followed her closely. And when Little Glory used death to awaken her heart, her lover was already in his grave. She thought that the last image of Little Glory she could seize was the child. She had many beautiful dreams about the child: undoubtedly, he would be male, the spitting image of Little Glory, naughty, clever, and precocious enough to understand love at a young age (so that he would love her as Little Glory did). She recalled a book about reincarnated Tibetan soul boys, which recorded the stories, one after the other, of reincarnations of living Buddhas; some even had photographs. Since a living Buddha could enter a fetus to reincarnate, Little Glory could also enter the fetus inside her. She consoled herself with this idea of a relationship between the fetus and Little Glory, as seen in third-rate "transmigration" novels or movies.

Little Beauty gave birth to a baby boy, yet it scarcely had time to breathe before it died. The doctor feared she would not be able to bear the shock and had just quickly shown her the baby's face before bundling it away. From start to finish, she did not hear her baby cry. But she had no understanding of this (it goes without saying). Moreover, the dead baby looked alive, just as Little Glory had done when he was fished up from the spring. During her post-labor fatigue, she sweetly thought that her good little darling was so well behaved: he was not noisy, had not even cried once, such a sensible boy. Before she understood the truth of what had happened, she felt unceasingly happy and proud of him.

Little Glory's grandma strongly believed that her great-grandson's soul would not leave his body until he had been baptized and insisted on baptizing him, choosing the holy name John. Then she gave him the last rites. Little Beauty dreamed that she saw the childhood Little Glory run up to her bed, flapping two small wings on his back. Smiling, he called to her in a soft voice: "Mama, Mama!" Little Beauty took his hands, put them on her warm bosom, and said: "Child, you have grown so quickly. You've grown up already and I still haven't had time to give you a name." Little Glory smiled and said: "I already have a name, which God gave me." Little Beauty asked: "Is it your name in heaven?" He nodded. Little Beauty said: "Tell me, otherwise how can I find you in heaven?" He said: "John. That's my name. I'm always in the last rank of the angels." Then he quickly flapped his wings and flew toward the heavens.

Little Beauty told me she believed in the "facts" (her choice of word) she had seen in the dream. Previously, she had not had so much faith. A power had mysteriously affected her, pushing her (she said it was the Holy Spirit). She went to the church to be baptized: Little Glory's grandma was her godmother.

Hot tears rolled down her face as she sat on the rotten branch in Triangle City's forest. She asked me if I remembered that her grandma had hanged herself. I nodded. It had been the first time I had witnessed death. She said that she became cold and withdrawn from that time. Her grandma had had the rope ready for a long time, and her parents had known, she said; yet they had neither urged her grandma not to do it nor thought of a way to stop her. After her grandma hanged herself, they felt relief as well as disgrace. She very clearly remembered a sentence her mother said: "Why didn't she go to the woods to find a tree to hang herself rather than do it here?" Her father just lowered his head, showing no emotion. She felt ashamed of them and herself. She had just turned five then, and the floral cloth bag she used for hopscotch and the floral padded jacket she wore had both been made by her grandma. From that time on, she had become withdrawn. Sixteen years later, the entrance and exit of two lives had opened the door to her heart.

Nowadays, if you attend mass in the Church of the Sacred Heart of Jesus in the center of Triangle City, you can hear Little Beauty singing. She is the lead singer in the choir. She has a very good husband now, and a treasured son who is already in primary school. Can you imagine: her husband is Little Iron.

Orphans of the Japanese Empire 日本遺民

Translated by Elisabeth Lund Engebretsen

1

In the United States of America there is San Francisco. Everywhere in San Francisco you will find the English, Scots, Germans, Israelis, Russians, Chinese, Hui, Mongolians, Malays, Japanese, Native Americans, and many other ethnic populations.[1] You could call the city an ethnic version of a natural history museum. But if you go to Tokyo and look through the Tokyo census, you'll rarely find any ethnic group other than the Yamato majority. The Japanese archipelago stretches far and wide but can't seem to reach out to the open-minded spirit blowing over the ocean. Small islands and small countries get pinched by small ideas. But oddly, they worship the big and powerful, going so far as superworship. So the Yamato are called the Great Yamato and their country the Great Japanese Empire.

The people there have small builds. Their diminutive scholars have written essays on the benefits of small stature, suggesting that it helps the tall Western races enjoy the sunlight together with the Yamato race: the sun ascends in the East, the country of the small-built people. This is called the land of the rising sun. Its small-built ethnic group can't block the sunlight and keep it to themselves. So they share it generously with those Westerners, who are so pitiful but whose tall height influences their high IQ.

Of course, in the Triangle City where I grew up, we had only the three seasons of spring, autumn, and winter, and it was nothing like the bustle

First published in *Youth Literature* (青年文學), June 1999; and in *Collected Works of Cui Zi'en* (崔子恩文学作品集), vol. 2 (Zhuhai: Zhuhai chubanshe, 2003).

1 Hui (回) are Chinese Muslims.

of Tokyo. But our city gate was wide open, welcoming each and everyone, regardless of whether they were good or bad, beautiful or ugly, notorious criminals or male or female prostitutes. In truth, to register as a resident of Triangle City was easier than blowing dust. But Tokyo, the center of the Japanese Empire, wasn't like that, and neither was Singapore. You had to use the weapons of sexual seduction and your gender. In other words, you had to seduce and marry one of them. Naturally, in Triangle City you were more likely to encounter sublime love.

With its thousands of different blooming flowers and fruits, snow-white Triangle City was as picturesque as a poem or painting. There were the Chinese, Hui, North Koreans, and Manchurians who were born and bred there; the Japanese left behind by their empire's invasion; all the Gallic peoples, the Scots, the Franks, and the Bavarians who came for missionary work; and the Russians, White Russians, and Ukrainians, who gave a hand with urban reconstruction and then lingered and forgot to go home. Any one of them could live there permanently, no questions asked. They could make a living, though the pay wasn't much. But at least they had secure work.

When I was two months old, my dainty mother carried innocent me to the Church of the Sacred Heart of Jesus to be baptized. Cleansed of original sin, I was christened Peter. The priest who baptized me was a young, handsome Pole. My parents were raised in the free Sacre-Coeur school, run by two Swiss priests, one old and one young. Half the doctors and nurses in the Railway hospital where my father was in charge were White Russians. When I turned fifteen, with the hint of a mustache emerging above my lip, the Poles, Italians, Swedes, Swiss, French, and Russians simply vanished overnight from Triangle City. Some people said they left voluntarily because they were homesick, or that the city was too pure and too dirt-poor for them. Others said they were kicked out, because their ancestral countries were rolling in wealth, so wealthy they threw their milk and bananas into the sea, and people from rich countries are as evil as the countries they come from. They're devils, foreign devils, people said. Starting with the Eight-Nation Alliance's invasion of China, nothing good ever came from them.[2] I had my doubts, so I looked through some history books and found out that Poland was one of the biggest victims of World War II, the nation destroyed and besieged by foreign powers. How could they be expelled from our city of sublime love?

2 The Eight-Nation Alliance (Germany, Japan, Russia, Britain, France, United States, Austria-Hungary, and Italy) invaded China in 1900 to repel attacks by the grassroots Boxer Rebellion on foreigners living in China.

One of our closest neighbors, Akiko Koyama, wasn't expelled. She was the mother of Little Bright and Little Red. Her old man was a train conductor. He was tall and hot-tempered. That these Japanese stayed on here, not wanting to leave voluntarily and also not forced to leave, made me suspicious. I once used the ancient prose from my schoolbooks to ask Papa: "Whence the cause?" Papa told me this was a political issue and was not for a medical doctor such as himself, who examined the condition of the human body, to diagnose the shifting trends of international politics. To this day, I'm sure he was entirely unaware that my idolization of him was completely shattered on hearing those words. If a person of intelligence cannot offer the truth in response to a question, then what's the difference between him and any common person? From that moment on, I always fought with Papa. My logic was the typical adolescent variety: a shattered mirror can't compare with common glass.

Papa used to get up at dawn every morning to listen on the sly to the English-language broadcast. I took advantage of this moment to annoy him by positioning myself not far from him and playing the clarinet, hitting the highest possible notes. My lung capacity was rather limited, and performing music on wind instruments was always fairly strenuous for me. Still, because my music teacher favored the well-behaved appearance of his boy student, I was given free rein to choose whichever instrument I wanted from the new ones they had bought, to take back home to practice. I chose the French horn, the trumpet, and the clarinet. Needless to say, I was blowing my lungs out on these glittering brass instruments. Before this, Papa had suggested I start playing the violin. Naturally, I vowed never to play any string instrument.

Before long, my breathless playing on the clarinet brought on pneumonia. As soon as the coughing erupted, I tried to muffle the sound by covering my mouth in order to avoid his stethoscope and thus avoid becoming an experiment for his medical practices. I no longer believed that Papa, who could not even answer my question "whence the cause?," could compare with my former high opinion of his medical expertise. Maybe he had just a smattering of knowledge, like those itinerant doctors. In the evenings he played his violin; he always played "River of Sorrow." Before, as soon as he began playing, I inwardly shed some tears. Now, as soon as he brought out the bow, I sniggered and then removed myself. Naturally, I left only after my derisive smile had been clearly seen by him. After all, I was in the prime of my youth. I resolved that the pneumonia was cured by covering over my mouth. However, provided that one believes in karma/cause and effect, the calcification of spots left on my lungs was the cause, and then later when I took the college entrance exams, I received the punishment in the health exam, the effect being that I was skipped over. Papa kindly but sadly fixed his eyes on me, my sniggering and derisive profile seen from behind. Sometimes I heard him sighing to himself, because of the shadow over my heart and the gradually deepening chasm between us. Neither of us foresaw that the pursuit of perfection leads to a person's first disappointment and final isolation.

As always, Papa went to the hospital during the day or at night, performing surgery on patients in the operating room. As always, in the mornings he surreptitiously listened to the English-language radio, and at dusk he played the violin, changing the tune to "Song of Nostalgia." Spring left and autumn arrived in Triangle City. Day by day, his expression and language became more desolate and thin, more indifferent. I became the strong one, clenching my teeth, refusing to allow mercy to engulf my spirit. Papa became the weak one, withdrawn, avoiding as much as possible any chance of meeting face-to-face with me. I took advantage of this opportunity to look freely at his hidden books, using the delicate letter paper and ink that he had preserved from his time in college to write with abandon. Most importantly, he no longer disciplined me. Whenever I felt like it, I could go to our neighbors on the left, to look for Little Bright or Little Red. As for the Europeans being completely swept out, while the Japanese remained calmly behind, I would independently find the answer to "whence the cause" outside of the government and among the people.

2

Akiko Koyama's old man drove the steam train. He was tall and sturdy and named Zhao Jianghe. He drank strong liquor at the drop of a hat, and then took turns beating and cursing Akiko Koyama, Little Bright, and Little Red. Our neighbor Old Zhouji once said that all Japanese men are sadists and all the women are masochists. I had a vague idea what he meant because he used bodily gestures to show me. The image of the flogger and the flogged stuck in my memory. I soon lost sympathy for Akiko Koyama, who endured the beating and abuse, weeping and wailing. But she always appeared unfazed when she walked down the street. And she used our same local dialect when chatting with Mama. Little Bright and Little Red were altogether different. They suffered under the leather whip. Little Bright went mute from time to time.

Little Red took to an extremely feminine appearance when she grew up, the type that men tend to like. She tried to guard herself with what could never make her safe; men didn't really love her, despite her impeccable beauty and gentle ways.

3

Akiko Koyama took full advantage of the Railway Bureau's special privileges for employees' families to travel free of charge. Each year on her one trip to Circle City, she took turns traveling with Little Bright or Little Red. The one left behind stayed with us; Mama and my sister fed and looked after them. She then used the last free ticket for herself to go once a year to Square City. As Little Bright and Little Red went on their train trips less often, when she went to Square City, she frequently deposited her two kids with our family. Those were the happiest couple of months of our childhood: all of a sudden, our normally strict mother relaxed her restrictions on me and my sister; we could eat, drink, and play as we pleased because Mama didn't want her good friend's children to feel the least bit uncomfortable. To pay us back, or maybe as a way to create a dependent bond between us, Little Bright told me his mother always stayed in a hotel in Circle City. There, she secretly met with a clean and neat Japanese man, always the same man. Little Bright felt disgusted by Japanese people. He said they were all bastards and perverts (though he was referring to that particular Japanese man). Little Red was even tighter with my sister. She confided in my sister that when she and her mother traveled to Square City, they always stayed in the house of a Japanese woman. This woman was so poor that every time they went there, her mother brought stuff from home to give her. Sometimes she even gave her money.

Without a doubt, as a child, I had a lively imagination. But before I started school, my actual knowledge of the world was limited to the trips I took with Mama once a year to Circle City to see my maternal grandma, with Papa to Square City to see my paternal grandma (I also remember both of them occasionally taking me on other travels), and to things I saw, heard, and felt while playing around in Triangle City. All I could really imagine was the small inn I knew from Circle City, trying to picture it as narrow and dark, with wooden walls, and imagine that man who met up with Akiko Koyama as short, with a long handlebar mustache. I pictured the woman living in Square City as looking like Akiko Koyama; probably she was her sister. Even those images wobbled on the horizon of my imagination. They quickly dissolved in my single-minded devotion to playing. Sometimes I pictured them as part of the theatrical-like scenes in our games. I was just too curious about too many things. I had to wait until I grew up to reach a level of writing via the symbolism of Chinese characters that allowed me to solve some of these mysteries.

4

After Little Bright and I taught ourselves how to count from one to one hundred using Arabic numerals, and knew it inside out, Triangle City's Railway Number One Elementary School agreed to let us in on account of our high IQs. Our mothers used my family's sewing machine to make us sailor-style school uniforms. Then they took us both on a trip to Circle City. I wasn't really interested. For one thing, when I went with Mama to register, I fell deeply in love with my primary school (it was much bigger than my house and kindergarten put together, like comparing the ocean with a creek). For another thing, Mama wouldn't let me wear my brand-new school uniform to visit Grandma (she said I wasn't officially a student yet). Third, I had drawn a pile of masterpieces with my crayons (like thirteen of them), but Papa hadn't paid them the least mind (he was swamped with his surgery).

But once on the train my scheme to act like a brat with Mama vanished like the fog. That's because Akiko Koyama and Mama generously fed us the presents they had brought for folks in Circle City. Akiko Koyama fed me Triangle City's famous Lao Ding Feng flaky-crust mooncakes. Mama gave Little Bright delicious black-currant jam and meat pasties. Little Bright was a year older than me and skinnier and taller than me too. But we shared a passion for eating sweets. If the train hadn't sped through the night, our two mothers would easily have arrived the next morning empty-handed.

Once we got off the train, Mama and I needed to take the number 1 tram. We said goodbye to Little Bright and his mother, who had to get on the number 11 trolleybus. When the tram started moving, I looked out the upper-level window onto the train platform. Seeing the backs of Little Bright and Akiko Koyama recede toward the rear of the tram, I suddenly felt a bout of tenderness, regret, and anxiety. Their silhouettes gradually grew smaller and then disappeared, revealing that most basic experience of separation. Like the first wet dream, the first kiss, a boy's first night, these memories have a special place. Grandma and Auntie could see the feeling of loss in my eyes. I didn't feel like going out to play, and gave the cold shoulder to my cousin Lin Lin. Unheard of for me, I hardly had an appetite. By the third day, Mama made Uncle take me to the inn where Little Bright was staying so that I could see him again.

The Sunflower Inn was so tiny it looked like a toy castle (now I realize the style was Eastern European). Uncle and I sat waiting on the vestibule sofa for well over two hours, all the way until the last number 11 bus was leaving to go back, but there was no sign of Little Bright and his mother anywhere. Feeling desperate, on the way back I dreamed up one horrible scenario after another. First scenario: Little Bright was hit by "the beggar's slap" (slang for child trafficking). Someone posing as a street beggar drugged him, put him in a canvas bag, and simply disappeared in the city maze. A distraught Akiko Koyama, hair disheveled, went looking for him all night until she, too, vanished. Second scenario: Akiko Koyama's "Japanese military police" guy was ruthlessly killed on the street, and now Akiko Koyama and Little Bright were holding a vigil for him in the funeral parlor. (This scene was a little fuzzy, since I'd never been to a funeral parlor, and I couldn't decide between the vigil in the funeral parlor or a mass in church.) Third scenario: one car after another, big and small, had forced Little Bright to stay on the side of the road, forever unable to reconnect with his mother on the other side. (This, in fact, was more of a snapshot than a storyline.)

After returning to Grandma's, I became feverish. Mama said my whole body felt like a piece of burning coal. Grandma wouldn't let go of massaging my hand, and occasionally put her face right up against mine. I didn't know if she was taking my temperature or she thought I was about to die and wanted to get in an extra show of her fondness for me (usually I didn't like it when older people kissed me). Younger Auntie skillfully inserted a thermometer in my mouth and then gave me an injection to bring down the fever after having disinfected the syringe by boiling it in the steel pot on the stove. (She was a nurse.) Before hearing Grandma scold Uncle in Circle City dialect for not taking care of me, I couldn't tell when I was awake or hallucinating. It was like the cyclical intermission when counting numbers—1 2 3 4 5 and, again, 1 2 3 4 5. But on hearing Uncle's rebuttal, I crashed back into an imaginary world. Everything was twinkling dots and lines and then more dots and more lines. The backdrop was mostly white, milky white, grayish white, and then suddenly changed to black, and then dark gray, and then grayish white again. Faintly colored lines swirled around dots into one vast plane; blood-red points appeared here and there, and maybe a yellow-painted five-pointed star, or even a field of sunflowers. Dizzy, ever dizzier, I fell gently through the air, lying on my back looking up. I wanted to vomit but nothing came out, and I still couldn't reach the ground.

5

When I showed up for my first day at school, I wore my new sailor-style school uniform. Little Bright was also wearing his, but his had been washed two times already, so it looked a little old. This was because school had already started two weeks earlier. I hardly needed to make any effort to catch up. I still thought the school was my own special paradise. Every day I left home really early in the morning (I was even willing to miss out walking with Little Bright) to wait outside the school under the old elm tree for the school janitor to open the gates, to be sure I was always the first to enter the classroom. I kept this up all the way until I graduated from high school. But at the university I became a pro at skipping lectures. I had another habit that followed me all the way from first grade to high school graduation but at the university also became "a thing of the past": I always had top grades (even if my scores weren't always perfect), in every exam in every subject, for the highest all-round year-end grade, in my own classroom and in my entire class. These two habits made me a bit conceited, I admit, but on thinking back as an adult, for a long time all I could remember was a childhood that was colorless and boring. I almost wrote an article once urging the "goody two shoes" students to put down their books and have a playful childhood by doing what they want and enjoying themselves, just like Little Bright did.

Little Bright was like a different person at school from at home. At school he was like a wild animal let out of his cage. He played in the classroom and outside. And he was like a fierce young leopard. He was ready to punch and kick anyone who provoked him. During those first two weeks when I wasn't there, he'd already secured for himself the position of "prince" (actually, he was a despot). As soon as I showed up, he put me under his protection, to prevent me from being bullied and humiliated on account of my delicate and weak look. But once he got home and had to face his father's violent drunkenness, he immediately changed into a pitiful small cock, pulling his head and chest into himself, unable to say a word. He'd run to our house looking for comfort from my mother. He really was two different people, living in two entirely different worlds.

By the second year of middle school—which coincided with my asking Papa, "Whence the cause?" and my former idolization of him falling apart—Little Bright was already as tall as his father and had developed the same violent tendencies as his father, matching his violence fist for fist, kick for kick. But Little Bright's youthful kicks and punches only resulted in him being badly beaten. Two neighboring father-son pairs engaged in war the same year—cold and hot: My papa and I were at a long, drawn-out impasse, getting tenser by the day. Little Bright and his papa, on the other hand, had explosive, earthshaking fights, but short-lived and shallow in comparison. Maybe it was as a consequence of this that he started to develop such different personas.

My friendship with Little Bright was firm but subtle. I was the better student. Sometimes I helped him with his lessons; occasionally I corrected his homework. Whenever we had exams, I helped him, or I'd just go ahead and write down the answers on a piece of paper in the middle of the exam, roll it up in a little ball, and make a strategic pass to him. Going by scores and grades, I was by far the best student, but I wasn't necessarily the best behaved. My blood boiled too easily. Even if I'd wanted to be teacher's pet, I couldn't get there. Deep in my bones I was a rebel. I disliked that the teaching was so slow, so I always picked out the teachers' mistakes. Each time the teacher assigned a topic for our essays, I always added a subheading to point out that the teacher's choices were too prosaic. (For example, when the teacher set the topic "Write about a work experience," I added the phrase "When it snows heavily, sweeping snow is futile labor.") I used to ridicule the class monitor, who loved to rat on students to the teachers.

My outward appearance was very delicate and pure, my clothes always spotless and neat. Sometimes I'd inherit my father's old clothes made of high-quality fabrics, which were re-tailored to fit me. This gave me a young, avant-garde look. Almost every new homeroom teacher took one look at me and chose me to be class monitor. But I resisted because what I wanted was to take on the duty of literary and arts committee member, usually reserved for pretty female students. Being a literary and arts committee member gave me many liberties, actually: studying by myself early in the morning, I could stand on the platform in the classroom and play like I was the teacher; singing or teaching myself a song, I could pace back and forth in the corridor; during committee meetings I could sit next to the most beautiful girls in my class (most committee members were pretty girls back then; who cared if some of them were tone-deaf). When I was on the committee, I got Little Bright to get up and sing and dance. His dance skills were fine, but he just didn't have grace and elegance (at the time, boy students were supposed to move their wrists like softly swaying silk). His singing wasn't bad, though. But when other students took on being a committee member, he never remembered his lines. If they tried to make him dance, they could be sure he'd smash the rehearsal to pieces like someone charging on his horse with a pike in his hand.

Sometimes after school he mysteriously disappeared with a few high school students. He didn't walk home with me then, and he never told me where he'd been. He learned how to smoke, but he never egged me on to share a puff.

6

One day in the first semester of the second year of middle school, Little Bright brought in his schoolbag for me a few candied fruits known as "ocean dates." He said it was to celebrate my leaving off that female stuff, as he called it. The day before I'd been kicked off the literary and arts committee because I'd rebelled against a male teacher. He always picked on me to be a model example to read out the study text to the class, and he took forever to give us back our homework notebooks. Using class recess to our best advantage, we went up to his desk and stuck our slimy hands inside to find the ocean dates he kept there and ate them. As I remember it, the sweet taste of the dates was second only to the mooncakes I'd savored on the train. Only thing was, the sweet dates carried a bitter aftertaste: as we were sucking up the sticky-sweet fragrance, Jasmine, who'd just become a committee member, suddenly appeared in front of the blackboard. Little Bright's eyes lit up and he called out her name, holding out his sticky hands with the sweets, inviting her to taste one. Even though she arrogantly refused the offer from such a "juvenile delinquent," I still developed a sudden, indescribable resentment toward her, Little Bright, and even toward myself. I stopped eating the dates and refused to take them from Little Bright's desk to mine, on the grounds that they weren't especially for me.

After school was out, I didn't move from my desk and ferociously did my math homework. The way we usually did things, Little Bright played soccer until just about sunset. I waited for him, and then we both took the number 22 bus back home together. But that day I figured out early on that I wasn't going to wait for him. As soon as he left the classroom with the soccer ball, I gathered my things in my schoolbag and walked out onto the road. Once on the bus, I almost felt what it's like for someone to come home from school all alone. It was a poetic sense of solitude: even without friends I could get through life.

As I approached the gate to my house, I ran into Little Bright's father, Zhao Jianghe. His face darkened with stubble, his cap layered with oily stains, he had the filthy look of someone who'd just got down from the front of the train locomotive. He knew I was a top student and liked me for it. Every time he beat up Little Bright, he'd add this insult: "Look at your neighbor 'Little Writer's' homework, how good he does. He gets every test perfect!" "Little Writer" was my nickname because the adults assumed I always got top scores. When he ran into me this time, he accepted my greetings and laughed lightheartedly, casually asking me: "My son didn't leave school with you?" "I don't know," I replied. I wasn't in the mood to be confronted with Little Bright's name or the recent events associated with him. When I got home, neither Mama nor my older sister was there. I found my towel and soap and went to the nearby public bathhouse. Little Bright and I always went there together. I needed to prove to myself that I could manage alone, that just because I was a "good kid" I didn't need the protection from a "juvenile delinquent." I could go out alone and go to the public bath alone. I could single-handedly face those tormenting hooligans, as well as the creepy, old fools in the baths who like pretty boys, and come out unscathed.

At supper that night, we heard crying sounds from our neighbors to the left and laughter from our neighbors to the right. Between the crying and the laughter, I couldn't concentrate on savoring the food. Behind Akiko Koyama's and Little Red's crying, I vaguely detected something even worse about to unfold. This premonition barely flicked through me when the crying next door was stifled by Zhao Jianghe's angry roar. Following that was a muffled sound of swearing. Then, all of a sudden, some sort of force brought the incessant cursing to an abrupt halt. A weak cry for help erupted through the silence. Mama put down her chopsticks. I followed her as she rushed into our neighbors' home on the left. There I saw Little Bright wrestling with his father, no longer willing to obediently accept the violence. Suddenly, he leapt forward in a move called "the lion's nod," a defense skill to overpower those taller and stronger. You use your opponent's body as the vector of support, slightly bend your legs, lower your chin, and then strike the center of your opponent's belly with the force of your rising forehead. The soccer term for "the lion's nod" is "sudden death." What Mama and I witnessed was a brilliant execution of this "sudden death": Little Bright aimed a perfect strike into Zhao Jianghe's solar plexus. Zhao Jianghe's eyes turned white, and he didn't utter a sound as he loosened his grip on Little Bright's hands. He staggered backward and crumpled to the floor. As soon as Little Bright had taken his revenge, he turned his back on his father and fled past us out the door. I was terrified. Akiko Koyama and Little Red knelt by Zhao Jianghe and shook his head. He slowly opened his eyes, unfocused and glazed as if he were already dead. Mama shouted at me: "Quick, go get Little Swallow! Get her over here!" Dumbstruck, I ran toward home. Once in our courtyard I yelled, "Sister,

sister!," but not a sound escaped from my throat. Only when I got into the house, aided by sign language and a hoarse imitation of my voice, was I able to convey my message.

Little Swallow resuscitated Zhao Jianghe. She learned this technique in physiology class and from Papa, who had taught her informally. Papa kept hoping one of us would follow in his footsteps and become a doctor. My sister acted amateurish and timid, so Mama had to bolster her nerves with encouraging glances from the sidelines. Finally, Zhao Jianghe started to breathe again, first one breath, then another. Then his eyeballs started rolling around. Due to oxygen deprivation, his stiff body came back to life very slowly. Akiko Koyama was crying. As soon as Zhao Jianghe was helped to sit up, he pointed at the bag of half-eaten dates on the table and said: "Take that thing, throw it away, and get it out of my face! That little thief will never again set foot in my house!" Little Red immediately grabbed the dates lying next to Little Bright's schoolbag, pushed open the window, and threw them into the courtyard. As I dragged myself through Little Bright's family courtyard to head slowly home, I couldn't help but notice the "scene" of sticky dates lying scattered on the ground. Beneath the light projected from inside their home, I could sense the "sticky" protest the dates were throwing my way.

I felt guilt and remorse. When I got to the old elm tree on the east side of the house, I suddenly knew he was hiding in the treetop. I knocked on the tree trunk a few times: "Little Bright, please come down. I was bad; I said it on purpose, that I didn't know where you went after school. I was being stupid cause I was jealous that you like Jasmine . . . !" Before I finished saying my apologies, Little Bright was sliding down the tree. It was like he hadn't even heard a single word I said. He just slapped my shoulder and asked, "Hey, pal, is he dead?" I knew he was talking about his dad. I just said, "No, my sister brought him back." In the dark I saw his grin, his canine teeth shining through: "Was it mouth-to-mouth?" I could hear the sexual hint in his question, so I quickly set him right: "No, no, she performed the chest-compression technique." I felt anxious using such a technical term for the first time. He said: "OK, so he's not dead, oh well. Let's go to your house." Saying this, he seized my waist with his arm. In the spot where he grabbed me, I felt a sharp tingling as if I'd been given an electric shock. The feeling spread to my whole body; my face felt like it was on fire. That night I didn't get in the same bed with him like we always had in the past. I slept on the floor while he slept in my bed. All through the night I tossed and turned, listening to his sound sleeping. I hardly got a wink.

7

Ever since Papa couldn't answer my question "whence the cause?," I became interested in historical material and exhibits on the Japanese-Korean war, the Sino-Japanese wars, Sino-Japanese diplomatic relations, and so on. When we wrote our essays for school, I'd add stuff on Japan to the topics the teacher set for us. When our teacher set an essay topic "My father," for example, I added "Imagine he is a Japanese orphan." Or when the teacher set the topic "A snowless winter," I added the subtitle "It always snows in Hokkaido during winter." Our second-year lit teacher really had a thing against me. He reckoned I was arrogant, self-satisfied, and a show-off. When Triangle City's eastern district museum opened a new exhibit about the Japanese military invasion of China, I went at least three times to see it. I even took detailed notes. Tatsuzō Ishikawa's *Soldiers Alive*[3] entered my bookshelf, and I added to that a lineup of authors who seemed to fit even better with my temperament (at least as I saw them), such as Yukio Mishima, Yasunari Kawabata, and Dasai Osamu.[4] Papa opposed my reading Mishima and Osamu because of their "suicidal complexes." In fact, Kawabata also committed suicide, but Papa really liked *The Dancing Girl of Izu*, so he didn't dismiss him as a "deviant novelist."[5] I didn't listen to him, of course. Actually, I regarded him with even more contempt than before. He hadn't even read these authors. He only knew how they died from listening to gossip. Although I admit my love of literature is probably inherited from him, he long ago exposed his "extracurricular" amateurish level of understanding, while I was already fully or at least three-quarters a "specialist."

3 Tatsuzō Ishikawa was a journalist embedded with the Japanese army in war-ravaged China. He witnessed the soldiers' march on Nanjing (known as the Rape of Nanjing). He subsequently wrote a deeply disturbing realist novella based on what he had witnessed that depicted the war's devastating effects on soldiers and civilians alike. The book was promptly banned in Japan.

4 Yukio Mishima: Japanese writer, 1925–70; Yasunari Kawabata: Japanese novelist, 1899–1972; Dasai Osamu: Japanese writer, 1909–48.

5 First published in 1926, *The Dancing Girl of Izu* is a short story about a twenty-year-old student from Tokyo traveling the Izu Peninsula during the holidays, where he has a chance meeting with a family of musicians. He is especially intrigued by the fourteen-year-old sister of the troupe's male leader and agrees to spend another day with them at their invitation. When he steps onto the boat to depart, he is both saddened and relieved.

In one way, I really hated Japanese people, judging from the museum exhibit. But, judging from Tōru Yasunaga[6] and Akiko Koyama, I really liked Japanese people. While I was studying Russian in school, I was also learning some Japanese from my father. (He was so busy, he just taught me a few phrases every now and then, and while I was his student for that short period, I went back to admiring him.) But I never crazily screamed out the Japanese word for "idiot" (baka) like other children did. True, I never cursed. Not one dirty word ever passed my lips. I remained a true disciple, even though our church had been closed down by the government by then and reading the Holy Bible was forbidden (my mother had taken to reading it underground/clandestinely). The angels came and went on the air of pure language I breathed out. I would've been too ashamed to utter even half a swear word and pollute my connection to them. After we started studying chemistry at school, I was really in my element with the periodic table. I excelled in math, physics, and chemistry and seemed to fit that ancient Triangle City proverb: "Those who excel in science can travel anywhere in the world." Because I was doing so well, Papa asked less and less about my schoolwork. He assumed I'd sit the entrance exams to Circle City Medical School (his alma mater) and inherit his profession. Once he even made special arrangements for me to enter an operating room to observe him amputate a young guy injured in a car accident. He didn't realize it was precisely this experience that made me determined never ever to specialize in any scientific discipline devoted to the human body. While Papa simply wished I'd be like him and become a happy amateur as regards literature and the arts, I set out to make it my life's profession, no matter that Papa kept trying to instill in me a thousand times the argument that "artists starve."

I was always troubled thinking about the Polish priest and the Swiss priest who'd been kicked out of the country. I gradually learned that Papa and Mama had actually been their students. They'd learned how to read in their church catechism classes. When they got to be adults, they became friends. My parents went to visit them after they'd been thrown into prison and beaten up. But it was impossible to persuade them to stay. The church members so much wanted them to stay! The strange thing was those Japanese, whom everyone hated and no one wanted to keep here, they were the ones who ended up staying. My neighbor to the right, senior high school student Zhou Ji, said, "The Japanese are the most despised people on the face of the earth. Take the Japanese who came here to Triangle City. Even if they wanted to

6 A character in Mishima's novel *The Decay of the Angel* (1971).

go home, people in Japan don't even want them, not to mention they don't even know their Japanese relatives' names and addresses." I thought Zhou Ji's answer to my "whence the cause?" was both simple and apropos. So I spent a lot of time around him that next year. I listened to him tell stories, and I borrowed his books. Some of the books I got from him contained explicit descriptions of "sex." Reading those books caused me to get excited, but because of my limited experience, I just didn't understand what it was all about. So despite my intense curiosity and strong erections, I couldn't make any headway.

After hearing Zhou Ji's disquisition, I felt pity for Akiko Koyama every time I saw her in the distance. Sometimes it was those few strands of white hair that got tangled up with her otherwise elegant hairdo. Sometimes it was her short and not so slender build. Other times it was those plum calves in the shape of an "O." She was without family or friends; an orphan, lonely, miserable, and helpless. (I hardly ever considered her familial relationships with Zhao Jianghe, Little Bright, and Little Red. I didn't know the word "multiracial" then. Instead, I thought of Little Bright and Little Red as Triangle City folk.) She had no home to go back to and a country she couldn't go back to. She reminded me of the old men in the lyric folk song "At Fifteen I Joined the Army."[7] Sometimes, lying in bed, staring at the ceiling, I'd burst into tears on her account. She hadn't left, not because she felt at peace with her lot but because in her own country she didn't have a friend in the world.

8

Our new semester started just as autumn arrived. The first three days we did physical labor: swept the classroom and pulled up the wildflowers and weeds in the sports field. The next three days we went to the countryside to "eat, work, and live with our farmer brothers." Naturally, Little Bright was much quicker than me in weeding; I was behind all the time. He used an iron shovel to dig up the weeds, while I used both my hands to gather up the stems and leaves and throw them at the foot of the surrounding village wall. I gathered up so few that when Little Bright finished weeding, he came over to help me. When we arrived in the village, the peasants didn't trust us a bit and wouldn't let us work in their vegetable fields. They only let us go into the cornfields that fed the livestock to carry out our "work game" (my term). So

7 This song is a Han dynasty (202 BCE–220 CE) anti-war ballad.

we basically sucked on the sweet and juicy stalks and stopped working very early in the evenings.

Little Bright and I were assigned to stay with a sturdy peasant family who bred large chai dogs. By seven at night, the local electricity was shut off. Our hosts gave us the inner room to sleep, while the husband, wife, and three small kids slept together in the outer room. Because we'd eat the local specialty of fresh vegetables and melons for supper, both of us had to go to the toilet as soon as we lay down. Peasants always have their toilets in the courtyard. Problem was, in their courtyard was also a really big dog. (I was afraid of all types of animals back then, especially rats, cats, and dogs.) Little Bright wasn't afraid of dogs, but he was afraid we'd wake up our hosts. He relieved the pressure by standing by the windowsill, pissing out the window, and letting it flow silently down the outer wall. I was too shy to do that, so I tried to hold it in until I almost burst. I pleaded with Little Bright to go with me to the toilet, so we tiptoed back and forth. We didn't seem to wake up our hosts, but funnily enough we never woke up that big yellow dog either.

Just as I was falling into the fog of sleep, I was suddenly awakened by cries next door. They sounded like pain and joy at the same time; they made me break out in a cold sweat. Gripped by fear, I moved my head over to Little Bright's pillow and parted the sheets so I could hold him. With all the loud, low moaning, cursing, thumps, and muffled sounds, I couldn't tell whether it was male or female, human or ghost. The hair on my body stood up straight (if, indeed, I had any body hair at the time). From between my legs I started to feel a strong, choking sense of excitement. Little Bright woke up, too. He brushed aside the sheets to hug me so tightly I couldn't move. Little Bright was taller than me; I could feel him pressed against me, a part of him right between my legs, getting hard. I immaturely reveled in the experience of being held so strongly by him. I still have dim memories of those young, intoxicating feelings. When he clumsily but somehow instinctively sought my lips, I was almost powerless to throw him off. But a feeling of shame pushed me to avoid his lips and break away from his embrace. I withdrew back beneath my own sheets.

Once back under my own sheets, the layers of cold made me feel lonely. I immediately longed for Little Bright's strong embrace again but couldn't bring myself to make a move. (Maybe this was a foreshadowing of my lifelong bashfulness about instigating sex.) The groans and banging next door became fiercer, a kind of indescribable fierceness that was both tenacious and alluring. In due course, Little Bright entered my sheets. Pressing against me, he kissed me forcefully and began to undress. He whispered urgently, "Take yours off too, quick!" But I didn't move. I waited for him to take his clothes off, and then mine. Both of us stark naked, he pressed down on top of me. He wrapped both his arms around me, causing my head to lean slightly backward. It was uncomfortable. He started to kiss me, his erect and bolt-upright youthful organ rubbing back and forth between my lower belly and my legs. I disengaged my arms from his. He then touched me all over. This was the first time I realized my skin was smooth as silk. He inserted himself between my legs and started twitching vigorously. We both felt the sore ache and pleasure of the friction; I lifted my face to accept his kisses. At this point, I felt an indescribable excitement building inside me that spread throughout my body, and liquid gushed rapidly out of my penis. My spasms caused Little Bright's semen to shoot out between my legs. I was fifteen that year; he was fifteen and a half. Our first sexual experience happened in an unexpected time and place and with an unexpected outcome. The following two nights we slept together naked, embracing each other (he basically sleeping on top of me), the initial impulse and intensity gone. We were together, experiencing a unique sense of warmth, intimacy, and peace. Without words, our young bodies communicated the kind of love that blurs all boundaries: brothers, friends, lovers, sweethearts, husband and wife, life and death; vast, pure, and brief.

9

Near the end of middle school, I had a premonition: once I started high school it would be impossible for a male student like me to fill the post of arts and literature committee member. (I had been reinstated to my former duty about six months earlier.) To make all the committee members feel overshadowed by me and also to bid my farewell to the arts world, I decided for the graduation ceremony to stage an independent ballet titled "The Elf and the Peach," an independent stage play titled "Memories," and some smaller performance pieces. I cast Feng Lili as my dancing partner in the ballet, with Little Bright dressed up as a giant peach. For the play, I cast Little Bright as the callous killer, a member of the Japanese military police. His character torments me, a brave and unyielding youthful victim, but is not successful in killing me. Feng Lili narrates "my memories" as she had witnessed those "past events."

On the day of the performance, my mother, sister, Akiko Koyama, and Little Red came to see the performance at the Railway Workers Club. They sat in the guests' seats. When "Memories" started, I was wearing a ruined costume and bundled on a pillar. The military policeman wore cavalry trousers and boots, with a big knife flung around his shoulder, strutting back and forth in front of me, flinging his leather whip to a deafening noise, and muttering the "red deer" curse. In that moment, I suddenly realized that Little Bright was that Japanese military policeman, that the military policeman was Little Bright. Even by the end of the evening, when our performances received first, second, and third prize ("Memories" was awarded first prize), this realization did not fade.

Of course, Akiko Koyama was Japanese, and so her son had to be Japanese too. I had previously assumed that only Akiko Koyama was Japanese and that her two children were Chinese, but now I realized they were "mixed-race" (I had finally found the appropriate word), since these Chinese people were also, simultaneously, Japanese. By investigating carefully, it was clear that Little Red resembled Zhao Jianghe, and thus looked Chinese, but Little Bright looked like Akiko Koyama. The refined and compact features of the Yamato ethnicity were unmistakably reflected in his lips, teeth, eyebrows, and eyes. Once I discovered this, I started comparing him with Mishima's Tōru character. I imagined his lonely but stubborn face inside Shimizu Port's beacon tower as he turned toward Izu Peninsula.[8] (His profile was like a flawless sculpture.) "A smile is the final sign of social intolerance; it is the arched arrow of cursing lips." Why was it that at the age of sixteen Tōru/Little Bright "their hearts were cold as ice, no love, no tears"? No. No. Little Bright was not like that, only Tōru. Little Bright did not shed tears, but he felt love. But who did he love, me or Feng Lili? And who did I love? If Tōru and Little Bright were standing before me, which one would I choose?

10

The transition from winter to spring was the time of school holidays in Triangle City and also marked the entrance point to the next grade level. After I had achieved the highest grades in middle school and advanced to high school, I spent the vacation traveling by myself to Circle City to visit Grandma. She was already eighty-three years old, but her health was still pretty good; she was even able to take me to the free market to buy live carp

8 Tōru worked in the beacon tower in Shimizu Port on the Izu Peninsula. There he was adopted by a retired judge who was convinced Tōru was the incarnation of his deceased wife.

fish. While my uncle and aunt were at work, I bought myself a monthly bus pass to go around the city, which, although I came every year, I was still unfamiliar with. First, I went to see the city museum's display of dinosaurs, as I was skeptical about the "dinosaurs were exterminated due to climate change" theory. The exhibition disappointed me greatly. The dinosaur skeleton fossil on display simply could not arouse my imagination; those dinosaur egg fossils looked as if they had been deliberately forged; there was no space whatsoever inside the egg for a little dinosaur.

Circle City had reserved a special spot for a Sino-Japanese War Memorial "Museum," which displayed many photos depicting scenes of Japanese military police slaughtering Circle City residents using guns and knives. It also displayed their cannons, guns, and military garments. Visiting this exhibition appeared merely to stem from habit and also my hobby in the history of ethnic relations. The question "whence the cause?" did not puzzle me anymore. Strictly speaking, my interest in "whence the cause?" now took on a far more personalized dimension (Why do people die? Why do people fall in love?), which cast aside my previous interest in this question with regard to national minorities.

Why was it that Papa became a doctor, why did he fall in love with Mama, why didn't my mother give birth until she was thirty, why was Zhao Jianghe beating and cursing Akiko Koyama, why did Little Red always look at me with such sad eyes, why was Zhou Ji so extremely interested in Eastern Zhou dynasty characters and stories, especially Jiang Ziya,[9] why was I hoping to be in a separate class from Little Bright in high school? In addition, why was I born a boy and not a girl, why could I not wear a flowery and deep-red-colored skirt, why could I not be a member of the literary and arts committee, why did I enjoy sleeping underneath Little Bright so much, why did I sometimes feel like I wanted to be really close with him but other times felt he was a stranger to me, why did Little Bright want to hang around with Feng Lili, why were there so many high school boys wooing my sister, why was she called Little Yanzi and me Little Pin?

Little Pin didn't know how he arrived at the entrance to Sunflower Inn, peering inside from the wide-open gate. I looked inside the vestibule (where I had once sat waiting on that old sofa); it seemed gloomy and narrow. The owner was sitting at the front desk, looking at me outside. His face was full of wrinkles, but his gaze cunning. Frightened, I did not venture to show my

9 Late Shang dynasty, ca. 1100 BCE, partly mythical sage advisor of King Wen of Zhou, purported author of the military classic *Six Secret Teachings*.

face again. I spent a whole day in the Circle City medical college, strolling through the entire campus. One by one I compared the real buildings with the virtual buildings in papa's old photos. I imagined how he flourished here: studying, rowing boats (the campus had a lake), playing ball, racing (he was a 100-meter sprint champion), dissecting corpses (were they male or female), and falling in love. That's right; who did he fall in love with? It was probably female students from the same medical college. (At that time, people in the railway system generally considered medical practitioners to be beautiful, poetic, and romantic.) Mama had not studied at the medical school. So my father had definitely had other women, a bit like Little Bright having Feng Lili in addition to me. (Had he really "had" her?) I heard that starting in his youth, Papa was the handsomest man everywhere he went. Between this kind of person always in the limelight and Mama's delicacy and piety, did they really remain loyal to one another?

I decided that if the security personnel asked my identity while I was strolling around the campus, I would arrogantly tell them that my father was a graduate of this college and now worked as head of surgery at the Triangle City Railway hospital. Upon saying this, the security guards would break out into a big smile and ask me whether I was planning to attend this medical school too. I knew that they expected me to nod and say yes. But I would instead shake my head and firmly announce that I was to attend a university which provided answers to all the "whence the cause?"

11

As soon as I returned to Triangle City, I heard that something serious had happened to Little Bright's family. The lecherous old Japanese man living secluded in Circle City, who professed himself to be Little Bright's maternal uncle, came to Triangle City to search for Akiko Koyama and was detained by the Public Security Bureau. Akiko Koyama had also been arrested. The official reason was that they were both spies. However, I had grown up by now and did not harbor the same level of trembling fear for this word as previously. Besides, I already had my own view on this: perhaps the man was a spy, but Akiko Koyama certainly was not.

Throughout this ordeal, Zhao Jianghe's behavior changed completely. He didn't touch a drop of alcohol, and every day he returned home straight from work to cook food for Little Red and Little Bright. According to Zhou Ji, Zhao Jianghe went to the police station every day to vouch for Akiko Koyama, to try to persuade them that she was no spy. She was simply a Japanese orphan, raised by his own parents. After they died, the two of them—"brother and sister"—got married in accordance with their parent's last will and testament. As for that Japanese man, he remained under suspicion.

Little Bright changed too; he became uncommunicative. He almost seemed like a good student: every day he arrived and left punctually, he did his homework and learned it well. We were still in the same class and grade. I did not want to be the class monitor, and Feng Lili had been appointed to the literary and arts committee. I was happy to keep my distance from the teacher and all that trendiness in extracurricular activities, so that I could knock people over with my brilliance in the college entrance exams. I would put everyone and everything behind me, including the teachers who were fond of me and who worked hard at their job (for example, Liu Wendong, our mathematics teacher who doubled as our homeroom teacher); including Feng Lili, whose eyes were as black as the deepest pond and whose voice resembled silver bells (a tawdry metaphor, to be sure); and including Little Bright, who hadn't even imagined going to university.

Since birth, the first time I felt discontent with my mother's moral character was when, to avoid suspicion of being a "spy element," she distanced herself from our neighbors to the left, using her behavior to let everyone know that she was not a friend of Akiko Koyama. After Jesus was arrested, his disciple Peter (incidentally also my Christian name) denied knowing his master three times before the rooster crowed. My mother, similarly, denied knowing her friend. In my heart, I have contempt for her, even though I also sought many excuses for exonerating her, such as she did it to protect her own children, or it is a woman's weakness, or maybe their friendship was never genuinely that close, maybe it was mainly due to the geographical proximity by being next-door neighbors.

In the second month of spring, Akiko Koyama was considered "innocent" and subsequently freed. The Japanese man, named Song Yuanxun, on the other hand, was forcibly repatriated back to Japan on the grounds of special spy crimes. My guess was that he, too, originally was a Japanese orphan who was later bribed by the Japanese right-wing faction to spy for them. I also guessed that he and Akiko Koyama were childhood sweethearts.

As soon as Akiko Koyama returned home, Zhao Jianghe returned to his old ways, drinking and beating up his family. But ever since Little Bright's "lion's nod" almost killed him, he no longer fought Little Bright. I don't know whether it was because he feared him or because he no longer had any reason to beat him. When Little Red suffered the beatings and curses, she ran over to our family to be with my sister. One of those days, I suddenly realized that Little Red did not resemble Zhao Jianghe at all but had grown to resemble more and more Akiko Koyama and Little Bright. And she was far more beautiful than Feng Lili in every way (hair, body, smile, voice). If I really wanted to insult Feng Lili (but why did I want to insult her and over what), I could pull out the trump card that Little Red (she was one grade beneath us) was my girlfriend. Just from the perspective of vanity, Little Red was the kind of beautiful girl that all the boys dreamed of. A pity she was not nearly as charming as her brother. In other words, I was not attracted to her in the least.

My father really liked Little Red. I had even heard him and my mother seriously discuss whether to go to our neighbors to propose marriage between me and Little Red, so as to avoid such a good girl falling into another family. This made me both bashful and angry. I felt I was subjected to extraordinary shame and humiliation: How could I possibly look for a girlfriend, how could I possibly get married and have children? I was rather arrogant and thought of myself as above others' common pleasures. I followed my own path, had lofty ambitions. I revered the model of the monks and priests. How could I possibly be with a girl who always accepted a thrashing, was pathetic, even if very beautiful?

At that time, I did not have a definitive or reliable understanding of people. In other words, I was conflicted and confused. I began to doubt everyone and everything, even God. (If He could do everything, then why did He allow the church to be closed down?) I prayed less and less, only occasionally, and then only because I was asking for something, like more pocket money so that I could buy those high-heeled leather shoes on sale in the department store.

12

In the second semester of the second year in high school, that is, before graduation and the college entrance exams (at that time senior high school was only two years), Little Bright and I became outright enemies. The reason was that I felt betrayed by him. How did he betray me? By having a date with Feng Lili. I was convinced that, given his casual way of following his inclinations and his nature, there was no way that their date would stop at just chatting and hand-holding. I was like a wildcat out of control. As soon as I caught sight of them flirting with their eyes, my eyes were ablaze. Many times, I felt like dashing up to Little Bright and slapping him in the face. My reason restrained me merely to this extent: that I must not manhandle him, that would be vulgar. However, a pivotal moment was approaching.

It was one day at the beginning of winter, a day I will never forget (we were to take the college exams in the depth of winter). I was the cream of the top students. Every day after school I went to the dean's office, where I received special tutoring from the dean himself. (He used to be the geography teacher; geography was my only weak subject.) On this particular day, it was dusk when I was done with tutoring. The sun set quite early in Triangle City during winter. By the time I got near the classroom, the light had so dimmed I could barely make out the silhouette of the corridor and the doorframe. I walked into the classroom and turned on the lights, thinking I would gather my schoolbag from my desk. As the lights came on, I heard a low cry of alarm: on top of a desk in the back of the room sat Feng Lili; glued to her, standing up, was Zhao Yaming (Little Bright's full name). Their faces were sweaty and red, a vacant expression in their eyes. Evidently, they had just disengaged from some form of physical contact. I don't know why, but I felt unusually calm. I marched firmly over to my desk by the window. I fetched my schoolbag from inside and in an unhurried manner packed my geography book and notebook, and finally buckled up my bag. I flung my bag over my shoulder and walked slowly onto the lectern. Just before reaching the door, I turned around. Facing them in an unmoving posture, with a quite theatrical, indifferent, and detached tone resembling a judge giving his verdict, I said: "I tell you, Zhao Yaming is Japanese. His mother's name is Akiko Koyama. His uncle's name is 'Koyama' Xun, a Japanese left behind, an orphaned spy. Not long ago he was forcefully repatriated back to Japan."

To this day, the ethnic group that residents of Triangle City despise the most is the Japanese Yamatos. To this day, I can vividly remember the transformation in Feng Lili's eyes, those eyes that were like a deep, dark pond, and how their expression turned from shock to hate. To this day, I remain both proud and remorseful about the fact that I deliberately changed Xun's surname to "Koyama."

From then on, Feng Lili never again spoke a word to Little Bright, and he never even looked at me. After he graduated from high school, he went on to work for the railway locomotive depot as a steam locomotive coal specialist, a "little stoker." He never sat the college entrance exam. As repayment for my arrogance, I did not top the arts scoreboard in my college entrance exam. And because of my bad lungs from blowing the horn, I was not selected to enter my first preference, Circle City University. I was only accepted by my second preference, Square City University. As chance would have it, Feng Lili was admitted to Circle City Medical School, becoming a younger-generation schoolmate of my father. A further fortuitous episode: when I took the train to Square City to register for my studies, it was Little Bright who was the stoker.

13

The always quiet Little Red was admitted to Square City University. To fulfill my long-held wish, I applied to the master's program in Japanese literature there upon my graduation. The world was changing. The image of Japan, now a developed country, was gradually changing among people in Square City, Circle City, and Triangle City. Little Red, whose looks were breathtaking, was also outstanding in her studies. Her reticent manner and insipid smile only served to increase her attraction to the opposite sex. According to what master's students in the Western languages who knew her divulged to me, the number of undergraduates, master's students, doctoral students, and professors of all ages pursuing her or secretly in love with her was more than ten dozen. Those divulging these numbers naturally counted among them.

Little Red often came to see me, and she always brought me food. She hoped that for the annual vacations we would travel back to Triangle City together by train. But I cherished my independence and never traveled with her. During the three years of my master's studies, my two grandmothers passed away in quick succession. A feeling of emptiness and postadolescent acute melancholy propelled me toward a belief in nothingness (though far from existentialism). I grew my hair long and wore shabby jeans. Both my outer appearance and my inner feelings were an ashen gray. All people die eventually. Why be born in the first place? Why walk in vain through this world? My youthful belief in Christ had been pushed to the very back of my brain and forgotten during my long period of so-called vigorous intellectual development.

In my dreams, Little Bright, or maybe a young lad looking just like him, still gave me affection. Waking up, I seemingly felt desire, yet no love. I did not want a family, did not want to propagate future generations. This belief, which was only a nebulous idea in my childhood, had by now become a firm principle. When Little Red came to see me and told me that Akiko Koyama, her, Little Bright, and that maternal aunt with a different name in Square City were migrating to Tokyo very soon, and Song Xiu had already handled all the formalities for them, and then inquired whether I wanted to go (implying I would become her husband), I resolutely refused. Little Red cried. This was the first time she asked why did I not love her? I was silent for a long time. I said, "I do not love anybody but myself."

The whole family left for Tokyo. Only Zhao Jianghe stayed behind in Triangle City. He was unwilling to go to "little Japan." On finding out that Little Red was multiracial, some of her admirers lost their fervor, but others stepped up their enthusiasm and sent her love letters nonstop to Tokyo. At last, someone more refined-looking than me, a young student with a pale visage, was chosen by Little Red. He went through numerous setbacks before finally getting his passport and visa. His name was Chi Binbin. He came to say goodbye to me when he was about to leave. Glancing at the limpid display of emotion in his eyes, I concluded that he would not fall in love with Little Red. I went so far as to warn him: "After you get to Tokyo, do not touch her brother!"

14

After obtaining the master's degree, I stayed in Square City to work at the Research Institute for Japanese Affairs. Once, my father came to Square City to honor my grandmother's and grandfather's souls in the Catholic Church's holy public cemetery there. He stayed in my room in the unmarried staff quarters. After he had seen several of my literary writings published periodically in newspapers and magazines, he no longer brooded about my not studying medicine. He even envied me: "Literature is the key to life itself." He probed whether I would write fiction or a biography and, if it involved him, would I "vilify" him. I offered a circuitous answer: "If I were to 'vilify' someone, I would rather not write about you, Father." Despite what I said, I could still detect traces of concern in his aging eyes. If I used the literary genre to depict my father, Little Bright, and myself, would I misrepresent us? After that meeting with Father, I ceased writing straightforward and simple works of pure fiction and took up essay writing. I must wait, wait for the rivers of time to clean people and things free of the dust and the smoke, wait for pure essence to reemerge. Only then can I touch it.

My older sister Swallow had married and given birth to a beautiful little girl. When their daughter was three years old, the three of them all traveled to Square City and stayed with me in my newly allocated flat. My sister told me that Akiko Koyama had returned to live in Triangle City. She vowed never to return to Tokyo again. Zhao Jianghe cooked for her every day. He seemed to have become a completely different person. Little Red called my sister frequently from Japan. They remained good friends. Little Red's temperament had undergone a big change. She talked a lot and was far more brazen. She told my sister that after she gave birth to a little boy, Chi Binbin divorced her because he had obtained Japanese nationality. She had recently met a German guy, younger than her by seven or eight years, who loved her very much. Maybe she would send her son back to Triangle City to be raised by Akiko Koyama while she went to live with him in Düsseldorf. Through my sister she asked whether I wanted to come to Tokyo as a scholar. Her lover was a Japanese university trustee. He had the power to arrange a post to research Japanese literature.

She did not mention Little Bright. After he went to Japan, nobody mentioned any news about him at all. The evening before my sister returned to Triangle City, I invited them all to Square City's most distinguished restaurant for a farewell dinner. During the banquet, her husband and I got very drunk. An eighteen- or nineteen-year-old waiter who brought us more beer reminded me strongly of the Little Bright of my former life. I asked my sister: "What about Little Bright, is he in Tokyo?" My sister hesitated, then said: "If I tell you, you promise not to be upset?" How could I possibly be upset, I replied. My sister then said: "After Little Bright went to Tokyo, he always saw himself as Chinese. He studied Japanese language pretty hard. But for several years, he couldn't find anything to do. Eventually he fled home and took up with the Taiwanese mafia." I ordered a new glass of beer, drinking and choking on tears. I put down my glass and told my sister: "Please could you call Little Red and tell her to ask that trustee to arrange an invitation for me for an academic visit, or research, or whatever. I need to go to Tokyo."

After I had finished speaking, I left the table and went to the washroom. There, I cried bitterly. I was still that same young boy, with the same pure and simple heart that was so easy to move. As long as I had one person in this world I had loved, I would not despair or lose myself.

The Silent Advent of the Age of Sexual Persuasion

言性时代悄然莅临

Translated by Petrus Liu

1

"Moon boy" is the nickname Yang Yang gave Kiki's new boyfriend, Shuang. Yang Yang had never met him. She could imagine him only through Kiki's words: a face as beautiful as the moon and a heart as cold as moonlight. He told everybody he would never be with a man, gay or not. Kiki's countless tears and pleas fell on deaf ears. But sometimes Shuang would coax Kiki, wiping the traces of tears from the corners of his eyes after he cried. That was only when Kiki threatened to break up with him. Nobody knew why Shuang had not actually left Kiki. As for Kiki, he was dead set on sticking to Shuang because of one thing Shuang said: "Screw love. No matter what, I have to get married and have a son. When we grow old, I'll ask him to take care of you too."

2

Shuang had a huge cock. "It's as big as *kunpeng*," Kiki said with pride.[1] Kiki's friend, Big Ma, was older than both of them, about twenty-five or twenty-six. Big Ma was curious about Shuang's legendary dick and was itching to try it. He asked Kiki to swap places with him in the dark of night without Shuang knowing. Kiki said, sourly, "No way. He's only eighteen. His dick is for sure the biggest in the whole of Square City. But even I haven't tried it yet. He's

First published in *Fairytales of Triangle City* (三角城的童話) (Hong Kong: Huasheng shudian, 1998).

1 Kunpeng is a legendary beast in the early Taoist philosopher Zhuangzi's fables.

still a virgin!" Big Ma couldn't argue with Kiki. The exact nature of Kiki's relationship to that big dick remained a mystery to all. If Kiki wanted to play guardian angel over Shuang's dick, there was nothing other people could do.

3

Shuang was a man of few words and he rarely laughed. He liked to carry a switchblade with him at all times. He had a bad temper and got into lots of fights. He had just turned eighteen. He called anyone who crossed him and even those who didn't "bastards." He always looked angry, even when he was not, as if everyone were a bastard, not to mention people he liked. His handsome face was a hybrid of urban cool and primal savagery. Zhang Qianqian, a poet who went by the nickname "Mahjong Table," described him as the "perfect blend of a modern city and a primeval field." That poet himself was an interesting story with an obsession; really it was a tragedy. He actually didn't know how to play mahjong, but he thought mahjong was very fashionable. So as not to feel like a detached bystander in the popular life of Square City, he bent over on all fours and let his friends, Black Donut, Wild Dog, Bamboo Dumpling, and Sugar Candy, use his flat back as a mahjong table. After his first service as a mahjong table, he delivered a lecture. He praised the ordinary people of Square City for using "the people always play mahjong" to passively counter the decadence in official culture. In Kiki's opinion, the poet was interested only in the differences between the "things" of the "classical age" and the "things" of the "modern age," but overlooked the people who caused those differences, be they men or women. His attacks on modern society, his enthusiasm for mahjong culture as an antidote, and his praise for Shuang's "perfection" all came out of his interest in "cultural studies." Kiki knew he had no need to protect Shuang from the poet like he did from Big Ma. What a slut. Whenever he thought of Big Ma drooling over young men, Kiki, who was normally calm, would lose his temper and his heart would burst into flames.

4

Ever since he turned sixteen and a half, people started saying "I love you" to Shuang. Whether they said it in English or Chinese, Shuang's big dick would immediately get hard. The first person was the older sister of his gang brother.

She was ten years his senior, and she didn't need to try too hard to get him into bed. One coquettish line lured him into her ample embrace. From that night on, Shuang became a "cool" person. He used to be a rambunctious and energetic boy. Overnight he became cool and quiet, though no one could tell whether his personality transformation was a tactic to seduce more women or to keep them at bay. When Kiki said "I love you" to Shuang for the first time when they were on a night bus together, Shuang instinctively raised his right hand and was about to slap Kiki's face. But he stopped himself. He had a hard-on in his tight jeans that was both itchy and painful; in fact, it was demanding so much of his attention that he didn't have any energy left to hit Kiki. He put his hand down and said furiously through his teeth, "Bastard! Who do you think you're talking to?" Kiki was unusually brave that night. He said softly, "I am talking to you. It's love at first sight." Shuang looked up and down and then added, "What the fuck? Are you a guy or a girl?" As it turned out, whether Kiki was a guy or a girl was not very important. Shuang took him back to his apartment and fucked him hard three times with his monstrous dick. Kiki was so sore afterward that he couldn't stand up.

5

Kiki didn't introduce Shuang to Yang Yang, because Shuang didn't want to meet anyone who might think he was attracted to men or was gay. Kiki only told Yang Yang the story about the fortuitous meeting on the bus. Yang Yang liked stories—romance, suspense, thriller, news, myth—whatever stories she heard, she was easily moved to tears. It was a great ego boost to tell stories to Yang Yang, especially for a man of Kiki's age. The young people of Square City were no longer interested in the jaded tales of "talented scholars meet beauties" from ancient China. They were now in a brand-new age, in which sex and pleasure could be openly discussed. The poet dubbed this century "the age of sexual persuasion."

6

Kiki was quite pleased with himself after his "adventure" with Shuang. Shuang's eyes were dark and mysterious, brimming with intellect and vitality. Whenever Shuang called other people "bastards," he couldn't help but bat his long, thick eyelashes at the same time, subtly changing his sinister pupils into upright ones, giving him quite the boyish look. Kiki laughed to himself: Who has seen a Daddy this young and innocent? From the moment they met, Kiki followed Shuang, treating him as his prized object of love and admiration. Kiki courted Shuang every minute of every day with tea, doing his laundry, shining his shoes, and cooking for him. Shuang was the center and Kiki the margins. However, the one dictating the terms of their relationship was Kiki, not Shuang.

Shuang rode a motorcycle. He took an ugly girl on the back of his motorcycle for a half-day joyride around and around the highway to the northwest of Square City. That ugly girl knew Yang Yang and let the cat out of the bag. Yang Yang told Kiki. Kiki gave a stock response: "He likes girls, that's the way it is. I wouldn't take that away from him, that would be inhumane." As soon as he left Yang Yang's, Kiki called Shuang. He told him he missed him so much and he felt so lonely. Within minutes Shuang was outside Kiki's building, honking his motorcycle horn for Kiki to come down. Kiki got on and put his arms around Shuang's waist. He felt the elastic material of the back seat and pressed his face against Shuang's strong but youthful back. They spent the whole day going around the city, riding on the highways—old ones, new ones, ones still under construction. After their ride, they got into the shower together. Kiki washed Shuang's big dick for him and told him "I love you" in German. His big dick understood the German and got hard. In the shower, Shuang's big dick grew wings. It soared through the sky like an eagle and landed on its prey, penetrating its body. The impact took Kiki's breath away and he almost fainted.

Every time Kiki got fucked, once they were done he would wrap an azure silk towel around Shuang's big dick and bury it like a treasure inside Shuang's pubic hair. He would then sing its praises, telling the big dick how much he adored it. The dick itself didn't seem to care, but Shuang was always beaming with pride. Shuang, who followed nobody's orders, became a good student. He always gave Kiki his full attention when Kiki worshipped his big dick.

However, a wild animal is, after all, a wild animal. Kiki couldn't keep Shuang from doing what he wanted to do. Everybody knew that. Big Ma said Shuang would never let Kiki keep him in a coop. He thought Shuang would never be devoted to Kiki and become a monogamist. That was true. Since he met Kiki, Shuang, in quick succession, got five different girls pregnant, some more than once. They all had abortions; two of them actually borrowed money from Kiki to get it done. Every time these calamities loomed, Big Ma would rejoice in Kiki's troubles and pat him on the shoulders: "See, you're better off if you let him fuck me instead. At least I'm a brother and wouldn't get you into this kind of trouble or make a fool of you." Kiki was determined to keep them as far apart as possible. "Hey, if women make him feel good, who am I to deprive him of such pleasures?" Big Ma had no comeback. He resented Kiki for getting totally in the way between him and Shuang.

Though he successfully blocked Big Ma's advances, the conversation with Big Ma still depressed Kiki. He threw himself against Shuang's hot and firm chest and started sniveling and crying. This kind of drama kept happening. Several times Kiki almost got Shuang to cry with him. Whenever Shuang felt Kiki's love, he was over the moon, but he was not given to emotional displays. He communicated his emotions with his semen. Kiki received his semen like a basin. He never ceased to be amazed at Shuang's apparently inexhaustible supply of ammunition.

7

One evening, in the middle of the night, Kiki was awakened by a light sound of the door unlocking. Moonlight was shining on his eyelashes; he felt like he was in a fairy tale. A shadow then blocked the moonlight; the odor of night wind and dust it carried brushed lightly against his forehead. He felt tears welling up in his eyes because someone had just planted a gentle kiss on his forehead. Shuang was kissing his tears, in a manner that was almost childish. His kisses deepened the scene of a fairy tale. Kiki closed his eyes and told himself: Only in a dream can a person experience this kind of love.

Shuang undressed quickly and got under the blanket. He held Kiki tight. His body was burning and shaking slightly. Kiki buried his head in his chest and licked his salty beads of sweat. He started crying; his teardrops gave Shuang an itch on his dirty chest. Shuang pushed Kiki's head and lips away, saying, "Silly girl, why are you crying again? I'm not dead. Not even hurt. At least not my head, face, and arms. I won't let anyone hurt me in places clothes won't cover. Otherwise, I will never hear the end of it from my parents."

Kiki felt a wound on Shuang's back. Shuang jerked slightly at his touch, from the pain. Kiki did not care about his injury. He only cared about feeling aggrieved: "You worry about your parents being upset. What about me?" Shuang looked at Kiki's face under the moonlight, saying, "I know how you feel about me. But that doesn't compare to my parents." Kiki glared at him like a mosquito's sting: "Tell me then. Who do you love the most?" Shuang answered like a good boy, "Of course my parents." Kiki pinched his back and Shuang squirmed in pain. Kiki said, "I'm asking you about love, romantic love." Shuang put on a serious, almost willful face. "That's what I'm talking about too." "You love your parents, romantically?" "Of course. Love transcends all. My love does not exclude my parents." Kiki pinched a different muscle. "Fine. Then I'm number what?" Shuang rested his chin on Kiki's head. "Whatever number you say you are. This is funny. What's the difference between number one and number whatever?" Kiki did not respond. He said with pain, "I knew it. I'm the last. Tell me, isn't that right?" Shuang was bored. He put his head aside on the pillow and said impatiently, "Then so be it. Whatever. You're funny. You ask me. Who do I ask?"

Kiki lay on Shuang's chest, pathetic and motionless, hoping to make Shuang feel how much he'd hurt him and how sorry he felt for himself. His actions spoke silent but deep words to Shuang. The moonlight had shifted to the wall on the eastern side of the room, but there was no response from Shuang. Not only that, Shuang actually fell into a heavy sleep. He hadn't even taken a shower, so his body emitted an intoxicating and disorienting male odor mixed with the smell of his semen that overwhelmed Kiki's senses. Kiki was so close to him but could not get through to him.

Kiki got up and turned on the light at the head of the bed. Under its pale, yellow ray, he daubed some antiseptic alcohol on Shuang's wound and breathed gently against it. Shuang slept through the whole thing, showing only an instinctive spasm when the solution stung his wound. Before he turned off the light, Kiki whispered to Shuang's naked body: "I love you." Who would have guessed—this confessional monologue woke up the slumbering giant cock. It stood up, fully erect and attentive, leaving the land of dreams, like an obedient schoolboy who sits with his back straight as a pen at the ringing of the assembly bell. Kiki turned off the light and started sucking his cock, taking in the whole shaft at once. He lay by his side. There was a stench from Shuang's pubic hair. Kiki sniffed the scent and fell asleep too, with Shuang's cock still deep in his throat.

8

When Kiki went with Yang Yang to entertain themselves in Triangle City, Big Ma and Mahjong Table seized the opportunity to take Shuang out for a few drinks at a bar called Yellow Pavilion. "Baiwei" beers were 99 yuan a bottle; the three of them finished off nine. Shuang drank the most and pissed a lot. Plastered from the beers, he walked like he was floating in space. Big Ma had the perfect excuse to suggest to Shuang that they spend the night at the hotel across the street—"since the little guy couldn't possibly get himself home."

Mahjong Table and Big Ma were completely sober. They put the wasted person in the center of the large bed and knelt down one on each side like two hungry lions. They took a moment to assess the situation. When they saw that Shuang was gaining consciousness, they pretended to be drunk and incapacitated too, twisting their noses and crossing their eyes. In the drunken atmosphere they faked, they brazenly stripped Shuang down to a pair of tight gray briefs—a gift from Kiki. The lions grew hungrier, because the outline of the big cock was already visible. At that point the poet felt a sting of conscience: "Holy shit, Big Ma, are we . . . is this . . . rape?" Big Ma had his eyes fixated on the big cock's outline and answered with muffled words. "What rape? We spent 1000 yuan on the drinks, plus the hotel—a total of 1600 yuan on this guy. How could he not know what we were after? We fucking paid for this." Big Ma thought to himself, Kiki's a stupid fool for bragging to his friends about the size of his boyfriend's cock. He's practically inviting his friends to steal him away.

The poet agreed with Big Ma and went after the gray briefs, but Big Ma stopped him, saying, "Who said you get to go first? Rock, paper, scissors!"[2] The poet couldn't argue with that, so he swallowed hard and put his right hand behind his back. They yelled, "Rock, paper, scissors!" at the same time and pulled out their hands. Mahjong Table was paper and Big Ma was rock. Before Big Ma could weasel his way out of the game, the poet's hand reached for Shuang's underwear at a speed one thousand times faster than he could write poetry and got first sight of the impressive view. He suppressed an "oh—" just in time to keep face in front of Big Ma and turned his "oh—" into poetry: "oh your towering cliffs oh!" Like thunder after lightning, Big Ma also made a hoarse sound in his throat, searched his brain for some poetry, and finally recited Kiki's words: "As big as *kunpeng*!"

Neither of them paid any attention to Shuang's face, though it was still as beautiful as the moon. The two men were lost in a simple, one-dimensional rite of penis worship. They used every method known to mankind to get the *kunpeng* to spread its wings. Ironically, the big bird kept sleeping, in a position that was noble and carefree. From midnight to dawn, it echoed the deep slumber of Shuang's own handsome face, body, and mind.

2 A game usually played on drinking occasions.

9

While in Triangle City, Yang Yang fell in love with a boy called Dawn. The two were immediately glued at the hip. She stayed in Triangle City and sent Kiki off on a Boeing 767 back to Square City. At Triangle City's newly built airport, Kiki pulled Dawn aside and gave him a kiss while no one was watching. Kiki told him he looks just like his own lover Shuang. What Kiki omitted was: I am wondering if your cock is also as big as *kunpeng*. Before he entered customs, he told Yang Yang: If you want to know what Shuang is like, just take a look at Dawn.

Kiki returned to Square City alone with gifts he bought for Shuang. On the entire flight he fantasized about Yang Yang and Dawn getting it on in the back seat of the car. It was as if the noise from the plane drowned out Yang Yang's scream, "It's as big as *kunpeng*!" Kiki was getting jealous even in his own fantasies, jealous of Yang Yang's big boyfriend in the big city.

Before dinner was served on the plane, Kiki adjusted the angle of the seat to make his own chubby body more comfortable. In a half-reclining position, he had a brief dream. In his dream he could no longer tell Shuang and Dawn apart, so he had to feel their cocks to determine their identities. But their cocks were equally thick and long. Kiki was confused—who was his true love? In the dream he had an idea. He said, "I love you!" in French; one cock got hard right away, while the other remained still and soft. Pleased with himself, Kiki started laughing. His laughter got louder and woke himself up. Sitting next to him was a Belgian man with an angular face. He heard Kiki's sleep talk and mocked him in French. He said "I love you" to Kiki with a naughty smile.

After dinner, Kiki remembered what the poet said about *yanxing shidai*, "the age of sexual persuasion." "Yan," to speak and to persuade, is a thought process; "xing," sex, is an expression of emotions and love. The age of sexual persuasion allowed people to talk openly about sex so as to be more honest about love, while the previous age, the age of romantic persuasion, only produced dishonest lovers.

10

Kiki shared his revelation on the airplane with Mahjong Table. The poet was moved to tears, seeing how a phrase he made up had received such thoughtful feedback. In this postmodern era, where talented writers vie for power, he was extremely grateful that an alternative phrase for this era he cooked up on a whim could gain public currency. His gift back to Kiki was a confession about what he and Big Ma had done to Shuang. Kiki knew that it was only a matter of time before Shuang's big dick got exposed to the public. What he cared about was a different matter: "Did he have an erection?" Mahjong Table said wistfully: "No, the big bird slept. Maybe it had a problem with our 'nests' and did not want to come in."

Kiki hurriedly called Shuang. Shuang picked up the phone and said, "Bastard! Who is this?" Kiki's pretty face was all red and twisted, but he kept his temper and humored him, "Daddy, it's me." Shuang recognized him and softened his tone. Every time Kiki came on the phone, Shuang expected him to say "I miss you," "I love you," or some kind of sexual talk. This time, Kiki skipped the greetings and came right to the point. "Tell me, did you sleep with Big Ma and Mahjong Table?" Shuang's expectations came to nothing, and Kiki had never interrogated him this way before. It was a huge blow to his ego. "Fuck! Yes, we slept together. What are you going to do about it?" Kiki spoke with more attitude: "Your cock is mine and mine alone. No one else gets to touch it!" Shuang talked back, taking a harder line: "Fuck you! It's my cock. I'll do whatever I want with it. I'll stick it in whoever's mouth, or honk at the sky with it, and it's none of your business!" Then he hung up by throwing the receiver against the telephone base, leaving Kiki with a series of "beep, beep."

Kiki wasn't dumb. He knew everything in life followed a natural rhythm. It was rare to be loved by a handsome, popular guy like Shuang. So long as Kiki, from the bottom of his heart, without any hint of a performance, told Shuang "I love you," Shuang would become gentler with him. Even if Shuang didn't want to end their argument so quickly, his dick would protest and state otherwise. Kiki decided not to call back right away and instead let Shuang stew a bit. He had to first show a thing or two to those sex-crazed sluts who seduced his boyfriend.

11

Kiki went by himself to the mahjong game looking for Big Ma. The poet was again offering his back as a mahjong table, while reading a new anthology of poetry on the floor. On the four sides were Wild Dog, Bamboo Dumpling, Big Ma, and Black Donut. They had been playing for twenty-four hours, and Bamboo Dumpling cleaned everybody else's wallet. Big Ma owed him 700 yuan. The poet was lost in the realm of poetry, every now and then uttering a couple of furious lines from his new anthology, such as "Your penis is a sign of your power / I castrate you / let's see what's left of you." Kiki was not interested in his poetry. He knew that phallic worship was built on a combination of castration anxiety and castration pleasure. He kicked the poet in his belly only for emphasis. The mahjong table fell flat on the ground; the tiles, paper money, and coins scattered everywhere.

The four gamblers, eyes red from their marathon of games, attacked Kiki like zombies with superhuman strength. They pushed Kiki down on top of the tiles and money and started beating the living daylights out of him. Kiki courageously attempted to bite Big Ma's left big toe off, showing great precision despite the cotton socks. Immediately, Big Ma screamed loud enough to wake the dead.

Big Ma was sent to the Square City Hospital with blood dripping from his left foot. The doctor took his socks off and saw that his big toe was already severed. Two doctors, a neurosurgeon and an orthopedist, worked together to save it and put it back where it belonged. The "chapter" that had been brutally separated from its "text" was re-sutured to it.

To pay off the costs of Big Ma's surgery, hospital room, food, and taxi, Kiki spent all the money he had worked so hard to earn from doing shows in Triangle City. Kiki became the famous "Sabertooth Cat." All five people who witnessed the tragedy, except the poet, were afraid to come near him, especially Big Ma. Big Ma's left big toe would start shaking uncontrollably at the mere thought of him. Since that day, people who knew Shuang couldn't help taking an extra peek at his crotch. Some tried to remind him tactfully: Be careful—Sabertooth Cat might bite it off and swallow it, too.

12

After he had taught those sluts a lesson, Kiki returned to Shuang's embrace and broke down crying. Shuang said their friend Skin could vouch for him; he never had sex with those "bastards." He even teased Kiki about the sabertooth story. Kiki didn't listen. He was crying his eyes out. His endless tears were a testament to the strength, intensity, thickness, and depth of his love. Shuang understood. He felt flattered and confused at once. His pride made him enjoy the scene and want it to continue. His bewilderment finally led him to kiss Kiki's tear-streaked face. He tasted the tears; they tasted bitter and tart and then thick with sweetness. He teased Kiki: "Hey, bastard, stop crying. Your tears taste kinda sweet." Kiki was like a big kid. Surprised, he immediately stopped crying and with the tip of his tongue reaching around to the side of his cheek tried to lick his own tears. For some reason, they actually tasted quite sweet. They were as sweet as peaches. Kiki stopped crying completely. He was now busy savoring the taste of his own tears. He laughed and said to Shuang, "Yeah, sweet as honey."

To pursue those sweet tears and that happiness, Shuang moved in with Kiki. He only went home on the weekends to see his parents and brother, whom he loved more than anyone else on earth. Shuang also announced he was breaking up with his regular, and irregular, girlfriends for the time being. He hid in Kiki's apartment all day long, telling him stories and jokes, playing chess with him, dancing with him, and playing poker with him. Kiki was not satisfied with these victories. He asked Shuang to make him a promise: "No girlfriends, no marriage for ten years." Shuang readily agreed. "Ten years then." Kiki got the answer he wanted, but he got tearful again: "So, after ten years, you're willing to leave me?" Shuang knit his thick eyebrows and thought earnestly for a moment. "Whether I have a girlfriend or not, whether I'm married or not, I'll visit you and fuck you every single week. Does that work?" Kiki persisted, "Until we grow old?" Shuang said, "Certainly. Needless to say."

In Square City, there was no tradition of boys crying for boys or boys saying "I love you" to boys. Kiki was an exception to the rule, and in that regard, he possessed a unique talent. Shuang was tamed by his tears and love. They started a new tradition in Square City. They were two geniuses. Their vows were greater than wedding vows.

13

When I was writing this story, Sabertooth Kiki and Moon Boy Shuang were attending the fireworks festival in Triangle City. Shuang let me borrow his motorcycle, and Kiki wasn't jealous at all. Kiki wanted me to exhort my readers: Never waste your talent if you're good at conquering men with tears! And don't hold back in declaring "I love you." Pay no heed to old sayings like "boys don't cry." Fuck them. Kiki wanted me to tell you, dear readers, that in this brand-new age of sexual persuasion, if you tell your man "I love you" and cry, he will become your slave immediately. Your tears will change from bitter to sweet. Kiki has one last reminder for you all: If you want to survive in the age of sexual persuasion, you must let go of the values of the old age of romantic persuasion, such as modesty, subtlety, and artifice. And don't forget to tell your man, "Your cock is as big as *kunpeng*!"

Men Men Men Women Women Women

男男男女女女

Translated by Yizhou Guo

0

It's a warm winter in Beijing.

1

Guigui has been living with his boyfriend, Chongchong, for a long time. They have been playing a game that makes them feel impressed with themselves. Guigui pretends their balcony is a recording studio and he is a radio host. He "broadcasts" on a recorder and gives the tape to Chongchong. Chongchong goes out on the street and performs the role of "audience."

On this day, Guigui prepares everything for "broadcasting" and goes in the "studio" on time. He puts on the big headphones, sits up straight in front of the recorder, and solemnly starts his broadcasting role.

"Public Toilet Time—Public Toilet Time! Dear audience comrades, this is International Red Star Radio Station. Your host, Guigui, is greeting you from Beijing, the capital of earth. As the only radio station about toilet culture on earth, we've received so much support and encouragement from you, our audience comrades, since our opening day. On this occasion of New Year's Day 1999, I'd like to represent all crew members in wishing you a smooth defecation

First published in *The Whereabout of Crimson* (胭脂的下落) (Kunming: Yunnan renmin chubanshe, 2007).

and a long flowing piss in the new year. To begin, I'd like to broadcast a personal ad from a lavatory comrade: XX Wang, thirty-one years old, healthy and strong, big penis, yet gentle and kind, is seeking a good-looking young male partner taller than 180 cm. Foreigners preferred. Please call 65547789, ext. 77800."

After broadcasting, he takes out the cassette tape and puts it in a case.

2

Chongchong strolls along the Sidaokou rail tracks listening to his Walkman. He pulls from his pocket the tape Guigui recorded, puts it into the Walkman, and hits play. He then puts the Walkman back in his jacket pocket.

He hears Guigui's voice coming from the earphones: "Dear audiences from around the world. Here's some public toilet news: On the eve of the Chinese Lunar New Year 1998 CE, the sole faucet in our city's public toilet no. 1069 was stolen. The thief was caught on the spot. During the day of December 30, 1998 CE, a wedding motorcade passed by public toilet no. 69. Both the bride and groom needed to pee. To prevent having them wet their wedding dress and suit, the officiator ordered the motorcade to stop. The bride and groom got out of the car to go separately to the men's and women's rooms on each side. But the guests blocked the path to the men's room. The groom ended up carrying the bride and running together with her into the women's room. This scared the shit out of those ladies who were pooping and peeing in the women's room."

Chongchong turns off the Walkman and makes a call. After it is picked up, Chongchong pretends to be excited and serious: "Hello, are you the host Guigui? You are? That's great, I'm so happy to get through to your hotline! Your hotline is so hard to reach. I'm an avid listener of Public Toilet Time. I love this show that your station launched this new year. I appreciate that you enrich all of our lives with color and hope. But I have one small suggestion . . ."

3

At Chongchong's place. Guigui answers the call while removing only one side of the big headphones: "Right. Right. Thank you. Your suggestion is great. We will definitely keep improving, providing more and better spiritual nourishment for folks who love our show. What was that? My voice is sweet? Of course, I look even sweeter... What was that? A date? We can talk about a date later. I have another incoming call. Thank you and thank you for your call!"

He puts down the phone, sits down, leans back in the chair, and, pleased with himself, starts eating biscuits.

4

On a busy street. Xiaobo, carrying his travel bag, approaches as if he were looking for something. He is handsome, wears a casual outfit, and looks a bit travel-worn.

He stops in front of Qingqing clothing store and a record shop. He looks up at the signs, hesitating before he uneasily strides in. He quickly comes out and enters cautiously the other door on the right.

5

Xiaobo walks timidly into Qingqing clothing store.

Sis Qing, the store owner, is helping two female customers try on clothes. She says to one of them: "This outfit suits you so well. You see, so nice, I didn't even expect that."

The customer clearly likes the clothes. She bargains hard with Sis Qing. After negotiating for a while, they come up with a satisfactory price. The two customers pay and, talking and laughing, cheerfully walk out with the clothes they bought.

Only during this moment of leisure does Sis Qing notice Xiaobo, who is standing cautiously by the entrance.

When Xiaobo sees Sis Qing looking at him, he immediately asks: "Ma'am, I am looking for Mr. Li, the owner."

Sis Qing responds coldly: "There is no owner Mr. Li here."

Xiaobo: "There isn't? Then what about the owner?"

Sis Qing: "I'm the owner."

Disappointed, Xiaobo turns around. He says: "Thank you, ma'am!" He walks out.

Sis Qing watches him go. Through the glass window, she sees him pace back and forth near the door and walk in again.

Xiaobo points to the phone and asks: "Ma'am, may I call someone?"

Sis Qing nods: "Sure."

Xiaobo dials a few numbers and speaks into the receiver: "Please page 8890. I'm Xiaobo. Phone number is"—he looks down and reads out the number on the phone—"62215637." After hanging up, he stands by and waits.

While putting away some clothes, Sis Qing asks: "Hasn't called back?"

Xiaobo: "No."

Sis Qing asks abruptly: "Do you want to work for me?"

Pleasantly surprised, Xiaobo asked: "You think I'm qualified?"

Sis Qing: "Where do you live?"

Xiaobo: "With someone from my hometown for now."

Sis Qing: "Then, how about moving here and watching the store at night? Yes?"

Xiaobo nods immediately and says: "Yes."

6

It's morning. Xiaobo slowly pulls up Qingqing clothing store's aluminum roll-up door. He carefully cleans up every corner of the store, then stands in front of the door looking out at the street views.

A taxi arrives. Sis Qing and her husband, Dakang, jump out of the car. From the trunk they pull out several loads of clothes.

Sis Qing glances at Xiaobo and asks him to come help. She directs him to move things into the store.

7

In Sis Qing's shower room. Xiaobo is taking off his clothes.

Sis Qing goes back and forth in front of the shower room and kitchen. She turns on the coal-fueled water heater, adjusts the temperature, and arranges Xiaobo's shower.

After setting the temperature, Sis Qing takes a new towel, walks into the shower room, and hands it to Xiaobo: "Xiaobo, this towel is for you. You can use it from now on. I set the right temperature for you." She turns on one of the taps and teaches Xiaobo: "You just need to turn on this one. If it's too cold or too hot, just give me a holler. After you're done, come to the living room to put on new clothes."

8

In the shower room. Xiaobo takes off his briefs, displaying his muscular body. He starts showering.

9

In the kitchen, Sis Qing deftly cuts vegetables.

Now and then she gets concerned and calls loudly to Xiaobo to ask if the water is too cold or too hot.

10

Sis Qing finishes cooking and takes all the dishes to the living room.

Her husband, Dakang, has already set the table. He sits across from Xiaobo. They wait for the meal to start.

Sis Qing puts the last dish on the table, hands chopsticks to Xiaobo, and says: "Here, dig in!"

Dakang, embarrassed, asks: "Anything to drink?" She ignores him, turning to ask Xiaobo instead: "What will you drink?" Xiaobo: "Anything is fine." Dakang, self-deprecatingly, says: "Let's have some beer." Saying that, he gets up and takes out a bottle of beer from the fridge. He opens it up and pours some for himself and Xiaobo.

Sis Qing sits down and puts food into Xiaobo's bowl: "Xiaobo, what does your fellow hometowner do?" Xiaobo absentmindedly says: "Who?" Sis Qing: "The friend you stayed with before you came to work at our store. Called Chongchong or something?"

Xiaobo: "Oh him... He's an accountant. He also writes when he's free."

11

Sis Qing is making Xiaobo's bed in the guest bedroom while speaking to Xiaobo, who is standing to the side not knowing how to help: "Xiaobo, you will sleep here from now on. It's cold in the store. Not to mention the security system is installed so there's no need to watch the store anymore."

Xiaobo rubs his hands and responds with a foolish smile: "Thank you, Sis Qing."

12

At night, in the other bedroom. Dakang has already taken off his clothes and lies down. Sis Qing is mumbling to herself while taking off her clothes: "It's hard to find a good boy like Xiaobo."

Dakang doesn't say a word.

Sis Qing turns off the lights, lays down beside Dakang. But she has her own quilt.

Dakang sits up quietly and moves his hand under Sis Qing's quilt. Sis Qing refuses: "Don't bother me." Disappointed, he moves his hand back.

13

Xiaobo hears the phone ringing in the Qingqing clothing store. He picks it up: "Hi, brother Kang. My sis is not here. She must be at Da Yang's place to chase down the debt."

14

It's dusk. Sis Qing is crying alone in the living room.

Dakang gets home and sees Sis Qing crying on the couch. He asks impatiently: "What's wrong? What are you crying about?"

Sis Qing ignores him and keeps crying.

Dakang gets agitated: "What on earth are you crying about?"

Sis Qing finally says: "Yang scammed me again. He wouldn't give me back my money."

Dakang pulls Sis Qing up and walks with her toward the door: "Let's find him and square this account!" He drags Sis Qing out of the house just like that.

15

Dakang and Sis Qing sit in a taxi. The streetlights are already on.

The taxi stops in front of Qingqing clothing store. Dakang gets out of the car, runs into the store, and calls out to Xiaobo, waving to him to come out immediately.

Xiaobo runs out from the store.

Dakang yells: "Close the store. Come with me!"

Xiaobo closes the door immediately. He pulls the roll-up door down, leaving the lights on, then follows Dakang into the taxi.

16

It's the third-floor hallway of Tianyi Restaurant. The hallway is a bit narrow, but the light isn't dim. Xiaobo and Dakang lead Sis Qing to room 302.

Dakang gently knocks on the door.

Yang's voice from inside the room: "Who is it?"

Dakang pinches his voice and pretends to be a pretty girl: "Excuse me, is Yang here?"

Yang opens the door. After seeing Dakang, Xiaobo, and Sis Qing behind Xiaobo, he immediately shuts the door.

Dakang and Xiaobo run into the door together, chase Yang to the bed, and start beating him.

Dakang curses: "You fucking pull that shit on my wife? Trying to steal money from a woman? What the fuck kind of man are you!" Xiaobo: "You dare to steal money from my sis?"

Yang begs them to stop their fierce beating.

They let go of Yang. He takes out a stack of money from his pocket and hands it to Dakang. Dakang gives it to Sis Qing and says: "Count it and see if it's enough. If not, let's beat the bastard again."

Sis Qing takes the money. She doesn't count it. She directly walks out. Xiaobo follows her right after. Dakang sees them, glares at Yang, and walks out as well.

17

Xiaobo makes himself busy in the clothing store.

Sis Qing is by his side, casually hanging clothes. All of a sudden, she says to Xiaobo: "Xiaobo, I'll introduce you to someone tonight."

Xiaobo: "Who?"

Sis Qing, satisfied with her plan: "Kiddo, don't you worry about it."

18

It's night. A mid-level restaurant. Sis Qing and Xiaobo sit across from one another and wait for someone. Two cold appetizer dishes are already on the table. Sis Qing mimics a shadowboxing gesture and says to Xiaobo: "You know how to do this?"

Xiaobo answers with a smile: "I practiced it when I was little, but not since then."

Sis Qing smiles: "I bet you do it well."

Xiaobo smiles shyly and doesn't say a word.

At this moment, Sis Qing's young friend Ah Meng walks in. She has short hair and a charming look: "Sis Qing, sorry I'm late."

Sis Qing gets up and gives Ah Meng a warm welcome, holds her hand, and pulls her toward the table: "It's not late. We're not hungry."

Ah Meng notices the handsome Xiaobo. Xiaobo glances at her, too.

Sis Qing takes this opportunity to make the introductions: "This is Ah Meng, my little sister." Then she introduces Xiaobo to Ah Meng: "He is Xiaobo, my little brother."

Xiaobo greets Ah Meng politely: "Hello."

Ah Meng responds: "Hello."

They both seem a little uncomfortable.

Ah Meng takes off her scarf and looks at Sis Qing with an air of mystery. Sis Qing suddenly screams: "Aiya, you cut your hair short! How could you not tell me before you did it?"

Ah Meng is gratified: "Not bad, huh. What about it, you want to cut yours too? Doesn't it look good? You want to do it too?

Sis Qing takes another look at Ah Meng's hair and compliments her: "Nice! But it wouldn't look right on me."

Xiaobo has obviously been yearning for the dishes in front of him for a while. While the ladies chat, he can't help but pick up his chopsticks. He takes a bit of food discreetly and starts eating by himself.

Ah Meng suddenly lowers her head and pulls off a wig. Her long, beautiful hair tumbles out. Sis Qing is dazzled and says: "What was that?"

Ah Meng laughs brightly: "That was fun, right?"

Sis Qing pretends to be mad: "That's not funny. You were just messing around." With this, she calls to the waiter behind her: "Hey, bring up the hot dishes as well."

At that moment, they both see Xiaobo sneaking the cold appetizers. They exchange glances and a knowing smile. Sis Qing gives Ah Meng another meaningful look to suggest she pay attention to Xiaobo. Ah Meng is a little confused.

19

Two red lanterns hang outside the restaurant. The three of them finish dinner and walk out. Sis Qing purposely drags Ah Meng to walk with her behind Xiaobo.

Xiaobo turns back to look for them. He sees them walking slowly arm in arm and says: "Sis, do you want me to go back first?"

Sis Qing takes a look at Ah Meng and says to him: "All right then . . . you can go."

Xiaobo responds, good-natured: "Then I'll leave now." He doesn't say goodbye to Ah Meng, just walks off into the night.

After Xiaobo leaves, Sis Qing takes hold of both Ah Meng's hands and asks slowly: "Ah Meng, what do you think of Xiaobo?"

Meng: "Not bad, pretty nice."

Sis Qing: "You like him?"

Ah Meng: "What nonsense are you talking! Shame on you!"

Sis Qing: "Seriously. I think Xiaobo is a fine person. You two would be pretty good together. What do you say?"

Ah Meng blushes, swivels her waist, and bumps Sis Qing with her hip: "We just met. You know, I'm just not the quick type."

Sis Qing smiles astutely: "Then I'll arrange for you guys to meet more."

Ah Meng doesn't say anything but lowers her head and smiles.

20

Xiaobo gets back to Sis Qing's place first. From the entrance to the living room, he sees the TV on. Fat Dakang is sleeping soundly on the couch. Xiaobo walks by him and accidentally wakes him up.

Xiaobo greets him with enthusiasm: "Brother Kang!"

Dakang asks: "Where'd you go?"

Xiaobo says: "Sis Qing invited us to dinner."

Dakang: "Dinner? What dinner? Why didn't I know about it?"

Xiaobo says frankly: "Sis Qing introduced me to a girlfriend."

Dakang stops digging for information about the dinner and becomes interested. He sits up and asks: "Girlfriend? How's she look?"

Xiaobo walks toward his bedroom and responds indifferently: "Not bad. We met for the first time, so not a lot of feelings."

21

Xiaobo flips through his photo album in the bedroom. Dakang walks by, stands against the door, and says: "Your sis is not back yet. Want to go play billiards?"

Xiaobo looks up: "Sure!"

Dakang adds: "We gotta go fast. Otherwise if your sis comes back and doesn't see us, she'll start a cold war with me again."

22

In the pool hall. Dakang and Xiaobo play billiards. They play a couple of rounds. Xiaobo wins them all.

23

Dakang and Xiaobo are walking in the hallway of the fitness center with heavy parkas on. They see an opening with a sign that says "public toilet." Dakang goes in. Xiaobo hesitates, then says: "Wait up, I gotta go too." He then runs clumsily toward the men's room.

Xiaobo approaches the urinal and stands in front of it. He pees alongside Dakang. Dakang finishes quickly and leaves. Xiaobo has tons of pee. Obviously, he was too into the games and held in too much.

24

Chongchong shows up with a backpack across a street. He waits until the traffic is clear, then crosses the street. He walks toward a sign that says "Public Toilet."

Outside a finely decorated public toilet, Chongchong stops a moment and looks at the wall. Then he walks into the men's room.

There's no one in the men's bathroom. Chongchong looks around and examines the walls and the inner side of the door. He finds words and drawings carved on the door. He takes out a notebook and jots them down.

25

Chongchong walks around to the side of the public toilet and sits down, with a notebook and pen in his hands. He stares at the sunshine as if he's pondering something. After a while, he starts writing in the notebook.

26

Under a steel bridge that spans one of the city's moats. Ah Meng and Xiaobo walk to get onto the bridge, one behind the other. Ah Meng starts a random conversation with Xiaobo: "Why did you wait until now to straighten your teeth?"

Xiaobo responds tepidly: "One of my friends wanted me to do it."

Ah Meng asks: "Does it hurt? Wearing braces?"

Xiaobo answers unwillingly: "No."

They both get on the bridge. Xiaobo looks at the dirty moat. He seems bored.

Not knowing what else to say, Ah Meng asks: "Among today's actresses, who do you think is the prettiest?"

Xiaobo: "I can't say any . . ."

Ah Meng: "What about Gong Li? Do you like Gong Li?"

Xiaobo: "I don't have any feelings for her."

Ah Meng mumbles to herself: "You don't even have feelings for Gong Li?"

Xiaobo walks toward the other end of the bridge by himself, leaving Ah Meng alone on the bridge.

After seeing Xiaobo walk off the bridge, Ah Meng, embarrassed, unwillingly follows him.

27

In a small restaurant. Ah Meng and Sis Qing sit across from one another, waiting for the food. After the waiter brings the dishes, Ah Meng blurts out hurriedly to Sis Qing: "I've got a feeling, something isn't right."

Sis Qing: "What do you mean?"

Ah Meng repeats: "I think something isn't right."

Sis Qing stares at her, perplexed, and waits for her to say more.

Ah Meng: "Xiaobo doesn't like me at all."

Sis Qing can't believe it: "Why?"

Ah Meng: "I think . . . he doesn't like girls much."

Sis Qing surprised: "What are you talking about? He doesn't like girls? That's impossible."

Ah Meng starts eating: "He doesn't. He doesn't like girls. He's not interested in me at all."

28

Bright sunshine spreads through the store's window. Xiaobo is changing the women's clothing on the mannequins.

Sis Qing pays close attention to Xiaobo's every movement. Obviously, she has doubts about him now.

29

It's night. Sis Qing takes off her outer layer of clothing in the bedroom. Dakang has already lain down and is reading the newspaper.

Sis Qing, worried, says: "What do we do about Xiaobo?"

Dakang turns toward her and asks: "What do you mean?

Sis Qing, almost talking to herself: "He doesn't like girls. Even a lovely girl like Ah Meng. This kiddo . . . is going to have a harder life than others." With that, she sighs, turns off the light, and lies down.

In the dark, Dakang puts away the newspaper and asks curiously: "You just said . . . Xiaobo is a homosexual?"

30

Chongchong walks close to the outer wall of a men's public toilet, carrying his backpack. He sees all kinds of words written on the wall. He takes out a notebook, carefully examines those words, and now and then jots down some of them. Then he walks toward the side of the women's bathroom and writes down some of the graffiti on that wall as well. Later on, he walks into the men's room.

Inside the men's room, people are shitting and peeing. Chongchong enters, writes down words from all around the walls, smiles to those people, and one by one gives them his card. He modestly introduces himself: "I am Chongchong, first-class toilet literature writer, chief editor of the magazine *Shining Public Toilet*."

Those who take his card try hard in the dimness to see what the card says.

At that moment, a handsome young boy walks in. As he stands in front of the urinal, Chongchong walks up to give him the card.

When he takes a look at the card, he blushes immediately.

Chongchong, as is his habit, goes on to introduce himself: "I am Chongchong, first-class public toilet literature writer, chief editor of the magazine *Shining Public Bathroom*."

The young boy unzips his pants with the card in hand, takes out his penis to pee, but for the longest time can't make anything come out.

31

It's an easygoing afternoon. Sis Qing and Ah Meng sit in an elegant café and chat. Their relationship seems to have undergone some changes. They appear exceptionally close.

Ah Meng: "Let's travel together this Spring Festival."

Sis Qing: "Sounds good. Where? You decide."

Ah Meng: "America or Europe. Maybe Europe. How about Paris?"

Sis Qing: "Such a cliché."

Ah Meng: "Where do you wanna go?"

Sis Qing: "I'd say Egypt or Vietnam."

Ah Meng: "I'd prefer Yunnan over Vietnam."

Sis Qing: "Yunnan it is. Better than staying in Beijing and getting bored."

Ah Meng: "If we travel, what about your husband? Doesn't he go crazy?"

Sis Qing: "Whose husband? Yours? I don't have one."

Ah Meng: "No husband, okay. Let me be your husband."

Sis Qing: "You're crazy. Acting all crazy. No wonder Xiaobo has no feeling for you. I tell you, Xiaobo is not a homosexual. It's just you're not appealing to him."

Ah Meng starts to throw her tiny fists into Sis Qing's left shoulder: "You're bad! If I can't get married, it's all your fault. I'd commit my entire life to you."

Sis Qing: "That's fine. I happen to need a maid to order about." Before she finished her words, she stood up and prepared to dodge Ah Meng's attack.

32

In a men's public toilet near Wudaokou. Chongchong continues diligently transcribing the public toilet literature on the wall.

A middle-aged man with glasses walks in, stops when he sees Chongchong, and discreetly looks Chongchong up and down from behind his glasses. Chongchong promptly takes out his card and introduces himself: "I'm Chongchong, first-class public toilet literature writer and chief editor of *Shining Public Toilet*." The middle-aged man cautiously takes the card. He doesn't go to the urinal but walks outside, perplexed. Outside of the door, he checks the card all over. Half to himself, half for Chongchong to hear: "Chongchong, first-class toilet literature writer, some kind of chief editor. Hei, I didn't even know there was this kind of magazine, *Shining Public Toilet*."

Inside the restroom, Chongchong hears him and smiles. He keeps copying into the notebook.

33

Guigui and Chongchong are burning the midnight oil in their living room, in a hurry to make a new issue of *Shining Public Toilet*. They divide their labors in this way: Chongchong sits in front of the computer and uses computer graphics to draw *Shining Public Toilet*'s cover. Guigui sits to the side proofreading. Sometimes, Guigui laughs out loud at the contents. Chongchong turns around to stop him, urging him to focus on work.

34

In the café that Sis Qing and Ah Meng had visited. Cuicui, dressed as a woman, sits alone at a table, elegantly enjoying a cigarette.

With his big backpack, Chongchong rushes in and sits across from Cuicui. Obviously, this is a pre-arranged date.

Once he sits down, Chongchong asks her: "Did you bring it with you?"

Cuicui gracefully takes out a piece of paper from a woman's purse and passes it to him: "Here are two pieces."

Chongchong looks at her: "Just two pieces? That's very little."

Cuicui responds: "You know we girls are more reserved than you guys. Bathroom graffiti is rare, other than one or two pieces. These two were already hard to come by." He takes the opportunity to move closer. His head almost reaches Chongchong's shoulder. He casts a warm glance at Chongchong and points to the sentences: "You have to identify them. Were these actually written by a man who sneaked into the women's room?"

Chongchong gives them a professional review: "The first one, 'Xiaoli is a little demon,' doesn't look like it. The second one, 'A fairy's cave is born in nature, the infinity scenes are at a dangerous peak,' this one could be. But that's OK. The more, the better. The more, the better."

Chongchong pulls out from his backpack the *Shining Public Toilet* finished the previous night and passes it to Cuicui. Cuicui takes the magazine, looking excited.

Chongchong shows her some entries from the table of contents. He tells her: "Look. The magazine is out. *Twenty-eight-year-old Beauty with a Creamy Body*, you're the author."

Cuicui fondles the magazine admiringly: "It's really here! It's got my name on it!"

He keeps browsing: "This magazine is pretty good. I'll write more stuff for you in the future."

Chongchong observes his expression and sees that he's engrossed. He smiles with satisfaction.

After a while, Cuicui asks: "Hey, Chongchong, is this the only one of its kind in the world?"

Chongchong answers with pride: "Of course."

35

It's morning. Xiaobo, wearing a short undergarment and long underwear, brushes his teeth in the bathroom.

In her own room, Sis Qing finishes her makeup and walks out. She enters Xiaobo's bedroom and puts 500 yuan by the side of his pillow. As she passes through the hallway, she efficiently straightens things up there and puts on her coat.

As she's about to go out the door, she says to Xiaobo: "Go check those teeth. Your braces need to be tightened. By the way, this is your salary for this month. I'm putting it on your bed." She enters the small bedroom and after a while comes out.

Xiaobo turns around, with foam in his mouth: "Thank you, Sis Qing."

Sis Qing: "Don't mention it."

When he sees Sis Qing opening the door, Xiaobo asks: "No need for stocking today?"

Sis Qing: "Stock what? There's no time right now. I'm going now. You can come later today. You should get those braces tightened. You hear me?"

Xiaobo answers "yeah" obediently. Sis Qing finally leaves home.

36

After he finishes brushing his teeth, Xiaobo combs his short hair with Sis Qing's comb. He walks to the hallway, gets down, and starts to do push-ups.

At that moment, late-riser Dakang walks out of the bedroom. He wants to leap over Xiaobo but stops. He looks at Xiaobo's buff and well-proportioned body, as well as his up-and-down rhythm. He suddenly shudders, as if he has had an electric shock.

Xiaobo counts the number of push-ups: ". . . 5, 6, 7, 8, 9 . . ." To cover up his reaction, Dakang joins the counting: ". . . 10, 11, 12, 13 . . ." All of a sudden, Dakang can't endure the electric waves inside his body anymore. He stops counting.

Xiaobo isn't aware of any of this. He counts to fifty-six, until he is exhausted, and lies down.

Dakang strains every nerve to control his impulse. He watches Xiaobo stand up panting, take off his T-shirt, and use it to wipe off his sweat. Xiaobo speaks while wiping: "Today's no good. I only did fifty-six. Such a loser."

Dakang can no longer control his impulse. He pounces onto Xiaobo, brings him to the edge of the bed, pins him down brutally, and tries to take off his underpants.

Xiaobo is paralyzed by such a sudden attack. He doesn't fight back until Dakang removes his underwear.

Dakang tries to insert himself into Xiaobo's body but is thrown off under the bed by Xiaobo suddenly turning over. His head hits the wooden bed board hard. He screeches out loud in pain.

After he wrenches himself away, Xiaobo pulls up his underwear, grabs the rest of his clothes and socks, and hurriedly runs to the living room. There he hastily puts on his clothes.

Dakang has a large bump on his head. He rubs the bump and lashes out at Xiaobo: "Who the fuck do you think you are? A rabbit, glass, a fairy with cock and cunt! You think I don't know, right? I just want to fucking try something new today. You'd better not think I'm interested in people like you! Even if you gave it to me, I don't want you! Look at yourself, looking like a man. Who knows what's inside your asshole! If I were you, I'd rather die. Why are you even alive? You're a fucking disgrace to men!"

Xiaobo can't bear anymore; he angrily stands up, grabs Dakang's collar, raises his fist while shaking: "You curse me again, I will beat you to death!"

Seeing how angry Xiaobo is, Dakang is stunned and shuts his mouth, revealing his true weak nature.

Xiaobo pushes him away, storms back to the small bedroom, quickly packs up, and puts all his stuff into his backpack.

Dakang listens to Xiaobo's movements from the living room and realizes he's packing. He worries that he will take valuables from the house. He quietly comes to the door and watches Xiaobo.

Xiaobo takes his toiletries from the bathroom, drapes the down jacket Sis Qing gave him over his shoulders, hoists his backpack, and walks toward the door.

Dakang gets up a little nerve again. He blusters: "Get out! You get out! As far as you can, never let me see you again!"

Xiaobo opens the door without looking back.

Dakang regains his fury: "Come back! Take off that coat my wife gave you!"

Xiaobo immediately throws down the backpack, takes off the coat, and slams it on the floor. He then picks up the backpack and dashes out.

37

Xiaobo walks on the desolate street in the cold wind. He wears only a sweater, hunches his shoulders, folds his cold arms in front of his chest, and carries his backpack.

He's still so angry he grinds his teeth and clenches his fists so hard they make clicking sounds. His eyes are filled with tears.

When he arrives in front of a row of trees lining the street, he can't hold it in anymore. He throws down the bag, punches and kicks a tree.

The pain in his legs from kicking the tree seems finally to relieve the humiliation and pain in his heart. He leaves off the trunk of the winter tree and meanders aimlessly in a directionless direction.

38

Xiaobo ends up coming to Qingqing clothing store. He knows that Sis Qing is good to him. He should not leave without saying goodbye.

A clearance sign hangs on the glass window that faces the sun. The winter sun casts a chilled light on it.

Separated by the window, Xiaobo sees Sis Qing and Ah Meng inside, busy helping customers. He waits patiently.

Inside, Sis Qing wraps up business with a customer. She notices Xiaobo outside the window. She opens the door, goes out, and calls to him: "Xiaobo, what's the matter? Come in and help! Did they fix your braces?"

Xiaobo stays where he is, unwilling to move. He mumbles: "Sis Qing, I gotta go."

Sis Qing senses something strange. She closes the door behind her, comes to him, and asks with concern: "What's wrong? Anything happen back home?"

Xiaobo mutters a vague "yeah."

Sis Qing, worried: "Then you'd better hurry up and go buy the train ticket now!"

Xiaobo: "I'm afraid I'll never see you again. I've come to say goodbye."

Sis Qing laughs: "Foolish kiddo. What a silly thing to say! How could we never see each other again!"

At that moment Ah Meng, holding up a piece of clothing, pushes open the door and comes out to ask: "Sis Qing, what is the lowest price for this camel's fur coat?" When she sees Xiaobo, she gives him a smile.

Xiaobo doesn't react. He lowers his head.

Sis Qing leans sideways to answer: "Up to you."

Ah Meng turns around and goes back inside.

Sis Qing notices that Xiaobo is shivering. She realizes he's not wearing a coat. She grumbles: "Why don't you put on a coat? You went out without a coat?"

Xiaobo wants to explain but on second thought keeps his mouth shut.

Sis Qing doesn't dig into it. She returns to the store and takes out a gender-neutral and nice-looking plaid tweed coat. She swiftly, as if in a whirlwind, comes to Xiaobo's side, grabs his backpack, and puts the coat on him.

Xiaobo takes a look at the coat, half embarrassed and half unwilling: "Sis, I'm not gonna wear it."

Sis Qing almost forces him: "Put it on! Don't catch a cold!" After he puts the coat on, she pushes him: "Go. Buy the ticket early and get on the train. Call me when you get home." With that, she pulls two 100-yuan bills from her pocket and squeezes them into Xiaobo's hand. She orders authoritatively: "Take it. Buy something to eat on your way."

Xiaobo retreats, as if exiting a stage lit by sunshine. With a swirl of emotions, he says: "Thank you, Sis Qing. I'm leaving."

Sis Qing doesn't grasp his intent, only urging him: "Don't go to scalpers. They're all frauds!"

Xiaobo sidles away. With tears in his eyes, he waves his hand to Sis Qing. To disguise them, he turns his head to face the buildings in the distance.

39

It's already afternoon. Xiaobo, with the plaid coat Sis Qing gave him and his backpack, continues to wander around. It's obvious he has nowhere to go.

He arrives at a street park. He watches the strollers, the vendors who sell balloons, and the old men with kids.

While looking at them, he begins to feel frazzled. He sits on a wooden horse for children.

Sunlight spills onto his handsome face. He closes his eyes and falls asleep. The way he sits and sleeps shows that in his heart he's still completely a child, innocent and pure.

40

Dusk arrives. During the evening rush hour, the flow of people and cars picks up.

By the side of a public telephone in a corner store, a few people wait in line to make a call. Xiaobo is one of them.

It's Xiaobo's turn. He picks up the phone and dials a number. The call is picked up. He's excited: "Hi, is it Bro Chong? This is Xiaobo . . . I quit my job . . . Sis Qing was nice to me, but . . . don't ask . . . the thing is, I still have to stay at your place . . . You welcome me over? Cool, I'm on my way." He puts down the phone. He feels relieved.

He leaves, only to realize before getting too far that he forgot to pay. He quickly walks back and pays for using the phone.

41

It's already dusk. Chongchong is typing in front of the computer in the living room.

There's a knock at the door. Chongchong hears it and opens the door. It's Xiaobo.

Chongchong pulls him in and greets him warmly.

Chongchong brings Xiaobo to settle on the couch and asks: "That job, why did you quit?"

Xiaobo lowers his head and can't help but say, aggrieved: "Don't ask."

Chongchong senses something and says promptly: "If you wanna quit, just quit. Just stay at my place. It's convenient. Still the same camp bed in this living room. It's the right moment. You can help me give away magazines." While saying that, he pours Xiaobo a glass of water and hands it to him.

Xiaobo: "What magazine?"

Chongchong takes out a magazine from under the couch and shows it to Xiaobo: "Here it is. I created it myself. Guigui helped. Take a look, what do you think?"

Xiaobo: "What is Guigui?"

Chongchong laughs: "Guigui is a guy." He points to the guest bedroom and says: "He lives here too. He's still in bed."

Knowing the right way to behave, Xiaobo tactfully stops asking further questions. He looks at the magazine: "This magazine is kinda special. Never seen it before."

Chongchong proudly: "If it's not special, would I do it?"

At that moment, Guigui gets up and asks from the bedroom: "Chongchong, who's here?"

With a guilty conscience, Chongchong answers: "Oh, just a fellow from my hometown."

With the sound of slippers on the floor, Guigui walks out, looking drowsy. As soon as he sees Xiaobo, he turns charming. Taking in Xiaobo from top to bottom, he says affectionately: "I've met you somewhere."

Chongchong immediately makes fun of him: "You? Who haven't you met?"

Guigui thinks seriously and says: "I must have met you somewhere."

Xiaobo becomes stubborn: "No way. Where did you see me before?"

Guigui insists: "I definitely met you."

Chongchong laughs: "Xiaobo, you don't understand. It was in a dream."

Xiaobo is perplexed: "In a dream? No way . . ."

Chongchong bursts into laughter: "He's saying you're his dream lover!"

Xiaobo naively and foolishly becomes even more confused: "I, I . . . am a guy."

Chongchong: "A cute guy is what he wants. Don't you understand?"

Guigui shoves Chongchong onto the couch and goes to the bathroom.

Xiaobo only half understands. He makes a silly smile and looks at Chongchong.

42

Still dusk. Sis Qing returns home, feeling a bit empty. She removes her coat. She goes straight to the bedroom where Xiaobo had stayed and straightens up the bed that Xiaobo once slept on.

After tidying up the room, she goes to the living room. She sees Dakang reading the newspaper. She asks him: "Did something happen to Xiaobo's family? He didn't even have time to put on the coat."

Dakang acts as if nothing happened, covering it over by saying: "How would I know?" He checks out Sis Qing's body language and realizes she doesn't have a clue about the conflict between him and Xiaobo. He becomes bold: "You took him in as your little brother. How would he tell me anything instead of telling you?"

Sis Qing stops talking. Desolate, she goes to the bathroom to wash her face. Obviously, she still misses Xiaobo.

43

It's morning. The sunshine spills into Chongchong's living room. It falls onto the face of Xiaobo, who has just woken up.

He pulls his clean and strong naked arms out of the quilt. He sits up on the camp bed, revealing his chesty body. He gets out of bed with only his underwear on. Displaying his nicely shaped, well-developed muscles, he straightens up the bed. He closes his suitcase and puts it on the couch. He then folds the camp bed and puts it in the corner.

At that moment, Chongchong walks out of his bedroom. Before going to take a shower, he peeks into the living room. He sees Xiaobo's already up, smiles: "You're up."

Xiaobo responds: "I'm up."

Chongchong suddenly becomes uncomfortable in front of Xiaobo's dazzling, half-naked body. As if fleeing disaster, he scurries to wash up.

44

In heavy winter coats, Chongchong and Xiaobo walk shoulder to shoulder on the sunlight-filled streets.

They come to the bus stop for bus number 56. At the stop, there are a lot of people waiting. A gust of chilly wind blows. Chongchong pulls up Xiaobo's collar and enjoins: "Get off at Shuangyushu stop, then change to bus 302, get off at Zhaolong Restaurant stop, then walk toward the west, you will see Sanlitun bar street."

Xiaobo: "Got it."

The bus arrives. Chongchong gives Xiaobo the bag full of magazines on his shoulder. Xiaobo takes it, squeezes into the queue of passengers, and gets on the bus.

After the bus pulls out, Chongchong continues watching after it.

45

It's the afternoon. The sunlight is bright. Xiaobo goes from bar to bar on Sanlitun Street to give out the *Shining Public Toilet* magazines. Some bar owners accept it happily, while others tactfully reject it.

After coming out of a bar called Boys and Girls, Xiaobo unexpectedly sees Sis Qing and Ah Meng coming out of the bar next door. Their arms are intertwined and they look extremely intimate, unusually so. They talk and laugh. They brush past Xiaobo without even noticing him.

Xiaobo's right hand, which he raises and prepares to wave, freezes in the air. He chokes back the greeting that is about to come out of his mouth. In a daze, he stands rooted to the spot, unsure of the best thing to do.

At a small intersection, Sis Qing and Ah Meng cross to the other side of the street.

Xiaobo watches them until they disappear into the crowd on the other side of the street.

46

It's dusk by the time Xiaobo gets back to Chongchong's place. Chongchong has just returned home as well. He takes the backpack off Xiaobo's shoulder and checks in with him solicitously. Then he asks: "How was it? How did people from the bars react to the magazine?"

Xiaobo answers: "Some owners didn't want it. They said this kind of magazine is too vulgar for the bar culture."

Chongchong continues: "How many did you give out then?"

Xiaobo opens up the backpack and counts the number of magazines left: "Thirteen."

Guigui, who is cooking in the kitchen, pokes his head out and says: "Only thirteen? That's not enough."

Chongchong hurriedly says: "It's not too little. Thirteen is fine."

Guigui takes this opportunity to come out of the kitchen and run to Chongchong's side, coquettishly: "Chongchong, I don't feel like cooking tonight."

Chongchong says generously: "Sure. If you don't want to cook, let's go out to eat. I just got my bonus."

Guigui gets excited: "You got the bonus, then we should eat something nice."

Chongchong turns to Xiaobo and asks: "Yes, I got a bonus. What do you like to eat?"

Xiaobo looks politely at Guigui, implying he should be the one to decide.

Guigui, not picking up on this, asks Xiaobo: "Right, he got a bonus. What do you want to have?"

Then Xiaobo, says, with the air of a child: "McDonald's!"

Guigui, disappointed: "Just McDonald's?"

Xiaobo, a bit looking forward to it: "I haven't had it yet."

Chongchong adds immediately: "McDonald's it is then! At least it's McDonald's."

47

It's the middle of the night. With only his underwear on, Chongchong gets up. Guigui, sleeping topless with him, is woken up by his moves. He hazily listens to Chongchong's movements.

After peeing, Chongchong carefully walks through the hallway, opens the living room door, and walks in. He comes to Xiaobo's bedside, leans down, and for a long time gazes at Xiaobo sleeping under the moonlight.

After a while, he can't help but kiss him on the cheek. Xiaobo wakes up with a start. He sits up for a second, then lies down again and closes his eyes. Chongchong kisses him again. He offers no response.

Chongchong goes back to his room as if he were a thief.

48

Riding a bike, Xiaobo carries on his back a bundle of *Shining Public Toilet* magazines in envelopes. He stops at the post office, locks the bike, and walks in with the magazines in his arms.

At the bulky parcel counter, he takes care of the mailing formalities. He walks out of the post office empty-handed, gets on the bike, and leisurely rides away.

49

It's evening. Chongchong puts on tango music in the living room. He patiently teaches Xiaobo ballroom dancing.

Xiaobo is not used to it. He can't get his feet to move right. Chongchong shows him how to do it while sounding out the beat.

They don't notice that Guigui comes back from outside.

Seeing Chongchong's eager attentiveness to Xiaobo, Guigui uncharacteristically becomes jealous.

He steps up, turns off the tape recorder, and mockingly says: "What are you doing? Being romantic? There's so much shit to do. All you care about is dancing!" Chongchong releases Xiaobo from his embrace: "Fine! Fine! I'll stop! Time to work."

Chongchong and Xiaobo sit down, like elementary school students who did something wrong. They obediently put the magazines into envelopes. One writes down the address, the other inserts Chongchong's card.

50

The same night. Sis Qing sits opposite Dakang in the living room.

Sis Qing says nonchalantly, while putting lotion on her hands: "I have to move out."

Dakang, surprised: "What do you mean?"

Sis Qing: "I'm saying, the apartment's yours. I'm leaving."

Dakang stands up: "You want to divorce me?"

Sis Qing: "Getting divorced or not, that's up to you."

Dakang: "Why?"

Sis Qing: "No reason. It's just someone else likes me."

Dakang: "Which means you're having an affair?"

Sis Qing doesn't respond.

Dakang, feeling he's right, becomes bolder: "For how long?"

Sis Qing: "Not very long."

Dakang: "Who is it?"

Sis Qing: "None of your business."

Dakang threatens: "You aren't gonna say, right? You're not walking out this door until you tell me."

The two confront one another for a while. Sis Qing finally says: "I'll tell you. Don't be surprised."

Dakang sneers: "I won't."

Sis Qing: "It's Ah Meng."

Dakang, stunned, jumps up: "What? It's her?" He walks back and forth, looking furious.

Sis Qing gives no explanation. She walks to the telephone, picks up and dials. She's calling Ah Meng. Sis Qing calmly says: "Ah Meng, it's me. It's all settled here. Come and pick me up. See you downstairs in fifteen minutes." She puts down the phone and unhurriedly starts packing.

Dakang stands there, dumbfounded.

51

Sis Qing walks out of her place, wearing a long coat and carrying a shoulder bag. The sound-controlled light outside the building comes on. She quickly descends the stairs and walks out the gate.

Outside the gate, a taxi is waiting. Ah Meng stands beside the car door waiting for Sis Qing.

Ah Meng takes Sis Qing's bags that she is carrying and puts them on the passenger seat. They get into the back seat from both sides of the car.

The driver starts the car, but it stalls out. The driver has no choice but to ask Sis Qing and Ah Meng: "Sorry. Can you give me a hand pushing the car?"

The two get out and smile at each other. They walk to the back of the car and start pushing. Under the streetlight, their shadows look beautiful.

The engine starts up.

They get in.

The taxi slowly drives away. In the dimness of the night, it disappears into the crowd of buildings.

52

It's midnight. Chongchong tosses and turns. He can't fall asleep. He leans over and checks Guigui's breath with his hand. He sees Guigui is sleeping soundly. He sits up and sneaks out of bed, naked.

Actually, Guigui is pretending to sleep. Once Chongchong gets out of bed, Guigui immediately opens his eyes wide and stares at Chongchong's back. He listens to Chongchong's steps and quietly gets out of bed.

Chongchong doesn't go to the bathroom but instead opens the living room door. He sneaks in and swiftly leaps onto the camp bed. He lifts Xiaobo's quilt, squeezes in, lies down next to Xiaobo, and starts stroking him. Xiaobo wakes up with a start. But he doesn't seem to resist too much.

Guigui stands naked by the door. He sees it all.

53

It's early morning. The light of the day is still dim. Guigui gets up early. He turns on the light. He appears to be gathering his belongings from the bedroom. He doesn't have much stuff, very simple.

He comes to the living room. He takes down off the walls the photos that belong to him and the two pictures he painted.

On the camp bed, Chongchong and Xiaobo are pressed against one another in an embrace. They look intimate and warm. Guigui deliberately turns a blind eye.

He goes back to the bedroom. He puts everything into a large red backpack. He zips it up, puts it on, walks to the door, and turns out the light.

He stands at the window in the light of the dawn. It seems he doesn't know what to do.

54

At last, Guigui bravely walks out onto the street. The sun is already up. The early risers mostly look like working people. Guigui is among them, carrying his red backpack. He appears to be in a hurry and in awe.

When he comes to an intersection between a road and the railway, Guigui turns toward the side of the railway.

Walking between the double tracks, Guigui takes out his cell phone. After the call is connected, he uses the cell phone as a broadcast microphone. He starts humming the "Wedding March."

55

The sun is out. Chongchong pushes down the speakerphone button. The lyric-less "Wedding March," sung by Guigui, is transmitted through the microphone. Xiaobo wakes up too, pricks up his ears, and listens closely.

56

Guigui sits on a rail track and starts "broadcasting": "Dear audience comrades, this is 97.7 FM megahertz, International Red Star Radio Station. Your host, Guigui, is greeting you from Beijing, the capital of earth. Due to global warming, an increase in endangered species, an unpredictable political climate, the endless and increasingly severe financial crises, all station crew members are infected with a grave spiritual illness and will die soon. For this reason, we have made this special episode . . .

"Next is a public toilet fable: when the Son of God Jesus Christ was made flesh, ancient Rome applied pseudo-democratic politics and forbade anyone to build a private bathroom, including the emperor. One day, the emperor was in an imperial meeting. He suddenly felt an urgent need to urinate. He hastily handed over leadership of the meeting to the regent and fled at the speed of a marathon to a public toilet across from the palace. While peeing, the emperor was attacked by two blind citizens. One groped his front; one groped his back. The emperor rebuked them: 'How dare you! You dare to molest the emperor!' As soon as they heard that, the two ran away in haste. Out on the street, the one who had grabbed the front said: 'It turns out that the emperor is just a soft meat ball.' The one who had groped the back retorted: 'No, the emperor's power is a hole.'

"Dear audience comrades, the life of a public toilet is beautiful. But love is cruel. To have an even more resplendent life, I, Guigui, the host of Public Toilet Time, will temporarily say goodbye to everyone, and go to Neptune to experience the public toilet life over there. Someday, you will hear an entirely new program I made from Neptune. I wish all of you good health and a great future. I hope you all grow old together in the bathrooms."

57

Xiaobo and Chongchong hear that the call has been cut off after Guigui finishes broadcasting. The brief cutoff tone comes through the phone receiver.

Xiaobo lies back in bed. He pulls the quilt over him. He looks like a small animal.

Chongchong, still motionless, sits on the edge of the camp bed. In the morning light, his fully naked body is revealed.

Men Are Containers 男人是容器

Translated by Casey James Miller

1

The city is the container of men, just as a glass is the container of wine, condoms are the containers of penises, and I am your container. Men are also the containers of the city, just as the mouth is the container of food, books are the containers of history, and you are his container.

Men are the containers of other men. One man is the container of many men. Just as the sea is the container of rivers, a man is the container of others, and others his container.

Square City used to be a container. It held me (they call me Peach) and those whom you are about to meet: Pear, Apple, and Banana; Bill, Georgi, Arai Sakuo, and Koyama Miyoshi. As it turns out, I am still the container of Square City, harboring its past stories and present experiences.

Being containers, Square City and I both possess similar organs, but it is still essential to differentiate between square and round, deep and shallow; between mouth and anus, heart and brains; between the different qualities of clay, metal, and flesh.

Containers can shatter. When angry or intoxicated, he liked to crush the delicate glass holding his sweet alcohol in his hand. Containers can overflow, can transcend containment. When pouring you a draft beer, I always liked to deliberately make the foam swell over the edge of the glass and flow swiftly down the back of your hand. Perhaps you still remember.

Contents can change their containers, and containers can change their contents. Men change men as regularly as they change underwear. We move from

First published in *Fairytales of Triangle City* (三角城的童話) (Hong Kong: Huasheng shudian, 1998).

country to country and from city to city without ever settling down in a single place. Generations flow through Square City like cards shuffle through a deck, yet Square City still is the same. I have liked you, liked him, and liked them too, but I continue to be a container, just as used and unused condoms are still containers.

2

Bill came from England, slender and tall with blond hair and blue eyes, covered from head to toe in a fine layer of golden fur. He studied history at Square City University and spoke fluently in the local dialect. He occupied room 307 in the foreign student apartments, which was across from Arai Sakuo, next door to Koyama Miyoshi, and diagonal to Charlie 5. Charlie 5, from Egypt, was of mixed race; his father was Irish and his mother Egyptian. He spoke Square City dialect extremely poorly: as soon as he became nervous, he reverted back to English or a mixture of Egyptian and the local dialect, which only added to his Latin lover charm. His boyfriend, a Spaniard, was a professor of European economic history at Circle City University. Every summer and winter break, when Bruguera came to stay in his room, Bill would stand mischievously outside the door of 303, imitating Charlie 5's high-pitched screams, making everyone along the hall nearly die of laughter.

The year that Pear, Apple, and I started school, Square City University implemented a mixed residence system: every foreign student was required to share with one undergraduate of the same sex a single room and a double bed. (When the apartment building for foreign students was still under construction, the administration, thinking that foreigners were all as tall and big as horses and worrying that the traditional Square City University single beds would be unable to accommodate them, specially purchased double beds for their use.) At first, Bill and Arai Sakuo objected, protesting the policy as "inhumane," "surveillance," and an infringement upon their freedom. After their protests were firmly overruled, they had no choice but to bow their heads to "power" and to stand by as the administration opened their doors and tossed Peach, Plum, Apple, Pear, Banana, and Jujube (a truly exceptional group of young men) into their rooms.

After the first night, Pear, Apple, and I gathered together in front of the big mirror that covered half of the bathroom wall, brushing our teeth and swapping stories of our experiences "sharing the same bed."[1]

1 A common phrase that usually means being married, though not here. The author is deliberately playing on its double meaning.

The three of us were all from Triangle City; I attended Railway Secondary School, Pear attended Army Secondary School, and Apple attended National Secondary School. We were also the toughest, naughtiest, and most trouble-making students at our respective schools. No one there had liked us, but no one had dared to stand in our way; only the boldest and most dissolute boys and girls had the courage to follow along at our heels. In terms of our physical appearance, we also looked rather formidable: Pear was tall and laid-back, brawny and handsome. Apple was hale and hearty, with a ruddy complexion, strong muscles, and sturdy bones; he loved to talk and laugh, to move around and cause a commotion. I, on the other hand, had a nimble and perceptive appearance, with an alert expression and lively eyes that concealed my innate pride. Although we were young, we thought that, if we relied on our charm, we would be indomitable. So, before the foreign students in 303, 305, and 307 had any leeway for racial discrimination, we started an anti-Western verbal campaign.

Pear said, "Georgi [the Bulgarian who lived in 305] is such a fucking narcissist! After every shower he stands naked in front of the mirror, examines himself from head to toe, does a set of American-style fitness exercises, and then inspects his stomach, arms, and butt for any excess body fat. Once men turn twenty-five, they're not so pretty anymore! If he thinks he can keep his skin as tight as a fucking drum, he's dreaming."

I said, "Bill uses so much cologne it's like being fumigated. As soon as he gets in bed, he cuddles his mouth up to my neck and starts tickling me with his breath. I manage to escape, but as soon as I fall asleep, he starts pressing his lips together like a platypus on me again. While sleeping, he sings Irish folk songs in at least two languages."

Pear said, "He is definitely in love with you. You've got to watch out, be careful he doesn't rape you! Actually, that won't do: you should put a bowl of water between you and him on the bed, just like in the story of Liang Shanbo and Zhu Yingtai."[2]

Apple said, "Why don't you just turn into a butterfly, eh? You don't have to get so classical, that time is long past. Get a load of my Charlie 5's ever-increasing affections; he's taking much more initiative than your Bill: as soon

2 The story of Liang Shanbo and Zhu Yingtai is a late imperial tragic folktale about a young woman, Zhu Yingtai, who dresses as a man so that she can study at school. There she becomes close to a young man, Liang Shanbo; they become "sworn brothers." Zhu Yingtai is then called home and is betrothed to someone else. She asks Liang Shanbo to visit her "sister" at their home. Liang thus discovers Zhu's female identity, but he is too late. He falls ill upon hearing the news of Zhu's impending marriage and dies. Zhu then follows him to his grave and dies from despair.

as the lights go out, he lets out a cold cry and starts drilling straight into my warm blankets. Once he gets inside, he starts rubbing his butt against my junk till I am rock hard. I can't get to sleep until I give him a whack on the head and kick him out of my blankets. Then I drift back to sleep while listening to his whimpering."

3

Banana wasn't born with his nickname. He was originally called Shi Dabo, and on the first day he entered Square City University he was thrown in to live and sleep beside Arai Sakuo in 308. The two had similar qualities: their facial features were well-proportioned (especially the bridge of their noses, which were both rigidly straight, suggesting that their respective penises were equally rigid and straight); they were both swarthy-skinned, athletically built, and with a thoughtful and taciturn demeanor. They even had matching heights of six feet two. As soon as I set foot on the third-floor hallway and saw Shi Dabo and Arai Sakuo coolly sizing each other up, my nimble and perceptive heart became happy: two such similar characters thrown together like this was guaranteed to produce some drama.

Georgi and Bill were good friends, frequently meeting up in Square City to stroll through its broad avenues and narrow streets and watch movies. They would attend every type of lecture or seminar having to do with Square City politics, arts, culture, or education, always sitting together but never speaking a word. Then they would go back to the apartments (usually returning to room 305) to earnestly exchange in English their opinions regarding the event. Georgi was writing his master's thesis, whose working title was "Square City's Affluent Classes," using anthropological methods. In comparison, Bill appeared idle and carefree, completely forsaking his elite upper-class English background. His only goal and source of pride was to become fully fluent in the Square City dialect. Perhaps it was due to his appreciation of antitraditionalism that, during the years we shared a room, in the moments before sleep when I was still conscious and awake, I seldom minded when he pursed his lips together like a platypus against my neck as he slept.

Arai Sakuo's friend was Koyama Miyoshi, who lived in 309. They had come to Square City together from Tokyo, where they had both lived on the Chūō Main Line, Arai in Kichijōji and Koyama in Kokubunji. They met each other one summer during a high school baseball league match. They both got into Tokyo University, later ending up in Square City after leaving university early due to the anti-imperialism and anti-corporation protests that were engulfing the youth of Japan. Despite being good friends, they seldom went out together (except for occasionally going to eat Japanese-style noodles at Ba Pan Noodle House) and rarely even conversed in Japanese. Like a pair of lonely trees, they took root inside rooms 308 and 309, sitting alone in front of their tape decks with their ears glued to their headphones, desperately studying Square City dialect. After Plum started living in 309, his exuberant energy enlivened Koyama Miyoshi and the two started shooting hoops, swimming, and hitting the clubs and bars together, where they separately pursued fleeting heterosexual affairs. Before long, Koyama's spoken Square City dialect became imbued with a highly amusing Circle City flavor, while Arai's proper Square City accent remained utterly uninfluenced by his roommate, Shi Dabo.

On the first New Year's Day after we fruit had all entered university, the plot that was unfolding on the third floor reached its first dramatic climax. First Koyama Miyoshi and Plum exchanged short-term girlfriends, and a rumor circulated that the girl who had originally been seeing Plum (who was now with Koyama) was a high-ranking nightclub prostitute who had once fleeced the president of Square City University out of 5,000 RMB, nearly driving "his excellency" to utter bankruptcy (or perhaps the collapse of his scholarly status). Then there was Square City University's New Year's Dance. Georgi, Bill, Charlie 5, and I all put on women's clothes and outrageous makeup. As soon as we arrived on the dance floor, we started tangoing and grinding with Arai, Koyama, Shi Dabo (he hadn't been nicknamed Banana yet), Pear, and Apple, temporarily reducing the audience into a dumbstruck silence until all of Square City University suddenly erupted into thunderous applause. While we were dancing pressed up against one another, Bill daringly kissed Shi Dabo on the lips and declared to him, "I love you." I stealthily nibbled Arai on the earlobe; he pushed me away in shock and then clutched me to his chest in a strong and unyielding embrace. Charlie 5 cuddled into Pear's breast with a long sigh, trembling and crying, pressing his tears all over Pear's face. After dancing like that for ages, as Pear dragged a tearful and bleary-eyed Charlie 5 off the dance floor, I wondered whether Charlie 5 was missing Bruguera, who was in faraway Circle City.

Before the clock started ringing to signify the New Year, the mood on the dance floor began to climax: everyone joined hands, forming two large, concentric dancing circles, spinning madly until the clock began to sound. At the first chime, the MC dimmed the lights slightly, and the dancing throng of people scattered like ants, hurriedly searching for the people closest to them that they most longed for, to share with them the first moment of the New Year. As the clock rung out a third time, Arai tightly embraced me from behind; through the silk fabric of his dancing clothes, I felt a hard, erect object pushing and radiating its warmth against my peach-shaped behind. I suddenly felt a change like an electric current take place in my groin. His breath puffed against the back of my neck, fragrant and arousing. I couldn't resist turning my head around and, as the clock cried out to announce the approach of the New Year, bringing my mouth up to his in a kiss.

4

Looking straight ahead of him, Arai took me by the hand and led me off the dance floor. His overcoat was draped over my dancing clothes. His body wore my own down jacket. In the middle of the frigid winter night, we frequently stopped to exchange warm kisses (his cool, rugged exterior concealed a passionate inner energy). A few times we almost slipped and fell onto the snowy ground. Stumbling forward, holding on to each other for support, we pushed open the main doors of the foreign student apartments. Mr. Cheng, the night watchman, deferentially nodded his head and wished Arai a happy new year, in English, while looking straight through me as if I weren't there (he was an ex-military English instructor who worshipped all foreigners as if they were gods but loathed the local people with all his heart). However, even this did nothing to dampen my spirits. We continued to kiss as we climbed the stairs. On the second floor, we could already hear the muffled sounds of Charlie 5's high-pitched screams. As we arrived on the third floor, his screaming reached a climax. Its precipitous, sudden stop made one feel a kind of loss, a sapping of strength, filling the night and the body with a wistful regret. Who had made Charlie 5's screams ring out and then caused them to so abruptly subside? If they might rise up once more, would it not mean that life itself was not ebbing away?

Wanting to observe Arai Sakuo's reaction to the screams (including their creation, crescendo, and collapse), I moved to kiss his face, but he averted his eyes. In that moment, I saw a glint of tears. I took his hand, scratching his palm, trying to make him turn his cheeks toward me, but he walked on toward 308, paying my harassment no attention. It occurred to me: the screams might arouse excitement in some people but might also unexpectedly move others to tears. What kind of softness was hidden at the center of the hearts of those who shed a tear?

Arai opened the door to 308 with his key, and I accompanied him inside, locking the door behind me. At first, we were both somewhat taken aback: underneath a pool of light on Shi Dabo's side of the bed was Shi Dabo himself naked (wearing only a pair of short athletic socks), legs arched, torso rhythmically rising and falling. Straddling him and covered in golden hair was Bill, lifting his firm, slim hindquarters in time with Shi Dabo's rhythm, squeezing tight, falling down, loosening up, in a wavelike motion. Putting Square City words to an English folk song tune, he sang as he was being screwed, "Your big banana's tasty and hot, its length hooks my heart and its curve hits the spot." After a brief moment of embarrassment, Arai confidently started to loosen his jacket and undo his belt. By the time he had teased off the last of his clothing, I was still standing stupidly by the door. He moved toward me, kissing me, like calming a frightened rabbit, then started pulling off my clothes. I surrendered to his actions, suppressing the child from Triangle City inside me who told me to resist, obediently allowing him to strip me bare and pull me to his side of the bed, laying me flat on my back in the place where he slept every night. He kissed me, kissed me all over my body, ardently caressing my chest, sometimes very roughly, almost to the point of pain. He lifted my legs apart, placing them on his shoulders. Penetrating long and deep, driving forward without restraint, he pierced right to the heart of my peach. My mind darkened from the pain, and it was only after a deathly faint that I finally regained complete consciousness.

I longed truly for only two things: one was to make him happy; the other was to close the deal as quickly as possible. In the course of my work, I discovered that Arai's happiness was like a tall and luxuriant tree with many branches: the distance from top to bottom was beyond the wildest stretch of my peach. All I could do was to go on playing the role of obedient child. Fortunately, I discovered another type of pleasure: observing the sex moves of Arai, Bill, and Shi Dabo (I had already given him the nickname Banana and was only waiting for the first day of the New Year to spread it throughout Square City University) and trying as hard as I could to learn a little of their mastery.

Shi Dabo and Arai were both that type of swarthy, strong, and hard man; Bill and I were more elastic. Bill was "enjoying the flowers of his rear courtyard" like a child at play, while I was experiencing it for the first time, still feeling rather tender and green, unenlightened about how pleasureful the game could be. Shi Dabo and Arai were no longer mirror images of one another. Shi Dabo was coolheaded and steady, his tempo neither fast nor slow; gentle and tenacious yet with remarkable endurance, the purity of his sensual indulgence only imparted through his panting breath. Arai however was valiant and bold, like an untamed mustang that had just been bridled, bucking against the bed, me, and his own body, unwilling to bow his head, unwilling to abandon his willful gait, unwilling to reveal the slightest gentleness. They both had the same flourishing, seemingly inexhaustible strength, except that for Shi Dabo the exertion of power was pleasureful, whereas Arai seemed to derive joy from its simultaneous summoning and destruction.

As dawn drew near, the four of us were squeezed on the one bed, Bill and I facing its head, Shi Dabo and Arai facing the foot; my own two splendidly sweaty and fragrant feet were stretched between the two hard men. Before they sunk into a deep sleep, I kept worrying that one of them might launch a sneak attack, might suck on or bite off a toe.

5

Banana's nickname and its accompanying English folk song rapidly spread around the third floor. Following my lead, Pear, Plum, Apple, and Jujube all started to sing "Your big banana's so tasty and hot" after Bill's faltering fashion. Shi Dabo took great pride in his new nickname, unexpectedly replying to Pear (the first person to call him "Banana" to his face), "Darling, just like your pear was imported from Triangle City, my banana was imported all the way from Thailand. Don't forget, the road was very long, and the fare is very high."

I called out Shi Dabo's name in the common bathroom, and he emerged from the waist-high wooden doors of his stall, water streaming from his body. Gripping his big banana with both hands, he drew near to me, raising himself up on his toes and saying as he closed in, "Oh, my dear sweet, juicy Peach, are you hungry? Do you want a taste? Don't forget, 'my big banana's so tasty and hot, it'll hook your heart and hit the spot!'" I ran, terrified, into another stall, hiding behind Charlie 5 and using him as a shield as he was taking a shower.

It turned out Charlie 5 had an open-door policy. Standing between the short wooden doors of his shower stall, he faced down Shi Dabo, beckoning and saying, "Come here, come on in! I've got a big container; my only fear is that your big banana won't touch the sides." Shi Dabo brought his hands together in front of his chest and, bowing slightly, spoke: "I submit to you, not to others, but only to you. As long as you are the true high-pitched screaming master, I must submit to you." After speaking, he went back to his showering. I, on the other hand, had been delivered from the claws of the tiger into the clutches of the devil: Charlie 5 lost no time in getting his hands all over my peach.

During the afternoon on the last day of the New Year's vacation, while Bill and I were using the coin-operated washing machines in the laundry room, we heard the muffled noises of a large group of people in the hallway. We went out to have a look. A small crowd was gathered outside the open door of 308, including two girls from Square City (one who charged a fee, one who came for free) who had been recently recruited by Koyama Miyoshi and Plum. I suddenly heard the distinct sounds of one and then another heavy, powerful thump. At once we ran over to look inside: Arai and Banana, each sporting a boxing glove on his left hand (they were both lefties), were squaring off in the center of room 308, trading punches, one after the other, each more forceful than the last, every fist smashing against his opponent's muscular chest. Blocking those blows with the strength of their bodies would knock anyone half a step back.

As the boxing match increased in intensity, a terrible look came into Arai's eyes, but Shi Dabo remained as cool and collected as before, maintaining his composure. It seemed as if neither of them had any intention of calling a truce. A feeling of dread slowly came over me: if this went on, they were going to beat each other to a pulp. I worked myself forward through the crowd, trying to get a better look. Pear and Apple, who mistakenly thought that I was trying to break up the fight, both held me back, Apple quietly saying, "Peach, don't do it. What has it got to do with you? If you do it, you'll ruin the show!" Pear, in a much louder voice, as if he was deliberately trying to make the two brawling men overhear, said, "What, are you trying to make this a three-way fight? Don't you know that when two men are fighting and throwing punches left and right, they are actually expressing their subconscious desire for each other? If you want a piece of the action, why not start with me!" Saying so, he landed a savage blow on my navel. Not wanting to seem weak, I punched him back on his lower belly. He fell to the floor of the hallway in exaggerated pain, shouting, "Charlie 5! Look over here! Peach just knocked down our baby!"

Although the encircled throng let out a burst of laughter, it had no effect on Arai and Shi Dabo, who were fully focused on trading their final blows as if they were about to climax (they looked as if they had rehearsed it countless times or had been programmed by computers). In all the many fierce struggles I have witnessed between two tireless athletes, whether boxing, Ping-Pong, badminton, tennis (so many athletes let out a deep, sexy roar when they hit the ball), freestyle wrestling, fencing, tae kwon do, or judo, the two athletes' love and hate, their fear and self-confidence, their domination and submission, their attack and its repulse, are all full of stimulation and arousal, analogous to the process of making love. Isn't the limitless pleasure that Shi Dabo and Arai derived from beating upon each other's bodies the same as what the soccer forward feels when kicking the ball through his opponent's goal, or the emotion a rugby player has as he falls to the ground clutching the ball? I suddenly couldn't resist keeping score: "1–0. 1–1. 2–1. 2–2. 3–2. 3–3. 4–3. 4–4. 5–4 . . ." As I reached "10–9" Bill squeezed by me, shoved me aside, and hurled himself between Shi Dabo and Arai, blocking their fierce blows.

My mouth slowly stopped moving as all the excitement and anticipation gradually dissipated from my body; if not for Bill's untimely interference, Arai and Shi Dabo, in the final moment of their struggle, turning from cold to hot, from hate to love, would certainly have embraced, their sweaty faces pressing together, their exhausted bodies propping each other up, left fists still weakly flailing, punching toward their opponent's chest but without enough strength to kill even an ant; just like two soulmates who, in flirtation's final moment, fall to the ground and lie panting in each other's arms (indeed, from that moment on, they became lovers).

6

At the end of the second semester of our second year, Pear got into a huge fight with Bruguera (who was already visiting during his summer vacation since Circle City University let out first), knocking out one of his front teeth, and was forcefully evicted from the foreign student apartments and given a disciplinary action. Charlie 5, as promiscuous as ever and still making his high-pitched screams, seemed unaffected by Pear's encounter with his former lover.

Bill and Georgi had already finished all their master's classes. Georgi, who successfully completed the program with his thesis, "Square City's Affluent Classes," had started packing up his things to return to Bulgaria's capital city, Sofia, and make it big. Bill had not even decided yet on a title for his thesis. He didn't have plans to return to England, and he seemed to have lost interest in everything (including the Square City dialect). He couldn't stop thinking about Shi Dabo (and his big banana), which as I had predicted had become the private property of Arai Sakuo. Bill deeply regretted not switching rooms with Arai when he had the chance: if he had moved into 308 first and made Arai, who became my lover, move into 307 instead, wouldn't everyone have been satisfied?

I also suffered for a month due to Arai's fickle affections. Although I always had a feeling that he and Banana would sooner or later go from mere mirror images to lovers, when what I had anticipated became reality, I became deeply depressed, lovesick, unable to eat or drink. The difference between Bill and me was that I didn't allow anyone to detect the sadness in my heart; with a rakish smile, I started flirting wildly with everyone around me, even my fellow Triangle City natives Pear and Apple. From that time on, I started frequenting Di Di Bar and the Square City clubs; I let whoever stared at my peach have a bite. In any case, Arai no longer wanted it.

The person who helped me escape my hopeless state was Charlie 5 (are you surprised?). One day, after we had spent the week together drinking at the counter of Di Di Bar, he told me that, because Bruguera would shortly be returning to Spain, he was thinking of getting back together with Pear. I thought that would be impossible, but he said, "Everything is possible, because men are containers; regardless of who they are filled by, they still must be filled. They can't stand being empty." Sure enough, soon it was Pear causing Charlie 5's high-pitched screams again. I often recall the words he spoke to me. Wasn't I also a container? Physically or emotionally, wasn't there someone who would be able to fill me?

Bill's broken heart finally became unbearable. He got a few pieces of expensive luggage and returned to London, swearing that he would never again come back to Square City or speak a word of its dialect. After he left, I asked Koyama Miyoshi to move in with me, and we started to "share the same bed." Today, I can proudly tell you that I am both emotionally and physically filled by my beautiful, brilliant Koyama Miyoshi, even if some maidens do occasionally show up in his container (I keep an eye on such proclivities, making sure that he doesn't start going for the same no-good girls Plum used to like).

7

The city is the container of men because the city holds men's pasts. Men are the containers of other men; therefore, men hold other men's pasts. One man can be the container of many men; a group of men can also be one man's container. One or many, many or few, it's not important; what matters is that men can contain each other. This new container theory subverts the "opposites attract and likes repel" concept of gender. After becoming aware of this new concept, I founded the Square City University Container Society to promote a new container theory. Our members include both men and women, and the mission of the Container Society is to overthrow that rotten and rigid idea of "opposites attract and likes repel." Our president is Charlie 5, himself a mixed-race person. Every Sunday, we all march through the broad avenues and narrow streets of Square City, giving lectures and posting flyers. We even started a telephone hotline. More and more Square City people no longer hold the binary gender theories of yin and yang, of opposites and likes, to be eternal truths. It makes me happy that this story of Square City University (no matter how common, coarse, and corporeal) was able to amend an ancient piece of conventional wisdom and expose a hidden mystery of gender.

Fire and Wolf Share a Fondness for Male Beauty　老火和老狼同好男色

Translated by Yizhou Guo

1

Fire went to Miami and "married" a young Miami white fellow. They gave birth to a mixed-race "surrogate" boy by mixing their sperm in a test tube. They were preparing to have a second child using the same method. Fire's mom set out on a journey all the way from Circle City across both the Pacific Ocean and Gulf of Mexico to arrive in Miami. She was ready to take on the role of grandma and childcare worker, in Circle City style, of the Miami children—the one that was already born and the one that was about to be born. She hoped that the temperature of her gender could warm her grandson's boring and monotonous life. Poor grandson. Neither of his monogender parents came with soft, plump breasts or abundant breast milk.

2

Wolf went to Moscow. At this point, he was living with a sickly young Uzbek boy. Wolf trafficked fashionable furs from Circle City to the Russian capital and had earned quite a fortune. The Uzbek boy's family was very poor. Fifteen times a month, on average, he stole Wolf's cash and goods and sent them back to Uzbekistan to support his parents and his book-smart younger brother in middle school. Wolf secretly felt upset, but all he could do was open one eye and close the other; the young boy also turned a blind eye when

First published in *Fairytales of Triangle City* (三角城的童話) (Hong Kong: Huasheng shudian, 1998).

Wolf occasionally cheated with those Kazakh, Ukrainian, or Tajik macho men of all ages. Wolf looked wizened, thin, and ugly; he overindulged in alcohol and sex and had turned bald too early. His biggest wish when he had been in Circle City was to have an affair with Qi Shishi, the most famous handsome man in town. Now that he was in a foreign country, his most ambitious plan was to live with a young, blond purebred Russian fellow—no matter if he was a top or a bottom, good-looking or ugly, so long as he was pure Russian blood. Based on his achievements so far, he had failed on both counts.

3

The reason Qi Shishi was considered to be the most handsome guy by the male-chauvinist men in Circle City had everything to do with his occupation. In general, those big macho men, due to an overindulgence in tobacco and alcohol and an excessive lust for power, always caught a cold or a fever. As he was the nurse at the outpatient clinic of Circle City Hospital, Qi Shishi had to use his bodily organ to come into contact with over a hundred male butts—for the obvious reason of saving lives—and give them exactly the same hypodermic injection. Viewed from the perspective of gender politics, most male chauvinists are political opportunists who blow with the wind: when they see a beautiful woman, they are prone to female beauty; when they see a handsome man, they turn to buggery. As soon as they entered the injection room of Circle City Hospital outpatient department, there was no way for their left or right politics, their superior and subordinate ideologies, to resist Qi Shishi's beautiful face and soft hands. Usually as soon as Qi Shishi injected the compound estrogen diethylstilbestrol (he often made errors at work by mistaking estrogen for a pharmaceutical to reduce fever), they got carried away and ejected body fluids like urine or semen inside their underpants. After they experienced orgasm or became manic or fainted in Qi Shishi's hands, these men would get sick on a daily basis, and every day they would rush into the outpatient building of Circle City Hospital. This eventually led to the "major outpatient incident," similar to those serious casualties on the soccer field, where everyone scuffles and tramples on each other. Since the incident was triggered by the male nurse's beautiful face and soft hands, Qi Shishi had to be transferred to the inpatient department, and, what's more, to the pediatric ward.

4

The year Qi Shishi transferred to the pediatric ward, a.k.a. the year of the "Circle City Hospital patient hooligan riot," Fire was fourteen and Wolf sixteen. They were both of the age that prefers to hang out with more mature young men. They had heard a lot of those young men's "portrayal" of Qi Shishi; often they couldn't help but add a few imaginative strokes to the picture.

Fire's home was north of the railway, Wolf's to the south. The two had never met. Fire was still in middle school when Wolf was in high school. Even though they went to the same secondary school, they never encountered each other on any occasion. Fire had seen a few thriller movies; he aspired to become a stuntman in Square City after he grew up. He often climbed to the top of the water tower to do all kinds of bird-flying movements. Sometimes he imitated parachuting by jumping down with an opened paper umbrella. The success of tower-jumping encouraged him: his second training project was to jump onto roadbeds or bushes from a fast-moving train. The first time, he succeeded without practicing. Unfortunately, the third time, he chose to jump from the roof of a passenger car, broke his left shinbone, and was admitted to the orthopedic surgery ward. Wolf, on the other hand, got a urinary tract infection from masturbation and was hospitalized in the urology ward. The two troublemakers annoyed the doctors and nurses. While still bedridden, they were transferred to the pediatric ward under the guise of "sickbed shortage" and became the oldest, the most pained, and the most lachrymose "big boys."

Whenever nurse number 003 Qi Shishi was on night call, Fire, from the easternmost room 101, cried loud and long about his shinbone, like a train taking off from the station. From the westernmost room 1011, Wolf wailed bitterly about his urinary tract, like a wild wolf. The children, whether they were severely sick or just slightly injured, were all hit by the sound of wailing and started to cry from all four corners. Fire and Wolf became the lead singers of the children's chorus, although their voices, especially Fire's, were kind of similar to a rooster who has just learned to crow. Qi Shishi was tranquil and elegant; he took his time to serve those kids who needed midnight medicines or injections. When he arrived at room 101, he smiled and called the fourteen-year-old stuntman "Fire." While inspecting the medicine in the IV bottle, he told him gently: With the progression of the times, the steam locomotive will become history very soon. You'd better seize the chance to jump from the top of the train to those frosty roadbeds, just like those car-jumping heroes and gangsters in the movies, before it is eliminated entirely. Going into room 1011, Qi Shishi called the slight and wizened juvenile "Wolf" while giving him urinary catheterization. He warned that if he howled like a wolf again, he would be sent to the gynecology ward.

After the lead singers' sounds disappeared, the chorus also stopped. What was left was the never-to-be forgotten nicknames, "Fire" and "Wolf." The nicknames' young owners had their wishes fulfilled from their misfortune: they got to meet the most handsome man in town when they were still young and vulnerable, and received his reprimands, touches, and other services more than once. They would be satisfied with this for the rest of their lives.

5

Five years later, in spring, Fire and Wolf once again entered Circle City Hospital's pediatric ward, under the supervision of nurse number 003 Qi Shishi. By now, they had robust voices and mature sexual characteristics. And they had gotten to know each other because they were both studying at Circle City University's Department of Foreign Languages, they both lived in the same dormitory, and they both slept in the same double-deck bunk beds. They both went to the hospital this time due to unrequited love. Their object of longing was the same person. They fought with one another and in their struggle severely injured each other. The occasion that led to their shared injuries and lovesickness (as well as sensual damage) was AIDS: not too long ago, the Epidemic Prevention Institute relocated Qi Shishi to Circle City University to administer an AIDS vaccine to those sturdy students and feeble professors. (The vaccine was a new product that only circulated locally in Circle City. It had not yet been sold on the global market.)

6

It was a deadly quiet midnight; Qi Shishi was on call. Without any forewarning, Wolf abruptly began to howl his heart out from room 101 on the hospital's east side. This time, his howl was mature and solemn, from his guts. In contrast, Fire made not a single sound. Each time Qi Shishi administered his medicine, he gritted his teeth in tormented pain. Even when large beads of sweat dripped from his forehead, he made no sound. He recovered very fast. Qi Shishi could therefore save his time and energy for other young patients. Wolf thought it was a good deal: Qi Shishi came to room 101 three times more than he visited room 1011. Before he left the hospital, Wolf thought the time was ripe to formally ask Qi Shishi out on a date. Qi Shishi went on the date but was unusually quiet. When Wolf threw himself on Qi Shishi and tried to tear into him, Qi Shishi slipped away, without making a sound, like a fox running across a desert on a moonlit night.

Wolf started to mimic being in love. At first, in the middle of the night he covered his mouth with the quilt and wailed, right under Fire's bunk. He didn't realize until his tears wet the quilt that this was an imitation of a brokenhearted woman. He then changed to writing poetry obsessively, in both Chinese and Russian, just like those men passionately in love from classical times. When he found it hard to shake off his crazed enthusiasm, he would ask Fire to help him with the translation (for this, he voluntarily knelt down to reconcile with Fire), so that his poetic flame would have three written forms: Chinese, Russian, and English. He sprinkled a few tears on them; if he couldn't squeeze out any tears, he substituted tap water or saliva. These poems were each sent one by one to the pediatric ward by Fire. Of course, no one ever knew if Qi Shishi actually received those painstakingly concocted love exercises. The third kind of mimicry of being in love was to keep watch on a rainy night. The pattering spring rain soaked him through and through. From dusk to dawn Wolf stood right outside Qi Shishi's home, regardless of being battered by wind and rain. Unfortunately, Qi Shishi happened to be on night shift. When he returned home in the morning, the sight of Wolf soaked by the morning rain frightened him, and he was too scared to go home. He ran to the phone booth on the street corner and invited Fire to go to the fitness center with him. The last imitation of love was closer to human beings' "death instinct": leaping to one's own death.

It was not unexpected that Fire was the one who finally won over Qi Shishi's affections by his perseverance, patience, magnanimity, and willingness to help others. After they quietly (and stealthily) started their secret love affair, the news eventually reached Wolf. He climbed to the rooftop of Circle City University's main building and alternately cried, laughed, screamed, and sang. He threatened to jump and smash his body to pieces. If he were in Triangle City, police would surely have come. Warmhearted people would plead and talk sense into him. There would be a hero climbing up the fire escape to grip his small waist from behind without startling him. Unfortunately, this was Circle City, where people's hearts were as cold as ice. People went to class, did their homework, ate and slept as usual. They sang and played music, traveled, made love, and raised kids as normal. No one cared whether a pining college boy was heartbroken because of falling in love with a man, or whether on top of the building he was playing the most tragic game of mad passion that men and women play. Wolf was miserable. He screamed, cried, hooted, and jumped around for three days and nights. He wore himself out, became all skin and bones. In the end he had to come down through the fire escape by himself, with his tail between his legs. He found a street food vendor and gobbled down a meal that had absolutely no meaningful connotation of love.

7

On the upper bunk above Wolf sat the man of both their dreams, Qi Shishi. Four lanky, youthful legs hung down, making shapes like a door gap in front of Wolf's bunk. There was a narrow door and a wide door. Wolf instinctively chose the narrow door between Qi Shishi's legs. He broke through them, climbed on the bed, and fell asleep immediately. Through his completely symbolic gesture, he satisfied his desire and slept with a delightful, unrestrained erotic dream. Those on the upper bunk were hugging and kissing. All Qi Shishi noticed was a chill autumn breeze that blew between his shanks. Other than that, all he felt were Fire's vigorous and fiery kisses and caresses, and the hard object standing nakedly erect from his open jeans zipper.

8

The swelling in Fire's midriff made him lay Qi Shishi down and lay himself on top of him. The following scene emerged on the double-deck bunk bed next to the western window of Circle City University student dormitory number 2, room 211: Below the lower bunk were a heap of men's shoes for different seasons, full of dust. Facing upward on the lower bunk lay Wolf, steeped in his erotic dream. He was extremely skinny, having just come down off the top of the main school building. He had made his own decision that he would reach Qi Shishi's beauty through a dream world. Under the surface of the upper bunk, he gave his body wholly over to what was happening above him, pointing his erect, erotic sense organ vertically upward. On top of the upper bunk, the "precious body" of Qi Shishi, the object of its erotic desire, happened to be face down. Above the precious body was the naked body of Fire, thrusting ardently. Fire focused his energy downward, repeatedly penetrating the focal point of his penis into the depth of the precious body. His buttocks nearly hit the snow-white limestone ceiling because he arched so much.

Perhaps out of pleasure and also out of pain, Qi Shishi felt like moaning but was afraid to alert the black-leather-clad dorm master. He resorted to using the pillowcase to cover his mouth, just as a nurse would usually do. Though Fire was a virgin, he was a natural at the "backyard walk" (similar to the moonwalk and the space walk). The result was a tremendous earthquake while he targeted Qi Shishi's beautiful butt. Qi Shishi had already fallen into the erotic net, physically and emotionally. He fully welcomed this "lover's part" inside his own body. When the orgasms came, the board from the upper bunk loosened, shook, and fell down. The board, Qi Shishi, and Fire, like a chamber music trio, all fell vertically onto Wolf, who, facing upward, was intoxicatingly asleep in his erotic dream. With the piling up of persons and board, board and persons, no one could really tell which groans, which smothered shouts, and which whinnying sounds were out of pain or satisfaction.

9

The dorm master, adorned in black leather pants, black leather jacket, and black leather boots, was inside his room, eyes and ears observant and alert in all directions. From the boys' noisy, tumultuous voices, songs, curses, snoring, clatter of footsteps, fisticuffs, commotion, and the sound of a six-stringed guitar; from the ponderous repression of lust, the deviant, impetuous urges, the rising tide of thoughts defying the impregnable power discourse of Circle City, he carefully distinguished his ideal objects and the perfect timing for him to "attack" them. This dorm master was not only healthy and sturdy but was fond of those masculine boys who were sturdy just like himself. Fire had long been his ideal mate for "spear on spear and club on club." He stood by the open door of his chamber, all eyes and ears. He first felt the floor shaking beneath his feet. He presumed he was like an ant, instinctively sensitive to earthquakes and even wind and rain. As soon as he felt the shaking floor, he immediately rushed to the fire escape and, as agile as a fireman, descended to the ground from the twenty-first floor in one breath. He then quickly "evacuated" from the shadow of the twenty-one-floor dorm number 2. While he continued to feel the ground's acute shaking, three sound waves transmitted from the top floor's easternmost room 211, conveying in great volume homoeroticism and its pains and pleasures. The "earthquake" was thus aborted. He then felt like an electric shock had gone through him. He got an erection, ejaculated, and fell limp to the ground all in no more than 3.7 seconds. He stood up, his crotch and left leg wet, staggered to the twenty-first floor and knocked on the door of dorm room 211. No response from inside the room. He eagerly looked forward to witnessing Fire in a scene of "adultery." He kicked up his black leather boot and shoved it onto the inserted door lock. The door swung inward and then bounced back, smacking the dorm master on his forehead as he charged inward, knocking him unconscious to the floor.

10

For the third time, Wolf went to the pediatric ward of Circle City Hospital. Under the meticulous care of nurse number 003 Qi Shishi, the traumas on his forehead, nose, chin, chest, knees, and toes gradually recovered. But one particular traumatic part had only one kind of phenomenological recovery but no sign of another kind: his penis, the stoutest and strongest part of Wolf's skinny body. Because that day its head stuck out the highest, it suffered the heaviest blow. Not only did his spring dreams fall apart, his phallic organ withered quickly and never regained its previous firm and upright demeanor.

The dorm master was shorn of his leather jacket, leather pants, and leather boots, all replaced with an infant hospital dress, and he was sent to room 101. Echoing Wolf remotely in room 1011, he showed symptoms of intermittent idiocy caused by his brain concussion and a strengthened erotic function. Every time Fire visited Wolf (for atonement), the dorm master, from his room all the way down the eastern corridor, would send a masculinist courtship signal toward the west: "Fire. Fire. I am 101. I am 101. Come have coitus with me immediately. Or you will be expelled from school under the charge of sodomy with Qi Shishi." In the west end, Wolf was contaminated by the masculine power from the east end. He threatened and coerced Fire to hand over his lover Qi Shishi's beautiful lips and his "backyard" (similar to the best anuses in Marquis de Sade's novel and Pier Paolo Pasolini's films) to help recover his erectile function. Otherwise, he would report them to the patriarchal authorities, as the on-the-spot witness of their "sodomy." Qi Shishi shuttled between room 101 and room 1011, wearing a white gown, a white nurse's cap, and a sky-blue, square-shaped surgical mask, looking tender and merciful. With guilt and natural kindness, he changed the medicines for Wolf's wounds and injected all necessary medicines into the dorm master's stout butt to balance intelligence and sexual desire. In terms of Fire, he was still devoted to him with all his passion. He anticipated "growing old together" with this young fellow.

11

The dorm master left the hospital first. Fire's schoolwork was not affected at all, the reason being that the dorm master was "fond" of Fire and Fire was smart enough to engage in "spear on spear and club on club" with him (though sometimes he felt queasy). Fire cared about the interest value of his "spear" but was resolute in his disregard for its preservation value, love value, reproductive value, and collection value. This paved the way for him later to be a male escort (of course, for the sake of making a living) for a couple of years when he was in Orlando.

Wolf left the hospital after the dorm master. That day, he didn't go home but went right back to room 211 of Circle City University's dorm number 2. As it was a Sunday, their roommates all went out to seek carnal pleasures. Only

Fire followed Wolf's "instructions" and waited inside. Naturally, Qi Shishi, who was infatuated with him, was there too, cuddling up to his fiery chest. Tears streamed down Qi Shishi's face and he gave Fire the "last kiss" and, right at that moment, Wolf entered the room.

Wolf needed Qi Shishi's "oral treatment" and "anal treatment" to cure his impotence. Fire needed Wolf to keep his mouth shut so he would not be expelled for his "love affair" with Qi Shishi. Wolf and Fire made an agreement: In the name of love, Fire begged Qi Shishi to sacrifice this once for the sake of Fire's future prospects. Qi Shishi was placed on the bedside of Wolf, like a docile lamb.

12

Fire thought everything was set up. He prepared to leave room 211 and his lover, to allow Wolf to have his way with him. But just when he was about to brush past Wolf, Wolf beseeched him to stay and observe the course of his treatment and recovery. Fire could not defy this "entreaty" and obediently remained. He sat on a mahogany chair in the middle of the room, facing the lower bunk of that double-deck steel bunk bed near the window facing west. He could see and vividly feel Wolf's penis, inserted into Qi Shishi's beautiful mouth, get hot, expand, gradually arise from its base, until it became fully erect and that mouth could hold only half of it. He saw a dark blackish penis that was thicker and larger than his. He saw it surge passionately through the "oral treatment" and impatiently enter the next treatment. It met with difficulty while entering because the entrance to the next treatment was too tight. He saw it repetitively knock and jerk about until eventually, by moving back and forth, little by little it inserted and moved onward into the depths until its thick base submerged there. The second treatment lasted nearly all afternoon. All Qi Shishi did was bury his head under the pillow, without a single sound or movement. He was like a corpse, letting Wolf stroke, bite, rub, throb, have spasms, attack, penetrate, and finally cum. While he observed from the side, Fire repeatedly suppressed his instinctive impulses. He remained silent and stunned. Even more, he was a bit envious and yearned for that penis, which was more enormous than his, and those movements that were more skillful.

13

Qi Shishi returned once more to Circle City Hospital's outpatient department. He had to use his nimble hands to do the injections for over one hundred men in their (butt) muscle. The relocation was for the following reason: he had withered and dropped off just like a spring flower. (It is not known whether it was caused by the ravaging of others or self-destruction.) He was no longer considered the handsomest man by those masculinist men of Circle City. Before this, Fire and Wolf had visited him in the pediatric ward over and over again. Fire visited "for the sake of love" and to apologize. Wolf visited for no other sake than lust. But it was as if Qi Shishi had become invisible; he never met up with them. When he took the position in the outpatient clinic, all the men who once adored him lost interest: his face looked the same, his body looked the same, his smile looked the same. His outfit became more stylish, his temperament became more tender. But he was no longer beautiful: somehow a flame had just suddenly gone out inside of him. Since then, all physical interaction between men in Circle City had become sterilized, absolutely safe behavior: they were no longer attracted to each other; they had no radiance inside.

14

In Moscow, Wolf repeatedly visited prostitutes, although he never managed to get any young man with purebred Russian blood and blond hair. No matter how much he would pay, they all refused to be with him. He began to hate them and believed that every one of them had secretly signed a "devil's contract" with Circle City's Qi Shishi. One day, about midnight, he tried to force a Russian young man to submit to him, just like he raped Qi Shishi that very year. This resulted in the young man stabbing him to death and running off with all his money.

15

In Miami, Fire was not able to "give birth" to the second mixed-blood baby because the white young man he had "married" dumped him for a new flame. Their first son was flown back to Circle City by Fire's mom, who endured all kinds of hardships to raise him by herself. Fire returned to Orlando (Orlando was the first place he landed when he arrived in the United States) and started a special rent business: he "emigrated" a couple of young boys from the East (they looked very much like Qi Shishi from the old time) and taught them the skill of intramuscular injection himself (he once learned that skill from Qi Shishi). Then he advertised on all sorts of men's magazines: "Handsome men from the East providing door-to-door testosteronum propionicum injection. Oral health care and anal health care from their own bodily devices also provided." It was said this business was flourishing. Almost all Orlando men who were fond of male beauty knew about the fame and reputation of "Fire's Specialty Store."

Teacher Eats Biscuits Thin as Parchment

老师吃饼薄如纸

Translated by William F. Schroeder

1

I had heard that student-teacher love was quite fashionable at the Triangle City Media Studies Institute, so when I was finishing graduate school I transferred there from Square City. My advisor played the loving father and urged me to stay. Square City is philosophy's paradise on earth; unfortunately, my advisor loved only his goodly wife, so I stood no chance. When I was getting my bachelor's in Circle City, I was young and nubile—but young teachers, middle-aged teachers, old male teachers, still not one showed the least bit of special interest in me. If Square City is philosophy's temple, Circle City is philosophy's fortress. But teachers in Square City and Circle City love only their reputations, not pretty boys, so I had just one option—become a teacher myself to fulfill my dream of student-teacher love.

Twenty-nine is a frightful age. Although I looked very young in the sunlight—like a nineteen-year-old—I became timid in the haziness of moonbeams and lamplight, that kind of haze that made me think I'd reached thirty-nine. Good scholarship only ever surges in fits and starts under moonlight and in lampshade. But lecturing in the daytime system of the university, one merely need bask in the flattering rays of the sun. Half-knowingly, that's one of the reasons I chose to dive into Triangle City's fishpond.

First published in *The Whereabout of Crimson* (胭脂的下落) (Kunming: Yunnan renmin chubanshe, 2007).

Thanks to Yu-chien Huang for her advice on some difficult passages.

The most irrelevant pleasure in this was being able to extricate myself completely from the tiresome company of women my age. From the time of middle school they had begun more and more to resemble tadpoles with their little tails, swimming in schools beneath my eyelids, nodding and swishing about. No one in the gaggle stood out as especially beautiful or ugly, and thus any variety in the life around me was hard to discern. I had heard it said that in Triangle City all the men and women of my era had been sacrificed to the Age of Innocence, each by that time having an insipid countenance and a pudgy corpulence, so they wouldn't have had the wherewithal to tangle with me. And not a one of those hoity-toity, glib, and vulgar geniuses at Square City would settle for the folksy hamlet of Triangle City. Thus I set out all alone, with an intention to stay out of the limelight as my strategy in the midst of that grand era. I have no other choice but to stay safely in a corner; it's my strategy to shelter myself in contemporary times.

2

As soon as I entered the Media Studies Institute, I found a whole new world. At this place, a truly epochal phenomenon existed: all the professors were at least ten years older than I, and the students all at least ten years younger. I was elated. Sandwiched in the middle, I was the one and only special personage who could range freely among them. As a result of a close investigation, I discovered that the students demonstrated a rather progressive consciousness and behavior, whereas the professors kept to their old notions—they were narrow-minded and conservative, beset as they were with their outdated knowledge. I deduced preliminarily that precisely those dialectics of vanguard and reactionary, stiff and vigorous, stagnant and fresh, corrupt and vital—these had driven the Sturm und Drang of student-teacher love there. However, my profound philosophical training reminded me that one shouldn't fetter one's vision on the basis of such superficially salacious phenomena; moreover, one shouldn't hastily turn observations into conclusions. Because I was a newcomer (young and good-looking) and had three degrees (bachelor's, master's, and PhD) my philosophy classes immediately spanned the course directory: Monday was the publishing department's first years, Tuesday the journalism department's second years, Wednesday broadcasting's third years, Thursday television's fourth years, and Friday the film department's graduate students. All of these were large lectures held in the biggest auditoriums on campus.

I recall that I reported for duty on a Wednesday, and for the first two classes the next morning it would be me at the podium. For that reason I did a bit of secret reconnaissance in the quiet of the night before. The limited space of the auditorium consisted merely of a sixteenth of Square City University's largest hall, but its windows were enormous, and it was otherwise completely outfitted with a PA system, television, video recorder, and movie projector. I felt an exquisite sangfroid. It would take me only three minutes to assume the best position, like a movie actor who gets into character to shoot a film. Relying on knowledge of my own body and its sensitivity to light, I quickly ascertained at which angle and in which position the greatest intensity of sunlight would shine on my face, making me likeliest to appear nineteen, and at which angle and in which position shadows would mark me, making me likeliest to appear thirty-nine. I had had a premonition that the first time I would ascend the podium the next day, I would evince, in that one place, at once and with my singular face, a gendered charisma that spanned twenty years. As for the female students' gasping admiration and jealousy and the male students' youthful passion and sudden courage, I hadn't much paid those a thought before I officially arrived.

That night, I slept deeply, slipping only occasionally into dreams. In any case none of them had to do with real life, rather belonging to the realm of philosophy. As soon as the sun rose, I sprang from my bed, completed my toilet, and dressed to the nines.

3

According to certain regionally focused schools of thought in geography studies, Circle City, where I was born, has eight seasons. Square City, where I did my studies, has the conventional four. And Triangle City, where I've dedicated myself to work, has three. The day I was to debut to the stares of the students fell directly on the cusp of spring and fall. A golden, half-springlike, half-autumnlike sunshine cast itself shaggily on my body, my face, my hair, just perfectly enough for this twenty-year span of a character to make his grand appearance on stage, despite having to face down his enemies as if on the brink of a demilitarized zone.

I entered the front door of the building, stepped into the elevator, and ascended sixteen levels of humanity to discover the students scattered about in the hallway, twisting those bodies that only nightclub girls and young tennis trainers could possibly have, listening to their music, reading their books, or straining their throats to broadcast some gossip, as if they'd beheld my knowledge, my beauty, and my erudition a million times before. I knew it was an act and that each of them in their bones was deeply concerned about everyone else's impressions. But I wasn't their audience—they were mine. I cast a lithe glance all the way to the end of the hall, allowing the shadow of my beautiful visage to reflect far enough down to rap slightly on the door of the auditorium. Just as at Square City University, I had to pass through a gauntlet of male students as if through an uninhabited land—the difference being that back then I had fixated on the male professors, not really believing the students existed, whereas now, these young men not only existed but intensely so. As if, entering that uninhabited land, I maintained a level of punctiliousness that ran quite in the opposite direction of my inner virtuosity.

I stepped on the podium a precise thirty seconds in advance. Part of the sun, having been refracted by the design of the window into large swaths of brilliant geometry, fell on the right half of my body and face. I flipped my elegant mane, gazing outside at the glorious day with my right eye, which was exposed to the brightness, while using my left eye, obscured in shadow, to scour the entire auditorium. The seats were filled not at all with the kinds of youthful faces and expressions I'd imagined. Students scattered themselves around the back of the room, regarding me half-heartedly, all strung about either in slouchy T-shirts and ripped jeans or decked from neck to ankle in chains of cowhide, cow horn, cow bone, and elephant tusks. I had heard a long time ago that they were a bunch of television cowboys, imitating their big-screen role models in some sort of new great Western style, even keeping in character with their best pals.

After thirty seconds, I decided to start the lecture. Latecomers made their way nonchalantly toward their places, which I took as meaningful provocation, though behind that must have lain curiosity and even reverence toward me. The last latecomer, a female student, closed the door behind her and, feigning timidity by sticking out her bright-red tongue, leapt lightly up the stairs like a panting cat until she could cuddle up beside one of those hard-bodied young men. Nobody showed the least bit of reaction to her behavior, almost as if they considered it a matter of course. Based on intuition, I suspected premeditation. They were busy applying a kind of practical knowledge gained over time, using their accumulated ability to manipulate an audience in order to challenge me.

In Pythagorean number theory, every calculation begins with the cardinal number one, and every number contains a dimension. My number one at Triangle City was this class, and from there on out, every dimension would root back to this one. Apparently, student–teacher love would have to commence through warfare. Their weapons were popular television waves; mine were the ancient, ancient impulses of philosophy. On the staging grounds of philosophy, I maintained utter confidence, and come what may, that most beneficial half-sunlight, half-shadow provided the perfect natural conditions for my graceful good looks. I decided to imitate Bertrand Russell's method and offered up the great Socrates. This move contradicted educational tradition, starting as it did with a grand gesture for a discussion topic: the critique of Socrates. But I had victory in my grasp. In all of televisionland, not one person could have jockeyed with even half of one of the white hairs on Socrates's head.

What I hadn't expected was that, on hearing I wanted to criticize a great master, they would all develop such a veritable enthusiasm. The first to approach the dais with his interjections was a young man called Bryte White. He had his hair shaved in the style of an American NBA star, cropped so close below the crown of the head you could see a reflection and above that a flattop with razor's edge. Inside his well-trained and astute body lay hidden a callous and crafty power. As soon as he spoke, I knew that having him premiere as their cardinal number gave them the advantage in this first round of the battle between students and teacher. He stammered a lament: Socrates was both wise and foolish, having chosen Athens and not California. He could never get along with career politicians and, just like his fellow wise men, used high-and-mighty philosophy to prove that leaders weren't as clever as they thought they were. Despite his shabby and nasty appearance and his habit of going around barefoot all day, he still got it on with young boys. Since ancient times his brand of Socratic love has been spread all around, until today it's quite the fashion. Among the young guys in the television department, there are twelve who've been homosexually harassed, and this isn't without a connection to Socrates's philosophy. It's also worth remembering that he didn't cherish his life—he could have fled before drinking the poison, but he didn't, and instead talked with his disciples about immortality.

After Bryte White had withdrawn, Armstrong Li cocked his rock star shoulders to defend Socrates. He believed that the master's greatest contribution was precisely that he succeeded in stubbornly loving young people. For transmitting his philosophy to those young people, he received not one little drachma—unlike Confucius demanding his jerky strings after class,[1] and even less like the way some of today's professors seize on the pure and youthful love of their students.

That feline girl was called Dreamy Yao. And just like a cat, she edged 'Strong Li out of his position. She renounced his partiality to Socrates, believing that in *Lysis* that shriveled old philosopher was just masterminding a scheme to deal with the inferiority complex of Hippothales by encouraging him to persevere in the actually undeserved commemoration of that fairy Lysis, setting an ugly precedent for Greece and humanity. Maybe it was that wafting influence of antiquity that was making her boyfriend distance himself from her and making her suffer so, too.

I could see that they were purposefully acting out this drama of a so-called modern criticism. Starting with Bryte White's proposition, they resourcefully and properly figured out a line of argument. But not only did it gloss over a half-minded understanding of philosophy, it also helped them establish a glib confidence so they could patronizingly dispose of philosophy *and* me, their new professor whose mind brimmed over with finely honed philosophical thought. With compassion for the disgrace of those philosophical tigers who had been subjected to such flat conventionality and dog's guile, I paced back and forth in front of the podium, along the same path and in the same posi-

1 *Shuxiu* (束脩), the ancient practice of paying tutors with ten strings of dried meat, has become a contemporary idiom for any compensation paid to a teacher.

tion as I had rehearsed the night before. However, my adversaries remained focused on the fate of Socrates's person, and almost nobody paid any special mind to the twenty-year span that traversed my face.

4

During the break, I went to the toilet, and Bryte White followed close behind me to use the neighboring stall. Having thought I heard sounds of his urination, as if he were pissing to the clouds, I felt the intermittent effects of constipation.

During the second half of class, I discovered these vigorously written chalk words on the blackboard: "Teacher eats biscuits thin as parchment." I immediately connected this phrase with my recent trip to the toilet. Who saw me go there? Bryte White. But maybe others did too. I shuddered at the thought. Those students I had had dealings with, with whom I had contrived countless love scenes, what way was this to treat and respect my elegant and learned bearing? "Teacher eats biscuits thin as parchment, eats them till finally they turn into shit. How wasteful, how wasteful, eating those biscuits—why not just save time and first eat the shit?" Were they using their disdainful gazes and this taunt from a children's primer to set the tone of our relationship? An unprecedented feeling of sorrow and desolation slowly and hotly percolated up from my nipples to my gullet to my jowls. Availing myself of the fact that this feeling had not yet entirely flushed out the composure my noble upbringing brought me, I rattled off decisively, "For the remainder of class we will continue our critique of Socrates."

As soon as I got to the hallway, the floodgates burst open to loosen my tears. As never before, the true face of my deep-seated loneliness and misery, my desperate frustration, showed itself exquisitely, as if piercing through that thin layer of self-admiration and self-esteem, as well as self-pity. We all dream of the character of past and future generations. We are nostalgic or avant-garde. We all suppose ourselves people of great virtue and prestige or full of youthful vigor. But we are only really ever able to hang suspended between things, neither up nor down—going to school, getting married, raising children, and dying off with the same age group. I had never wanted to be like that. I had always wanted my visage to be a beacon, to break firmly in my private life from those of my age cohort. I had wanted to detach even the deepest elements of my body from the passage of the eons to attain a kind of historical elasticity, to become a new breed of man with a time-spanning philosophical capacity. I had never imagined that when I needed to coordinate with former or future generations of men there would be so many impediments. But I wasn't about to give up.

Leaving the bathroom mirror, I again mounted the podium. The television cowboys paid absolutely no mind to my absence and instead were eloquently spewing their criticisms of Socrates as if he were some plebe to be publicly humiliated. Quite apparently, they were undertaking Aristophanes's project. But this time I was anything but courteous. I slammed my fist on the podium, and the whole place went utterly silent. Those white-faced young vaudevillians in front of my podium, once radiant with delight, scattered sheepishly back to their seats. In a kind of heroic mood and with an authoritative yet youthful tone, I began to narrate for them all the glorious periods of philosophical thought, now broad and expansive, now meandering and complicated. Though I had not yet exhausted my speech, and with the audience still rapt, the final bell sounded to signal the end of class, and of a sudden there rose a clamor of applause in the auditorium. I feigned disapproval, gathered up my books, and crept swiftly away.

5

That afternoon, Bryte White skipped his class to come knocking on my door. At first, I greeted him frostily, but he was skillful and patient enough to get me to let him in and even offer him a seat and make him a cup of instant coffee. He said he had had a very special feeling he wanted to tell me about. I listened attentively while he told me that he had noticed from my face and body an elasticity of time that only top-billing actors who've been thoroughly made up could have. Yes, he actually used the phrase "elasticity of time." That feeling he described melted me. So when he followed up by embracing me and kissing me, I didn't play hard to get. He continued kissing me on the nape of my neck, then stripped off my shirt and twisted my nipples with marked force. He went on, impatiently removing his own clothes until all that remained were the thick, white athletic socks on his feet. He held me all the way to the bed.

From afternoon till dusk, dusk till midnight, I made the experiential journey from nineteen-year-old to thirty-nine-year-old under his tutelage. When I saw him off, the stars and moon shone especially beautifully. I had fallen in love with him, and he said he loved me too. That student–teacher love I had eagerly awaited for so long never did happen between me and my professors but rather simply and enchantingly appeared right there between me and my first lot of students. Of course, before parting, he and I held each other, unable to bear our separation, kissing tenderly and making an oath of eternal love, promising another rendezvous the next day.

6

The lecture for the graduate film students was in the afternoon. At lunch Dreamy Yao sat at my table on purpose. She ate her food while at the same time observing me from the chest up, staring of course. When she had almost eaten her fill, she threw a grin my way, saying: "I heard that before yesterday you were a virgin—no wonder you've still got such good skin and such a nice figure. But you'd better keep a little distance from that White fellow, or else he'll use his special powers to destroy the faith in love someone like you probably has." I had no energy left to chew. Apparently Bryte White had broadcast our little affair to everyone. Dreamy Yao slurped up her last sip of soup and prepared to get up. But seeing me there drained of spirit, she consoled me: "Don't worry. Among us students, who's a virgin or vice versa is all public knowledge. See, we already consider you one of us. Those other old codgers won't hear the slightest thing about it. You want to get promoted or make money? Do it with whatever identity you think fits you and it won't influence how you interact with them. The way I see it, if you were in charge, we'd all graduate with excellent appointments."

When I had returned to my room and finished rinsing my mouth, I had no heart at all to prepare for the opening lecture about game theory in philosophy. I had to do some philosophizing myself about my feelings for Bryte White and my desire for him, as well as my humiliation at his betrayal. That afternoon, as soon as class was over he would come looking for me. When the time came, I was going to teach him a lesson or two about the dignity and respect a doctor of philosophy deserves. I wanted him to get a good taste of humiliation and then get the hell out.

During class that afternoon, my heart obviously wasn't in it. I simply relied on some verbal techniques I had perfected during ordinary moments of idle chatter, as well as the novel conditions that game theory had created for me, to try to gain a little reverence and esteem from those future film greats. But when they gave me those all-knowing looks, their expressions made it clear that the previously historical fact of my chaste bachelorhood had fallen on their ears like thunder.

In my room later, thinking of that fuzzy-headed young hooligan betraying the details of our coital bed, I was angry enough to bite through jade. My habitual constipation revisited me once again, which dissipated my enmity somewhat. Doing absolutely nothing, neither skipping rope five hundred times as I normally did, nor even touching the works of any great philosopher, I was of one mind to wait for that evil young thing's arrival.

Time passed—seconds, then minutes, then days—and Bryte White never came back to see me. At that very same moment every day, my constipation returned. Each time I ran into him, he uttered a refined and courteous "Afternoon, Teacher," as if nothing had ever happened. Every week when I lectured, he participated in the discussions as always, and each time he spoke he did so with more of the true qualities of philosophical thought. I heard Dreamy Yao tell of the seven successive girlfriends he bucked through like a stallion, living together with each of them for one or two weeks. He even sat for graduate school entrance examinations, to my surprise in philosophy. But that all this was his doing really wasn't very odd. He was a dandy by nature, some sort of Don Juan, a specialist in trafficking with demons, a specialist in destroying humanity's faith in love.

7

During the spring of my second year, when it was coming time for an epilogue to that period, the age-span on my face had already begun to converge on Pythagoras's one. The more I lacked opportunity, the deeper my despair; the worse my constipation, the more intense my love and hate for Bryte White. He tormented my soul, my heart, my face. One after another august year shriveled in the sunlight, nineteen years turning to twenty, twenty to twenty-one. On the passage of New Year's Day, I began to feel that if ever again I wanted to bestride that great river of time, I'd only be able to gain inspiration at the age of forty or fifty. A distinctive maturity had made me full-bodied. The vicissitudes of love had caused wrinkles to creep along my forehead. Though I continued to teach the television school cowboys, my composure had begun to fray at the seams. Nevertheless, as a form of revenge, I now and then had the pleasure of taking flight with some of the buckaroos from the journalism department, the publishing department, broadcasting, and even other television school cowboys.

On the evening before graduation, Bryte White started to come around looking for me again. Each time he came, I refused to see him. He was as charming as before, and as ever cracked his callous smile. But none of that sufficed to eliminate the indignation I'd stored up for a whole year. In the end, he hung a small sign of white pasteboard around his neck announcing his concession, on which he wrote in bold brushstrokes: "Students eat biscuits thin as parchment." In the same vein as he had criticized Socrates, he continued his "modern criticism" to engage in his own bit of self-condemnation. I made him stand there from afternoon till midnight, as if in reference to the way he had used his lance on that day during those same hours to slash through the glamour of my twenty-nine-year-old bottom.

At midnight, my originally unflinching intentions began to waver. I grew unsure of whether, after all that, using an entire year to punish his offense toward my long-cherished ideal of student–teacher love was entirely wholesome, not to mention the fact that my never-before-experienced affliction with constipation was tormenting me like a red ant on a hot kettle.

Borrowing the glow of the moon and the stars and some lamplight, I let him come in. He with his unfazed youth and I with my inelastic maturity, we kissed each other's lips over the placard. He let the sign fall and sat himself down with sincerity. Just as sincerely, he brought out Square City University's acceptance notice for the master's philosophy program. Sincerely again, he began talking with me about Socrates's early philosophy; Socrates's, Plato's, and Aristotle's philosophies; and the myriad "new" philosophies that had come after these men. When we had thoroughly excavated these topics, he announced that his advisor was Gan Liang, exactly the same advisor I had had for my master's. He told me that when he was finished with his master's, he would go on to study for the PhD, choosing again exactly the same advisor as I had had. Then finally he announced he loved me, uttering those brittle and shrill words like a slap across the face. During the first glimmers of dawn, we finally used the strength of philosophy to restore the balance between love and hate, longing and revenge. By way of mellifluous and intoxicating sex, we traversed the generational cold war and the attraction that arced between the two poles of that spectrum to open a new page in the book of student–teacher love.

8

As of today, we've lived together for ten years. During those ten years, he's finished his master's and gotten his PhD, even returning to the profession he was born for: writer-director in the cultural section of a television station. He tells me that his decision to study philosophy came entirely as a response to my challenge and the love at first sight he felt for me. And he admits that what really motivated him wasn't my erudition or my genius but that boundless springlike warmth and autumnlike coolness, that half-feminine, half-masculine presence about me when I first appeared in the auditorium that day. He loves me to the best of his ability in order to banish my formerly cultivated habits of loneliness and desolation. But as for that one year's emptiness and humiliation, I still bear a grudge. We don't discuss philosophy anymore. Each time he kisses me, when I want him or he wants me, I always force him to call me "teacher." Sometimes he's obedient, very, very obedient, complying with my order. But sometimes his fiendish nature emerges and, after he calls me teacher during our lovemaking, he adds his own flourish: "Teacher . . . eats biscuits thin as parchment." My constipation problems have resolved themselves completely of their own accord, and I've almost forgotten what that felt like altogether. But no matter how old I become, I'll always want him to call me teacher. If we didn't have that student–teacher antagonism, we wouldn't be able to love each other or grow old together. And this is my unshakable creed.

Platinum Bible of the Public Toilet

公厕白金宝典

Translated by Wenqing Kang & Cathryn H. Clayton

1

"Dear Friends, this is the International Red Star Broadcasting Station. Your host Guigui is wishing you a happy new year from the capital of the globe, Beijing.

"At this critical juncture, our staff at the radio station are all very concerned about the world, with global warming, increasing numbers of endangered species, political instability, and rampant economic crises. I, Guigui, greet you with foresight into our future, wishing all of you constipation-free shitting and smooth pissing in the new millennium.

"At this moment, as we move away from the old and everything is changing, I, Guigui, am filled with a multitude of new thoughts and sentiments. Since the founding of this radio station, the only one of its kind in the world that specializes in public toilets, 97.4 FM has become a beloved capital of radio stations and an exciting public cultural center. Every day we receive numerous and invaluable letters, telegraphs, phone calls, and emails from all over the country, beyond the straits, and from abroad. Though there are hundreds of thousands of languages in the world, they all share a single origin!

"Here, on behalf of all the staff of our station, I would like to express my sincere gratitude and heartfelt admiration to you. As an additional token of appreciation, I am throwing you 2,000 loud kisses on your pretty organs for peeing and shitting. Muah! Muah! Muah!

First published in *Gay Spot* (點GS), 2017.

"In order to improve all of our station's programs, after careful planning and production we have decided to put on our first revised program at midnight on January 1, 2001. It includes the following: first, a two-and-a-half-hour program called *Public Toilets at Midnight*, in which we present to everyone the Fermented Stool Symphony composed of materials our reporters have collected from public toilets, both old and new, in different parts of Beijing. The second is called *Darkness before Daybreak*, a reading of the famous novel of the same title by Chongchong, first-class writer of public toilet literature. The reading is provided by Fan Tiantian, famous public toilet performer. The third one, *Morning Prelude of the Capital*, is a series of close investigations of those who go to the toilet in the morning. The focus is on social issues, such as the shortage of public toilets, the difficulty of using public toilets, toilets with coarse interior and exterior designs that are devoid of artistic taste, insufficient and ill-matched cleaning facilities, and low hygienic standards. *Morning Sun*, broadcast at 8:00 and 9:00, is a music program of pop songs for public toilet cleaning workers with intervals of some international news and gossip. At 10:00, the most popular audience-participation program begins. To enter the Public Toilet Romantic Music Competition, listeners can dial my hotline 99575. The first prize is a free trip to Singapore, Malaysia, and Thailand for three people, who could be same sex or different. *Public Toilet at Noon* is a replacement for those half-hour programs at noon last century, mainly to satisfy listeners' craving for news. We report state leaders' chance meetings at public toilets and their unexpected happy endings, their long embraces and wet kisses, and those equal or unequal treaties they reach afterward, which benefit the globe and all of mankind.

"Our mission at International Red Star Broadcasting Station is to showcase the prestigious position of public toilets in the field of international politics, economy, culture, literature, and art, to promote mutual understanding and adultery between developed and developing countries, and to whet every listener's food and sexual appetites. Opinions and suggestions are welcome.

"Thank you very much!"

2

Darling, I need to tell you a multilayered truth. There are more good people than bad people in the world. Note that all genuinely good people are considered bad people, scum. Most genuinely bad people are celebrities and rich people who turned from bad to good. Also note that good people have strong destructive desires and bad people are conservative.

Darling, do you understand my philosophy or not?

I am Guigui, the famous anchor of the public toilet program, a paragon of humanity. I chose public toilets as a lifelong research topic, as the basis for my spiritual foundation and professional career, because I am a good person through and through. When I was young, year after year I received the school rating of a "good" child. Year after year I maintained a reputation of a good student and a good neighbor. Year after year I was regarded as a refined person in my upbringing, manners, and education. I was a person with no enemies.

I think that good people are the only forces driving society forward, because they alone possess the indomitable will to destroy and sufficient means to rebel. By contrast, those bad people who were once bad and wild children are quite unreliable, because as soon as mainstream society waves at them and butters them up with a couple of words like "you're terrific," they immediately cave to the corrupt and degenerate orthodoxy. Moreover, they always want to join the highest social classes so they can feel better than their peers.

After spending thirty years with my eyes at times open and at times closed, sometimes dreaming, I find myself surrounded by so many people who want to call themselves good. But the only good people who can be considered self-aware and humble are Na Long, Fan Tiantian, Zhang Fang, Chongchong, and myself. Moreover, at the present, Na Long and Chongchong are history, which means they were bad once but later rectified themselves and never again wavered in the position of the awakened.

Darling, I nag you about these big ideas that bear little relevance to the fancy plot of the book. I'm not trying to bore you or make you curse; I'm doing this because I care about you. You should understand that what I'm saying is the truth. Never believe those bad people, because they are not really bad. Meanwhile, do believe those good people, because they're not only really good but are also determined to do bad things without mercy. That we set up the International Red Star Broadcasting Station to propagate public toilet culture is the most notorious example.

3

Na Long is tall and cool. And he has a pure heart. He has integrity and has never lied. Even on the brink of orgasm during our lovemaking, when I repeatedly ask him whether he loves me, he'll never say anything he is not absolutely sure of just because his semen is surging. Sometimes I will coldheartedly make him pull out and reflect on what I want to hear. He does as I say, but in the end, he tells me, "I'm still not sure whether I love you, because from the very beginning until now, I still don't know your real gender. If I love a person, I must make sure she is a woman." This is typical of Na Long, starting everything from the public definition. He can't accept anything that doesn't have a public definition, rejecting his own thoughts and feelings. I can't do anything about that, so I just let him penetrate me at will while I wallow in self-pity. After a round of hard banging, he goes to sleep and I stay awake.

Since I was born, I have always been considered a queer child. My body and my features do not have any characteristics that conform to the gender norms of thousands of years of history. Men take me to be a girl and women take me to be a boy. Sometimes men take me to be a boy and women take me to be a girl. Therefore, since I was young, I have been able to go freely in and out of men's and women's public toilets and men's and women's public bathhouses. Of course, "freely" does not mean "smoothly." In the toilet and the bathhouse, I still face some discrimination, although sometimes the situation can be the reverse. Generally speaking, discrimination depends on who first occupies a strategic high ground. If I get to the designated space for defecation or washing up first, s/he or they would think that s/he or they might have entered the wrong place and flee in panic until s/he or they find the big, gender-orienting character sign that says Men's Toilet or Women's Toilet or Men's Bathhouse or Women's Bathhouse. They enter again gingerly and demurely. I, on the other hand, am experienced and comfortable in either men's or women's toilets and bathhouses, like a fish in water, meeting the unexpected with equanimity, like a seasoned general commanding a battle.

In the fifth year of my cohabitation with Na Long, I found an advertisement in the public toilet on the south side of Wangfujing New China Bookstore. It was written bilingually in Chinese and English with pink chalk. The

Chinese is as follows: "Advertisement. Half a month ago, I was fucked eleven times by XXX's big cock. Last night, I was fucked ten times by XX's super-sized big cock. If you don't believe me, please contact XXX and XX for verification. Their email is zizien@fm365.com. Jade Trumpet of Beijing." XXX in the above text is a very popular singer at the moment, enjoying a wonderful reputation in homosexual circles: First Whip of Beijing. XX is a Hong Kong movie star and television and music entertainer, known among gossip-loving homosexuals as the "First Cannon in East Asia."

Though this advertisement was not very well crafted either graphically or verbally, it nonetheless made me feel extremely sexually frustrated. I did not expect that it would have such a big impact on me. Because it shook me so much, I reevaluated my outlook on life and my values. I resolutely decided to quit my position as a college professor and change my relationship with Na Long into a business transaction, so that he could fuck me at will, by any means, at any time. With his money, I established the International Red Star Broadcasting Station to spread the true feelings and desires of toilet-users all over Beijing, all over China, and to every corner of the world. If E.T. likes it, he can also listen free of charge.

The above is my confession of why I set up this public toilet radio station.

4

I told Na Long I had to work the whole day at the broadcasting station. Not only would I have no income, I would need to purchase a large quantity of high-resolution, high-power equipment. Moreover, I would need to take up the time, on and off work, of friends who are experts on public toilet life and ask them to help me collect materials for the program. I would need to buy them a fancy dinner once a month at his cost. I would also need money to pay for advertising costs on all kinds of mainstream media so I could raise people's public toilet consciousness and promote the International Red Star Broadcasting Station.

Being the real man that he is, Na Long agreed without hesitation. His only condition was that he would not be involved with my thoughts on public toilets, never endorsing or opposing my public toilet ideology.

At first, I did not intend to be the host myself. I planned to invite my one-night stands (of passion or sex) who were famous actors to show up so that the program would instantly catch the public's eye. My inspiration came from successful television soap operas: no matter what you are doing, first you need one to five popular stars to shore up the facade. All other issues are of secondary importance.

Unfortunately, even after I had slept with so many famous people, the host position of the International Red Star Broadcasting Station remained vacant. The reason was nothing other than the fact that while those celebrities never hesitated to lick and bite my excretory organs in bed, they were completely tongue-tied when it came to talking about the smell and style of toilets in public. They feared that the audience would confuse what they talk about on the radio with their private lives.

As a result, I had to step up and shoulder the burden of hosting the show. I had no idea I would become famous throughout the world because of it.

5

At the peak of my career, a bad person called Chongchong fought his way with talent and determination into my circle of friends.

Chongchong was a rascal who had drifted from Fengtai to Xicheng. In the second year of his studies in the computer department of Beijing United University, he had to drop out after failing all seven of his courses. He's the pretty type and would do very well as a twink. But once somebody like him gets past a certain age, it's hard to say what kind of market value he still has.

I almost went to bed with him when we first met. The "almost" was because neither one of us had a condom on us at the moment. And we knew we would have plenty of chances to hook up later. We also knew the law of intercourse is that the sooner you start sleeping with someone, the sooner that relationship ends. So we didn't feel like we had to get started right away.

When Chongchong met me, he had already transformed himself from someone constantly turning tricks for wine, meat, and sex into a fairly popular writer. He was knocking on the doors of all kinds of literary journals with a medium-length story. He got a major boost in confidence after meeting an editor who was conservative in his own life but strangely fond of rascals. The story was published all right, but nobody showed any interest. The only difference it made was that Chongchong went from a writer with nothing to show for it to a published writer. Luckily, Chongchong did not care much for the story itself. He only cared about what his fame could bring—fan letters, public interviews, and book-signing events.

When we met each other, he had just published his debut work, which sold for 15 yuan each. I bought one on the spot and asked him for his autograph. I was the first idiotic reader at the book-signing event, and also the last one to this day. With irrepressible enthusiasm, he instantly accepted my invitation to join in the cause of public toilet culture and became the first freelance writer of the International Red Star Broadcasting Station.

Ever since he was young, Chongchong has had an excellent hobby: prowling women's toilets. Unlike most other aficionados of women's toilets, who are only interested in the people using these toilets and their exposed body parts, Chongchong is only interested in the naming and architecture of women's toilets, which represents an ultimate transgression. Prowling women's toilets was Chongchong's way of challenging authority through action. One after another, other aficionados of women's toilets who were active at the same time were arrested and sent to the police office and security bureau. The coolest one of them all was sentenced to thirteen years in prison. Chongchong was very lucky; he sidestepped that minefield. As public toilets gradually became modernized, privatized, and corporatized, he stopped immediately and remained at large. According to his own estimate, he is the only one who escaped among his group of toilet rascals. Now acting as the principal public toilet freelance writer, he feels more or less that he has picked up his old profession.

Because of the solid foundation laid down when Chongchong was young, I give him many important topics and columns to plan and write. When he needs to relax, I take him to dinner, to the sauna, and to swimming pools. I cover all these activities with Na Long's money. Another type of entertainment is to make love with him. This has nothing to do with Na Long. I use my own body. There is only more or less a half-inch difference in girth and length between his and Na Long's; their styles, however, could not be more different. Na Long never makes any noise when making love, not even heavy breathing. No unnecessary words to either begin or end. He's too shy to use language to represent, conjure up, or present the tide of his body fluid. Chongchong, in contrast, has a very strong desire to dominate. His style is to change positions repeatedly, flipping over from bottom to top and top to bottom, maximizing the limited space and length to make waves. The actions of his lips, tongue, and teeth are like the string of a bow, jumping around with exceptional skill. More importantly, he has the talent and passion of an Olympic Games commentator. From the initiation of sexual lust to the burst of the final current, he always pauses to express his opinion, which could be coolly observant, a distinctive perspective, or a passionate evaluation, making the atmosphere no different from that of the Olympic Games.

Na Long does not have the slightest idea about the fact that I use my spare time to exchange skills illegitimately with Chongchong, who, nonetheless, knows clearly my seemingly legitimate sexual intercourse with Na Long. Chongchong thinks of Na Long as the most outstanding man in world and is very proud to share one beautiful organ, or more than one, with such a man. Every time Chongchong jumps around fanatically, making speeches, I can feel strongly and clearly, from the frequency of his sound, eruption, sight, and touch, that he is saluting Na Long in this very particular way. I suspect that he, in the darkness and unconsciously, also directs the storm of his desire to Na Long.

I know if Na Long found out how Chongchong and I entertain ourselves, he would resolutely banish his friendship with Chongchong and the love between us. This is potentially very damaging and I have never worried about anything as much as this in my life.

6

After Zhang Fan joined in, an expert at making connections, the International Red Star Broadcasting Station officially declared itself a strong army.

Except for Na Long acting clandestinely as back-seat boss, Fan Tiantian, Chongchong, Zhang Fan, Wang Xiaoyi, and I each have unique skills, although we cannot be described as able to wield both the pen and the gun, or as being both talented and virtuous. Right away, we had our program for morning, afternoon, and evening, day and night; twenty-four-hour broadcasting was ready. We moved all our broadcasting and recording equipment from my home to Chongchong's.

Chongchong has a huge apartment, three bedrooms and one living room. Both of his parents went to New York, living a very luxurious life painting portraits exclusively for rich foreign devils. Upon finding out this fact, I instantly leaned my young body and young radio station toward the foreign power so as to alleviate our economic exploitation of and political discrimination against Na Long. Before that, we had been spending Na Long's hard-earned money but begrudging him for not being willing to participate in our great public toilet culture activities.

After we moved our radio station into Chongchong's home, I suggested finding a name for our little clique. The International Red Star Broadcasting Station is a mass-media organization, composed of machines and people. The machines already have names like Philips and Sony. We have more options to name the people. After several rounds of heated debate and repeated discussion, we delivered a verdict by three in favor, one absentee, and one veto that the name would be "Public Toilet Utopia." One of the best rewards for people who support me is to gaze at them with my soft eyes exuding tenderness and love; another is to feed them meat whenever they want. As a result, Chongchong had yet another experience with me that broke Olympic records, and the fine-looking Zhang Fan claimed my "first night" after I revirginized myself. Because of that, Zhang feels he owes me something for the rest of his life and has since obediently kept my company.

7

When Zhang Fan was inducted into my "first night," he was only eighteen. When he smiles, he shines magnificently. He is as beautiful as any current pop star. He is interested in all the topics that do not fit his look and age. In other words, the topic he is passionate about is always irrelevant to him.

He speaks slowly with clear punctuation. The superficial impression he leaves people is that he tends to nag. But his work is exceptionally efficient, and usually he can finish a week's work of reporting and editing within two or two and a half days. Wang Xiaoyi, who is in charge of on-the-spot reporting about women's toilets, looks like a quick and neat worker but always has a hard time finishing her task on time. Gradually, Zhang Fan has had to take over part of Wang Xiaoyi's work.

Because the gender system in the global capital Beijing is as complete and indestructible as always, Zhang Fan still faces quite huge judiciary obstacles to entering the women's toilets to do on-the-spot reporting and investigation. In order to avoid pledging his youth to the prison market prematurely, he can only wait outside the women's toilets, wisely so. Disguising himself as an American-born Chinese, he uses foreign-accented Chinese to address the women who, having just tightened their belts, are on the way out of the women's toilet—mami, sister, or grandma—before introducing himself as an anthropology student from the University of California. He asks their generous help because his advisor, Lisa Rofel, suggests that he explore the topic of the public toilet in Beijing, and the completion of his degree depends on them. He immediately takes possession of the lonely hearts of these female interviewees with the united fleet of his East-West fusion identity, the blinking but ostensibly weak expression in his eyes, and his casual but not alternative hairstyle and clothes. One after another, they offer him help, filling his recording machine with what they saw, heard, thought, and said without any reservation. If need be, a mami or a sister is always willing to reenter the toilet for him, never minding the foul smell, to record sound effects into his machine, such as the sound of pissing, the noises made when releasing, the clatter when putting on makeup in front of mirror, and laughter in the public toilet.

For a while, the material Zhang Fan collected for the women's toilet program was more valuable than what he collected for the men's toilet, anthropologically speaking. Accordingly, the radio station opened a three-week-long special program, *Anthropology of the Women's Toilet*. For the first time, Zhang Fan broadcast to his audience as an anchor, explaining to them the bodily and spiritual experiences of women of different ages, different social statuses, different ethnicities, different mother tongues, different neighborhoods, different facial features in terms of beauty, different weights, different sizes of bladders, different lengths of urethras, different tightness of the anus and intestines, different sexual orientation, different color preferences, and different dreams of Mr. Right, during the time they were in the toilet and after. According to a survey, the worldwide reception rate of this program was as high as 59 percent. After careful discussion, we decided to make the program permanent until the study of anthropology could encompass all human phenomena.

8

"Dear Audience, Ladies and Gentlemen, and Dear Comrades, you are with the International Red Star Broadcasting Station. Coming up is the *Public Toilet Fable Program*. I am Fan Tiantian.

"During an epoch when God's son Jesus Christ was born, ancient Rome was practicing fake democratic politics, in which it was clearly stipulated that no one was allowed to have a private toilet. Those who did would be crucified, including the emperor.

"One day, Caesar was holding an imperial meeting when he suddenly felt the urge to piss. He immediately passed along his presiding rights to his regent and ran into a public toilet opposite the imperial palace in the style and speed of a marathon. Due to the long period of withholding his piss, he experienced difficulties opening the gate of his bladder, leading his urethra, face, and ears to turn all red.

"At that moment, two blind citizens entered, holding each other. Caesar asked them to use their dexterous massage skill to help him release. Out of the principle that one finds it a pleasure to help others, the two blind men got busy. One was in charge of the front and the other the rear. They made the emperor feel not only the urge to pee but also the urge to ejaculate. Not able to withhold his urge, he yelled as if he were ready to go to Gaul to fight, 'How dare you sexually harass Caesar under the sun?' Upon hearing this, the two immediately ran away without even having time to put on their pants.

"They finally stopped at a fountain square, catching their breath. The blind man who had touched the frontal part of Caesar said, 'I find that emperor to be a lukewarm meat pole, sometimes soft and sometimes hard.' The one who touched the rear part of the emperor disagreed and said, 'No. That's not right. The emperor is a very deep hole, with a weird nasty smell.'

"Dear listener comrades, the name of the fable is 'The Blind Men Grope the Emperor.' It was written by William Billy, a British citizen, currently living in Beijing and working on sexual health research commissioned by UNESCO. He also did the Chinese translation himself; the original English version can be found in his work 'KY.'"

9

In the early fall of my seventeenth year, I met Na Long in Twin Beauty Park, where we both took photos of withered flowers. We caught each other's attention because we both held the same domestically made Seagull cameras. The two cameras were so completely identical they made the two of us particularly stand out. Both of us were beautiful adolescents, full of curiosity and fantasy about the power of unconventionality. Until then I had never met anyone so muscular. He was wearing shorts, a T-shirt, and sneakers, with a tight jacket on the top to showcase his solid body. As a result, my blood was running hot; for a moment I even felt suffocated. Later, Na Long told me that his heart beat faster, too, when he first saw me. So much so that he could hear his heart beating heavily amid the noise of the birds and insects.

Among all the flowers in Twin Beauty Park, the purple and Chinese roses were the most abundant. In the early fall, the purple rose was still flourishing, but the Chinese rose had begun to wither and look old. Both youths focused the camera on the withered flower. In a later autumn afternoon when the sun was setting and daylight getting dim, this picture was really moving.

Before long, we perchance met again in a photo shop. Our developed pictures could not be more different in style. His purple rose apparently lacked exposure and looked dream-like and illusory, thus defying withering, as if withering were only a fiction and, instead, the luster that dazzles the eyes was irrefutable fact. In contrast, my purple rose almost exploded out of the picture, the fatigue and relaxation after being in full bloom, like a series of mourning songs. The shot was very close and made the flower have a touch of heroism.

We looked at each other's efforts and, by the time we were leaving the photo shop, talked as if we were old friends. "I love the fall season," I said. "Fall is moving," he responded. These two comments led us to become friends. In other words, our relationship changed from chance meetings to seeking each other's company.

10

On a holiday afternoon in fall, when Na Long's parents weren't around, we clumsily tasted the sweetness of each other's lips; on his still-childlike bed, the action quickly transformed into inexperienced intercourse. That was our first experience. I really felt the pain and he was nervous. When the pain lessened, I began to imagine that my experience was similar to the blossoming of the purple rose. Gradually, I felt that I was beautiful and Na Long was doing the work of dew and bees.

11

In the global capital Beijing, anchor is a newly emerging profession. It requires that the person not only have diarrhea of the mouth but also know how to take a dominant position when it's not appropriate to do so. In addition, the person has to be expert at dealing on the spot with a diverse audience, protecting both personal privacy and the well-being of the city and the country. As an anchor, I aim to reform the superficiality and hypocrisy of this profession through my bodily behavior. When taking phone calls on live broadcasting programs, I stick to one principle: absolutely genuine material, answer all questions, and no false facts.

A hotline phone call came in, and on the other end was a zealous young man. He said his name was Michael, a typical Beijing native, born and bred in its alleys. He spent a lot of his telephone fee on narcissistic self-description, reporting to me the statistics of his height, weight, beautiful features, outstanding body, waist, hip size, penis girth and length. Hardly had he finished describing himself when he said to me, "You have a beautiful voice. You must be very inexperienced. I want to fuck you, and fuck you to death, in a toilet." I did not want him to feel that I was either surprised or shocked and responded quickly and smoothly, "How do you know that I am inexperienced?" He paused for a second before he said urgently, "Whatever, I want to fuck you, fuck you to death in a toilet, because I feel like coming when I hear your voice." I laughed this time, telling him it's been a while since I was a virgin. After a long silence, he said, "What a pity. I am obsessed with virgins and only fuck virgins. Your voice is too fucking deceptive." Before I hung up the phone, he added, "Before this phone call, I masturbated every day while listening to your virgin-like voice. Now, it's over."

On the "Hotline Telephone Log" of the radio station, I wrote: "As of 3:30 p.m. December 30, 2000, Guigui is very sorry that he cannot continue to provide free sexual service with his virgin-like voice for a Beijing native named Michael." Wang Xiaoyi, whose work followed mine, saw the log entry and immediately gave me a nickname, "Voice of a Virgin." Because of this, I was famous in our radio station for a while. The bad guy Chongchong sent a congratulations message to my pager: "The Voice of a Virgin is more destructive than the Voice of America."

12

At the turn of the new millennium, the International Red Star Radio Station began to air a singing party and a talk show with invited guests, entitled *Public Toilet and Me*. Both are live broadcasts. The first program was hosted by Fan Tiantian and me; the second was the cooperative work of me and Chongchong. In the living room of Chongchong's home, where our broadcasting took place, I couldn't help laughing whenever I heard the phrase "turn of the new millennium," because it always made me think of "intercourse of the two centuries." Nobody knew why I was laughing. But the laugh was contagious, and some singers and guests would laugh with me. In the hours before the New Year's bell rang, our broadcasting space was full of skin-tickling laughter.

13

"Sunlight streams purple mist off Incense Peak. Far away, the waterfall is a long hanging river flying three thousand feet straight down like the milky river of stars pouring from heaven."[1] After Momo composed a tune for this seven-word quatrain poem by Li Bai and turned it into a song about the public good of public toilets, we invited the popular star XXX to give a live

1 Poem by the famous eighth-century poet Li Bai.

performance. We received a phenomenal response. XXX was the protagonist of the "Advertisement" on the wall of that huge public toilet south of Wangfujing Bookstore. When he was invited to our broadcasting hall in the new millennium, he had already retired from the two fronts of film and television, only maintaining his reputation as "evergreen tree in the music field." To assure the glory of his last spectacle, he outdid himself. In the millennium party broadcast live by the International Red Star Broadcasting Station, he sang in praise of human beings' pissing function and gestures, while demonstrating his famous organ, "the number one penis of the capital city," to all the staff in attendance, who thanked heaven that they have eyes.

14

Na Long and my home is located in the Jimen neighborhood north of the Jimen Bridge, on the top floor of a twenty-two-story building. We moved in together not very long after we first met, when neither of us was yet twenty years old. The International Red Star Broadcasting Station was set up half a year later. By the time we broke up, ten years had passed. Time flew between the two of us, weaving a seemingly solid net. But in the end, the only thing the net could catch was memory.

Our breakup was not a foregone conclusion. It came instead from the interference of external forces. A doomed love usually begins with sexual frigidity. This was not the case between Na Long and me. Our sexual love can almost be said to have been unmitigated in those ten years. Every time we glanced at one another, we could not help pouncing on each other. Every time we thought of one another, we yearned to hold each other in our arms. This kind of situation used to create a variety of existential crises for both of us.

In the early days, I was pale all the time. The reason was either damage to my mucous membranes or an excessive loss of blood. He began to skip classes, taking me by bike to the Third Hospital of the Beijing Medical School. He swore he would not touch me again until the mucous membrane had healed. But hardly had we got home with my prescription when we began to kiss nervously, hold each other, jump on each other, and tear off each other's clothes. We ended up copulating, stuck to each other like glue. Sometimes I felt pain and he felt good, and sometimes we both felt wonderful. After a while, a miracle happened. My membranes became more and more resistant and durable; they had adapted to the practice. We happily said goodbye to the bike route to the Third Hospital and, clinging to home, used the same diligent postures to cultivate the love that came from our bodies.

With the end of my "first night" with Chongchong, Zhang Fan, and Fan Tiantian, and the arrival of "the Twelfth Night," I had accumulated some experience, which enabled me in a very academic manner to compare the differences and similarities of making love. My comparative study led to an important discovery, worthy of a report at an academic conference. The title of my report could be "Everlasting Love Lies in Unchanging Love-Making Gestures." Chongchong, Zhang Fan, and Fan Tiantian are change-loving people, no matter how big or small the change is. A few fans of my program, with whom I had a one-night stand, are the same. They have to subvert a bit, more or less, as if they have to negate our initial lovemaking gestures with a new one so as to reach orgasm in the end. Among them, Fan Tiantian excels. He wouldn't forget to change his body position even at the moment of ejaculation. Once he was like a screw rotating around on my body. The most valuable academic lesson is, although each of them has their masterstroke and, in terms of change, consummate skill, I never expect anything from them. If we meet by chance, I can happily accept them (and reminisce about their performance around and inside my body). But the next time I look forward to sex, there's only one object of my anticipation; that is Na Long.

Before Na Long and I moved in together, his parents occupied the apartment at Jimen. It was very difficult to use sunlight or moonlight there to channel our desire. Out of necessity, we invented an efficient route for action, going to the public toilet. Because my sexual features are ambiguous and Na Long's are absolutely distinctive, we decided to "smuggle" ourselves into the men's toilet. From then on, I was more familiar and felt more intimate with men's toilets.

According to Na Long, he was often able to witness men watch and touch other men's sexual organs, and men perform oral sex on other men. Generally speaking, people were not surprised at the familiar, strange behavior. Although China is a patriarchal society, men in fact are very repressed. Unless he wants to be seen as a hooligan or a sex maniac, it's basically difficult for a man to say to another man he's interested in: "I want to fuck you." Generally, "I want to fuck you" needs to be perverted into "I love you." If the relationship is not that close, it will be perverted into "I like you." Even though the Chinese language is so perverted this way, the men who speak this language still need a long period of time being involved with a woman before they can figure out whether they have hit on the good fortune that can answer the deep riddles, such as whether he can ejaculate, in what way, ejaculate in due course or wait a little longer, ejaculate inside or outside, on the hands, breasts, or butt? Unless you are a capable rapist, all is decided by the woman. As a result, men begin to rebel secretly. They take advantage of the convenient space of the public toilet to fondle each other in a timely manner, to make sure their erupted fountain of semen is always fresh and fragrant. This is exactly what Na Long and I did to take advantage of the understanding and care between men. We snuck into men's toilets to appease our thirst and hunger.

I once asked Na Long why we never changed our position when having sex. His answer to me was terse: we acquired it in the toilet. I did not probe. In fact, our first time was at his home, during a brief period when his parents weren't there. Maybe that gap in time is the same as the toilet in terms of space: narrow, people entering and leaving at any moment, you can be seen or caught at any moment. Excessively open and wild positions are not appropriate for that environment.

15

The night that the old and new centuries had intercourse, when I was busy with my broadcasting, I thought of Na Long, missing his generous temperament, his strong, handsome features, his tobacco-infused smell, his straight, virile penis, and his consistent thus easy-to-remember lovemaking. Muttering to myself, I concluded this truth: simplicity and consistency are most memorable, diversification and renovation are the easiest to forget.

In fact, since I broke up with Na Long, I have not been looking for a new sexual partner. Every time I imagine sex, the object of desire is consistently Na Long. I know this is love. For Na Long, more powerful than love is dignity.

Na Long's sign is Leo, which has a physical affiliation with the sun's passion, the god Apollo's nobility, and a king's supremacy. Both of us believe in this. He needs a feeling of being irreplaceable, and, accordingly, he is my only love. I did not take care to protect it, thinking it inevitable that his semen would flow to me steadily and inexhaustibly as rivers go to the ocean. I never thought it could end. The reason is very simple: Zhang Fan spent a night in our home. Not being able to suppress his desire, Zhang crawled into the bed belonging to Na Long and me and made love with me. Half awake and half asleep, I was naturally lustful. After witnessing this scene, Na Long quietly left. His departure was the dénouement of our love. Later, Zhang Fan said to me, if Na Long had joined in, I would have played with him, too. That would have been sublime. He is still confused as to why it could not have been a ménage à trois.

16

After Na Long and I met in the autumn when we were seventeen, he became a vegetarian. He does not eat beef, lamb, pork, dog, rabbit, chicken, bird, or ant, scorpion, locust, vole, snail, shrimp, crab, fish, or any eggs, including chicken eggs, bird eggs, insect eggs, fish eggs, and tortoise eggs. He does not suck honey or eat the penis of any animal, raw or cooked. He eats vegetables, fruits, and grains. Accordingly, I named his semen plant protein. When I missed him, I would call to tell him that he should give me some plant protein to drink. Can't you see disaster victims lined up for your soup?

Na Long's mother likes to listen secretly to his telephone conversations. Time and time again, she heard that I requested plant protein from her son. She began to search his room; the main target was Na Long's bottles. She thought that, as class representative of the biology course, her son had invented a new type of dietary food, which had not been tested and named by national scientific research departments. She mobilized her husband, who was also a fan of the slim body, to negotiate with their son. The strategy was that they would invest 1,000 yuan to buy Na Long a pair of Nike basketball shoes, which he had dreamed of for a long time. In exchange, Na Long would provide them with plant protein to drink.

Na Long warned me that I was not allowed to call him asking for his bodily material. When I asked why, he was very embarrassed to tell me the story. Upon hearing it, I was shocked. But gradually, I began to appreciate the inherent humorous relationship between language and material, father and son, and son and mother. I was in a state of schizophrenia for three days and could not stop laughing. I did not eat, drink, or go to the toilet, only laughed:

big laugh, wild laugh, playful laugh, charming laugh, odd laugh, smile, giggle, naughty laugh, slutty laugh, sinister laugh, mocking laugh, faked laugh, guilty laugh, coquettish laugh, boastful laugh, boisterous laugh, sincere laugh, twisted laugh, lustful laugh, innocent laugh, suppressed laugh, contented laugh, all kinds of laughter. I exhausted all the laughter I could in this world.

Na Long naturally kept me company, watching me laughing, listening to my laughter, and sharing the pleasure with me. In the end, of course, it was he who was troubled and hurt by these laughs.

17

On the premier day of the debate program *A Universal Principle of the Public Toilet* created by Chongchong, everything that came out of my mouth was fine prose, because I had drunk a lot of Na Long's plant protein. Chongchong, in contrast, was sluggish and out of character, speaking with no logic, because his animal protein had been sucked off.

The topic of debate: Should the toilet system be abolished?

On one side of the debate are five artist debaters. Their position: the public toilet system should be abolished. The five artists are Liu Wei, Yan Lei, Qin Qin, Xi Xi, and Wen Wen. On the other side five college professors: Zhang Xiaoqiang, Fang Yanyan, Wang Tong, Liu Jiang, and Ding Fei. Their position: not only should public toilets not be abolished, the practice should also be applied to the animal world.

Chongchong has been dating a rich slut in her thirties, the age of raging lust. Her small and slim husband far from satisfies her, a salted fish bone that doesn't even fill the gap between her teeth. After she picked up Chongchong at the Boys and Girls Bar in Sanlitun, she fed him a ton of milk every day and had him eat half-cooked steak. Before long, Chongchong had become a meat eater. His new dietary habit is to drink milk or liquor when he drinks anything, never touching tea or water. Both of them agree that foreigners grow big and last long in bed because of their reasonable diet. In contrast, Chinese men eat grassfed breast milk.

By the time Chongchong became a meat eater, it had been over three years since Na Long had become vegetarian. On the last few nights of the twentieth century, I was on duty for the Night News of Public Toilet. Because for a while Steel Hammer Gang was rampant on the streets of Beijing, I was too scared to go back to the Jimen neighborhood.

Since the beginning of last year, a group of unidentified people from outside Beijing appeared on the street, using steel hammers to kill people. They don't rob the rich to help the poor, or attack the powerful. Their targets are consistently passers-by, single women and young men. They are well disguised and skilled. One knock on your head—even if you don't die, you will become an idiot.

I used the opportunity to stay at Chongchong's home, and he strongly recommended his animal protein to me. After the careful cultivation of that rich slut, Chongchong's performance apparently became very different from in the past. While in action, he constantly asked me about the taste of his body. I intentionally gave him a hard time, telling him salty, bitter, and sweet alternately. He was most happy when I said sweet but shocked when I said spicy. I asked him to taste himself. But he felt utterly disgusted by protein that he himself produced. Therefore, he will never know into which school of cuisine it should be classified.

18

After the Utopia of the Public Toilet crumbled, I grabbed all the stored records, including 3 CDs released for souvenir, 58 recording tapes of news, 1,031 recording tapes of installments of the public toilet fiction series, 2,324 copies of the Public Toilet Jokes, 23 copies of the Public Toilet Fables, 75 copies of the Public Toilet Legends, 8,011 copies of the Amorous History of Public Toilets, 10,321 copies of the Songs for Public Toilets, 3,083 copies of personals, 10 copies of the Debate on the General Principle of Public Toilets, 110 copies of the Public Toilet and Me, 10 copies of the singing party, 700 copies of the hotline program, 6 copies of the Anthropology of Women's Toilets, 2,002 copies of the Midnight Drama of Public Toilets, 15 copies of the Skills for Men's Public Toilets, 49 copies of the Autumn Selection in Public Toilets, and many other recordings that had been produced but not yet broadcast.

Zhang Fan grabbed the equipment. Chongchong kept his property rights, which is the three-bedroom apartment on the east side of the Workers' Stadium. Wang Xiaoyi was noble and did not want or take anything with her, only shedding some dry tears. Fan Tiantian rented a container truck from a moving company, taking away a Xinghai piano, an electronic bass, a set of drums, a microphone, a microphone pole, a microphone stand, a sound control system, a waterbed originally belonging to Chongchong's parents, all the blue velvet curtains and the tablecloth, a water filter, and a wood toilet lid. Chongchong had thought to keep the toilet lid, because it was the witness to different styles of bodily friendship between him and me, as well as some other sexual partners. But Fan Tiantian argued that the mirror in front of the toilet could revive every piece of Chongchong's memory, and he was the only person who could not part with the toilet lid. Without it, he could not release or ejaculate, as an emperor without his throne cannot use his executive power.

Fan Tiantian had been a virgin before joining the International Red Star Broadcasting Station, a fact that surprised many, considering the reason that he was kicked out of the Central Academy of Drama was "unlawfully living in the female students' dormitory." He was kicked out of Beijing Film Academy because he was caught naked in bed with a female student. He was banned permanently from Shanghai Academy of Drama because he damaged the campus grass while lying down kissing a female student. He framed the three delinquent notices against three scenic oil paintings and has kept them with him ever since. When he was interviewed at our station, it was exactly these three certificates that he showed us. At that time, he claimed that the participation in media work of people such as him, an expert in both the arts and heterosexual love, would greatly elevate the media work in the eugenic sense.

Chongchong had looked up to him a lot, believing that his hubris came from his vast experience with heterosexual sex. He must have treated beauties as easy to get as grass and popular stars as catkin. In Chongchong's mind, anyone who has ever shown up in a film must either be a beautiful woman or a handsome man. He would have no regrets for the rest his life if he could get drunk with them just once.

As long as Fan Tiantian appeared at Chongchong's home, he was treated as a royal guest. Sometimes, when chatting with Chongchong, Fan Tiantian would touch and hug him. This was the moment when Chongchong was most anxious, not knowing how to respond. As a result, the damaged one was not Chongchong but Fan Tiantian. He thought he was a somebody, putting on the air of a star. Even his talking became more theatrical, like the sound of thunder in his throat, or a thunder after a thunder, the so-called resonance.

Fan Tiantian once generously loaned to Chongchong his female classmates from the three art institutions he attended. But Chongchong could not handle them. Every time he met a starlike female student, he would instantly collapse. His heart would beat faster, and he was barely able to move. Three female students from the three institutions led Chongchong to lose control three times. The first time was urine, the second was prostate fluid, and the third was semen. For more than a half year, he would not hang a picture of a star in his room, watch TV or a film, or read magazines with pictures of stars in them because, once he saw them, he would have a wet dream, ejaculate prematurely, or have erectile dysfunction. According to internal sources, it was Fan Tiantian himself who eventually cured Chongchong's sexual weakness. As they say, it takes the one who made the knot to untie it.

Because of this rich history behind him, Chongchong naturally could not say anything when Fan Tiantian expressed his interest in keeping the toilet lid, although Chongchong showed tremendous contempt when Fan Tiantian's secret was then revealed.

19

The revelation of Fan Tiantian's "real content" is very similar to the story that Dr. Chuan of Qingdao told me. Dr. Chuan has been engaged in research on sexual health and education, editing a monthly journal in his spare time, funded by the Ford Foundation of the United States. He is the eldest among my friends. Dr. Chuan's story is as follows. There was a young couple from a certain village, a certain township, and a certain county of Sichuan Province. The man was big and strong, and the woman tiny and pretty. Being married, they loved each other tremendously and lived a bountiful life. One year later, the marriage was not as perfect anymore. Two years later, things further deteriorated. Three years later, the couple began to fight. The husband accused the wife of being barren, and the wife complained that the husband was impotent. The reason is that, after three years of marriage, they still did not have any children. After clamoring back and forth, the wife suggested they go to the hospital to have a fertility test to determine who is the original criminal. They did not trust the township hospital, and the county hospital could not figure out what was going on. After a long journey, they arrived at the provincial capital, Chengdu, and went straight to the special division of fertility at Sichuan Medical School Hospital. The separate tests found that the husband was totally healthy, and even possibly had high fertility, but the wife was still a virgin. The experts on both sides met and compared notes, finding a shocking fact about the procreation-centered human being: for three years, the couple had been practicing anal sex, imitating cock and hen in their position and gesture. Every time they had intercourse, the husband would hold in his mouth a pinch of his wife's hair. Three years later, a large area on the back of the wife's head was bald.

The true story of Fan Tiantian is as follows. He is a very shy person by nature. As a result, his relationship with different women in the past only developed into the stage of sleeping naked together, no more and no less. After joining the Utopia of the Public Toilet, he became bolder. He fell into a sexual relationship with an enthusiastic audience member named Liwuer after she pursued him persistently. In the beginning, they slept in the same room but not in the same bed. Next step, they slept in the same bed but did not take off their clothes. Next step, they took off their clothes but not their underwear. Next step, they slept naked together. Once the frequency in which they slept naked together exceeded what Liwuer could withstand, she began to ask him to have sex. Thus, Fan Tiantian went all out to make her pose as a hen and himself stepped over her back, completely disregarding his own safety. His head and face were as red as a red cockscomb, with his butt rising up. What they did was anus-to-anus intercourse. Using the definition of female homosexual behavior, it could be called "mirror rubbing."

The person who revealed Fan Tiantian's postmodern sexual intercourse mode was Wang Xiaoyi. Completely unlike Liwuer, who could adapt to and even enjoy rubbing around with a person, Wang wanted to demonstrate to Fan Tiantian through her actions how to do it properly so that he could change sexually from being a cock to a man. But Fan Tiantian would rather die than succumb. For this reason, Wang Xiaoyi filed an application to withdraw from the Utopia. In the approval meeting, in Fan Tiantian's absence, she had to explain the reason for her withdrawal. That was how the story of Fan Tiantian became public to the Utopia of the Public Toilet.

20

Based on utopian idealist principles, we vetoed Wang Xiaoyi's resignation request and immediately followed up with a resolution: mobilize all the people to save the comrade who had taken a wrong turn in life.

On a dark windy night, after finishing the day's broadcasting task, all the members of the Utopia got together. Accompanied by relaxing toilet music, we opened a bottle of XO and each one had a drink. Zhang Fan added some ice to his, and Wang Xiaoyi added some boiling water. Fan Tiantian, learning from the yokels who add Sprite to red wine, intended to add some Coke to XO but was stopped by Chongchong. Using this opportunity, we casually took turns to talk to Fan Tiantian.

Chongchong: Hey, Fan Tiantian, this is whisky.

Fan Tiantian: What's wrong with whisky?
  Zhang Fan: Yeah, what's wrong the little bird?
  Fan Tiantian: What little bird?

Guigui: The little bird flying in the sky, swimming in the water, and running on the ground.

Chongchong: The little bird flying in the sky, swimming in the water, running on the ground, and sleeping in the crotch.

Zhang Fan: The little bird flying in the sky, swimming in the water, running on the ground, sleeping in the crotch, and outside the crotch adding Sprite to the liquor.

Fan Tiantian: Do you sons of bitches want to get fucked?

Wang Xiaoyi: Right, are your assholes itchy?

Chongchong: You! Want to get rubbed?

Guigui: Yes. I want to get rubbed. Try me. I'm afraid you haven't mastered the skill yet.

Chongchong: Who has? Show me.

Guigui: Wang Xiaoyi. She is a natural expert at rubbing. Plus, someone has given her special training.

Chongchong: Actually, it is better to bring the master out directly.

Zhang Fan: Who is your master?

Wang Xiaoyi: I don't want to say.

Guigui: I will say it for you.

Wang Xiaoyi: No. I am so embarrassed.

Zhang Fan: Quickly say who the master is, so he can resolve my ten years of itching.

Chongchong: Stop! How old are you? You have been feeling itchy for ten years? Maybe I could say that I've been feeling itchy for ten years.

Zhang Fan: Don't worry about how many years. It's itching anyway, and the itch needs to be rubbed so that it's not itching anymore. To do that, we need the master of rubbing.

Guigui: Then bring out the master of rubbing in a grand appearance, please!

Chongchong: The master of rubbing, please.

Infuriated by wave after wave of language arrows, Fan Tiantian took off his pants in front of everyone, posing his butt in the shape of an arch to take turns rubbing the commune members. We followed his lead with our hands and mouths, provoking the stuff behind the mirror to explode.

Appreciative of Guigui, they left all opportunities related to a first night to the famous lover of the first night. Therefore, Guigui came first, putting Fan Tiantian's snakelike, long-neglected, and nearly defunct organ officially on the right track.

After that first night, Fan Tiantian was so thankful to everybody that he was overcome with tears. He said, "If I hadn't joined the Public Toilet Utopia, my life would have stopped at the level of my hip." His comrades not only put him on the right track. They also recycled his body fluid, which he had thought worthless, turning it into something precious, an expensive nutritional supplement. He said he was greatly honored and extremely happy. His desire was fulfilled and his whole body was relaxed and satiated.

21

"I am Guigui, the chair of the broadcasting debate on *The Universal Principle of the Public Toilet*. On my left are the representatives of the defense team, and on my right is their opposition. Today's topic is whether we should abolish the public toilet system in human life.

"To guarantee the academic quality of this debate, our station specially invited the famous professor of Beijing University, Ms. Dai Jinhua, to chair the academic evaluation committee. She is sitting in front of me.

"To guarantee the fairness and validity of this debate, our station has invited notaries public from Beijing Haidian District, Wang Shuishui and Zhao Qiangbin, to certify our debate. They are sitting behind me, one on my right and one on my left.

"The defense team on my left is composed of five popular artists who are very hot at this moment. They are Liu Wei, Yan Lei, Qin Qin, Xi Xi, and Wen Wen. They will argue the position that the toilet system should be abolished, both public and private.

"The opposition team on my right is composed of five knowledgeable and academically recognized college professors and associate professors. They are Zhang Xiaoqiang, Fang Yanyan, Wang Tong, Liu Jiang, and Ding Fei. In the debate, they will not only argue against abolishing the toilet system but will also argue for actively extending the toilet system into the animal world.

"I, as chair, solemnly declare that in this debate, the nature of the positions on both sides is absolutely real and absolutely fictionally real. That is to say, the speech of these debaters might be heartfelt and might also be rhetorical.

"Let's welcome the premier debater of the defense team to state his basic position in five minutes."

"Chairperson, chairperson of the academic evaluation committee, notaries public, ladies and gentlemen, comrades:

"Hello everyone. I am Liu Wei; Wei means 'bright.' When my name appears in the debate on *The Universal Principle of the Public Toilet*, it means the light of the public toilet, and that is the principle of the public toilet!

"What is the light of the public toilet? The true light of the public toilet is a lamp or a window. Should it be sets of eyes flickering in the darkness, coveting each other? No. Absolutely not. The real light of the public toilet destroys walls, throws away the tiles on the roof, saws the rafters, and fills the shit holes so that the earth on which our humankind lives, from day to day and month to month, can recover its original appearance under the sun, preventing any darkness from obstructing our freedom to view afar, even when we are pissing, dumping, and having intercourse.

"Not very long ago, public toilets provided us with shelter from the wind and rain and also helped us to hide the filthy and the foul. They provided us with shade but also attracted shit-eating flies and piss-crazed mosquitoes, which bit thousands of our sisters and brothers and infected them with dysentery. When the time of AIDS arrived, they spread HIV+ wildly.

"Also, not very long ago, public toilets were a place where we met perchance and the best place for neighbors to exchange greetings, convey information, and expose their private parts. Many bad habits and traditional customs, cherished over the years or that stink to eternity, were passed down erroneously precisely through the uniform and unchanging posture of shitting and pissing.

"Generations upon generations of people come into the world, shit, piss, and die. Generations upon generations of people make public toilets, or private toilets, their home and final destination. According to item 7891 of the most authoritative and statistically meaningful *Encyclopedia of Six Thousand Years*, the difference between the number of people who died because of their addiction to their posture on the toilet and the number of people who died in their hospital bed is only 0.0345. This figure is a lot higher than the ratio between people who died in war and those who died in car accidents.

"No doubt, the space of the public toilet as a type of public space, free from government authority, like the refuge for the Hebrew people, has provided asylum and support for prostitutes, thieves, heroin users, oral sex lovers, anal sex experts, and explosives specialists. After the onset of the internet age, it has become a dangerous zone that is closely scrutinized by the police and easily sought out and destroyed by the authorities. If those female thieves and male prostitutes do not understand this change and still use public toilets as their happy home, they will surely become ensnared. In the internet age, if we continue to keep the space of the public toilet, we will be assisting the devil for sure and (precariously) putting what barely survives of humans' avant-garde spirit under the purview of the mainstream perspective.

"Not very long ago, two intolerable problems appeared in the public toilet. To eradicate them, we must simultaneously get rid of the public toilet system; otherwise we only replicate the problem. The first problem is that for a long period of time, there has been no one to clean public toilets, creating a buildup and loss of shit. This kind of phenomenon not only pollutes the air and the living environments of urban and rural residents but is also susceptible to the spread of pandemics. Moreover, we cannot underestimate the loss that this has brought to agricultural production. We can imagine the shit of millions of people left to evaporate in the public toilet because it is not channeled back into the fields in a timely fashion and cannot become the organic resource for food, vegetables, and fruit. What kind of corruption and waste this is! The second problem is that some public toilets are so spotless, they look like reception halls for distinguished guests, with a fragrant smell and lovely music. They cost a lot of human and material energy, increase the use of cleaning water, cause chaos in the labor market, and waste human resources. Do you know elite talent like me, while in college and graduate school, cleaned toilets? What a waste of youthful years and artistic talent! You can imagine if toilets continue to be erected on earth, how much water, energy, emotion, and talent has to be wasted on cleaning toilets.

"In a word, the public toilet system and its derivative, the private toilet system, must be abolished and eradicated by our generation. Otherwise, we would be disloyal to our ancestors and descendants, would not be able to face friends and neighbors, and would not have the courage to see angels and god after we die.

"This is my speech. Thank you for listening!"

"Next, the first representative of the defense team will expound the opposing position. The time is five minutes. Welcome Zhang Xiaoqiang!"

"Hello, I am Zhang Xiaoqiang!

"I guess people must know the proverb when the lips are gone, the teeth will feel the chill. This proverb comes from 'The Fifth Year of Lord Xi' of *Zuo Record*. In this story, the kingdom of Jin intended to attack the kingdom of Guo. To carry out this attack, Jin had to ask the kingdom of Yu to use their road. The king of Yu could not decide whether he should allow the Jin army to use his road. His minister, Gong Zhiqi, wrote to him and strongly urged him to refuse the Jin army permission to pass through their territory. Gong recognized that the kingdom of Guo was the neighboring kingdom of the Yu. The geographic and historical relationship between the two countries was like the dependent relationship between lips and teeth. If the kingdom of Guo was wiped out by the kingdom of Jin, the kingdom of Yu would be burned afterward. Gong felt that if there were no lips to protect the teeth, the teeth would succumb to an overwhelming chill.

"I repeat this classical story here not to show how knowledgeable I am but to introduce the original meaning of the public toilet. The word *ce* (toilet) in *gongce* (public toilet) belongs to the category of "厂" in classical writing. It looks like a mountain cliff under which people can take shelter. So it relates to a house. Toilets are necessary for people's lives. It is a long, glorious tradition that, as long as there have been houses, there are toilets. This tradition, so far, has been deployed not only in every imposing and decorative piece of famous architecture but also widely used in small residential homes. Toilets are one space which human existence relies on. Destroying toilets is tantamount to destroying the lips of the architecture. When the lips are gone, the teeth will feel the chill. After the destruction of toilets, where will human beings go to use their urethra and colon to conduct their monologue and dialogue freely? What is self-defeating? The motive and the strategy of destroying the toilet system is the beginning of human beings' self-defeat.

"Lao Tzu said in chapter 80 of the *Dao de Jing*: Reduce the size of the country and reduce the population.[2] Even if you have the biggest and most

2 The *Dao de Jing* (道德经) is a classic text of Daoism, written around 400 BCE and credited to Lao Tzu.

beautiful things, you should not put them into use. Let everyone cherish their own life instead of thinking that wandering around everywhere is a good thing. If we extend Lao Tzu to the contemporary age, I believe we should reduce the country into the home and reduce the home into a toilet. In the toilet we could put televisions, telephones, computers, refrigerators, and washing machines to sit idle, using them only as evidence of the wealth of our home and our country. I still insist that we stay within our household, while we let the modern city return to the primitive state, which could provide wild animals and other species on the verge of extinction with living space. In the process of implementing this brand-new concept, the toilet will be the only key word and the only object for practical use, the synthesis of the signifier and the signified. It will be the turning point from one structure to another, the basis and the origin of the new human being, and the country within the country, the city within the city, and the home within the home.

"Based on the aforementioned understanding and position, the four of us suggest changing the global capital, Beijing, into a gigantic toilet, and let everyone spit, shit, piss, kiss, and make love anywhere at will.

"We also suggest that everyone should give up their homes by opening them up as public toilets for wild and domestic animals. Meanwhile, everyone should be mobilized to teach all kinds of birds, animals, fish, and insects to adapt to the environment of the public toilet and stop them from making love in the wilderness and defecating nutritious and nonnutritious material everywhere in the open air so that they will not spoil the scenery and pollute the green, green grass.

"Ladies and Gentlemen, extending the public toilet system to the animal world will be a complete revolution. In the past, we humans have killed each other and revolutionized each other. This time, as big brothers and sisters of the animal world, human beings will not only consider the benefit for their own group, but they will do a heavenly deed, that is, to open an alternative and safe path for little brothers and sisters of the animal world to have intercourse and defecate.

"Ladies and Gentlemen, we will name this position of ours the Global Co-Prosperity Concept. The only way to implement this concept is to abolish human beings' hierarchical system. Put every person at the entrance of the public toilet as a certified custodian for entering animals. The main task of human work will therefore become both simple and interesting. Our aristocratic taste will escalate to the highest point. The everyday work we do will become unprecedentedly noble and transcendent. Our duty is to guide those animals into the toilet according to their sex and sexual orientation so that they do not run into a bathroom of a different sex or sexual orientation, and so that they will not be sentenced by the Beijing police as offenders of sexual harassment, sexual voyeurism, or sexual violation.

"Through our efforts, the will to power, the hierarchical concept, and the difference between rich and poor that have been deeply rooted in the human mind will collapse. Particular attention paid to how and what animals defecate will inadvertently liberate our human visual sensibility, mind, and soul. This is exactly what is meant by getting rid of the bondage of a thousand years: everything is reborn in the ruins, and ten thousand boats are bound to set sail.

"Due to the fact that every day, we witness and touch bountiful and diversified types and shapes of external animal genitalia, we humans can also push the orgasm of sexual liberation to a brand-new level. By then, we will not have to indulge in sexual voyeurism surreptitiously or experience trepidation about a ménage à trois, intergenerational love affairs, or the love of boys. We will no longer have any restrictions or taboos on sexual love. In other words, liberating animals is the same as liberating humanity itself.

"Therefore, on behalf of the opposition team, we solemnly condemn the irresponsible point of view of the defense team position. We oppose the abolition of the toilet system. We oppose pushing human beings back to the times of wildness, and we oppose disregarding the big picture of human beings and revolution as a whole by talking only about reform and innovation within a limited small framework. We must not and should not lose these beautiful lips of the public toilet. Moreover, we should, through our close relatives—birds, animals, fish, and insects—make these lips more voluptuous so that our sharp teeth-like humankind will be forever protected by the saliva in between and be bright and nourished forever.

"This is my speech. Thank you, Chairperson."

22

The time during which the first round of the public toilet debate was broadcast happened to be the anniversary of my first night with Na Long. I got some money from Chongchong and went to the Moscow Restaurant to have a Western dinner with Na Long. We went dutch. I was still very young the first time I went to the Moscow Restaurant and was disgusted by its famous red cabbage soup. The person who brought me to the restaurant was my father. He was a surgeon in the Beijing Railway General Hospital. My father's generation experienced the Second World War, the war of liberation, the war to resist US aggression and aid Korea, the anti-leftist struggle, and the Cultural Revolution. And owing to the whimsical changes in Sino-Japanese relations, Sino-Russian relations, and Sino-US relations, they also had dealings with the Japanese, the Russians, and the white and the Black people of the United States. The relationships which my father's generation had could be characterized as unequal. My father is a person of integrity, unthreatened by any type of authority. Therefore, he dislikes Japan and the former Soviet Union. He dislikes even more the conceited United States. He believes that a state is a symbol of power, and therefore he is disgusted with any type of state politics.

The reason he brought me to the Moscow Restaurant was that I was the top student in my class that academic year. This time I chose the restaurant; otherwise he would have definitely brought me to a cheap but nice Chinese restaurant. It's not that my father doesn't like Western food. Compared with the people in our neighborhood and my mother, my father seems particularly interested in food such as bread, butter, steak, and pork chops. This particular fondness of his was usually criticized by my mother. If it were not me who insisted on going to a Western restaurant, my father would have definitely not been willing to annoy my mother.

When Na Long and I walked into the Moscow Restaurant together, the autumn noon sunlight shone through the great windows onto the tables and floor, providing an impression of brightness. Hardly had I sat down when tears blurred my eyes. Na Long stood up in front of me and walked behind me and held me tightly; he lowered his head and kissed me. He thought I was moved to tears by the autumn noon. His kiss was very powerful and very hard. The memory of that "virgin noon" has a beckoning power from which neither of us can escape. He gently shifted his body and positioned the mid-part of his body between my shoulder blades. Through his autumn clothes, my shoulders felt the unique passion and firmness of his erection. The memory of us at seventeen, the pressing force and the stickiness between virgin and virgin, has excited us almost as if it were another person's story. I wept out my tears and could hardly find time to tell him another tale of "bittersweet times." I simply told him I needed to go to the bathroom. He then accompanied me from the southwesternmost window of the restaurant through the rectangular hall into the square hall and walked down the steps to the public toilet in the middle of the stairs. We entered the men's toilet together. At that moment, a young guy was walking out while fastening his belt. As soon as he saw me, he was so surprised that he stopped what he was doing. He then followed me with his eyes while closely checking me out, estimating my gender and value until I gave him a proud and demure smile. Only after that did he zip himself up and quickly walk out. Na Long and I "picked up our old profession" and began our quiet but earthshaking kissing, fondling, and fucking in the public toilet of the Moscow Restaurant. When he entered my body, in and out and muddling inside, tears burst again from my eyes. My tears dropped onto his hands and arms. I also felt his body fluid drop on my neck, and they were tears. I turned around and let him hold my flaming tongue in his mouth. Our tears mixed together, cleansed our faces, and made them glow.

If someone were to ask me what is love, I would instantly answer him inside the partition of the public toilet. Love is when one person moves in and out of another's body, with no constraint and with abandon. My father entered my mother's body, and a result, I was born from my mother's body. Then Na Long entered my body. Love is just like that: it has to do with the entrance of in and out, the action of in and out, the methods of in and out, and the intensity of in and out. It is just like a chain: every link must be connected. When Na Long's memorable flame burst forth in my night sky, I heard the sound of breathing and the irrepressible groan coming from the next stall. A vertical crack in the partition clearly framed a sneaky eye and a masturbating hand. At the moment our eyes met there was no embarrassment nor flirting between us. He was so immersed in the violently moving waves that he was not at all affected by the fact that I saw him. He bravely moved forward and aimed squarely at the crack before erupting. With the sharp moan of a wild animal, he shot his body fluid directly at me through the crack, hitting me in the belly, and splattering down my underwear and jeans. One drop even fell on my suede sports shoes.

Na Long and I walked out of the stall together. The door of the adjacent stall was also open. The young guy we met when we entered turned around and faced us. One of his hands still rigidly held his penis, which was moist, blurry, and in a limp state. But he held it firmly in place without any intention of showing off, only holding it solemnly as if holding a child's toy, unwilling to give it up. He was extremely serious even when he used his other hand and arm to send us a flying kiss. I even noticed tears glistening in his eyes, not knowing whether they were the remains of happiness or gratitude for the happiness. At that very moment he deeply moved me. I told Na Long I even fell in love with him.

23

Na Long and I had a beer, which was not brewed by the Moscow Restaurant but was a Beck's, made in Germany. After he had two small bottles and I had one, I began to tell him about my father, the first time my father took me to the Moscow Restaurant, my father's life story, and his death. Perhaps it was not the first time I told him about my past.

He never met my father. He didn't know whether my father would like him or not, or if my father saw him, if he would think he was a good match for me.

My father's hometown was Pingduo, Shandong. I don't think I have a hometown myself. Where I was born and where I grew up, that counts as my hometown. My father came to Tianjin with my grandfather, and then later they arrived in Beijing. Father's family was very poor and lived in a big courtyard with many other families. When my mother married into my father's family at the age of nineteen, his family could be described as only having an empty house. The empty house was also crowded with too many people. I will not describe to you the details of that time because they would be my invention, or the retelling of a legend, the retelling of my father's or my mother's memories. There is no evidence to support it. My father was a man of integrity, very proud and capable. He passed the college entrance exam and got into Beijing Medical School with only an elementary school education. He was a surgeon since he graduated. Because my father was poor when he was young, he was careful with his money and things. He rarely spent more than was needed from day to day. He changed all the money he saved into gold. Before he died, he gave my sister a gold ingot. I was sixteen then and hadn't met you yet, so no one paid any attention to me. Because my father's teacher was a Russian, he had a special attachment to Western food. The time my father brought me here, he ordered red cabbage soup to share with me. I almost spit it out when I tasted it. I had never had that heavy taste before. But I forced myself to swallow it down and then waved my hand, gesturing that I wouldn't touch it again. Even looking at it was torture for me.

My favorite dish is this, what you ordered for me today, mixed grill with butter. I still like to eat it. You can see people's tastes are quite particular and obstinate. It's the same with Chinese who came to the United States; they still wanted to eat Chinese food. This is what they call a Chinese stomach. Even the stomach is nationalized and ethnicized.

That day, my father gave me a small glass of dark beer. That was the first time I had alcohol. I instantly got drunk and fell asleep in my chair. According to my father, I looked like a lotus flower when I was asleep. After I woke up, I went to the toilet. That was the same toilet we were in just now. An uncle touched my face and then also touched my butt and said that I was "extremely beautiful." He looked as if he wanted to devour me. I didn't tell my father about this episode, afraid that my father would disapprove. He never knew this. Actually, I should have told him, and he might have given me some instruction. In that way, I might have been able to grow up a person of another sexual orientation.

My father suffered from colon cancer. When it was diagnosed, it was too late to treat. Before the diagnosis he often groaned in pain throughout the night, a kind of groan that was suppressed by his willpower. He didn't want me to hear this sound. When he was alone with my mother, he didn't care. Maybe he felt my mother should share embarrassment, glory, hardship, and happiness with him, but my sister and I should only enjoy his protection.

My father's ashes are dark in color. It is said that in the last stage, cancer gets into people's marrow and erodes the bones. We sent his ashes to the Catholic church in Xibeiwang in the western outskirts, to put them in a columbarium facing the sun. Believers think this is closest to heaven. But I think my father had already ascended to eternity when he closed his eyes.

24

Diagonally across from our table sat that young guy. Just prior, we had indirectly shared an orgy in the toilet. His face was still glowing. His intermittent gaze toward me looked anxious. From a medium-range view, his hand, the knife and fork in his hand, the chopping with his knife, the salad on his fork, the glass he held in his hand, and the napkin wiping his lips all seemed to be slightly shaking. I consider these phenomena to be a lingering mist surrounding the remains of passion. His expression and state had a certain potentiality. He looked like a bird flying closely above the water, constantly grazing the water's surface, leaving the shadow of his flight and the color of his feathers reflected on the water, changing the water's image. He was a UFO in my past and present. It seemed like he was standing beyond the past and the present, but it also seemed that he was in between them. If I think about the Moscow Restaurant, his profile is unavoidably mixed in. This is a human relationship uncannily united and dispersed and uncannily memorable and forgettable.

25

Chongchong received a remittance from the United States that was the blood and sweat of his parents' hard work. Zhang Fan borrowed US$100. Wang Xiaoyi took away US$10 as a souvenir because she had never seen US currency. Chongchong took me out, bought me a pair of 1,000-yuan Nike running shoes and a French dinner at Maxim. He said this was my reward. I asked him why he wanted to reward me, and he shamelessly complimented my sexual service, which had been improving day by day. I replied, "It is you who are my servant."

In fact, he is indeed my servant. He will give me whatever I want. Sometimes, even before I realize what I want, he already provides it in a very appropriate way. When I want to concentrate on my love affair with Na Long, he instantly disappears without a trace. If I need company, he fills in and "provides me with excessive pleasure."

Our relationship has been like this for a while: intense bodily communication from every direction but with less intense emotional balance. As for responsibility, when I'm hungry he feeds me. When he's thirsty, I let him fetch water from the well behind my house. No more, no less. Chongchong's vital weakness as a wanderer is still his desire for approval and acceptance, even before and after lovemaking. He always asks me something like this: How do you feel? Are you comfortable? Am I the number one stud in Beijing? Have you ever had any tool this big? Have you ever experienced such a long time during which a pipe does not leak? Tell me are you happy to death? When he diversified his actions and I was indomitable, how could I disappoint him? So I encouraged him as if to encourage the firework-launching engine of National Day and let him effloresce all over the city: East City, West City, Xuanwu, Haidian, Congwen, Shijingshan, also including Fanshan, Changping, Daxing, Miyun, Huairou, Shunyi, and Tongzhou. The far-flung outskirts and counties also need a whole night of mounting the horse, without a break, unquenchable, without extinguishing the fire.

Chongchong's and my interactions were initially very limited. While reading his book *The Past in a Glass of Wine*, I could see both his hooligan side and his will to a normal life. I once asked him, Are you a hooligan? He said, Who am I afraid of since I am a hooligan? I hit right on his weakness, which all hooligans have throughout history. I told him in all seriousness, Hooligans are afraid of no one, only the government and the police.

From then on, he began to examine himself and would never say he was once a bad kid, nor that he kept company with hooligans. Two years later, I heard a rumor that Chongchong claimed to everyone that he was a top-rate student from kindergarten all the way to PhD. He was always in the top three. Someone came to me to verify this because the year in which Chongchong said he graduated and the school he claimed to attend was the same as mine. I know that I am responsible for Chongchong embarking on this fictional road. He pursued nothing before the age of thirty. He only wanted to act like a rebel, the more complete the better. After he realized through me that only a talented person with knowledge and integrity could possibly truly rebel, he began to draw the history of himself toward that enlightened path. Facts are not important. What is important: "memory" can also be created.

Looking back on his past at Beijing University, I no longer believe the story that he failed seven courses, was a computer science major, and didn't really graduate. I made a joke with him by doing an experiment. The title of the joke and the experiment is: Does a man have a sign indicating his virginity or not? If yes, when did he lose it?

Chongchong unequivocally admitted that men have a virginity sign, but whether it has been broken or not, only each man knows. Female virgins are a different case, since there is a unified standard of the "hymen." Although both are physical characteristics, hymens are already there, whereas men's "virgin liquid" develops later. He thinks male virgin signs are a kind of behavior, which has a clear aim: a penis inserted into another's body, which ejaculates inside for the first time in his life. I asked him whether inserting into another's mouth would qualify or whether inserting into an animal's organ would qualify as well. He hesitated for a while, then nodded affirmatively.

Naturally I did not give up investigating his "first night." He had to confess that he completed his first night very early on, in fifth grade. The object was his physical education teacher. He also confessed, in addition, that his first night was spent in the mouth and was thrilling and surprising.

The second step of my joke and experiment was two months later. That day, we all acted as if we were jealous that Chongchong had an excessively intimate relationship with an overzealous listener. When the broadcast had finished, Chongchong invited me to have a late dinner. I absolutely refused, showing my intention to go back to Jimenli that night. But on that day, Chongchong just didn't want to leave me.

So I asked him again how he had spent his first night. He said it was a beautiful night with a bright moon and few stars. He was seventeen, as was his object. The location was the exercise grounds of Beijing Number Four Middle School. I suppressed my laugh until the third step. As in the first and second steps, I asked him the location of the first night. He totally forgot what he told me last time about the first night. After careful reflection, he decided his first night was with me, with condoms. The location was my temporary apartment in Xiaoxitian.

I laughed for a while. From then on, I called him Derrida, a name with deep deconstructive interest in the hymen and hymen reconstruction. "Between desire and fulfillment, between insertion and reflection, the hymen, although contaminated by evil thought, is still sacred: expectation here, looking back there, in the future, in the past, in an illusory moment of the present, a mime performs. His action is constrained by a permanent illusion without destroying the hard ice or the mirror."[3] Borrowing this passage from Derrida, I used my virgin voice to eulogize Derrida's innumerable first nights, praising his nightly renewable new virgin fluid: between desire and fulfillment, between insertion and reflection, the male virgin fluid, although contaminated by evil thought, is still sacred, expectation here, looking back there, in the future, in the past, and in the present.

26

Na Long and Chongchong became acquainted because of me, and indeed became friends. For a while, their relationship developed to the extent that they shared everything, a characteristic of communists. In fact, for a while they "shared Guigui." It was just that only one party was clear, while the other was not.

When Chongchong began to write his popular fiction, he totally worshipped a very famous senior writer, who had published seven or eight bestsellers, adapted seven to eight TV dramas based on others' works, slept with one wife, and had extramarital affairs with three girls. Chongchong both respectfully and jokingly called him "Old Cannon." After finishing his first novel, Chongchong paid a typing office to type his manuscript neatly and presented it to Old Cannon by mail. Chongchong was traumatized by his lack of response. Because of that, he didn't write for three years, after which he could not suppress his strong desire for novel writing and made a second attack. This time he changed his pseudonym and consistently imitated Old Cannon's writing methods. After *The Past in a Glass of Wine* was tidily typed out, he presented it to Old Cannon himself. At this time, he hadn't yet had the opportunity to show me his virgin liquid.

Hardly had Old Cannon finished reading the beginning when he patted Chongchong's neck and head, saying, "I have a successor now. My hooligan literature finally has a successor." The patted one was so honored and surprised,

3 Derrida borrows from Greek and Latin mythology, in which "hymen" refers to the God of matrimony and to a hymeneal song. Derrida argues that the hymen's protective screen, as an invisible veil, stands between the inside and the outside of a woman, and consequently between (male?) desire and fulfillment. Derrida, *Dissemination*, 209–18.

he said immediately, "Master, spare me. I don't think I deserve it." Therefore, Old Cannon mentored and helped Chongchong publish his first flop. That was the book for which I was the only one to ask for his signature. From then on Old Cannon became his Empress Dowager Cixi, giving orders for his life and career from behind a screen. In return, Chongchong presented beautiful girls he knew in the film academy through Fan Tiantian to his male empress dowager.

When Chongchong published his second novel, Old Cannon began to uncharacteristically attack him. Old Cannon openly cursed this son of a bitch as a sodomite and criticized his writing as one that makes sexual intercourse too direct and too seductive. Moreover, Chongchong's writing confused who is a man and who is a woman. Old Cannon formally refused to recognize Chongchong as his disciple. He said, "A traitor came out of the modern fiction family. You, son of a bitch, should take Sade as your father." In addition, he called every publisher and demanded that every channel of distribution for the book, *Degeneration of the Plum Blossom*, be blocked. When Na Long learned of this, Chongchong's book was already lying in his drawer, hibernating for half a year.

Na Long smoothly invited Old Cannon to the bar at number 50 Yellow Pavilion. In front of a group of flattering new-budding writers, Na Long slapped him twice, echoing through the whole bar. That girl from the film academy that Chongchong slept with and later dedicated to Old Cannon was also there. It is said no one present dared to make a move. They were all shocked and dumbfounded by Na Long's transcendent nonchalance.

Very soon after the sound of the slap, a middle-aged woman editor from a publishing house paid three visits to Chongchong and took away his manuscript of *Degeneration of the Plum Blossom*. Up to the disintegration of the Public Toilet Utopia, however, we hadn't seen the book printed or published.

27

The story of Old Cannon's beating quickly became the headline of a small newspaper. A picture was taken on the spot by a clever, insightful entertainment reporter, nobody knows who, and published with a red frame around the headline. The eye-catching headline: "Master and Disciple Become

Enemies, Hooligan Writer Suffers the Poisonous Hand from a Public Toilet Writer." This small newspaper and that entertainment reporter deserve credit. Exactly because of that report, Chongchong found an accurate position for himself in the literature field—Public Toilet Writer.

Humiliated, Old Cannon left for the United States. Legend has it that, for a while, he was desolate in New York and was rescued by Chongchong's parents. To return the patronage and kindness, he attended Chongchong's mother in bed with his middle-aged body, was inadvertently caught by Chongchong's father, and was kicked out of their house. From then on, as a model of the rebellious generation of new China, he wandered around the European continent, venting grievance and wrongdoing to big shots and ordinary people about the fact that no Chinese writers had won the Nobel Prize.

Na Long's two slaps brought about the success of two writers from different generations, old and new. Because of that, I rewarded Na Long with my body, flesh, and blood. The reward time I chose was noon, the brightest moment of the day. Before the reward ceremony, I uncharacteristically played solemn and imposing music: symphonic music by Tchaikovsky. After entering the formal rewarding procedure, I said to Na Long, who held the cup of my body with his hand, that he had achieved the highest honor around the globe, including art, literature, politics, economics, astronomy, geography, mathematics, physics, chemistry, peace, and progress—that is the prize of the Guigui Court.

Na Long, holding his cup in his hand, made an acceptance speech that I remember to this very day. He whispered in my ear: How deep is this Court?

28

To return Na Long's cavalier favor, Chongchong didn't touch me for three months. Out of an instinctive yearning for normativity, he took chastity as the highest state and used it as the utmost salute to Na Long. No matter what, he treats me as Na Long's and characterizes the relationship between himself and me as illegitimate.

After three months of virginity training, Chongchong's way of talking took a reverse course. In the past his speech while making love was always improvised. The rhythm and flow were usually very smooth, like floating clouds and running water; even during the interval of changing positions he would have something akin to a musical interlude during ballad songs, totally colorful, not one imperfection. At the beginning of his change, I had a hard time adapting. His style of lovemaking was still free and whimsical, but his oral skill seemed rigid and abrupt, as if he were reciting a text or monologue. Particularly startling was that he constantly changed characters, to which he sometimes gave names and other times was totally mystifying. The identity, age, and sexual orientation of his characters were difficult to identify and were often conflated among themselves, as if multiple characters simultaneously crowded into his throat.

At first, my response was rhythmic disorder; I didn't know what to do. I was used to listening to music and following its rhythm and tempo, swaying my body, gyrating my hips, turning my head, waving my hands, and kicking my legs accordingly. Once the frequency of his words of command and his body positions split and became unsynchronized, I was instantly confused and disordered: If I corresponded with his voice, I couldn't correspond with his position. If I corresponded with his position, I would mess up the tempo, mistaking 4/4 as 3/4. For a time, I became depressed, sweating in his sometimes powerfully vociferous and sometimes dry and withered monologue and recitation of text, thinking the warrior in the bed of the past had become a clumsy bear in the bed of the present.

Fortunately, I hold a doctoral degree; I have both a high IQ and a high-tech methodology, am well-rounded and willing to make an effort in research and practice. After the failure of the first time, I began a kind of "reverse exercise" procedure. I constantly contemplated the functionality of my own body, making it possible for a "smooth turn," "reverse thinking," and awkward positions, so that I could reach a state of an unharmonious erotic beauty.

I began my training by walking, one step at a time. At first, I swung my left arm while stepping with my left leg, and then swung my right arm while stepping with my right leg. In this way I walked forward. My "smooth turn" took me from Jimenli to Da Zhongsi, from Da Zhongsi to Shuangyushu, from Shuangyushu to Sitong overpass, and then turned to Dangdai Shangcheng (modern commercial city), from Dangdai to Haidian Theater, from Haidian Theater to Jade Palace Restaurant, from Jade Palace Restaurant to the

Center of Family Planning, from the Center of Family Planning to Xuezhi Kou, from Xuezhi Kou southward to Jimen Hotel, from Jimen Hotel to the Jimen neighborhood. In five rounds of exercise, I only made seven mistakes in total. The mistakes were very obvious because I adapted to the thread of the crowd, correcting my step, complicating my "smooth turn."

The second field of my training was calligraphy with my left hand, eating with chopsticks in my left hand, fondling Na Long's hard breast and back with my left hand. The motive of this exercise was to train myself to become a clever lefty. For someone with a PhD, who was accustomed from childhood to using his right hand to do everything, the left-leaning approach would undoubtedly bring confusing ugliness to the calligraphy, a big mess to the food, and bruises to Na Long's chest and back. Those details are not pretty at all. I had to use the memory of a college classmate to erase them.

That college classmate of mine was very short, but he was fresh and energetic all day. The minute he entered college, he had made up his mind to become famous. He was originally very mediocre. In order to change, or to challenge and attack his natural-born character, he valued tremendously whatever his tall classmate said. That tall classmate opined: all geniuses in the world are lefties. He was surprised this joke became someone else's mantra. Feeling undeservingly flattered, he contentedly observed the shorter practitioner in the bunk below him. He witnessed the whole arduous and extremely prolonged process as his bunkmate changed from a righty to a lefty. Due to his natural-born deficiency, from the beginning to the end, that shorty took two whole years and eventually became a lefty. The only thing that could prove the colorful achievement of the lefty's talent was: he did not drop his chopsticks when using his left hand to eat and could write a complete character with his left hand. Except for that, his grades were still under 80 in every subject. Every heterosexual or homosexual object he was violently pursuing had escaped from him as quickly and as far as possible. Until his graduation, this short student who changed from a righty into a lefty did not show any symptoms of supernatural powers. In the graduation exam, he was miserably eliminated at a very early stage. In a fit of pique, he ran to Shenzhen to engage in business, determined to become rich and become the envy of the whole school faculty when he would return to Beijing.

That Na Long's chest and back were as smooth as before proved that I had achieved the goal of my second field training. In all, it took me exactly nineteen days. I can't help but be secretly contented: compared with my college classmate, I am a fast-track lefty.

My third field of self-training was the reverse twist. It was the final and most difficult barrier. Passing it, I would achieve my goal. Failing it, I would become a dilettante. Chongchong would not be happy, and I would be regretful for the rest of my life.

I was born to be a person who pleases his friends, angers his enemies to death, and offers endless praise to God. No matter what, I wanted to pass this barrier by transcending my past.

The reverse-twist training, first of all, required borrowing space technology. This means when people on the ground hear the noises of airplanes or space shuttles moving, they should not look in the direction from which the noises emit. Instead, they should turn in a thirty-degree acute angle and look at the noiseless sky. At that moment, we can see a silver-colored, child's-toy-sized, model-like space industry product emitting smoke and fog in the blue sky. The advantage of this kind of borrowing: when Chongchong emits noisy language, I do not necessarily need to follow and think the real body is right under or above the noises. I have plenty of time and space to keep my lower body stable, while only moving my head thirty degrees either to the left or the right. In between this movement, I can anticipate the precise rhythm of Chongchong's midsection.

Reverse-twist training, secondly, required borrowing astronomical phenomena. The relationship between lightning and thunder is half to one measure slower. When rainclouds hit one another, they generate electricity and thunder simultaneously without sequence. Because the speed of light is faster than the speed of sound, we see the lightning before we hear the thunder. As for the rain, it lags behind even more. From the transmission techniques of light, thunder, and rain, in this sequential order, I have learned the "lagging behind strategy." In the battle with Chongchong, I used the technology borrowed from the space industry, saying one thing while doing another, to establish a complete coordinate system. Phonetics made by Chongchong from any angle would instantly appear in this coordinate system, which analyzes its trajectory, then receives and analyzes the trajectory and frequencies of his body's movements, and, in the end, directs my ear to pursue his sound waves and directs my body to respond to his body's waves, each one having its own responsibility, avoiding total chaos.

Of course, reverse-twist training also combines the principles of abstract math, pulse, and ultrasound diagnoses and, despite all odds, catches up with the stride of the digital age.

29

Because the reverse-twist exercise induced and utilized large quantities of my energy, physical strength, and time, after a serious investigation of ratings, Public Toilet Utopia held a meeting that night to critique the programs that I produced. What saddened me was that Chongchong was the first to accuse me, using the harshest language to criticize me.

I secretly made up my mind that I would not dedicate my first night to him after my training.

Chongchong said, Guigui has been absentminded recently, soulless, half-awake and half-asleep. Nobody knows what he is trying to do, totally ignoring the international reputation of the International Red Star Broadcasting Station. Guigui should therefore be fully responsible for the sharp drop in ratings of the Time and Space of the Public Toilet.

I stood up and performed my smooth turn for everyone. I performed my self-choreographed outer space dance that was even more in outer space than the usual moonwalking, making gestures of lightning and thunder, and listening to and watching airplanes awkwardly out of sync. Zhang Fan, Fan Tiantian, and Wang Xiaoyi looked like they were falling into a fog. Chongchong, on the other hand, changed from looking dumbfounded to looking drunk and stupid. Not being able to control himself, he rushed toward me and lifted me up, quickly carrying me to his bedroom. I struggled to use my left-handed reverse-twist method. As a result, he became even more irrepressible. Once we entered the room, he locked the door immediately and began to talk.

I continued to practice what I learned from my training according to my plan. He caught me by surprise, and I did the same to him. I made him ejaculate on the bedsheet as soon as he took off his clothes, like ink that accidentally leaks from a fountain pen. When he started with his violent poetry, I had already resumed from left hand to right hand, from unsynchronized to synchronized moves, from reverse thinking to direct thinking. This made him look like an ant in a hot pan, crawling all over and stumbling out of bed several times. But he wouldn't give up, returning to bed each time, crawling all over until he finally fell, dealing with his ink while murmuring to himself.

30

I dedicated my left-hand, smooth-turn, reverse-twist, and reverse-direction first night to Zhang Fan. My zealous passion, master skill, and solid confidence kept an appropriate distance from his vapid personality and extremely beautiful face and body. After a period of twisting and mediation, the sunshine in his face gradually faded and dusk vaguely took shape. My distance methods made him extremely excited at the beginning. His youthful heart, youthful lungs, youthful gaze, and youthful penis, no matter how tender, could not resist his straightforward urge. Surprise, insecurity, anxiety, disappointment, and fatigue were written all over his dusk-filled face. For him, the skill and the situation I meticulously managed had become flirtation, deception, and torture. He was constantly murmuring to himself. Anxiety did not enhance his desire all the time.

I had become dominant. I let him speak or sing, but when he spoke or sang, I evaded the rhythm so he couldn't reach me. That was how he fell. The most pleasant rhythm for Chongchong seemed out of place in Zhang's bed. By dint of my bodily skill, I could totally make smooth turns or otherwise, every once in a while, synchronize with him and compromise with conventional smooth moves. The only reason I wouldn't compromise was to guarantee the completeness and purity of the reverse-direction first night. I didn't compromise; the power of youth would not let him bolt. Hence, the only one to adjust the frequency of his moves was him.

He temporarily went into panic mode; in his small, narrow, rented room he practiced smooth turns, using his left hand to repeatedly put on and take off condoms and saying one thing and doing another. He is smart and quick-witted. He mastered the basics and skills of reverse lovemaking within three hours. From the moment that he screamed with abandon "light up the fireworks," we had reached a new harmonious order. After his fireworks burst forth in my anus, we felt like we had just had a sauna, sweating all over our bodies.

Long after the first night, every time we met, we couldn't help watching each other carefully as if we were strangers. Sometimes I would ask him if he had enjoyed himself. He would instantly change his countenance, looking in anticipation and horror. He would constantly nod his head only to then shake it. If I added another sentence asking whether he wanted one more time, he would constantly and definitively nod his head, saying no, I dare not want more. I could understand him. Including the passionate drama that led to the destruction of the relationship between Na Long and me, Zhang Fan and I never again did anything against stream.

Sometimes the rules of sexual games should remain consistent.

31

"Dear audience comrades, this is Zhang Fan, your special host of the International Red Star Broadcasting Station, greeting you from the global capital Beijing.

"Based on the principle that everyone is equal and that there should be no difference under the sun between the noble and the debased, the host has visited big streets and small lanes in Beijing, particularly the women's toilets on the big streets and small lanes. The visit that I took the effort to make has born ample, breast-like fruit. Here I dedicate it to you.

"To make it easy to remember and search, I name this program *Anthropology of the Women's Toilet*. I hope you all like it.

"My name is Zhang Fan, please don't ignore my glorious name.

"Recently, Zhang Fan has visited Beijing Music Hall, Chang'an (Eternal Peace) Theater, Workers' Cultural Palace, Zhongshan Park, Tiananmen Square, Jade Among Jade Health Center, Beijing Experimental High School, Beijing Normal University, Beijing Broadcasting Institute, the Office of State Consul, and the Houku (Rear Storage) Office of the People's Congress, conducting a wide and in-depth survey and on-the-spot interviews on the issue of the difficulties female citizens experience with city toilets.

"Two thousand survey forms were distributed in total this time. One thousand eight hundred and two were returned. The return rate is 90.1 percent, far exceeding my expectations.

"According to official statistics, China is a developing country, and its female population is slightly more than its male population. For such a large country that privileges men over women, this kind of situation is incomprehensible. Women lining up for public toilets is a spectacle that can be seen all over the country. Why is it so difficult for female citizens to go to the public toilet?

"The first question of the survey is: Do you think the core issue is the absence of urinals in women's public toilets? 58.5 percent answered yes.

"The second question of the survey is: Do you think the area occupied by the women's toilet should be bigger than that for men's? 87.5 percent answer that it should. Someone also added: In the field of toilet architectural arts, we should not stick to the principle of equality between men and women. Privileging women over men in this respect is conducive to social stability, personal edification, and overall development.

"The third question of the survey is: Should women's toilets be immediately adjacent to the men's toilets or not? The answer to this question was very divided. There are two major different opinions, the first one 43.3 percent, the second 42.5 percent. The ratio is very close.

"The first opinion is that women's public toilets immediately adjacent to men's toilets easily causes women's sphincter to tense up and delay urination and other symptoms. In China it has been consistently the case that there are more male hooligans than female. There are more men who peek into women's toilets than women who peek into men's toilets. Women's delayed urination and constipation are mainly caused by the crowdedness of the women's toilet. To resolve this unrefined spectacle of a long line in women's toilets during rush hour, first of all, we need to build men's and women's toilets separately so that men won't smell women's fragrance once they enter into the toilet and become turned on, breaking into or jumping over the wall into the women's toilet.

"The second opinion is that women's toilets should be immediately adjacent to the men's toilets, just like the marriage model, one man and one woman, a husband and a wife. The most important thing is that they like each other's foul smell and that they can hear one another. People of this opinion think the delicate design in which each sits closely, separated by only a partition wall, helps women and men respond to each other and stimulate each other's passion for release. People of this opinion deny any connection between the difficulties that female citizens have in public toilets and male citizens and men's toilets. One returned survey employs a famous clothing brand name and its design to eulogize the beautiful picture that female and male toilets are close neighbors. That brand of clothes might be at this moment on the body of one our listeners, called Back-to-Back.

"The fourth question of the survey is: What is the gender of the authors who write licentious words and graphics on the wall of the women's toilet? Does the work of those graffiti artists waste a large amount of useful time in the women's toilet? 81.2 percent believe that the licentious writing and painting are authored by men. But only 23.5 percent of the people believe graffiti artists have illegally occupied the space of the toilet that leads to the long line of the women's toilet. In the comments column, some people carefully explain how the two questions within question four are contradictory. As they illustrate, women's toilet lovers among men would definitely not choose the rush hour to author their specialized work. The best moment for them to sneak into the women's toilet is in the middle of the night when nobody is there or in rainy or snowy weather. Whether they come or leave usually does not affect the rush hour volume and the turnover rate in the women's toilet. Zhang Fan believes that this school of opinion is quite objective and fair.

"The fifth question of the survey is: Does the excessive amount of menstrual paper in women's toilets constitute an inconvenience in traffic? Only 1.5 percent agree, and all the other 98.5 percent disagree. Among those who disagree, someone pointed out that the people who raise this question definitely do not have periods themselves. The question itself has bias, very, very nonfeminist. 20 percent of those surveyed think that the origin of the phenomenon of rush hour crowdedness in women's toilets is overpopulation in China. 18 percent think that female clothing is more complicated. The process of putting on and taking off clothing while in the bathroom is accordingly more complex. 12 percent think that the female biological structure leads to the situation that the persons entering the toilet cannot separate urination and defecation, unlike men who produce more, better, faster, and cheaper. 43.5 percent believe the main reason that causes the long line is that the people who are inside the bathroom carefully read the public toilet literature on the walls and the doors while they urinate and defecate. Among those of this opinion, someone suggested we should create a special kind of newspaper or periodical, collecting and organizing public toilet literature, and sell it on the street where people can buy it at any time. In that case, readers who are passionate about this kind of literature can save precious time in the toilet, leave the toilet vacant to more people who have a greater urgency, and bring the toilet literature back home to enjoy in bed.

"In this investigation, Zhang Fan found there are more women than men enthusiastic about going to the toilet, and more men than women enthusiastic about peeking into toilets. Zhang Fan also found that in the toilet, among strangers, women like to talk to each other. Between men, they like to scrutinize and evaluate the depth and the thickness of each other's organ. Zhang Fan also found that generally, female citizens like to spend some time and effort memorizing public toilet literature so that they can carefully reminisce later at home or at work. Male citizens, on the other hand, like to consume public toilet literature right on the spot. The method of their consumption is close to how they read erotic fiction, that is, masturbating while reading. Their eyes are bright while their hands are fast.

"The way Zhang Fan distributed the survey forms was by waiting outside of toilets and picking up the surveys at people's homes. Because all participants left their home phone, cell phone, or pager numbers, gathering the surveys was fast and convenient. Here I want to reassure every beautiful woman that your phone number will not be leaked, especially not to those well-dressed, nice-looking, womanizing men. While gathering the surveys, Zhang Fan was fortunate to have the opportunity to conduct 1,801 on-the-spot interviews out of 1,802 participants. The only woman who did not participate in Zhang Fan's interview had already entered the hospital for gynecology and obstetrics. She entrusted her very youthful twenty-three-year-old husband to turn in her survey to me. Because his heart was in the delivery room, her young husband declined the skillful request of Zhang Fan for an on-the-spot interview.

"In the follow-up interviews, Zhang Fan got the following information, which has important anthropological value: 1. Sexual activities that occur in the women's toilet are not as seldom as we estimated; 2. Women's toilets are the place where female underwear fashions are first displayed; 3. Weight-loss foods, medicines, and other similar products are publicized in women's toilets; 4. Mothers generally tend to bring their preadolescent sons to women's toilets so that they won't be left alone, get lost, or be abducted and sold by human traffickers; 5. Women who are fond of male beauty usually cannot help dolling themselves up, especially when taking off their skirts or putting on their pants; 6. When women want to assess others' economic ability or family situation, they usually start from the brand of their hygienic paper or cloth; 7. For many women, once they pass the threshold of the women's toilet, they instantly feel the comfort of absolute security. They generally believe that the place with the sign of the women's toilet is the most secure place for women's privacy; 8. Over 90 percent of the participants considered the women's toilet to be a liberation area for women, where they can finally relax and not feel measured or constrained by the male gaze, a place where they can feel more carefree than at home; 9. College-educated women tend to hide their jewelry and valuable accessories in their home toilets more often than those without a college education; 10. Over 80 percent of women think that planning their everyday expenses while in the toilet is much more enjoyable than shopping at department stores; 11. 100 percent of women who took abortion pills dumped their fetuses into the shithole or the toilet . . ."

32

For a while, a chaotic situation occurred outside the International Red Star Broadcasting Station. The reason was that two starstruck fans waited outside day and night.

The one who arrived at the foot of the building where Chongchong's home was located near the east entrance of Workers' Stadium was a woman of over thirty. In a fluent Shandong dialect, she insisted on meeting the host of *Anthropology of the Women's Toilet*, Zhang Fan. When we looked down from our balcony, we could see how ferocious she was. Together we colluded to not explain the true situation to Zhang Fan to see how he would make a fool of himself.

Soon it happened.

One day, when Zhang Fan came to work, he began to flirt with that woman at the entrance. I ran downstairs in slippers pretending that I was worried that Zhang Fan would be seduced by her, abducted to an isolated spot on Tai Mountain, gang-raped, and then killed. Hardly had I reached the building entrance when I heard the dialogue between the flirting expert and the woman passing through the intense sunlight. I stopped in the shadow of the hallway and held my belly to prevent the sound of my laughter from surfacing.

33

Zhang Fan: Are you looking for the International Red Star Broadcasting Station? What a coincidence! I am looking for it, too. I heard that this is the area of their activity. The scope of their activity is rather widespread. It's just like a guerilla war. How rampant this kind of underground station is! Why are you looking for them?

Bai Yuejuan: My name is Bai Yuejuan. I specialize in the silk business in Qingdao. I make quite a bit of money but I'm spiritually impoverished. By chance, I heard the program of the International Red Star Broadcasting Station and felt they were so audacious. I myself was born unafraid of death and naturally love audacious people and things. So at the spur of the moment, I left my business to my son and came to Beijing to join the revolutionary army.

Zhang Fan: Your son? How old is he?

Bai Yuejuan: Seven years old, called Bai Yang. He can do the accounts perfectly ever since he was very young. What do you do?

Zhang Fan: I'm also a fan of the public toilet.

Bai Yuejuan: What do you mean you're also a fan of the public toilet? You make it sound like I'm also a fan of the public toilet. I'm a devoted listener of the public toilet program of the station, but not a fan of public toilets. On this issue, we need to draw a clear line.

Zhang Fan: Yes, yes, yes. Yes, yes, yes.

Bai Yuejuan: Young man, you look sharp and handsome. Why don't you have other obsessions? What about sex? It's still better than your obsession with toilets. It's not that your elder sister is teaching you; I'm telling you that if I had a younger brother like you, I would push him to drown.

Zhang Fan: Push? Where to?

Bai Yuejuan: Push into the public toilet to drown. Who taught him to waste such a beautiful face. And nice body. I'd drown him. Then let's see if he dare not take on some real work!

Zhang Fan: I am concentrating on my real work.

Bai Yuejuan: You are? Have you ever seen Zhang Fan, the anthropologist of the women's toilet? When I say concentrating on your real work, you have to reach that kind of level. Could you do it?

Zhang Fan:...

Bai Yuejuan: Now you're quiet? Listen to Zhang Fan's voice, how sexy, how metallic, and how erectile! Since I was born, I've never heard such a voice of content and character, filled with blood, and with such strong personality as Zhang Fan's. His voice contains so much ridicule of the normative life and disdain for a lifestyle of debauchery. It also conveys such rich humanism and great empathy! But your voice only has this sticky fluid character and lacks metallic sturdiness.

Zhang Fan: That's because I'm not using a microphone, and the sound isn't filtered...

Bai Yuejuan: Here you go, this is the golden microphone I specially purchased as a prize for my white knight prince. It won't hurt for you to try it and let it filter your voice to see if it contains real gold.

Zhang Fan: So your golden microphone is gilded with gold.

Bai Yuejuan: How dare you say that! I could slap you. The microphone is gilded with gold? Look at it carefully. I can let you see me bite it.

Zhang Fan: Don't bite it. That will hurt. Can't you see it rather looks like a big cock?

Bai Yuejuan: That's none of your business. The more it looks like that, the more I want to bite it. Look at these teeth marks. It's pure gold, 24K. How can I be as cheap as CCTV, passing gilded microphones off as real gold?

Zhang Fan: It is really pure gold, I accept it.

Bai Yuejuan: Give it back to me!

Zhang Fan: Aren't you coming here specially to present it to me?

Bai Yuejuan: Did I say it's for you? Is your name Zhang Fan?

Zhang Fan: Yes, my name is Zhang Fan, and I am the white night prince that you dream of day and night.

Bai Yuejuan: Don't fucking bullshit me. There are lots of Zhang Fan in the world; the Zhang Fan I'm looking for is not as childish as you.

Zhang Fan: That's because when I broadcast, I play deep.

Bai Yuejuan: Resident ID, work ID, and union member ID, pull these three IDs out and show me!

Zhang Fan: Hey, it so happens, it's traffic control day today. I have all of them with me.

Bai Yuejuan: Is the person in the picture you? It looks like a little kid!

Zhang Fan: That was taken when I was sixteen years old. They wouldn't give you an ID before you reached sixteen. It will be the same for your son in the future.

Bai Yuejuan: You seemed sexier when you were young.

Zhang Fan: Maybe you have a tendency toward pedophilia? If you really like boys, I can introduce one to you. I have a colleague in our station named Guigui, who has a baby face and nobody can tell whether he is male or female, adult or child. If you date him, I can guarantee you will enjoy a never-ending spectacle of childhood for the rest of your life.

Bai Yuejuan: Don't bullshit me! Your membership card shows that you are an athlete. Aren't you a host?

Zhang Fan: Uh... Uh...

Bai Yuejuan: You are totally not the anthropologist Zhang Fan. Here are your IDs. Go take a hike. Don't block my view. I have to keep surveillance on everyone who passes by this area within three days, and I am determined to bring Zhang Fan to Rome.

Zhang Fan: Along the Silk Road?

Bai Yuejuan: Yes, of course.

34

Zhang Fan arrived safely back at the lair of the Public Toilet Utopia. I went back into the broadcast booth, covered in a cold sweat on his behalf. Chongchong, Fan Tiantian, and Wang Xiaoyi all crowded onto the balcony, completely disregarding the safety of their ally. Fan Tiantian picked up a microphone on a long pole, as if to record some sound.

At this point we were broadcasting a previously recorded program. When the broadcast wasn't live, everyone could move a little more freely. The broadcast booth was soundproofed; through the thick pane of soundproof glass that shut out all noise from the outside, I could see the three of them out on the balcony, doubled over with laughter, but I couldn't hear what they were saying. I got the feeling something fishy was going on.

Zhang Fan took off his jacket and began preparing for the 12:00 live broadcast. I quietly left the booth, crossed the narrow corridor into the break room, and emerged onto the balcony. Someone was yelling my name, loudly and clearly, as if reciting a poem or singing an aria: "... Oh Guigui, my Guigui, I dream of you night and day! My angel, my sprite, my phantom of delight! I am bewitched by you, I've lost my wits over you, my soul swoons at the sound of your voice, my heart trembles at the thought of you! Oh, Guigui, come out of your maiden's chamber, lift up your bridal veil, and fall into my virile embrace, my Guigui! My alpha and omega, my Guigui ... !"

It was a total practical joke, a prank played by the members of the Utopia's inner circle. The only way to deal with them was to ignore them completely. If they wanted to keep on like this, I'd keep using their own tricks against them and keep fishing in troubled waters.

I went back into the broadcast booth and checked the watch on my wrist against the Beijing time shown by the clock on the wall. Noon was the "golden hour": fifteen minutes of *Public Toilet News Roundup*, fifteen minutes of *The Echo Wall*, which was mostly letters from or live interviews with listeners; and then a half-hour program called *Naughty Jokes from the Public Toilet*, hosted by Chongchong.

I sat up straight in front of the microphone and cleared my throat, waiting for Zhang Fan to give me the "on air" signal. I glanced over the prepared script. When I got the signal, I began reading at newscaster's speed: "This is International Red Star Radio's noon *Public Toilet News Roundup*. Today's top story: on the night of Mid-Autumn Festival, Public Toilet 1069, Beijing, Planet Earth, was the site of a robbery. The thief stole the only cast-iron faucet in the facility, causing the water pipes to burst. This in turn flooded half of Public Toilet No. 1069 and caused its neighbors to be overwhelmed by a toxic stench just as they were gathered together to enjoy watching the moon, leading several of them to come down with enteritis. The theft of the faucet was discovered by a passerby who reported it to the police. By the time this story went to press, the water situation at Public Toilet 1069 was under control, but the perpetrator's whereabouts are unknown. The authorities have assigned police detectives to the case, and all leads will be rigorously pursued."

I paused for two beats, then continued: "In other news: in Beijing this morning, 893 new couples officially entered into a state of marital bliss. The story of one of these couples caught this reporter's attention. The groom, who is from Chaoyang district, picked up the bride from her home in Fengtai in an enormous luxury automobile. Halfway from Fengtai back to Chaoyang, both bride and groom were suddenly and simultaneously overtaken by the call of nature. When the bride ordered the driver to stop in front of a pay toilet on the Third Ring Road, all the rest of the cars in the entourage stopped as well. The guests all tumbled out of their cars like silk off a spool and decided to turn the public toilet into a prenuptial nuptial chamber. One of the guests gave the bathroom attendant a 100-yuan note and told the groom to carry the bride over the threshold of either the Gents' or the Ladies' Room. The bride insisted on the Ladies' Room, while the groom held out for the Gents'. During the argument, the bride brought out her ultimate weapon: 'If you don't take me into the Ladies' Room,' she said, 'I'll divorce you right now.' There was nothing the groom could do but carry her over the threshold of the Women's Toilet. The guests were delighted and turned this particular public toilet into a party space. Someone blocked the entrance to the Women's Toilet and refused to let the couple out until they played 'Pass the Apple,' bowed to each other, drank wine from each other's glass, and so on—all the usual wedding reception fun. The whole crowd was ecstatic. According to International Red Star Radio's special correspondent Cuicui, this is the third pair of public toilet newlyweds in the history of Beijing, and the third public toilet wedding. The first two public toilet weddings occurred on October 2, 1949, and July 1, 1976, respectively. Reports have it that the first bathroom couple has already celebrated their golden wedding anniversary, while the second couple has emigrated to America, where they have long since given birth to two chubby and fair-skinned male American citizens, one of whom was conceived right there in the public toilet and is now a tall, strapping twenty-three-year-old, currently a benchwarmer for the NBA."

A quarter of an hour passed like water, and then it was time for *The Echo Wall*. I hadn't had time to step out of the broadcasting room when I heard Chongchong's buttery voice: "Dear listeners and friends, this is Chongchong. Thank you all for listening to International Red Star Radio's odoriferous programming during your precious lunch hour. This morning, two enthusiastic listeners from far, far away managed to find the station's address and express their adoration for our host Guigui and our brilliant new talent, Zhang Fan. Let's listen to a live field recording from them. May it help you wolf down your lunch all the more quickly." What he played next was nothing other than the recording of those voices shouting "Guigui, my alpha and omega." They had added a saxophone tune on a barely audible background track, which highlighted the sappy romantic air of the whole thing.

35

Guigui's admirer was from Urumqi and looked to be around thirty years old. He had the body of a mafia goon and the face of a vampire, which was emphasized by the two canine teeth that stuck out of his mouth. Looking down at him from the balcony and hearing his mutton-scented cries, we found him simultaneously terrifying and comical.

I didn't dare go downstairs to return to Jimenli. Zhang Fan said he didn't care if he were followed. He said, "Anyway they only recognize our voices, and they're all just like Lord Ye and the dragon—in love with an image. When they come face-to-face with the real thing, they go all soft."

Gripping me by the shoulders, he swaggered down the stairs with me. At the door to the building, Bai Yuejuan glanced briefly at him and ignored him completely. He deliberately kept on walking, saying in all sincerity, "I say, Miss Bai, it's getting dark out. Why are you waiting for that bum Zhang Fan? Go home already, and beware of sex maniacs." He pointed with his chin toward the guy from Urumqi. That little gesture didn't make a difference; the vampire from Urumqi was striding toward us. I wanted to run away, but Zhang Fan held fast to my right shoulder and wouldn't let me go.

The vampire grabbed the collar of Zhang Fan's jacket. Zhang Fan laughed in the face of such danger. He said, "Hey, punk, you got a problem. You can't tell the good from the bad from the ugly. I'm the one who's bringing Guigui to you. This here is Guigui." This time he used his sharp chin to point to his right, toward me.

The vampire's eyes were bright and beautiful, very mixed-race. When his gaze landed on my face, it was as if those two canine teeth had plunged into my jugular. My whole body trembled. He looked at me for a moment, let go of Zhang Fan's collar, moved his enormous body directly in front of me, and unambiguously stretched out a hand, saying, "I'm Genet. I'm a huge fan. Please do me the honor of shaking my hand!" Without thinking, I stuck out my left hand, which he shook warmly.

His hand was strong and warm and dry; in it I felt passion, sincerity, and yearning. I was almost moved by him. He made his request without letting go of my hand: "Ever since I first heard your show, I have had only one wish. Please help me fulfill it." I didn't dare open my mouth or utter a sound, for I still half-planned to pretend that I wasn't Guigui. But I found myself unable to deny it; I could not bring myself to lie in the face of such honesty. Directly behind him stood Bai Yuejuan, that ever-suspicious groupie who, even though she had already seen Zhang Fan, refused to recognize him. Compared to her, Genet exuded a strength that was impossible to negate.

Impishly, Zhang Fan asked, "What wish? Speak up, don't be polite. Guigui is a person who grants every request." Genet replied straightforwardly, "I just want her to go to the bathroom with me. The public toilet, OK?"

So I couldn't escape being identified as Guigui. And as a member of the Public Toilet Utopia, the one thing Guigui could not refuse anyone, regardless of whether or not he was a member, was to accompany him to the toilet. Genet's request would have seemed ludicrous to anyone else, but to a member of the Public Toilet Utopia, it made perfect sense.

36

The problem came at the bathroom door. I thought when he said he wanted me to go with him, he meant that for once in his life he wanted to boldly and openly enter a women's toilet. But instead he insisted on going into the men's toilet. His reasoning was that we should take advantage of the fact that no one could tell what gender Guigui was. Zhang Fan and I both argued that going into the women's toilet would also be taking advantage of this fact. But he insisted that that would not be fair to him; it was too risky, and anyway his wish was simply to go to the bathroom, not to create unnecessary problems for himself. From this it was clear that to him, the women's toilet was as sacred as an empress, a space that could not be violated lightly.

After several rounds of discussion, we still did not see eye to eye. Genet dug those canine teeth into his craggy lips, went silent for a moment, and then suddenly said that maybe it would be better to go back to his room at the guesthouse of the Beijing Office for Urumqi Affairs, and I could go with him to that bathroom, which was unisex. When I heard that, I grabbed his arm and steered him into the men's room, with Zhang Fan right behind us cheering me on. Neither of us dared to go into his territory. Once there, there was no saying what else he might want us to do with him.

In the men's toilet, he had me stand by the wall and immediately broke into a Xinjiang folk dance. In the light of dusk, his movements were very fluid, very professional, with a uniquely Xinjiang kind of humor to them. They attracted the attention of a kid who was taking a leak and a young man crouched over a squat toilet taking a dump, both of whom stuck their heads out to watch the action while they went about their business. I ran out and dragged Zhang Fan in, so we could watch the public toilet dance extravaganza together.

By the time Zhang Fan arrived, Genet was already in the first stage of a striptease routine: he'd taken off his jacket and was whirling it around his body. It looked like a piece of brightly colored silk being whipped around in a tornado. Just as the tornado reached top speed, he tossed the jacket away as if it had been carried off by a gust of wind, and it landed squarely on the guy taking a dump. He winked at the guy with his right eye and, having thus reached a cooperative agreement with him, began taking off the next item of clothing. When he had stripped down to his string-bikini underwear—which looked like it had come straight off the shelf of a men's porn shop—and a pair of leather shoes, his movements suddenly became softer, slower, more suggestive. I could tell at a glance that he was imitating the moves in the Filipino film *Sibak: Midnight Dancers*.

He danced for a while longer. After he had thoroughly excited our voyeuristic impulses, he asked me to piss in front of him, and to do it standing up, not crouching. I didn't have the slightest need to piss. Zhang Fan bravely offered to stand in for me instead, and the skinny kid who had just finished pissing, but who had evidently become quite inspired while watching the striptease, also offered to do the job. Even the guy crouched over the trough stood up and prepared to take my place, but Genet wouldn't have it. His reasoning was hard to refute: it was Guigui who had promised to go to the toilet with him, not some lowlife from who-knows-where.

I wanted to run away but met with opposition from all the heroes on the scene. They accused me of being ungrateful. When it was time for the hero to save the damsel in distress, not one of them ran away; they all stepped forward bravely. But when it came time for the damsel to save the heroes, how could Guigui be so indifferent to the desires of so many young, virile heroes? Then the skinny kid said something that clinched it. He said, "You have to get him to take off everything that can be taken off."

I stood pencil-straight by the side of the urinal, facing the wall with my back to the dance floor. I quickly undid my trousers and just as quickly lowered them below my butt. My intention was to attract their attention to my beautiful ass, so that Mr. Urumqi wouldn't ask me to turn around.

My strategy worked. The room went completely silent except for the sounds of cars flying by on the street outside like a backstage band. Using every ounce of skill in my body, I finally mustered a small urge to piss. Unfortunately, there wasn't much of it, so rather than extending itself lengthwise into a respectable stream, it came out in a disappointing dribble, turning my trousers and the floor into one big urinal. The real urinal, built carefully of ceramic tile by a skilled construction worker, was entirely forsaken by my urine.

Having thus failed to do justice to the physical and mental effort that the construction worker and architect had put into building that urinal, I didn't dare pull up my trousers with any great fanfare. As I slowly fastened my soaking-wet trousers, I heard a long moan; it was coming from the guy squatting over the pit. I turned my head toward him and saw a clean white light coming from the torch he was holding at his crotch; the beam it emitted was long, almost long enough to reach my back. Just at the moment that it seemed the beam would reach me, but before it actually did, it somehow suddenly took on mass and curved downward under its own weight, like a white snake soaring through the air to pounce on its dinner suddenly crashed to earth, and turned into a thick, sticky white stream. I clearly saw the stream splash onto a pair of dusty, travel-worn black dance shoes nearby.

The owner of the black dance shoes became aroused and removed the last remaining item that covered his body, revealing a thick, long, mixed-race penis and a luxurious patch of pubic hair, as well as a narrow ass covered with curly black hair and a deep, dark, mysterious ass crack.

37

As the five of us were leaving the public toilet, I heard a sobbing sound. At the door of the bathroom, in the golden light of dusk, I saw the skinny kid, his face streaked with lustrous tears. In that moment, I felt my heart enveloped by a warm strength; it felt like a piece of soft candy sucked on by a pair of passionate lips. That was my soul suddenly warming up, sucking in my heart. It was also sucking in the dusk, this kid, this public toilet, this public toilet performance, this piss and semen and tears. But what else was it?

38

Thus one dedicated groupie left, and left satisfied. Before going, he gave me his address and phone number in Urumqi and in all sincerity invited me to visit him at his home. He said he had a Uyghur father, a Han mother, a Russian wife, and twin sons all living at home.

The other dedicated groupie did not leave; she remained at her post with a perseverance that had already become quite institutionalized: she'd put in an eight-hour workday and take two days off. Neither rain nor snow nor gloom could keep her from her duty. Soft-hearted Zhang Fan would rush downstairs and show her his ID card to prove that he really was her idol and could satisfy any demand she might have. The drama of the whole thing was that she simply refused to acknowledge him, insisting that her idol certainly would have nothing in common with that group of schoolgirls; he was certainly not some teenage heartthrob.

On two separate occasions, both the sweet-hearted Chongchong and "the last virgin" Fan Tiantian tried to impersonate Zhang Fan, each declaring in Zhang Fan's name that he wanted to be Bai Yuejuan's Prince Charming. But their performances were judged, respectively, too frail and too smarmy, and both candidates lost that particular election.

But with me, Bai Yuejuan was friendly and familiar. Whenever she ran into me as I was coming in or going out, she would always call out my stage name. She, like the vampire from Urumqi, hadn't the slightest doubt that I was Guigui and Guigui was me. The weird thing was that she just believed that Guigui was Guigui; she didn't believe what it said on Guigui's ID card and ignored the fact that Guigui and Zhang Fan always came in and left together. She blindly followed her heart, no matter what it told her.

Given this experience, Zhang Fan and I both decided to change our names. I wanted a name that, when someone read or heard it, would sound nothing like me; the more different the name and the person, the better. Zhang Fan, in contrast, wanted a name that sounded exactly like him, so that when people heard it they would immediately imagine his face, and when they saw him or heard his voice would be able to guess his name.

39

One morning when it was snowing lightly, Bai Yuejuan didn't show up to her post on time. By coincidence, Na Long, who had promised to give me a lift to Wangfujing, didn't arrive on time either. I called his cell phone, which was on but constantly busy. Annoyed, I called a Xiali taxi, went home to Jimenli, went to bed, and slept. When I woke up, it was already dark out. Naked, I went to the window and saw that everything outside was white. The snow was still falling, and falling hard.

I'm one of those people whose passions are ignited when it's raining or snowing; the harder it rains or snows, the hornier I get. Na Long wasn't back yet; if I kept burning up like this, I was sure to blow a fuse. I called him, but it was after hours so no one answered the phone at the office. I called his cell phone, but it was still busy.

As soon as I put down the phone, it rang, startling me. I let it ring twice before picking up. The person on the other end was named Zhou Jie; he was a client of Na Long's company. He had come to deliver a box of navel oranges to thank Na Long for his help.

Soon the doorbell rang and Zhou Jie came in. He looked very clean-cut, and although he was wearing a heavy black overcoat and carrying an enormous wooden box, he had a sort of wispy demeanor about him.

I invited him in. His snowy feet left snowy prints on the floor, which soon melted into rings of dirt and water. He put down the box, looked back at his own footprints, and laughed shyly, making a gesture of wiping the floor with a rag. I told him not to worry about it; if he really wanted to do some physical labor, there was something more important he could do. He immediately took off his coat, revealing a coarse gray woolen shirt that was ragged around the wrists, which made him look like a fallen prince.

I led him into the bedroom and invited him to carry me over to the bed. But the room was small enough that we both just sort of fell onto the bed. I like to imbue every first night with a little atmosphere of the classics, so I asked him to go up, down, left and right, forward and backward, baby do it again.

I kissed him. On his face grew some sparse stubble, like a few tender shoots of grass; it made me think of a spring night. I asked him if he wanted to turn out the light, and he nodded. I am an aficionado of the much-celebrated "first night"; I like to remember each detail, each sequence, each beat, each rising and falling of the curtain. One day, if I ever want to become an author, I could write a book called *First Nights* that would leave Chongchong in the dust, not to mention the illustrious Lao Pao.

While we were taking off our clothes, I said to Zhou Jie, "When *First Nights* comes out, thirty million celebrities will be instantly washed up."

He looked at me, puzzled, stopped taking off his clothes, and began to kiss me passionately, ripping open my shirt and practically jumping on me; when he entered me he did so in a frenzy, as if he wanted to cudgel me to death. His hands clutched me, pulled me, tore at me; he bit me, sucked at me, head-butted me, kicked me, and kneed me, and from time to time he arched his muscular ass into me, scratching me with toenails and fingernails and reaching his tongue deep into my throat. In short, his "first night" style was completely out of keeping with his clean-cut bearing. Even the way he came was startling: he didn't come inside me but instead pressed his thumb on the tip of his dick like a child playing with a water pistol, so his come sprayed all over the place as if from a shower nozzle.

On our "second night," which followed immediately thereafter, I didn't let him do that. I said, "I'm on fire inside, I need a high-pressure hose to put out this fire." He teased me mercilessly, first pouring a mouthful of his saliva into my mouth and making me swallow it, and then pissing into me. While he was pissing I thought of a sweet rain falling and moaned about the rain and the dew and the sunshine and the moisture and other such doctoral jargon, until my mouth was so full I barely even had time to empty it.

That is how I became friends with a total stranger. A box of navel oranges and a series of fire drills quickly turned two strangers into friends who could ask favors of each other.

It was a snowy, windless night; Zhou Jie lay asleep under the covers while I peeled oranges and ate them under the lamplight. I wanted to say a few words to the city outside my window, including some lectures worthy of a PhD. But before I could open my mouth, the telephone rang, loud and insistent.

40

Na Long was in Qingdao. Bai Yuejuan had decided he was her Zhang Fan and had had him kidnapped. Her goal in kidnapping "Zhang Fan" was very specific: she wanted him to go see her only son and to teach him, from a young age, how to love and respect the individuals who used the women's toilet, so he wouldn't grow up to be a male chauvinist.

Na Long got back his cell phone SIM card when he had only half finished the job. He met the seven-year-old boy, a clever little devil who knew how to do math and manage silk production—a real precocious type. Bai Yang was not as favorably disposed to Na Long as his mother was. And as for his knowledge of women's toilets, he was clearly a step ahead of Na Long. He told Na Long that International Red Star Radio should invite him to be a special guest host of a program called *The Anthropology of Girls' Toilets*. Na Long declared again to Bai Yuejuan that he was not Zhang Fan; he could not take on the responsibility of educating the next generation. Bai Yuejuan thought he was just playing hard to get, so she held a banquet in his honor and made her male secretary take him to a sauna. On the phone, Na Long didn't tell me about the sauna episode. I guess he must have been accompanied by a soft, juicy woman.

I urged Na Long to turn Bai Yuejuan's strategy against her and play the part of Zhang Fan to the hilt. As for his knowledge of the anthropology of women's toilets, he could listen to International Red Star Radio's rebroadcast and could go online to check the Public Toilet Utopia's email, zizien@fm365.com. "If necessary," I told him, "you can download some articles, and if you read straight from the text, you might be able to fool the kid. But whatever you do," I said, "don't come back home."

At the phone terminal in Qingdao, Na Long sounded hesitant. He said that the real Zhang Fan should go to Qingdao in his place, since forcing him, Na Long, to pretend to be a devotee of public toilet culture was a little like raping his personal philosophy. I explained patiently to him that it was useless, that Zhang Fan had long since revealed his identity to Bai Yuejuan, had even shown her his ID card, but she simply refused to recognize him. In her heart she had her own Zhang Fan, even if it was entirely the wrong person.

Na Long, discouraged that his cries for help were in vain, dejectedly asked me where and when International Red Star Radio's program on the anthropology of women's toilets would be rebroadcast. I told him it was at 97.4 FM, every Monday morning beginning at 6:30, rebroadcast every Wednesday afternoon at 14:30. He sighed and said, "From the looks of it, I'd better go ahead and accept the week's salary." I asked him what week's salary. He said that Bai Yuejuan had hired him to be Bai Yang's personal tutor for US$1,000 a week. I cheered and ordered him to drag it out a little longer, to stay in Qingdao a few more days, or better yet, a year or even two. "If you get too starved for sex," I said, "I can fly down to see you. Anyway, we'll have plenty of cash."

41

I came up with reams of new stage names for myself: like Moon Phase, Solar System, Infinite Sky, Baby Universe, Big Bang, Black Hole, the Uncertainty Principle; like Little Fish, Big Bird, Kafka Bug, Eastern Phoenix, Butterfly Fan, Dragon Mother, Jurassic Fossil, Bali Tiger; like First Empress, White Lady, Fifth Little Maid Wang, Miss Liu San, Little Miss Rice, Pockmarked Granny; like Classical Love, Post-Alien, and Meeting at Orchid Court. But when the inner circle of the Utopia voted, each one was executed by firing squad in its mother's womb or in the cradle.

Zhang Fan was more conscientious than I. The names he came up with for himself were generally more dignified, not as farcical as mine. Of the six groups, ABCDEF, he himself preferred the D group: this included allusions to Tang and Song poems, such as Like a Dream, Water Melody, Slow Slow Song, Eight-Rhyme Ganzhou Tune, and Partridge Sky. Aware of his painful experience with names that did not correspond to reality, the members of the commune were quite conscientious about voting for his new name. After three very serious discussions, groups A, B, D, E, and F were discarded, leaving just group C, which led to another discussion: it was between Cat Level, Dual Mouse, World of Enduring Honor, Good Girl, and Gradebook. I was leaning more toward Cat Level, Chongchong liked Good Girl, Fan Tiantian was partial to Dual Mouse, and Wang Xiaoyi thought Gradebook captured the reality of Zhang Fan perfectly, since there were places in which he was

100 percent, and others where he was failing or even zero. Eventually everyone agreed that Zhang Fan's stage name should be changed to Gradebook.

Originally at this point the whole thing could have been declared over and done with, but the instigator, Zhang Fan himself, began making waves. He declared that when he came up with the name Gradebook, he had only been thinking about it in terms of excellence; he hadn't thought of Wang Xiaoyi's interpretation. He said that "failing" and "zero" did not reflect his style of work in the least, and thus the Public Toilet Utopia's vote for "Gradebook" should be immediately nullified. Otherwise, if the name were used publicly, it would only do harm to the reputations of both the station and himself.

This proclamation left everyone at a loss. Finally, Chongchong suggested that the whole idea of Guigui and Zhang Fan changing their names should be scratched and the two instigators punished: Guigui should be fined one day of sweeping out the broadcast booth, and Zhang Fan fined one dinner out for everyone.

By a margin of two against three, Zhang Fan and I were in the minority; we had no choice but to follow the majority. Not only did we not get to change our names, we also had to use our own money and labor to pay our fines. While I was sweeping out the broadcast booth, I muttered angrily, "In the norms and practices followed by the Public Toilet Utopia, the majority should have to follow the minority! We should be the opposite of the hegemonic, hierarchical mainstream society! If our method of decision-making plagiarizes the mainstream, then what kind of utopia are we? Might as well change the whole name of our club. Public Toilet Shmu-topia! Public Toilet Doo-doo-topia! Public Toilet Twinkl-opia!"

Zhang Fan somehow found a way to pay for dinner for the whole crew on his empty wallet, and during the hot pot meal repeated to the rest of the table what I had been saying as I swept: if we didn't adopt the system of the majority following the minority, we might as well call ourselves Public Toilet Shmu-topia, Public Toilet Doo-doo-topia, Public Toilet Tinkl-opia. Because he made a gesture of falling water when he said "Public Toilet Tinkl-opia," I knew he meant something different than, or had misunderstood, my "Public Toilet Twinkl-opia." Since the whole discussion was just a matter of explaining the principle of the thing to the others in the group, I never expected to enter into a discussion with him about such details. But, being ever so sensitive, he guessed my disapproval from the look I gave him. After we'd drunk and eaten our fill, he asked me to take a walk with him around the outer wall of the Workers' Stadium, crunching the remnants of the winter snow beneath our feet as we looked at the moon.

42

Guigui: The moonlight on a winter night is even colder than the night itself.

Zhang Fan: It's ice.

Guigui: Natural ice.

Zhang Fan: Who says? It's man-made ice.

Guigui: You're misreading me again.

Zhang Fan: What do you mean "again"? What's wrong with "Public Toilet Tinkl-opia"?

Guigui: I said "Public Toilet Twinkl-opia," as in "Twinkle Twinkle Little Toilet" or "a twinkle in my eye."

Zhang Fan: I was emphasizing the sound of pissing. Tinkle tinkle tinkle. That's right in line with your wish.

Guigui: What wish?

Zhang Fan: You've already forgotten? You really are a hypocrite. What did you say in your opening address for International Red Star Radio?

Guigui: I didn't say anything.

Zhang Fan: Didn't you say that Beijing was the capital of the world?

Guigui: Yes, I did, but what I meant was, the population is so huge, the city so immense, the merchandise so plentiful, and the pool of talented homosexuals so vast.

Zhang Fan: And didn't you also say "May your number twos always pass smoothly and your number ones flow forever freely"?

Guigui: I'm going to say that on millennium New Year's Eve, not before.

Zhang Fan: You said it three whole years ago.

Guigui: Nonsense! I only thought of it this year, and I won't use it for another two.

Zhang Fan: I beg to differ. Anyway, "tinkle tinkle" is the sound of number one flowing freely; without "tinkle tinkle," your number one isn't going anywhere.

Guigui: Who says that's the sound of number one? And who said that taking a piss is "number one," while taking a dump is "number two"? Who made up that order?

Zhang Fan: As verified by Zhang Fan at the east gate of the Workers' Stadium, in the circus, the clowns come out at the start of the show, so they're called Act One, while the lions and elephants only come out during the main performance, so they're Act Two. By the same logic, pissing is often a prelude to the main show: it's quicker and easier and takes less time than taking a dump, so that's why it's called number one. So if you take some time to examine the question, you see that the nickname "number one" has a real structural basis to it. Then again, they say humanity has always had a phallic complex. You're a PhD, so you must know that "phallus" means penis, and the penis represents reproduction. Same for the vagina. So, continuing in the same vein of analysis, we see that nicknaming the urine that comes out of the reproductive organs "number one," rather than promoting it to the status of the "main performance," is actually a way of diminishing its importance and therefore of deconstructing phallocentrism.

Guigui: So according to your theory, the nickname "number two" is actually a way of celebrating and raising the status of the anus.

Zhang Fan: That's right. The anus has always been neglected by the reproductive-centric view, because it can't make babies.

Guigui: So anal sex has also been denigrated, considered inferior to vaginal intercourse, even seen as abnormal or perverse.

Zhang Fan: And so the term "number two" is a way of reclaiming the anus. "Number two" usually takes a long time and a lot of effort, and produces a solid substance that is dark in color and has a strong odor. It also occurs less often than urination, and that which is rare is more valuable, right? So on this basis we may reconstruct the status of a devalued organ and the action of that organ. In this way we may argue that the ranking system used in toilets, and the language that is used to express it, stands in opposition to the culture outside of toilets and is a contestation of official ideology.

Guigui: No wonder anal sex so often happens in bathrooms.

Zhang Fan: And so when I say Public Toilet Tinkl-opia, it may be different but accomplishes the same thing as your Public Toilet Twinkl-opia.

Guigui: In that case, when you say Public Toilet Doo-doo-topia, you must mean "doo-doo" as in "shit."

Zhang Fan: Exactly right.

Guigui: But my Public Toilet Doo-doo-topia is a reference to singing a song, "doo doo doo," while on the toilet. Doo-doo, doo-doo, doo-doo, doo doo doo . . . don't you know the song?

Zhang Fan: Doo-doo, doo-doo, doo-doo, doo doo doo . . .

Guigui: So which "doo" are you using now?

Zhang Fan: I'm not telling.

Guigui: If you won't tell, I'm going back. You can enjoy your man-made ice moonlight by yourself.

Zhang Fan: No, don't. I always get especially lonely on moonlit nights, and I especially need you. You're my flesh and blood.

Guigui: Who is?

Zhang Fan: Do you know why people make love?

Guigui: No.

Zhang Fan: To connect their flesh and blood to the flesh and blood of another person.

Guigui: What's so great about that?

Zhang Fan: That's another very philosophical question. You've heard that once upon a time, humans were double what we are now, with four legs, four arms, two pairs of eyes, two noses, two mouths, four ears, four breasts, four balls, and two penises?

Guigui: Yes, I've heard that. Plato said it.

Zhang Fan: Do you believe it?

Guigui: "Believe" is a strong word.

Zhang Fan: So how do you explain desire?

Guigui: That's a gigantic question, bigger than the heavens, bigger than the ocean. In other words, it's bigger than any number two and deeper than the deepest asshole.

Zhang Fan: That's why I want to ask you.

Guigui: Then you have to buy me a drink at a bar. I want a gin and tonic and a glass of tequila. I'm parched.

Zhang Fan: I say, my dear, we've just finished our lamb dinner. I'm clean out of cash.

Guigui: Don't you know how to earn some quick cash?

Zhang Fan: You want me to sell myself!

Guigui: It's such a quick and easy way to make a buck.

Zhang Fan: You obviously don't love me. You only love Na Long.

Guigui: I obviously love you very much, otherwise I wouldn't be talking in such depth with you about making love.

Zhang Fan: What if, in the process of selling myself, I end up falling in love instead?

Guigui: Then I'll settle the bill myself and go on back to Jimenli alone. You're free to do your own thing.

43

We walked all the way to a sumptuously decorated bar somewhere behind Sanlitun. I very professionally sussed the location of the bathroom and then found a table for four and sat down. From my seat, I could look to the left and see what was happening at the bar and to the right and see people going in and out of the bathroom.

Zhang Fan and I were both new to this bar. As we entered, found our table, and sat down, all the regulars stopped talking and stared at us with bright eyes, as if we had just discovered a new vein of precious minerals and they were all prospectors hoping to find a treasure.

Given my sharp senses, I could tell right away that they were quietly becoming excited, or more accurately were preparing to pounce. They were pointing not at me but at Zhang Fan. A young guy with a dancer's body walked flamboyantly past us over to the bathroom door but didn't go in. He whistled, echoing the decadent sounds emanating from the sound system behind the bar, his body gently swaying, his eyes never leaving Zhang Fan's face.

A short, good-looking young man with a red bookbag slung over his shoulder came over and asked if he could sit at the empty seat at our table. I nodded and he sat down, a half-empty bottle of Corona in his hand. They say that Corona is a gay drink. When the waiter arrived, I changed my mind and ordered a Corona instead of a gin and tonic. Zhang Fan took stock of the situation, confidently judged the price he could get for his body, and extravagantly ordered a vodka and orange juice.

The good-looking young guy struck up a conversation with us. He said he was an actor, that he had been in the television series *Don't Cry at Seventeen,* and that he was a second-year student at the Central Academy of Drama. I had seen that series because one of our loyal listeners had a major role in it. The personage sitting in front of us had never once appeared in any of the episodes. He also spoke Mandarin with a thick southern accent, while the Academy of Drama and the Acting Department at the Film Academy required their students to speak perfect standard Mandarin, as Fan Tiantian had demonstrated to us repeatedly.

I asked him his name, and he said it was Wu Wei, "Wei" meaning "raging fire." It didn't sound like a fake name he made up on the spot. In his southern drawl, Wu Wei began telling a story. He said that in his hometown of Huaiyin, he had had a lover who was like an older brother to him. They had been together since he was fifteen, until two years ago, when the lover had had to get married, and Wu Wei had tried to kill himself by slashing his wrists. He showed us the scar on his left wrist. I reached over and caressed it lightly; he pulled it back as if my touch had hurt him and, eyes shining with tears, said, "I've been waiting for him ever since. He said he would get a divorce and come find me."

As Zhang Fan drank his vodka, the rims of his eyelids began to turn red. He said, "If I were that kind of person, I would never marry." At that, a tear rolled down Wu Wei's face. Wiping the tear dry, he raised his beer bottle to Zhang Fan and finished off the whole thing. Zhang Fan asked the waiter to bring an empty glass; he mixed some orange juice and vodka in the clean glass and gave it to Wu Wei.

I saw the dancer guy at the bathroom door brandish his fist at Wu Wei. Wu Wei smiled briefly and carelessly at him, and the dancer opened the bathroom door and went inside.

Wu Wei drew out a pack of Zhongnanhai cigarettes from the red bookbag slung over his shoulder. After offering them to Zhang Fan and me, he stuck one in his mouth and then bent over and lit it from the red candle that was burning in a glass on the table. His smoking posture was adept and graceful, clearly very practiced, quite at odds with his youthful age and appearance.

In a small cleared space in front of the bar, some people started a drag show. I went over to watch, and two fierce-looking, short-haired women came over and stood close behind me. One of them touched me rather boldly. I looked back and smiled at them, a very erudite smile, hoping that would get them to lose interest. I never imagined that an erudite smile was just the kind they liked best. They closed in on me from both sides and swept me over to the bar. I peered back at our table and saw Wu Wei already sitting right next to Zhang Fan, both of them looking enraptured. Maybe it was the vodka.

Before the drag show was over, I extricated myself from the circle of people with the excuse that I had to go to the bathroom. At the door of the bathroom,

I met the handsome young dancer. I wanted to pass in front of him, but with a brilliant smile he stopped me and asked, "My dear, would you like to buy me a drink?" I looked back and saw those two sturdy short-haired women following me. I gestured back at them with my thumb and said to him, "Sorry, man, someone's already buying me a drink. Next time." He dropped his smile and collapsed against the wall in such a dejected way that it made my heart ache.

44

The bathroom was unisex, and it was only one room, perhaps meant to attest to the bar's androgynous frame of mind. There was a single squat toilet, one urinal, and a faucet mounted high but not too high, for cleaning up. The walls were covered with cartoon strips and scraps of paper with jokes written on them in Chinese and English. Above the urinal was stuck a small hawk, with one claw extended down and outward, saying to whomever was standing there, "I can make your python soar!" Above the bolt on the bathroom door, a blue fairy with laughing eyes was saying, "Hurry up and lock the door, I've already followed you in." On the frame of the mirror above the sink was a pornographic picture of two young men; each one had a little bubble coming out of his mouth, crammed full of the words "oh oh oh oh."

I first impatiently drained the entire Corona I had drunk into the urinal. This time the stream was plenty strong, so I didn't wet my pants. Then I squatted over the toilet and sent down my lunch of KFC homestyle chicken, roll, french fries, ketchup, and mashed potatoes, leaving space in my intestines for the lamb dinner. After I had been working at this latter task for a while, someone knocked at the door, a panicked knock that sounded like whoever it was couldn't hold it in any longer. The sound made me think of the time I took the train to Guangzhou.

Whenever I take the train I get constipated. It usually happens in the morning, just at the rush hour when all the passengers wake up and need to use the toilet. The time I went to Guangzhou was before they had the new high-speed trains, so the trip took two days and a night. After the first long night, my constipation wasn't too bad; I only squatted in the toilet for forty-three minutes, and when I opened the door, there were only thirteen people waiting in line. But after the second long night, I squatted in that toilet until my legs ached. The constant knocking at the door only made my problem worse. As soon as I managed to gather a little strength in my rectum and was about to give it all I had, a knock at the door would startle me and all that strength would instantly evaporate. I imagined that every single passenger on that train car must have been lined up outside the door. The more I thought like that, the more anxious I became; the more anxious I became, the more bloated my intestines got and the tighter my anus. Suddenly the lock on the door shot open, and in rushed an attendant. He hastily pulled out his tender white penis and pissed out the window over my head. When he was done, he smiled apologetically at me, showing his little canine teeth. When he left, he locked me in again. With my left arm I grabbed the railing, and with my right I reached around to feel my back, but there wasn't even a drop of piss on me. Full of admiration for his pissing abilities, I finished my excretory exercise, in a satisfactory but not particularly enjoyable manner. The odd thing was, when I came out of the toilet, there were only three people waiting in line. The young canine-toothed attendant told me, from under his oversized hat, "I sent everyone who was waiting in line to use the toilets in other cars."

The bar, however, was not a train car; it didn't have that rhythmic rocking feeling, and the people who came here weren't as purposeful as those on the train. No, it was more like a waiting room at the train station, where everyone waiting for the train was young, and it was always evening, and everyone was waiting for the overnight train, and if they didn't manage to get on it was no big deal, it wasn't like they were going to miss any life-and-death occasion, any once-in-a-lifetime celebration. As I straddled the toilet, I heard through the door the strains of the song "Tonight's Loneliness Makes Me Beautiful," and began swaying ever so slightly, my soul eclipsed by some kind of narcissistic beauty. As for the rapping on the door, I simply ignored it, so as not to allow anything to interrupt the continuity of this beautiful feeling. Tonight's loneliness makes me so beautiful, please don't interrupt my grief and my joy. Tonight's beauty makes me so lonely . . . I quietly hummed along, letting images appear before my mind's eye, one after another. In all the forcefulness of their appearance and disappearance, I couldn't tell if these images were memories, mirages, dreams, or pure fantasy. Following the rhythm of the song, they flew by in riotous profusion only to fade into the distance; a new one would emerge in the foreground only for another to send it flying noiselessly into the abyss—a hidden abyss, where there seemed to exist a black hole, a black hole of dreams and illusions.

45

Those two women "kidnapped" me and took me back to their place. One of them made tea to sober me up while the other one poured liquor to get me drunk. The tea wasn't strong enough to fight the liquor, especially Black Label whiskey, and soon my limbs were soft as cotton, my mind fuzzy, and my lips numb.

In this state, I vaguely felt my clothes being peeled off my body like skin, but because it didn't hurt, I didn't yell. Skinless, I was carried into a white boat that was full of clear water, but there were no fish; fish don't like water that is too clean because there are no microorganisms in water that is too clean, no vegetation, no little water bugs. I began to laugh, laughing at my own stupidity for ever having expected there to be fish in pure water, mineral water, distilled water. Humans without their skins were the fish here; my appearance would give them new life and strength. Lifeless mineral water, distilled water, pure water, here I come; I am a fish, I am a fish aficionado of first nights.

The voice of a person or a fish said to me: I am too, I am too, I am a fish aficionado of first nights, I also like first nights, my beautiful first nights. Thus, into the white-sailed boat swam two fish, two mermaids who were very beautiful, but their beauty was overwhelming, not the least bit gentle. The boat was rocking back and forth, about to tip over but not quite tipping over. My PhD-trained mind thought, *I've taken a white steamship to the land of the mermaids. Their territorial waters are narrow but very pure and clean. If they didn't stir it all up, there wouldn't be any blood; I don't know if it's my menstrual blood or theirs. Once I smell it I'll know.* Some tonguelike grass wrapped itself around me, and I felt hot, and said to I don't know whom: "You snakes, either let go of me or lock me up tight, I can't take it much longer." The snakes' tongues paid no attention to my plea, they kept coiling around me, slippery and oily, neither tighter nor looser than before. I said, "You tongues, don't, don't lick me there, is that any kind of place for snakes to lick?" No one paid me any mind; the tongues became harder and licked faster. They made me dizzy, my whole body started burning, and the fire had started from my crotch and my lips. I was afraid my pubic hair would get scorched, but I didn't smell anything burning. I told myself, *OK then, burn on. It's not me, it's the mermaids.*

A voice said to me, "Please remember us, we're your good little Sisters, not mermaids."

I felt sad that my body was on fire. I started crying and sobbed out, "My dear listeners and comrades, this, this is, International Red Star International Ray-Radio, I am your host Guigui. Do you remember Guigui? Your host Guigui doesn't care if you remember or not, in any case it's time for the *Public Toilet News Roundup*. Tonight the wind is blowing at force two or three; the south wind will change to a north wind and blow at force four or five, there will be scattered snow showers, with a low of minus three centigrade and a high fever of above zero, a fever that will burn uncontrollably. Your host Guigui's temperature is very high, it's a high fever that could easily spark a fire. Would the relevant authorities please take every precaution to fireproof the public toilets, to prevent forest fires that could destroy the delicate ecosystem of the public toilet . . ."

46

When I got back to the Utopia's base camp at the east gate of the Workers' Stadium, it was already 2:00 in the afternoon. The radio station was broadcasting, as scheduled, a public toilet symphony concert, and Zhang Fan, looking exhausted, was curled up on a chair sound asleep. He looked like a monkey. Fan Tiantian glanced over at me; in one movement, Chongchong scooped up the chair and Zhang Fan in it, and carried them toward our banquet hall.

What we called our banquet hall was actually our shared-use kitchen and dining hall, which we usually used to eat instant noodles, box lunches, or boiled eggs. Well aware that I had erred, I obediently moved a folding chair into the banquet hall and sat down in front of the door. Wang Xiaoyi solemnly announced, "The Sixth Plenary Session of the Fifth Representative Assembly of the Public Toilet Utopia is now in session." Fan Tiantian announced the agenda: 1. A public hearing regarding the dereliction of duty charges brought against Zhang Fan and Guigui; 2. Changes to the programming schedule and hosts; 3. Discussion of the strategy for corporatizing and internationalizing our media outlets.

Because Guigui and Zhang Fan had gone AWOL, they had both missed live broadcasts that they were supposed to have hosted, causing irreparable damage to the station's reputation. This was judged a serious crime that could not be defended and had to be punished. Wang Xiaoyi suggested that Guigui and Zhang Fan, but especially Guigui, should be taken off the air and given a position behind the scenes, working on editing and program logistics, for a probationary period. Zhang Fan and Guigui didn't have the cheek to contest this decision. The first item of business on the agenda was thus quickly closed.

The motion that Fan Tiantian take Guigui's place as program host passed unanimously; the names of the three programs *Morning Public Toilet News*, *Noon Public Toilet News*, and *Evening Public Toilet News* were changed to *Daily News*. All other arts and entertainment programming would be broadcast under the name *Tiantian's Studio*. Fan Tiantian came up with the idea of a new program called *Public Toilet Inspirations*, which would feature interviews with notable artists, politicians, military men, educators, diplomats, sociologists, and other famous figures who would be invited to discuss their views on the public toilet as a space of inspiration and creativity. The meeting passed this measure unanimously. Zhang Fan's companion program to *Anthropology of Women's Toilets*, *Anthropology of Men's Toilets*, would be taken over by Wang Xiaoyi, and from here on in, Zhang Fan would make a clean break with anthropology; that field would belong exclusively to Wang Xiaoyi.

The third item on the agenda had an unexpectedly bold and decisive outcome: we all unanimously agreed with Chongchong's suggestion to create an "International Red Star Radio Public Toilet Culture Media Corporation." The CEO and vice CEO would be Chongchong's mother and father, who were living in America, and Chongchong would be general manager. The corporation would comprise the radio station, a newspaper, and a magazine. Although the idea of establishing a television station and a school was as yet premature, that plan would be included in the long-term corporate objectives. Guigui suggested that the newspaper could be called *Red Star Radio Weekly*, while the magazine could be named *Oh Toilets*. Zhang Fan seconded Guigui's suggestion. The other three were wary of the two criminals, and quashed the idea unanimously. Fan Tiantian suggested that the newspaper be called *Urination and Defecation Weekly*, and Wang Xiaoyi suggested that the magazine be called *Brilliant Toilet Blossoms*, while Chongchong changed it to *Brilliant Public Toilets*. These ideas were knocked around endlessly, until finally a measure was passed, with a majority in favor and a minority opposed, that the official name of the newspaper be *Urination and Defecation Weekly* and of the magazine be *Brilliant Public Toilets*.

Suddenly it seemed that the future prospects of public toilet culture were very bright indeed. Everyone's wintry hearts warmed and surged like the summer sea. Chongchong decided to put out a table full of instant noodles to celebrate.

47

It wasn't until I had a chance to see Zhang Fan alone that I learned the ending of his story in the bar.

Zhang Fan had been caught up in misconceptions from the beginning. He thought that whoever made the first approach was the customer, while the seller should be the one to sit tight, knowing his selling price. As a result, he thought the good-looking kid, Wu Wei, was a sex-starved potential buyer, and all those complicated and beautiful stories he told were intended to win the seller's heart, making him more than happy to sell his body and mitigating any mistaken notion he might have that being bought and sold was somehow dirty.

This I had not expected. Had I known, I would have enlightened him in advance.

But once Zhang Fan had set foot in the wrong direction, he only strode deeper and deeper into trouble. When he saw me carried off by those two mermaids, he had originally planned to straighten up, step up, and, in view of the handsome, willing big fish that was sitting right in front of him, give me up and go after the fish.

Big Fish Wu Wei told him, "Whenever I'm out on the street, there's always someone following me. If they manage to catch me, they always say they saw my fantastic performance on *Don't Cry at Seventeen*, give me fresh flowers, ask for my autograph, maybe even take out a camera and ask to have their picture taken with me as a souvenir."

Zhang Fan was about 70 percent drunk. He mistily eyed the male beauty in front of him. His heart trembled. He couldn't believe his luck was so good that even when he was preparing to sell his body, he would happen upon such an attractive customer. After he had drunk some more, he told Wu Wei the whole story of the Public Toilet Utopia, to justify a higher asking price.

Although he was drunk, Zhang Fan was alert enough to sense that when Wu Wei heard the story of the Public Toilet Utopia, a sly look came over his face as if he thought the whole thing was a tale out of the Arabian Nights. To prove that the story was true and not something he had invented on the spot, Zhang Fan drunkenly dragged Wu Wei over to the bar and asked the bartender to switch the sound system over from CDs to the radio. When the dial was set to 97.4 FM, over the airwaves came the light music program broadcast by Beijing Music Radio every night.

Wu Wei laughed generously, like an older brother. It was unusual to see such an expression on his face. It put Zhang Fan on the defensive, and he began to wonder if the bartender was playing tricks on him. He himself slipped behind the bar and expertly twisted the dial. It spun around under his fingers, but the speakers refused to play the sounds he knew and loved so well. There was no voice saying "This is International Red Star Radio."

Sinking back into his seat, he suddenly began to doubt his own experience. International Red Star Radio didn't exist; he had never actually encountered such an entity, had never heard its voice late at night; it was all just an imaginary memory, more imagination than memory; it was the shadow of an illusion.

The bar seemed less noisy than before. On the faces of customers who were talking in whispers or who already had somewhere to go was reflected the waning light of the night outside. Wu Wei leaned lightly on the table and quietly reached his left hand out toward Zhang Fan, who was seated on his left, swatting at his crotch like he was swatting at a butterfly that had just landed on a flower—a gentle gesture, as if he were afraid of squashing the butterfly. In his drunken stupor, Zhang Fan thought, *Finally, some cash is coming my way.*

He half-drunkenly moved a bit closer to Wu Wei, so the height of the table and the shadows in the corner would better hide their actions. There was no longer any distance between the two beautiful young men. They huddled close, shoulder to shoulder, cheek to cheek beneath the light of the candle, each of them converting youth and beauty into renminbi, each of them viewing the other as a money tree waiting to be shaken. For Zhang Fan, it wasn't a big tree; as long as a pile of small change came raining out of it, enough to pay for the drinks he had just consumed, that would be the price of one erection. This was an improvised price, one that could fluctuate depending on the time and place. When he got it up, one hand wasn't enough to hold it; it was like a glossy, robust pigeon that can only be held fast with both hands, and which even then tries to stick its head out, crying coo-coo-coo, singing its unpleasant song to the blue sky outside its cage.

Zhang Fan's pigeon sang and sang until its throat got sticky and its voice trembled. In the end it got choked up with thick spittle and sent its song upward out of its throat. As it solemnly spit, he grabbed his glass on the table and began to sing in a repressed voice: "Tonight's loneliness makes semen beautiful..."

His song and its song came to an end. Wu Wei's hand, sticky with the fluid of the song, appeared in the candlelight. He said to him, "My dear, it's time to settle the bill." Intoxicated in two different ways, he answered, pleased, "If you want to settle the bill, go ahead and settle it." He drunkenly looked at the leftover alcohol on the table. Wu Wei stretched his song-soaked hand out in Zhang Fan's face, waved it, and said: "Mister, maybe you aren't familiar with current market prices. So let me tell you. A hand job is 300, blow job 500, winter swimming 1,000." He asked, curious, "Winter swimming?" He said, "You're not ready, maybe next time." He shook his head, saying, "No, you're wrong." The other said: "I have to go wash my hands. Let's settle the bill first, that's one of my rules." So he drunkenly called the waiter over. Wu Wei's sticky hand rifled through his pockets but only came up with a single 1-yuan coin.

Wu Wei took his ID card with him and left Zhang Fan a phone number and one sentence: "ID card, deposit 300 yuan." The bartender wouldn't let Zhang Fan leave and was going to make him work to pay off the drinks. Luckily a fat, pale middle-aged customer offered to pay for the 630 yuan worth of drinks so that Zhang Fan could get out of there. Of course, this time he really did have to sell himself, winter-swimming style, which not only paid for the drinks but also got him his ID card back from Wu Wei. After he and Wu Wei had exchanged the cash for the goods, Wu Wei suggested a winter-swimming freebie. He said no thanks.

48

"This is International Red Star Radio, and you're listening to *Tiantian's Studio*.

"I'm Tiantian, and this is the *Public Toilet Inspiration Hour*. In the next hour, I'll be playing you some recorded programs written and edited by International Red Star Radio's own special reporter, Fan Tiantian. Today's program is called 'Careers in the Toilet.'

"Good evening, comrade listeners. I am sociologist Wang Li."

"Mr. Wang Li, hello. I am Fan Tiantian from International Red Star Radio."

"Hello!"

"Have you heard our programs?"

"Yes, I have. I'm a frequent listener."

"Which is your favorite?"

"My favorite is a program hosted by Guigui—what's it called, it's a news program, *Public Toilet Karma* or *Public Toilet Storybook* or something."

"*Public Toilet Storybook* is hosted by Chongchong."

"Sorry, I'm confusing them."

"Why do you like the programs hosted by Guigui?"

"It's just a feeling, there's no special reason."

"Surely there must be some reason? Why don't you summarize it for us, using some inductive reasoning. When I was at the Central Academy of Drama, the teachers always said that no matter what you do, inductive reasoning is key."

"Let's put it this way: I find Guigui's voice very attractive. Why is that? It's very androgynous. It embodies a certain disdain for, even rebellion against, the clear gendered division between men's voices and women's voices that has been prevalent for hundreds or even thousands of years. I like things that are a bit rebellious."

"And?"

"And the program Guigui hosts is very philosophical. I'll give you an example. That fable about the Roman emperor going to the toilet, that was very philosophical."

"That fable is called 'Blind Men Grope the Emperor.' When I was a student at the Beijing Film Academy I acted in a short play called 'Blind Men Feeling the Elephant.'"

"Mr. Fan, you've studied at two different universities?"

"More than two! I also studied at the Shanghai Theatre Academy, which we called 'SHAT' for short."

"Congratulations!"

"Thank you! Now let's get down to business."

"Fine."

"I've heard your mother and your wife say that since you were a child, and still today, you've been fascinated by public toilets, especially those that are numbered 3-681, 6-757, 9-430—what we call food-court toilets . . ."

"I'm sorry, what is a 'food-court toilet'?"

"Oh, that's our professional terminology."

"It wouldn't refer to a public toilet with stalls selling kebabs and seafood stew, would it?"

"No, no, not at all. We use the term to differentiate between toilets that have walls dividing the space into stalls and those that have no dividers but just a row of squat toilets."

"I understand. So 'food-court' refers to the completely open style of public toilet. In that case, it's true, I am fascinated by them. I don't know if Mr. Tiantian shares this fascination?"

"Yes, yes, of course I do."

"In that case, may I ask why?"

"It's intuitive, just a feeling, no special reason. And yourself?"

"I find them well-ventilated and easily surveyed at a glance; the cross breeze is good, and one's relations with one's neighbors are excellent. Everyone squatting there can light each other's cigarettes, and if one runs out of toilet paper he can get a little bit from someone else, thereby avoiding any source of grievance to the anus. And one important thing is, one can feast one's eyes on things that are rarely seen in other situations."

"You could achieve this last objective at a public bath too."

"You could say that, yes. But in point of fact, in terms of convenience and speed, there is simply no comparison between visiting a public bath and visiting a public toilet."

"How so?

"First, in Beijing, there are public toilets everywhere. A few years ago there were even more. Every ten steps you could find a small outpost, and every hundred steps you could find a garrison—they were as thick as trees in the forest. This is why the rate of sex crimes in Beijing has always been lower than in any other major metropolitan area. It used to be even lower a few years ago."

"Why is that?"

"I'm sure you know why, Tiantian, I've no need to tell you. Thick as trees in a forest."

"In other words, when there's an outpost every ten steps and a garrison every hundred, people don't dare act out right there on the street. This is one reason. Another reason is that all sex acts that take place in outposts and garrisons are protected by law; they don't fall within the purview of criminology. So Beijing's excellent sexual public security has long been an example to the world."

"This is also an important sign of Beijing's status as capital of the world."

"Second, from an environmental point of view, because there are so many food-court public toilets in Beijing, there are few blind corners in them where flies, mosquitoes, maggots, and worms can breed; that's why travelers, city folk and foreign guests alike, used to always take care of their business there. In Beijing, the number of people who use public toilets must be ten thousand times greater than the number of people who use public baths."

"I agree."

"Third, when you're going to a public bath you have to bring a towel, soap, shampoo, as well as beverages both hard and soft, and you have to make sure to go when the facility is open—you can't just go wherever and whenever you want, whenever you're taken by the urge. Also, going to a public bath costs money, and the baths themselves use an enormous amount of energy, water, and fuel, thus representing an unnecessary burden both to the individual and to the natural environment."

"I agree. Going to a public toilet is so much better. Urine washes out the urinary tract; urine itself cleans the waste products out of the body, while simultaneously producing fertilizer that directly benefits soybeans, sorghum, paddy rice, corn, apples, pears, dates, and tomatoes, and indirectly benefits chickens, ducks, geese, pigs, dogs, cats, cattle, sheep, and horses, as well as endangered species."

"Fourth, people who work for a living can make money by going to the toilet, whereas they have to pay to go to the public bath . . ."

"What do you mean?"

"... Going to the toilet takes up work time, which means that even while you're not working, you're still collecting your salary. So isn't going to the toilet the same as someone just giving you free money?"

"Brilliant! Brilliant!"

"However, we must face reality: public toilets do have a negative influence on the development of a society. First, the more toilets a people or a nation has, the longer people will spend in them, which leads to an increase in passivity and slack work habits; and the more of these idlers there are, the more the entire nation will suffer from inertia. The old proverb says it best: put a lazy donkey at the grindstone, and it will spend a lot of time pissing and shitting. There are more public toilets in Beijing than stars in the sky, many more toilets than there are fast-food restaurants or elementary schools. Although this is admittedly convenient, it also encourages laziness and lethargy and leads to frequent urination, diarrhea, and constipation. This is why some scholars suggest that the public toilet question should be studied from both sides."

"So what you're saying is that we should build more public baths, to stimulate the masses' desire to go to the baths, and that this would make them more diligent at their work?"

"Well, that's close to what I mean, but not exactly. But this is a public toilet radio station; are we allowed to talk about public baths?"

"Of course. The public toilet is really just a focal point, one which naturally gathers and refracts the collective life of all humanity, the sensibilities of the times, the accretions of history, even our dreams. Recently, the station has been considering introducing a new program called *Public Toilet Dreams*."

"I'd gladly listen to a program like that."

"Mr. Wang, could you please talk a bit more about your views on public baths?"

"Certainly. In recent years, we have seen an increase in the practice of charging money to enter public toilets in Beijing. This has, to a certain degree, inhibited people's enthusiasm for going to public toilets and has led some lower-income citizens to become aware of the vice of overly frequent toilet-going. At the same time, pay toilets are intended to provide a source of funding for the city's economic development, especially in the area of environmental and hygienic services; they are also intended to provide new employment opportunities for laid-off workers.

"Consider this rough estimate: Beijing has a total population of 5,690,000. On average there are 0.15 public toilets per resident, meaning that there are approximately 85,350 public toilets in the city. If each of those toilets began to charge a fee, there would be 85,350 laid-off workers with a new source of employment.

"I've heard that many Beijing residents feel it's beneath their dignity to work as public toilet attendants."

"So then we should build more public baths. Public baths have a greater market awareness and a greater market value than public toilets. You can say they are a public space, but in fact they take money out of the pockets of working people; so the only sense in which they are really public is that they provide a space in which the public can get naked and watch others get naked at will."

"Do you mean that public baths stimulate consumption?"

"Exactly. Think about it: saunas and rubdowns, pedicures and spas, massages and sexual services—the entire industry today is nothing like it used to be. When I was a boy, five cents would get you into a public bath. Then it went up to ten cents, then thirty cents, then fifty, then 1 yuan, and these days 10 yuan is considered inexpensive, while 200 or 300 is not unheard of. Of course, this question also has two sides to it. In terms of consumption, public toilets can't hold a candle to public baths, but at the same time, in terms of labor turnover, nothing compares to the pay-toilet system. Public baths require professionally trained, skilled employees: the capital investment they require is young, good-looking, and knows how to give massages and pedicures, how to work the muscles of every part of the body. And they need a lot of them; one public bath requires eight or ten such young employees. This is why my next study will examine the possibility of transforming public toilets into public baths . . ."

49

Na Long came back to Jimenli full of sunshine and sea air. He didn't ask me to pick him up and wasn't as exhausted as I thought he would be. Seeing him, it was as if a tropical beach had suddenly extended itself up here into the Beijing winter. With an intentional double entendre, I asked him whether or not he had gone for a winter swim while he was down at the Yellow Sea. Imitating Wu Wei, I asked him, "Mister, how much does it cost for one winter swim?"

He looked blankly at me and responded: "It's free." I burst out laughing. He looked perplexed.

I held out my hand toward him. He put US$5,000 in it. I said, "We're rich! We should put the money toward our great new enterprise." So we went together to the Shuang'an Shopping Center and bought a Sony Handycam. He said he wanted to use it to film me sleeping and to film us each time we made love, so that when we got old and couldn't do it anymore we could watch a different film every day, to keep up with our old custom of making love every day, so we could spend a youthful old age.

When we got home, he first arranged lights on our big bed—those popular lights that give off a very orange glow—and then found a position for the Sony from which he could film at a downward angle. He set up the camera, turned it on, and rolled around on the bed alone, as if he were making a one-man film. He rewound the tape and watched as the little screen played back the time and actions he had just wasted. When he saw himself rolling around, he excitedly yelled to me, "OK!"

We tangoed into the picture, singing our own tango music. Our flesh was the turntable, the record, and the needle; it was both the amplifier and the music; we were the dancers, the actors, director, and cinematographer; at the same time, we followed the director's intentions, dancing from the floor up onto the bed. My movements were slow and erudite; his were quick and repetitive—a difference that reflected our different professions and upbringings. We danced from the bed back down onto the floor, sometimes moving out of the picture, then moving back in. I took off his tie and shirt and threw them off camera, like in a classic porn flick. Facing his muscular chest, his sturdy shoulders, and his hard, reddish black nipples, I was barely able to control the rhythm of the dance; but I had to relax and control it. Alternately controlling desire and giving in to desire is the key to the rhythm and structure of a porno flick. I used the tango music to say to him: making a porn movie tastes of both the sea-blue sky and a wild night on an isolated island.

50

Having that Handycam was like having a new kind of cultural capital. I risked betraying the Public Toilet Utopia and, holding this new pair of eyes, wandered alone down the avenues and alleyways of this world capital, Beijing. Whenever I found a public toilet, I would sneak inside, raise the eyes inside my bookbag and film for a while. Sometimes I filmed people: standing, squatting, taking off their pants or skirts, fastening their skirts and pulling up their pants; people in the act of pissing, just before pissing, just after pissing; people grunting, gasping, pushing hard; squatting and smoking a cigarette, squatting lost in thought; small children, old geezers, beautiful young maidens, stout middle-aged women, thickset men, wiry youngsters, white-haired grandmothers, giggling middle school students, young wives who poured their hearts out to each other while peeing. Sometimes I filmed scenes empty of people: external shots of public toilets, their number plates, entrances and exits; interiors of "food-courts" and stall dividers, the filth in urinals, the lines formed and the sound made by streams of piss; piles of fresh shit, the shapes and colors of squat toilets, the walls and the ceilings, the windows and the window lattices, the bare light bulbs, the flies, the mosquitoes, the maggots, the graffiti and slogans on the walls, the notes arranging rendezvous, the baskets for toilet paper.

The first public toilet manuscript I filmed went like this:

> "Person on person
> Flesh inside flesh
> Rocking up and down
> Boundless joy—
> "Hint: an action.
>
> "On woman's body is a river
> The water flows all year long
> Grass grows lush on the banks of this river
> Where monks come often to wash their hair—
> "Hint: a quality.

"If you can guess the answer to this riddle, please send it to Ouyang Xiao, PO Box 24-5, Beijing University of Aeronautics and Astronautics. Generous prizes available. All intelligent, beautiful, capable individuals, male or female, are welcome to claim a prize.—Ouyang Xiao, waiting by a tree stump for a rabbit."

These riddle-poems were written in blue ink with a soft calligraphy brush on the inside door near the window of the third-floor men's room at the

Outpatient Clinic of the Third Hospital of the Beijing Medical School. They were arranged such that the first riddle formed a kind of matrix above, and the second riddle another matrix directly below the first, with a space in between. The two matrices were very neat; the third passage, however, was neither in the form of a poem nor in the form of a matrix; it looked like a cheerleading squad running pell-mell after two regular army units. Ouyang Xiao's soft-brush calligraphy was not at all bad; I reckoned he was a student or professor at Beijing University of Aeronautics and Astronautics. That he was a man was obvious. Tacked up next to the text was a picture of a three-dimensional penis drawn onto a coordinate system; the coordinates mapped out the length, the diameter of the glans, and the diameter of the shaft: length, 21 cm; glans diameter, 7.5 cm; shaft diameter, 5.7 cm. In my analysis, the drawing had a strong industrial flavor to it; Ouyang Xiao was probably a gifted engineer, as well versed in draftsmanship as he was in classical poetry.

As I finished filming the text and its drawing, I had the sudden impulse to send in the solution to the riddle and to meet this riddler. I wrote out the answer with a soft brush on a piece of *xuan* paper, in calligraphy that deliberately imitated Ouyang's. I addressed an envelope but left off the return address; I included only my pager number, so as to avoid the danger of being harassed at home. I stuffed the letter into the back pocket of my jeans and walked out onto the street. The stiff envelope chafed against my butt cheek, so I took it out of my pocket, looked at the name, address, and stamp on the front, and suddenly felt like I was on trial. The crimes I was indicting myself for: dereliction of duty, using my official position to seek personal gain, and violating professional ethics.

What were my professional ethics? I would not sleep with people I interviewed or filmed, just as a teacher cannot sleep with his/her students, a doctor cannot sleep with his/her patients, directors cannot sleep with their actors, actors cannot sleep with their fans, and animal trainers cannot sleep with their animals.

I tore up the envelope and threw it into a trash can. I would not send the letter to Ouyang Xiao; let him be an already-discovered secret, the opening scene in a cliff-hanger that would remain unfinished. Perhaps he would thus disappear forever; perhaps one day he would once again float to the surface, like dirty oil or pure oil on water, affecting one's perception of the mouthfeel of life.

51

The Sony distanced me for a while from the Public Toilet Utopia. When children get a new toy, they have to play obsessively with it until the first addiction has passed; only then can they emerge from that state of intoxication. But while they are immersed in it, their parents' "do this" and their teachers' "don't do that" only strengthens their will to defiance and intensifies their obsession. I was like that: as soon as I was done with my work, I'd sling my bookbag over my shoulder and leave the "radio tower." Hiding in the bookbag was my beautiful, beloved new toy. We were as inseparable as form and shadow, the camera and I; our silhouette could be seen in every street-side public toilet in town. It seemed that the streets we took and the places we went were not my own ideas; I would simply follow it wherever it wanted to go, accompany it to see whatever it wanted to see. I was its vassal; my hands and body were its captives; it led me along like an animal on a tether.

It brought me a new career but also a peck of trouble. All told, it got me into trouble seven times—not too many, not too few. In honor of the seven deadly sins, I call them my seven deadly disasters.

The first disaster: a public toilet on the southwest corner of the Baizhifang Bridge. Daytime. Protagonist: a middle-aged migrant worker. With him I adopted a hidden-camera approach. I squatted on the toilet opposite him, aimed the camera hidden inside my bookbag at him, and, when he wasn't looking, set up the shot as a close-up, filming a special feature on masturbation: the motion of his hands on his tool, the expression on his face. The architecture of this particular public toilet was quasi-food-court in style: waist-high walls separated each stall from its neighbor, but the stalls had no doors on them. Thus, there were two rows of five doorless stalls facing each other: very convenient for face-to-face observation. While I was filming this protagonist, his eyes were "filming" the words and pictures scrawled on the half-walls to his right and left. His X-rated performance lasted so long that my squatting legs started to ache and go numb, and I had to lift my ass and straighten my legs briefly before getting back into position to continue filming.

The disaster happened just after he ejaculated and left. After he was gone, I hitched up my trousers and went over to the stall where he had been squatting to film the graffiti he had been looking at. He turned back and, in a thick Henan accent, asked me coldly, "Are you from a TV station?" Panicked, I immediately denied it: "No!" This denial both disappointed him and pissed him off. He said, "If you're not from a TV station, why were you filming me? Are you making a VCD to sell?" I denied it again. He stretched out a rough, semen-covered hand and said, "Give me 100 yuan! I thought you were from a TV station and were going to put me on CCTV's evening news. I saw right away that you were filming me. If you're going to make money off me by selling VCDs, you have to pay me first!" I obediently gave him the only 100 yuan I had in my wallet. It took me three hours and forty minutes to get from Baizhifang Bridge back home to Jimenli on foot.

The second disaster: the Qiran Hotel in Taoranting District. Nighttime. Zhou Jie had been discovered by a talent scout and was starring in a film called *Men Men Men Women Women Women*. One scene took place in the Qiran Hotel, and they needed someone to act opposite him, so he paged me to come over to the set to play a character named Cuicui. In the film, Zhou Jie's character's name is Power of the West; he arranges to meet Cuicui in the coffee shop on the right-hand side of the hotel lobby. When they meet, it turns out they are both wearing the same dark-red wig and are both dressed in the same androgynous, cutting-edge style. The extras in the hotel scene were instructed to have an exaggerated reaction to the pair—staring gape-mouthed, or pretending it was beneath them to notice, or finding the whole thing curious and somehow charming. Power of the West's purpose in meeting Cuicui is to try to sell her a new product called the Power of the West. This new product's functions include firming the vagina, constricting the anus, numbing the receptor nerves for pain and pleasure, and thus doing away with orgasms and the exhaustion that follows. Cuicui is a prostitute by trade as well as something of a leader among unlicensed sex workers; it is her job to try out new products that might improve the work efficiency of her brothers and sisters in the trade. Upon meeting, they each order a cappuccino and then get up and walk out, leaving two steaming cups of cappuccino in the frame. The next scene shows Power of the West going into the women's toilet with Cuicui, where he helps her stuff the Power of the West up her vagina and anus so she can test its efficacy. If it is as miraculous as he says it is, they'll close the deal right then and there and will maintain a long-term business relationship; if it doesn't work at all, or if it is only marginally effective, Power of the West will pay Cuicui for her services as a test subject in a dangerous experiment. The disaster happened in the women's bathroom. I had hidden the Sony in my breast pocket in advance, cleverly thinking that I would document the making of this film. As I was taking off my skirt, I secretly focused the camera on Zhou Jie and the rest of the crew on the set. When the director chirped "Cut!" the log keeper discovered there was an extra prop on the set. The Sony was thus discovered and confiscated, and the scene filmed again; so once again I had to drop my skirt, while Zhou Jie took the hemorrhoid suppository that represented the Power of the West and rammed it up Cuicui's ass. After they finished filming the scene, the production crew penalized me: they fined me 1,000 yuan and told me my name would not appear in the credits. I had endured two days and two nights of filming only to see my expectations of a 1,000-yuan profit and my chance at the Golden Chicken Award for Best Supporting Hooker go up in smoke.

The third disaster: Dongdan Park, daytime. There's a fake rock hill in the park, and along one side of the hill is a kind of secluded corridor that is shady and green and filled with lovers or people looking for lovers. Those looking for lovers can be seen frequenting the pay toilet on the western end of the corridor so often that one might think they all had enlarged prostates. This time I went with the flow, dressed as a man with a platinum earring in my left ear, not brilliant enough to dazzle the eyes, but neither too dull. I handed over my twenty cents and went into the men's public toilet, using the eyes in my bookbag to film two pairs of men engaged in oral sex. One pair was a graying older man servicing a beautiful youth; the other pair was a beautiful youth servicing an ugly, rough-looking type. When the older man was finished, he came over to me; in order to escape him, I had to get out of there. The second time I paid and went in, the middle-aged attendant gave me a knowing smile—a smile which showed that he knew the "secret" of that bathroom but which also conveyed a certain sense of anticipation and the gratitude of a businessman. From the looks of him, it seemed that he liked it when people came back often. It crossed my mind that I should be happy for him: each night as he cleaned out the public toilet, the garbage he collected must have been very protein-rich, richer perhaps than any food sold in a supermarket; so among all the public toilet attendants in the city of Beijing, he could be ranked highest—a veritable professor of public toilet attendants. This time when I went into the toilet, I only filmed a guy squatting over the pit toilet, shooting me a sidelong glance. The third time I went in, someone followed me. I didn't turn around but heard his footsteps, like a cat's. I calmly stood in front of a urinal, and as soon as I undid my trousers, a hand reached out and equally calmly touched my ass. I turned my head and saw a kid who looked like he must have been in middle school, half a head shorter than me, with hair cropped short along his neck and temples like a schoolboy, a tuft of bangs dyed blond, and cool eyes. There was no one else in the room. I slowly moved his hand away; he didn't resist, but when I let go of his hand, he once again calmly stretched it out, this time letting it come to rest inside my cotton underwear. His hand was cool to the touch, his fingers like five small snakes; his middle and index fingers played lightly along the lips of my anus and then slipped inside. I laughed, saying, "I'm still just a chick." He laughed and, in a voice that was still changing, responded, "So am I." I said, "So show a little respect and remove your hand." He caught the slight menace in my meaning and responded in kind, "Oh yeah? What's in your bag, you want to take it out and show me?" This stopped me cold: he must have already discovered that I had been secretly filming. I didn't want the tape to be stolen, the magnetic ribbon ripped out or torn, or the whole camera seized or smashed. I had once seen something like that happen, in the famous West Palace, the huge public toilet on the western side of Tiananmen Square. He ordered me to lower my head and kiss him; I obeyed. At first, I looked at him while I was kissing him; he stopped and ordered me to close my eyes. I obeyed again, though I kept my eyelids open slits so that I could secretly see what was going on. Through these slits I could glimpse his face, which was very dark and still had the roundness of a child's face; the sharp edges and corners were just beginning to take shape. When he opened his heavy-lidded eyes, his gaze was unusually resolute. He used his middle finger, first finger, thumb, and fourth finger to "gang-rape" me; the last to join in the rape was his pinky. It was sharper and pointier than the other four, and tore my skin a few times, drawing blood. It was so sharp it had a fingernail like a razor.

52

After provoking these three disasters, I had planned to take a bit of R&R. I never imagined that I had set into motion something I couldn't stop or that my luck could be so rotten. After careful strategizing, I decided to print up some business cards for myself and, always thinking of the greater good, quite selflessly used the name of International Red Star Television, conferring on myself the titles of Host, Public Toilet Special Programming, Senior Writer-Director, PhD in Media Studies, etc. When I had finished designing a prototype of the card, I took it to the Vast Skies Quick Copy Shop in Xiao Xitian, where I ran straight into my fourth deadly disaster.

The manager of the copy shop was a woman in her early fifties who ran the place with the help of her twentysomething son. By rights I should have given the prototype of the card to my beloved Na Long, but I didn't want him to see the pretentious titles I had invented for myself, so I came to Vast Skies instead. After the manager had pocketed the money and given me a receipt, she smiled and asked me: "You're Guigui? You're quite the celebrity around here. You host that public toilet show—it's my son's favorite." Thinking that I had happened across another die-hard public toilet fan, I showed off a bit, asking in response, "You mean *Public Toilet News Roundup*, or *Public Toilet Topics*?" She looked back at her son sitting docilely in the corner and said, "Neither. Xiaogang, what's the name of that show you like?" The young man named Xiaogang spoke quietly from the shadows: "*Public Toilet Fairy Tales*." I laughed a laugh that must have sounded very condescending and said, "Oh, that program. It's mostly children and children-at-heart who like that one." His face sank back into the shadows thrown by the curtain. His mother, out of my line of vision, said, "Yes, that's the reason my son is still just a big baby."

As I was leaving, I felt a strange sense of unease. Three days later, this feeling was confirmed.

That day I went to pick up my business cards, and behind the counter sat a plainclothes policeman. He was smoking, chatting, and laughing with the manager. At first I thought he was her husband or her lover. I handed over my receipt; he looked me up and down, took out a box of business cards, thrust them at me briefly, and asked with a twitch of his eye, "Are you the illustrious Guigui?" Hamming it up, I nodded and bowed from the waist: "At your service." He said authoritatively, "Come with me!" I still thought it was all playacting, so I responded in grand dramatic style, "But sir, where are we going?" He waved impatiently at me, wrinkled his solemn brow, came out from behind the counter, and stepped outside the shop.

The manager's melancholy son stood up from the shadows. He didn't move out of the shadows, but the glint in his eyes was like light reflecting off water. Like a massive wave surging in my direction, some of it rippled over me, while the rest of it flooded over the wall, the door, the window, and the view outside the window. I left him, left that little shop, and went into the teahouse across the street.

His name was Li Ming. That's what it said on his work ID. He said the police station had received a complaint from the public and had sent him to investigate. I ordered a hot chocolate for him, hoping that this feminine beverage would soften his authoritative air. For myself I ordered a cup of Mingqian Maojian tea, with its immature, bitter flavor. I said, "Some friends and I are preparing an installation for an art exhibit. My installation is a TV station, and during the performance I'm going to hand out business cards to the visitors." He asked me, "Why did you use the phrases 'Red Star' and 'Public Toilet' in the same title? Are you intentionally making a mockery . . . ?" I explained that this was avant-garde art, and avant-garde art always throws completely unconnected things together, allowing people to interpret it however they want.

He kept one of my cards and gave the other ninety-nine back to me, saying: "I might page you at any time to see what you're using these business cards for. Don't even think about not responding; otherwise, watch out!" He got up and walked out without paying for his drink, leaving me sitting in an insipid shadow. I felt like I had been blacklisted.

53

The fifth, sixth, and seventh deadly disasters have all assumed the character of photographic negatives in my memory—negatives that I have never dared develop. I'm afraid of seeing their original colors and shapes. I'm hoping that if I hold on to them and keep them under wraps they will "accidentally" go all damp and moldy, the emulsion will dissolve, the images lose their fidelity, and past events become distorted beyond all recognition.

Please forgive me if I can't tell you about these three most strange and terrifying disasters. Please forgive me, dear listeners and friends.

54

While I was wallowing in the Sony and the disasters it brought me, Fan Tiantian initiated the expansion of the Public Toilet Utopia. Given Chongchong's friendship with Na Long, he nominated him as the first candidate. Fan Tiantian had another candidate, a smooth-talking, emaciated artist and angry young man whose name, Wang Yumian, combined his father's surname, Wang, and mother's surname, Yu. Wang Yumian's background was similar to Fan Tiantian's. He was born in Xinyang, Henan Province, had danced in the

Railways Song and Dance Troupe, and then not long after getting into the Beijing Dance Academy had been kicked out, after which he drifted aimlessly among Beijing's eight main art schools, scrounging food, board, and sexual partners, be they male or female. Before being recruited into the Public Toilet Utopia, he had been dancing in the chorus of the Dongfang Song and Dance Troupe and had traveled with the troupe to Congo, India, Mauritius, Saudi Arabia, Costa Rica, Israel, and Ukraine.

Recruiting Na Long into the club was entirely Chongchong's idea; I knew that Na Long himself had no interest in it. When it came time to vote on the new member, I voted for Wang Yumian. As a result, Wang became a member of the Public Toilet Utopia by a margin of three in favor and two against, and Na Long avoided entanglement with "the organization" by a margin of two in favor and three against.

To celebrate the addition of the new member, we had a little party in a private room at the Shengchang Nightclub's KTV; Fan Tiantian paid for the drinks with money he had gotten from a sponsor. Wang Yumian performed for us a dance piece he had choreographed himself, called "The Urination Dance," set to the music of the "Dance of the Four Cygnets" from the Tchaikovsky ballet *Swan Lake*. In the dance, he imitated in an exaggeratedly joyful but true-to-life manner the movements of men, women, old folks, children, dogs, tigers, lions, donkeys, horses, yaks, elephants, and mice urinating, which made the people who had voted against him blush with shame and made those who had voted for him especially proud.

55

I invited Wang Yumian to Jimen District to do a live video recording of the "Urination Dance." I also encouraged him to create a "Defecation Dance" but suggested that the choreography should not simply remain at the level of imitation: it should strive for a deeper spiritual meaning and more philosophical themes. It should evoke, like Socrates, the spiritual dimension of physical activity and excavate, like Freud, the relationship between the unconscious/ego/instinct and sitting and squatting, defecating and playing with excrement, anal sex and anal pleasure. Wang Yumian promised to start researching it the very next day, so that as soon as possible he would have created a new, philosophically inclined dance piece.

I reminded him that Freud had written several letters to a person named Fliess on the topic of the repressed, dated May 31, September 21, and November 14, 1897. I gave him a copy of a section of the last letter, for his reference. The translation of that section reads as follows: "To put it crudely, the memory actually stinks just as in the present day the object stinks; and in the same manner as we turn away our sense organ (the head and nose) in disgust, the preconscious and a sense of consciousness turn away from the memory. This is *repression*. What, now, does normal repression furnish us with? Something which, free, can lead to anxiety; if psychically bound, to rejection—that is to say, the affective basis for a multitude of intellectual processes of development, such as morality, shame, and the like. The whole of this arises as the price of extinguishing (actual) sexuality."

Wang Yumian said, perceptively, that he already understood that the structure of the movements in his Defecation Dance should be designed around a central axis formed by the head being in close proximity to the thighs and should eschew upright postures and the possibility of anything noble. I added, "Yes, walking upright is the root of humanity's becoming noble, the root of discrimination. Because of upright walking and the popularity of modern toilet and bath facilities, the human sense of smell is lacking one significant stimulus—the rank odor of our own bodily functions. Thus, the human spirit is becoming increasingly depressed, its existence increasingly meaningless and tedious. The only way to awaken and restore vitality to the human spirit is to surround and fill our senses of sight, hearing, and smell with the stench of the human body."

56

Na Long's and my "last night together" happened as the Sony observed our sexual journey, after Wang Yumian created his Urination Dance but before his Defecation Dance.

It was a beautiful spring night. Zhang Fan and I came out of the bar and walked over to the base of the twenty-two-story tower. It was late, so the elevator had stopped working, and I suddenly became terrified of the dark corridor. Coquettishly, I asked Zhang Fan to accompany me upstairs. He threw his arm around my waist and walked me up the stairs as if he were carrying a piece of freight. Our ascent was powered by the force of the alcohol and the night, of youth and the good life. So were the passionate kisses we exchanged all along the way.

When we got to the twenty-second floor, I didn't have the heart to send Zhang Fan away alone, so I invited him in. I thought Na Long would have long since gone to sleep, so I opened the door with my key as quietly as I could and didn't dare turn on the light. Suddenly a naked figure embraced me from behind the door, and before I could cry out in surprise, sealed two burning hot lips over my mouth. He carried me across the living room and tossed me onto the bed under the flickering lights of the bedroom. He turned on the Sony, stripped off all my clothes, kissed me, caressed me, entered me; our movements were just like they had always been, nothing had changed. I moaned. Zhang Fan stood in the shadow of the doorway. He looked bigger than usual, his gaze as limpid and lovely as starlight.

He pulled it almost all the way out and plunged deep inside again; from the edges to the center, from the surface to the core, from the outside in, from the shallows to the depths of the ocean. It was like a smooth, powerful shaft of light, piercing the darkest recesses of my body from behind, penetrating my whole body, setting it on fire, like crystalline ice and like cleansing fire. I felt the brilliant light and the dark night all fade into a uniform dimness; there were only our bodies, our bodies linked by that shaft of light, as luminous as the sun.

After a particularly furious thrust, he suddenly stopped for about three beats; then he let out an uncharacteristic roar and released a powerful jet of heat energy into every cell in my body, opening my every pore. I could not help shouting for joy; my cry was sweet and bountiful.

I fell into the ravine of sleep.

When I woke up, the shaft of light had disappeared, and disappeared forever. In its place was a shaft of muscle and flesh. It moved in and out of my body slowly, gently, mellowly, in time with the rhythmic sounds of heavy, euphoric breathing. When I closed my eyes, I felt like the character Kika in the Almodóvar film, sound asleep as a thief with a physique like an ox stole into her home. Half-dreaming, half-awake, a sweet syrup of passion stuck my eyes shut; my blood turned to honey, flowing sluggishly through my veins, tingling, tickling, producing a dense and dissolute thrill. From his rolling, gyrating technique and his penchant for jabbing and thrusting like a boxer, I was hazily aware that it was not Na Long. I let out a songlike moan. I opened my eyes, and the dappled light thrown by the lamp revealed Na Long's cold stare. I turned my head to one side and saw clearly that the person behind me was Zhang Fan.

Sometimes his eyes were closed, and sometimes they were open; when they were open, his gaze fell directly upon Na Long's face.

When my consciousness finally awoke fully and took in that cold stare, it felt that it should somehow hide, that my body should dissociate itself from the body joined to it from behind. But my body refused to cooperate; it was still asleep, still intoxicated, unwilling to leave the space of that viscous, beautiful dream. It was not until well after Na Long had turned off the Sony and quietly left that the shaft of flesh shrank and softened and broke away, and that once-beautiful space became empty and meaningless.

57

Na Long sent a brief letter by courier service. It read: "Goodbye forever, my love. My heart is aching, and my dick swollen. When you move out, page me on my pager. Na Long. Today."

I didn't have much to pack. We had bought most of the stuff in the apartment together, using his money, so it was only right to leave it for him. The only thing I took without permission were the videotapes we'd made with the Sony, and because there was no time to make copies of them, I just divided them in two and took half. I packed a knapsack, for the last time swept the floor of the room clean of every last speck of dust, and left him a letter full of all kinds of good wishes. I didn't cry while writing the letter. That was a miracle. From that point on I thought of my own death. I constantly imagined being on death's door; like distilled water, death permeated my life with a boundless darkness. People may spend their entire lives on crowded, bustling streets, but death is like the wilderness, like the cold moon, primitive and deserted, lonely and eternal. Before I die, I thought, I will pour out all the tears that are filling my heart, so not even one teardrop will be left to return with me to that eternal desolation.

I picked up my bag as if I were departing on a long journey to distant lands. For the last time I looked around this room where I had known only joy, no pain, and bid farewell to my first love. Suddenly my heart twitched and then struck a wild blow at my soul. The pain pumped out my tears like a clear-flowing spring, and they bathed the final moments of my youth.

Before walking out the door, I took the key to the apartment off my key chain and put it on the refrigerator. As I left, I locked the door behind me. I skipped the elevator and made my way into the dimly lit stairwell. I descended slowly, as if I were descending a ladder from the heavens down to earth. In a flash, thirteen years. Thirteen years of love were now nothing more than a memory, nothing more than the past. A past that would never again have a future. The wellspring of my tears washed clean its roots, which were already history.

I dried my tears before exiting the ground-floor door to the building. The springtime afternoon sun was hiding outside that door, as if lying in wait. Under it, the city's torrential tide of humanity surged and rushed, always onward. In fact, they weren't really moving forward or backward; they were simply running in circles around the Second, Third, and Fourth Ring Roads. Yet they were still rushing like the current of an endless river. As I emerged from the building, the sun dried the ashes of my tears, imprinting them on my heart like a photographic image of the domain of love. Then I walked toward the crowd, unable to keep my steps from faltering.

58

"It's the Public Toilet Comedy Hour, Public Toilet Comedy Hour, Public Toilet Comedy Hour!"

"Greetings, dear listeners. Please forgive the strong flavor of urine and urine alkali in my voice today. I apologize! Just as a person's urinary tract gets full of gunk if he or she does not wash it for a long time, so Guigui's speaking tract has gotten rusty because it's been such a long time since Guigui has spoken with you about the laughs and lives of public toilets.

"For a long time now, your survival has depended on the multifarious sounds of my voice, just like flowers depend on sunlight, ghosts depend on life, and fantasies depend on reality. I fear that my recent neglect of my career in public toilet broadcasting may have caused many among you to spurn life and go down the road of suicide. I also fear that as you grow in the absence of my attentive care and my nurturing in the ways of the public toilet, you may stray from the righteous path and become the sacrificial lambs of bureaucrats and politicians, cultural elites, mass consumerism, fashionmongers, or purveyors of witchcraft and evil ways.

"Next up, we have two amusing anecdotes about public toilets.

"The first comes from a film called *Who Has Ever Seen the Wild Animals Day*. This was an independent film that never saw widespread distribution on the mainland. It was directed by Kang Feng, a graduate of the Directing Faculty of the Central Academy of Drama. The main character, Jiangzi, played by actor Wang Xin, is a young man of few words and a very sexy body. The story takes place outside a public toilet in Tiantan Park, and it goes more or less like this: Jiangzi and his friends Laoda, Wolfman, and Monkey are rambling around the city during their summer holiday, when they happen to ramble into Tiantan Park. Jiangzi goes to the public toilet by himself to take a leak, and there he meets a middle-aged man. In the light cast by the flame of his cigarette lighter, the man takes a good long look at Jiangzi's member and then gropes his ass. Wolfman calls this a homosexual encounter. Jiangzi, horrified at being called a homosexual, steals an exercise rod, dons a mask, and goes to seek revenge on the middle-aged man. The ending, though, has a twist: as soon as the man sees the masked, club-wielding Jiangzi, he drops dead. This scares Jiangzi so much he runs off to the reservoir on the outskirts of town and, panicked, refuses to go home. He seeks out a lawyer, is examined by a court-appointed physician, and in the end is declared innocent but mentally ill, with a mild case of obsessive-compulsive disorder.

"This is clearly an example of black humor. Our next story is what we might call red humor. It's one that Guigui heard on the train to Haila'er.

"During the War of Resistance against the Japanese, the Japanese army had spread throughout the three northeastern provinces, which they, in a spectacular bit of wishful thinking, preferred to call 'Manchukuo.' In the areas under occupation, the Japanese made every effort to promote the Japanese language, just like the Nazis tried to make everyone in occupied Europe speak German. In one small town, an elementary school teacher who hoped the Japanese would appoint him mayor was especially diligent in studying Japanese and practiced constantly, even when he went to the bathroom. As it happens, he wasn't very good at languages, and he was at that age when his memory was in decline, so whenever he learned a new word, he had to repeat it out loud at least 5,000 times. Now, just when he began learning the word *oishii* (meaning 'delicious'), a new principal, Japanese name Shimamura Masaki, took over the elementary school where he taught. Shimamura didn't have any real interests outside his work; his only passion was for food—in other words, he was something of a gourmand. On his first day on the job, he heard, emanating from somewhere deep inside the school, a hoarse, overexcited kind of bellowing, a voice repeating over and over again: *'O—-i—-shi—-i, o—-i—-shi—-i.'* Dying of curiosity, the principal left his office, passed by the sounds of the pupils reading aloud from their texts, and finally came to the wooden outhouse at the back gate of the school. He found that this repetitive hymn of praise for a well-prepared meal was in fact emanating from inside the outhouse. *'Oishii, oishii, o—-i—-shi—-i, o—-i—-shi—-i.'* The principal burst into the outhouse and saw the schoolteacher bellowing at his own shit. The principal shouted back at him, *'Dame zen zen dame!'* ('No, it's not!') But the schoolteacher just kept dumping those fresh, fragrant turds into the pit. So the gluttonous Japanese principal charged boldly ahead, jumped into the pit, and ate his fill of the schoolchildren's excrement, thus dying a martyr for a noble cause.

"My dear listeners and friends, humor and laughter are the secret to long life and eternal youth. Those of us who love public toilets, who have taken as our companions the public toilet artists who find their inspiration in public toilets, those of us who would raise our glasses and talk with them about everything under the sun, will understand perfectly what this means. In our eyes, every citizen of earth who steps into or out of a public toilet might be the author of a public toilet cartoon, a public toilet fable, or a public toilet curse. Everyone goes to the toilet; everyone has the potential to be a public toilet artist, or at least a viewer of the permanent exhibit that is public toilet art. Thinking about this simple truth, Guigui's heart is choked with love for humanity. If earth were not our home, if we were just tourists on this planet, passing through on our way to somewhere else, then public toilets would be relay stations on our travels through life; we would deposit our feces there and in return would receive the joy and eternal aftertaste of a public toilet art that is truly of the people, the masses, the folk.

"Comrades, if you have some sorrow, some shameful secret that you cannot reveal to anyone, if you have thoughts of suicide, if you're so rich you're dripping oil, if you're so poor you have nothing but the four walls around you, if you're lascivious, or frigid, or if you're impotent, if you're oversexed, if you're compassionate, if you're cruel, if you're afflicted with high blood pressure or heart disease, if you're an Olympic champion or an Oscar award-winner, if you've seen an atomic bomb exploding, if you've been infected with AIDS, if you like mountain climbing or watching the ocean, if you're a child-lover or have a taste for older folks, if you'd like to get your hands on the warm gun of a foreigner, if you want to sleep with a Black person, if you're prejudiced against whites, if you hate being an official, if you abuse your own son, if you're a little insane, if you have epilepsy, if your EQ is high and your IQ low, if you talk a blue streak, if you never eat your words and you're never late for anything, if you aim too high, if you're stingy, if you're unusually clever, if you're perfectly average, if you're all dried up inside, if you're a conservative, if you've ever raped someone, if you drink urine and eat shit, if you're a top student, if you run a low fever when night falls, if you believe you've lived previous lives, if in a previous life you were a sheep, if you've been cuckolded, if you go naked in winter and wear pants in the summer, you must keep on living! You are the material for my comedy; for my sake, please take good care of yourselves, keep on living—even if your beloved has left you and gone far away, please don't jump off a building and kill yourselves.

"These anecdotes and everything else I say—you must promise to remember it all!"

59

"My dear listeners and comrades, this is International Red Star Radio host Guigui, here in Beijing, the capital of Planet Earth, extending my greetings and bidding farewell to you all.

"Thanks to global warming, the steady increase of endangered species, the unpredictable political situation, recurrent ethnic warfare, and the daily intensification of economic crises, the entire broadcast staff of this radio station has contracted a chronic illness and is not long for this world. Thus, on behalf of the entire creative staff of International Red Star Radio, I bid you all a tearful farewell. We shall accept the invitation we have received from the people of the planet Neptune to recuperate there. We hope that on a different planet we might find a cure for all that ails our hearts and souls. Someday we shall return to Planet Earth, at which time we shall relive the good old days with you all.

"My dear friends, comrades, gentlemen, ladies, young women, married women, children, the public toilet life is a beautiful one; but the reality of life and love outside the public toilet is cruel. In our ongoing quest for an ever more brilliant public toilet life, we shall study the new architectural concepts and skills of the people of Neptune. Once we have mastered them, we shall return and help make the world a better place by turning every public toilet on earth into a spacious, well-lit, all-glass space, just like a waiting room at the train station, so that our children and grandchildren might live brighter public toilet lives than we.

"Finally, I wish all of you beautiful bodies and bright futures. May we all grow old together in the public toilet!"

Interview with Cui Zi'en

Petrus Liu & Lisa Rofel

ROFEL: Let's start with a simple question: your background. What books and films would you say influenced you the most while growing up?

CUI: I started with reading simplified Chinese. In the beginning, I read Marx, Engels, Mao Zedong, and Lu Xun. These were the only texts that were available to me and naturally the ones that influenced me the most. But I started to read in traditional Chinese since the second grade. I liked *The Dream of the Red Chamber* and *The Prayer Book* the most. My mom secretly had a copy of *The Prayer Book*, which I read. And later on, I started to read traditional Chinese vernacular novels about talented scholars and beautiful ladies in my dad's collections. These works written in traditional Chinese characters left a deep impression on me when I was in the third and fourth grades.

LIU: You were born in 1958 in Harbin. When the Cultural Revolution started, you were in elementary school.

CUI: Yes. Around 1965–66.

ROFEL: Other than books and films, what aspects of the socialist government during this time influenced you and your work?

CUI: At that time, workers, peasants, and soldiers were the politically elevated classes. My family was not from these backgrounds, so I received a reeducation about their cultures. Our neighbors were mostly railway workers, so I had been paying close attention to their lives.

ROFEL: So what was your family's background?

CUI: My father was a surgeon; he was the chief of surgery in a hospital. My mother was a member of the Catholic Church. Although most people of her generation did not know how to read and write, she had basic literacy thanks to the missionary school she attended.

ROFEL: How did your mother become religious?

CUI: From her parents, my grandparents. They became religious first. My mom and my dad met through their religious families.

LIU: Can you talk about how Catholicism has played a role in your literary work?

CUI: At that time, the Catholic Church had to remain underground and hidden from the socialist state, just like the "feudal" culture of literary works in traditional Chinese characters that I was reading. I was caught between two competing civilizations. The surface civilization belonged to Marx, Engels, Lenin, Stalin, Mao Zedong, China's great proletarian revolution, and the culture of workers, peasants, and soldiers. On the other hand, I was exposed to another, underground civilization of Christianity, which was rebelling against the dominant ideology on the surface.

LIU: When did you decide you wanted to be a writer and start writing yourself?

CUI: When I started to learn how to read and write, I knew I had to become a writer myself. As early as the first grade in elementary school, I was chosen as the speaker for my class at a workers' conference. But I didn't know how to write at that time, so my two sisters wrote for me and I just read what they wrote out loud. After third grade, I learned how to write and started doing so by myself. My eldest sister helped me to revise. I was on my own after that. In fourth grade, I started writing speeches all by myself.

LIU: What was your first published piece?

CUI: The first thing that got published was something I wrote in junior high, in a Harbin local newspaper called *Trains in Motion*. If we are talking about real publications, those came relatively late. The first would be the novella I published in the *Flower City* magazine in the 1990s, which was part of the series of "pseudo sci-fi stories" that you have translated. The first piece was called "The Imprisoned Einsteinium and Magnesium."

LIU: What about films? When did you start making films?

CUI: In terms of filmmaking, that started after 2000. *Men and Women* came out in 1999, but I was not the director. I wanted to pursue writing and filmmaking separately. My writing was literary, but my filmmaking was probably better called video activism.

ROFEL: Between writing and filmmaking, do you think one is better than the other for expressing what you want to say? Is there a difference?

CUI: In the beginning, there was a very clear distinction. But now I think that distinction was a product of my bourgeois mental hygiene, so I'm accepting more messiness in my life now. There was a time when I insisted on keeping those two spheres of production completely separate. It was as if the words I wrote had a fidelity to the medium that could not be translated into images.

LIU: That's why most of your literary works have never been adapted into films, and the films you did produce were not based on your own scripts.

CUI: Yes, none of them were adapted. Actually, the films I produced were unscripted. Well, most of them did not have a script. There were works that shared a name: for example, I wrote a story called *Enter the Clowns* and also made a film of the same name, but the film only used about one percent of the material in the story, and the story itself is made up of many, many fragments. The film re-created a fragment from the story, but only after that fragment itself had been further broken down into other pieces.

LIU: Other than your creative fiction, you have also written works of literary criticism and essays about culture and politics, including *The Tragedy of Youth: A Human Topic in World Literature* and *On the Fiction of Li Yu*. Can you talk about what you had in mind when you wrote these and what roles they played in your growth as a creative writer and filmmaker?

CUI: After I was admitted to the university, I discovered a lot of literary and social theories. I decided I was not in a rush to become a creative writer; instead, I first wanted to absorb these theories of what literature was and could do. Although my creative writing was not interrupted, my focus shifted to research at that time. I started reading a lot, and four years in college felt like four decades because I was reading in the library all the time. This habit of reading widely stayed with me for life. My research at the time was focused on the notion of world literature. Before I had to worry about completing a formal thesis, I published my preliminary research in book form as *The Tragedy of Youth*.

LIU: Then you wrote *On the Fiction of Li Yu*.

CUI: Right. I was actually planning on using it as the basis for a PhD. After I finished the manuscript, it was published quickly.

LIU: What about *The World of Artists* and *Desire, Drugs, and Roses: Traveling in World Cinema*? When did you start working on those?

CUI: I started writing *The World of Artists* around the time I was about to finish my master's. I had already decided to leave the system of academic research and pursue creative writing instead. I thought I could join the Writers Association and find a full-time salaried position to support my writing. Once I had figured out a path, I started thinking earnestly about my own identity.

LIU: You didn't want to become a government official. You didn't want to become a scholar or researcher either. So you became a full-time creative writer and started publishing novels?

CUI: We're not there yet. After I finished graduate school, my first job was at the Beijing Film Academy. My major was not in film studies; I majored in literature. So in order to teach at the Beijing Film Academy, I had to teach myself a lot of things about film production and analysis. I ended up spending a lot of time watching films and studying different national cinemas around the world. I began thinking about different kinds of cinematic languages developed by different societies and what I could possibly adapt for my own purposes or pass on to others. A lot of these ideas went into *Desire, Drugs, and Roses: Traveling in World Cinema*. I was working on this book and *The World of Artists* almost at the same time. They overlapped a lot and created a feedback loop with my teaching. I taught my ideas and findings in my classes, and what I discovered through teaching became new material for these two books.

ROFEL: I wonder if you could tell me more about how Chinese socialism—its theories and practice—shaped your writing. In the special issue Petrus and I edited, you mentioned that queer people were the true Communist International in China.[1] What did you mean by that?

CUI: That's right, let me explain these first: I have a theory that China has three imported cultures. These come from the West but not limited to Western Europe. The first is Marxism. The second is Christianity. Marxism is atheist, while Christianity is a religion. The last one is the imported culture of homosexuality. When I spoke of homosexuality in my earlier work, I was referring to this queer culture from abroad. Of the three imported cultures, only Marxism became mainstream in China; the other two became marginalized and had to go underground. In terms of the culture of Christianity, I would say that Jesus was the first postmodernist in history, and I would say that homosexuals were the true Communists. Why? The kind of socialism that was propagated by Chinese officials was false; it was full of lies. In China, what traveled under the name of socialism has always been a mixture of ideas, some of which were derived from Confucianism, Buddhism, and Taoism rather than Marxism. This is why when Petrus later asked me these questions about what Marxism and socialism meant for me [in preparation for his *Queer Marxism in Two Chinas*], I said that to understand how Marxism took root in China you have to first understand Confucianism, Buddhism, and Taoism.[2] These traditions were mixed with Marxism and created a seemingly novel discourse. But in reality? It is still Confucianism, Buddhism, and Taoism under the guise of Marxism. True Communism, and true socialism, never manifested in the brand of Marxism that was popularized in China. That's why later I made a documentary, *We Are the . . . of Communism*. The ellipsis signifies that most Chinese people are actually omitted by what was called Communism in China. Since our childhood, everybody was packaged by a fake kind of Marxism.

LIU: But in your writing, you clearly distanced yourself from Confucianism, Buddhism, and Taoism and embraced Christianity. You distanced yourself from China's revolutionary and class politics and instead foregrounded the politics of the body. Can you talk about how your writing engages these different forms of politics? I am thinking of your "Peachy Lips" as an example, which seems to offer us a counternarrative to both heteronormative worldviews and fossilized class politics in China.

CUI: What "Peachy Lips" articulates is the spirit of "anti-collectivism." By this, I am referring to the possibility of defining one's identity and values away from China's culture of collectivization since the May Fourth period. Unlike Lu Xun, I am a loner. Queer writers like me do not have literary associations or political revolutions to join. My most important resource is myself. To get any queer writing done, first I must block out all the noises and lies of Chinese socialism. Fortunately, I had been preparing for this for a long time. *Peachy Lips* was the result of years of thinking and research in the language of cinema and the language of creative fiction, neither of which fully dominated my imagination.

LIU: I think we are talking about an extremely important and complex issue: how to write a literary work that can simultaneously address all of these issues within a coherent setting. You have talked about how literary writing provides a means to resist the mainstream narratives the state has fabricated about modern China's history or economic transformations. In your formulation, literary writing, especially queer writing, seems to find itself in constant tension with the values of mainstream society. When Lisa and I began working on this current volume, we decided not to include "Peachy Lips." But we did include "Uncle's Elegant Life," "Intrigue like Fireworks," and other stories that explicitly explore the intersectionality of overlapping modes of oppression and identities, including gender, class, and sexuality. Can you give us some examples from the stories in this volume of the literary strategies you developed for promoting this kind of critical consciousness against mainstream values?

CUI: When I became a writer, I was already certain that I was different from mainstream society, that I had a different perspective to share. Otherwise, I would not be writing at all. "Peachy Lips" was the product of a mental lockdown. Its universe was quarantined from mainstream society and its lies. It was also quarantined from the influence of so-called high literature in China. I wanted to keep these impurities out of my work. Generally speaking, I tend to be susceptible to the influence of film more than that of literature. That is because film is worldly; it tends to reflect and takes its inspirations from a broader universe than fiction. So my first task is always to block out the influence of mainstream society and politics. Then I have to block out the influence of other films. As for the canonical writers of China, I find most of them to be too normative. To me, they are not literary enough, because they are all obsessed with earning a Nobel Prize from the West and seeking its approval, just like filmmakers are seeking the validation of the Oscars. I don't share that mentality. I feel they are writing from a position of debasement and writing for the sole purpose of earning a Nobel Prize. They think they are close to getting one, but they are actually far from it. Since I was a child, I never bowed down to the authorities. I had no problem saying no to Marx. I had no problem saying no to God. Why would I have trouble saying no to the Nobel Prize?

LIU: That's a really helpful way of characterizing your project. I think you and your work are truly "queer" in multiple senses of the word. You are antinormative and antiestablishment. You want to keep a critical distance between what you write and what is held to be natural, heroic, inevitable, desirable, or simply true by most people. This sense of queer in your writing exceeds homosexuality and sexual oppression, and I think you are doing a very rare and important kind of queer work.

CUI: Yes, and I have to be highly vigilant at all times. In all the things I do—from writing to filmmaking to social activism—I have to make constant judgments. For example, when the June Fourth student movement started, I did not join it immediately. I could not jump on the bandwagon before I had a clearer sense of whether it was revolutionary or pro-democracy or revolutionary and pro-democracy at the same time. And when I did participate in it, I knew that my involvement was more than spiritual. It was bodily, even as a passive observer.

LIU: So which social movements in China in recent history do you support and identify with? Which ones have you participated in?

CUI: Well, I tried to participate in Charter 08, but they kicked me out. They just wanted signatories. Constitutionalism in China is quite close to civil society. When Liu Junning wrote about neoliberalism and conservatism, I thought that he had ideas that were very important to China. He participated in Charter 08, and so did I. We both signed it. But then Liu Xiaobo and the others kicked me out because I am a queer writer. So in the end my name was not on the petition. Charter 08 was probably the only movement other than the queer movement that I strongly identified with and supported. But later on, I discovered that it was not really a movement; it was more like a political party. What its leaders wanted to do was to establish an alternative party through a social movement.

LIU: It sounds like in your work you often stand at the crossroads between different social movements and communities. I am curious to know: today we are publishing a translation of your short stories and making them available to English-language readers for the first time. How do you want them to see you? And how do your original readers in China see you?

CUI: It is strange here in China. People in literary circles are afraid of discussing literature with me. People in film are afraid of discussing film with me. And people in sexuality studies are afraid of discussing sexuality with me.

ROFEL: Why are they afraid of you?

CUI: Most people think of me as an expert, because I was trained by an academic literary studies program, with an emphasis on classical literature, and they are a little nervous about my expertise. As for film, people know that I am teaching at the Film Academy and my classes are popular there, so they think of me as a film expert. They are also afraid of me and my sexuality. And they know I am friends with Lisa Rofel, who is a real expert on sexuality. And of course, I have read many books in the field of sexuality studies and use a lot of theoretical jargon about sexuality in my writing, and I'm also a "practitioner," so of course they don't want to talk to me about sex. I am very excited about this translation project because I think it will open new doors for me to have discussions about these things with a different audience.

LIU: This is an interesting paradox. On the one hand, you are marginalized because many Chinese intellectuals are afraid of you and see you as an outcast. On the other hand, you are very well respected and influential among minority groups in China. An example that comes to mind is the establishment of the Beijing Queer Film Festival, in which you played an instrumental role.[3] So although you describe yourself as consistently marginalized and antiestablishment, you are also clearly a leader and a cultural icon, at least in queer circles. How did you create community while espousing values that were not widely shared by many? How did you survive and even flourish in a hostile environment?

CUI: This actually brings us back to *Desire, Drugs, and Roses* and *The World of Artists*. Having published these two books plus my teaching at the time created a public image of me as a film expert. I acquired a lot of visibility in the mass media and came to be seen as an evangelist of elite cinema of sorts. That was also because the Chinese film school at the time lacked knowledge of Western cinema. Everything that was already in the system was derived from the Soviet-controlled Eastern Bloc or socialism. So as soon as I started teaching there, I was elevated to the position of an expert and given a lot of privileges. I had access to a lot of films that were banned. I also happened to be the most popular instructor at the academy, because as soon as I started screening some banned titles in class—like Visconti, Fassbinder, and Bertolucci—they also felt enlightened. Before taking my classes, the students had some basic knowledge of those directors through readings but had never seen any of their films. So my classes established me as an authority—but I am using that word sarcastically. Many people in the first generation of independent filmmakers like Zhang Yuan and Wang Xiaoshuai were students of mine from that era. When they were making films, they were also thinking of an image they projected onto me, and I became an echo chamber for many of them. They wanted to show me their work before it was finalized and get some feedback from me. They wanted me to help them connect to other people or to find funding. I didn't start out doing queer work or queer activism. My role was more in the world of underground or independent filmmaking. My visibility in the print media was limited to a periodical run by the Nanjing Arts School. I had a column there called Chinese Underground Filmmaking. I wrote the column for about two years in the 1990s. The Berlin Film Festival was a by-product of this work.[4] The organizers showed a dozen independent films from China and used my article (translated into German and English) as an introduction. When we all met up again at Beijing University for the independent film festival, people asked, What is our next project? I proposed that we do a queer film festival, and it really happened. It started out as a joke, and at that time I didn't know we would be treading on a topic that was even more politically sensitive than what we had taken on before, and that the material would become such an important rallying point for minorities against hegemonic culture.

LIU: You are really prolific and multitalented. Just in terms of your movies alone, you have taken on at least three distinct genres. First we have narrative films like *The Old Testament*, *Enter the Clowns*, and *Feeding Boys,*

Ayaya. Then we have the "pseudo sci-fi" film series, which includes *Star Appeal* and *The Narrow Path*. Finally, we have realist films, including *Night Scene, Queer China, "Comrade" China*, and the *We Are the . . . of Communism* we just mentioned.

CUI: There is actually a fourth category, the completely experimental one.[5]

LIU: And your fiction writing is just as varied. Can you talk about how you work across so many different genres and whether you feel like you are addressing a different audience with each style?

CUI: For fiction, indeed I was working on stories of different genres all at once. The story of my filmmaking was not this schizophrenic. Most of them were made at different times, and even if the work schedules overlapped a bit, there was a clear sequence. For example, *Feeding Boys, Ayaya* and *Night Scene* were filmed at the same time and actually were originally meant to be one film. I cut the footage into two because the first one was too long—it took six hours total for me to capture the story I wanted to tell. In the end I thought it was way too long, and it was too similar to "Enter the Clowns" (the short story version), which itself was already quite fragmented. At one point I thought of discarding what I had produced because it took on two rather different topics: money boys and male breastfeeding, which Lisa has discussed.[6] I thought both topics were important but perhaps didn't go too well together if I had put them in the same film. To keep things separate, I ended up putting the documentary part about male sex workers in *Night Scene*, but to me they are also "breastfeeding" in a social sense, so I took a different approach to the topic. The focus of *Feeding Boys, Ayaya* is how men learn breastfeeding from women so they can nourish others. I also mixed in elements of Christianity, like the end of the world and saviors. After some editing the film didn't feel too busy. In any case, making an independent film was a relatively fast task, so it didn't keep me from other tasks like writing film criticism, education, and broadcasting. Fiction writing is an entirely different thing. It takes a lot of concentration and dedication. I spent ten years doing nothing but reading and writing. The decade I spent doing films was by contrast much more relaxed, and I had time to be involved in other activities including queer activism.

LIU: Some readers in Chinese find your novels difficult to understand, saying they are too postmodern or experimental. This may have something to do with the fact that their expectations of what a "queer" text should look like are cultivated by popular queer films like *Lan Yu*, *The Wedding Banquet*, and *Formula 17*, all of which are commercial works aiming at a mass market, with a palatable plot and an attractive cast. You are giving us something very different. You have always described your work as a rebellion against the narcissism of homonormative texts focused on gay pride and middle-class wholesomeness.[7] Can you give some examples from the stories included here to show us how you resist the narrative of gay pride?

CUI: For example, while some of my stories deal with queerness in a more expansive sense, others feature homosexual characters in the traditional sense: "Fire and Wolf Share a Fondness for Male Beauty," "Men Are Containers," and "Platinum Bible." While the figure of the male homosexual is the theme here, that figure is more of a parody than an occasion for pride and celebration. That figure invites ridicule instead of respect. He may happen to be the narrative focus of the story but does not command any kind of moral importance. He is both on the margins and the center of narrative interest. He is both liked and disliked, ridiculed and worshipped. The reader is not encouraged to see the protagonist as a role model or a site of identification; instead, the story may simply feel somewhat familiar, as if it is concerned with your best friend or a family member, even somebody you would not hesitate to offend. But what I want to emphasize the most through this kind of setup is the possibility of leaving the so-called gay point of view behind. I am not trying to give people an authentic gay story from the viewpoint or experience of a gay person. In fact, when I reflect on my own life, I often feel that it was the heterosexual perspective that taught me more. It was the heterosexual perspective that taught me the importance of distancing oneself from China's revolutionary ideology. In high school, it was through that perspective I began to get to know my own body, my interests, my world, my life, and what comes after life. I realized that I was part of a living, breathing world. But the people I was surrounded by, my educated youth friends, were all kind of sad. We were the same age, about sixteen or seventeen. But all of my classmates believed that their futures were determined by their reproductive organs. They were recruited and assimilated into a bodily system that promised them pleasures and an identity. They couldn't rebel against their bodies. I had many sex partners when I was that age. When we spent time together, I felt sad for them. They were in the prime of youth but victims of a biological determinism that amounted to nothing but sadness and despair. Lying next to their bodies, I began thinking about and writing the stories of

"Uncle's Elegant Life" and "Intrigue like Fireworks." These were among the first stories I wrote. They were inspired by the situation of those friends I knew. I felt that in China, maybe in the world, people who based their identities on what their reproductive systems told them were the saddest. If we look at the world from their point of view, we would see that the world of trans or gays was full of life, full of possibilities. By contrast, their world was so rigid, always at risk of breaking, but they needed to guard their masculinity no matter what the price. They were like worker bees, conditioned to follow a routine without thinking. Their identities and roles in society were fixed; if the beehive comes under attack, they were also conditioned to sacrifice their lives defending it. They carried the mandate of heterosexuality in China. Do I think heterosexual hegemony exists in China? No, it does not. China has patriarchy and chauvinism, but no heterosexual hegemony. I am eager to correct these misunderstandings about China and Chinese culture through this translation [this volume] and your influence in the anglophone world. Hopefully people will have a revised understanding of how the hetero-/homosexual binary works in China. I have always had ambivalent feelings about imported terms like *heteronormativity* in the context of China but didn't know how to express my reservations until you proposed this interview today. Last time when the three of us did the "Queering What Is Left of Queer" workshop at Duke University [April 14, 2021], I began making this point but ran out of time. I hope this translation gives me a second chance. If my writing makes a contribution, or I should say the largest contribution it makes, it is a rethinking of the categories of trans and gay within a heterosexual language.

LIU: This is why translation is such an interesting task. I feel that translation is a dialogue between the translator and the author. It is never simply about the technical process of finding an English equivalent of a Chinese word. It is a clash of cultures and assumptions. It is about crossing linguistic and conceptual boundaries. It is also about giving an existing work a second life, bringing it to a different discursive and political context for a transformative purpose. On that note, could you tell us something your hopes for this book's future readers? What would you like to say to them? What is the ideal response you'd like to see from your English-language readers?

CUI: Well, so far the only "English readers" I know are you two and some of the contributors to this project. You are all scholars in academia. I am hoping this book will disrupt the "episteme" of the English language, or what we call the queer episteme. By that I don't mean there is anything wrong with the order of things or organization of knowledge in English or that it is too Western. That's not something I would say. What I mean is that in the West there is a queer episteme that is enclosed in an even more chauvinistic universe, and that queer episteme is treated as the basis of civic liberty or a vehicle for a minority group to express itself and influence others. But that civic liberty is fake. It is similar to how empty notions like democracy and freedom don't mean anything in China. This is probably a digression, but I am also thinking of how Western missionaries built a limited space of religious freedom in China. So later we imported Western notions of democracy and freedom into China and only did a half job. We never converted anyone or made any real changes around here.

LIU: That's why we need to use fiction to build a more inclusive, a more multivalent sexual politics.

CUI: Hopefully this volume is a beginning. Even if it is only a beginning.

LIU: Lisa and I encountered some issues while translating your stories. Maybe you wouldn't mind shedding light on some of those here. These are not problems but more like interesting puzzles, and might have something to do with the conceptual and linguistic challenges your work presents that we just talked about. Many of the characters and places in your stories seem to have a fable-like quality. Are they allegories? Allegories for what? Another thing we noticed is that stories that have nothing to with each other may share characters or settings of the same name, especially the allegorical-sounding ones like "Square City" and "Triangle City." I wonder if some readers might have simply read it as a roman à clef, assuming that one is code for Beijing and the other for Shanghai, for example. And we keep meeting a character named Xiao Bo in different stories—can you explain that?

CUI: "Square City" and "Triangle City" are locations I use to organize the stories in this series, but in other series I use other terms. For example, the pseudo sci-fi series uses planets in the solar system like Mercury, Jupiter, Venus, and Mars. These are clear. In this series translated here I also use real-life places like Beijing. "Platinum Bible" and "Men Men Men Women Women Women" are both set in Beijing, not Square or Triangle City. In "Intrigue like Fireworks" I explain why these cities are named this way; I won't repeat it here. So yes, many of these elements are repetitive by design. But even when I use the same name for a location or a character, I employ a different perspective or introduce some other kind of variation, such as a different sexual identity for the same character. For example, in "Uncle's Elegant Life," a nephew decides on a sexual identity before he is of age. Later he meets a classmate called Wang Zheng with a nickname Wang Xiaohua and that person is trans, and this encounter has a transformative effect on the main character. In the end he wants his uncle to hug him one more time. He feels that he is on the verge of leaving one culture and falling into a black hole that we call the adulthood of heterosexuals. That's the ending of the story. "Intrigue like Fireworks" is also focalized through a coming-of-age narrative. The main character plays skirmishes with the mother of the girl he likes. Later he ends up marrying this girl, but when he returns to Triangle City again, the partners he plays skirmishes with are two childhood friends, White Eyed Wolf and Butterfly. The story has a hint of a normative, safe, and stable heterosexual life. It also hints at the possibility of a life on the side, one that is as tension-ridden as his relationship with his mother-in-law but for an entirely different reason. His wife, for all we know, may have a life on the side that others don't know about. And the partners in the exchanges enjoy a wide range of pornography: gay male ones are fine; heterosexual ones are also good. They are just looking for visual simulation. Their bodies are set up to receive both gay and heterosexual sex. The boundaries are blurred, and it is unclear whether the stability of heterosexuality is limited to visual pleasures or lifestyle. I think these two stories successfully dramatize the heterosexual perspective I have been talking about, and do a better job at this than "Men Are Containers" and "Old Fire and Old Wolf." I say better because these stories have a broader range and relegate heterosexuality to the borders of LGBTQ possibilities.

ROFEL: Maybe you can also explain to our readers why you want to talk about the toilet.

CUI: The toilet is a simple concept about equality and social justice. My stories are playing with this. In Chinese society before LGBTQ entered our language, there were only men and women. And women did not truly exist as social subjects. Despite the story of how the Communist Party liberated women, women were never free. Chinese society has always valued men more than women, and that inequality is visible on all levels. Since I was young, I have observed how women had to wait a long time to go to the public toilet. That was partially because they took a long time, having to squat for both number one and number two, while men could simply urinate standing in a row and not having to occupy a stall each. You realized that there was a great deal of inequality in the world—why can't they build more toilets for women? I thought about this when I was a kid. When I grew up, the first thing I wanted to do was give literary expression to this kind of inequality in the world. In my first movie, *Men and Women,* I also used the toilet to talk about these issues. That was not just about what is going on between men at public bathrooms. It was more about privilege. Actually, before I made that I was working on a short video called "The Pros and Cons of Public Toilets." I was working on that project and "Mass" at the same time, and didn't turn to *Old Testament* and *Enter the Clowns* until I was done. Those four films were part of a series, which I completed within six months. "The Pros and Cons of Public Toilets" was about the ideology of toilets, which I point out again in "Platinum Bible." These include public debates surrounding toilets and ways in which feminists try to "occupy" men's bathrooms and so on.

LIU: Right. So the toilet is a space of false equality. It is a relic of a binary system that divides people into "men" and "women" but also affords them different rights. In your fiction and films, we see you challenge a variety of false notions of equality, from Communism to socialism and gender. In those discourses, people are assumed to be equal or said to have been liberated, but your stories reveal the extent to which these equalities are either contingencies or false asymmetries. Your stories show us what is omitted or left out in the official scripts of Chinese socialism, or what has been rendered invisible precisely because of a limited understanding of how power works. It is wonderful we can learn so much from a discussion of toilets. In "Platinum Bible " the most hilarious episode for me is the one where international and local scholars hold a debate about different cultures of toilets in the world. And we meet Lisa Rofel and Dai Jinhua as characters![8]

(Laughter)

May 11, 2022
Boston/Ponte Vedra Beach/San Francisco

Notes

1 Cui, "Communist International of Queer Film."
2 Liu, *Queer Marxism in Two Chinas,* 48–58.
3 See our introduction, p. xii, for Cui's role in the Beijing Queer Film Festival.

4 The Berlin International Film Festival (Berlinale, for short) is a major international film festival held annually in Berlin.
5 See the examples Cui offers on p. 266 of this interview.
6 Rofel, "Traffic in Money Boys," 425–58.
7 Liu, *Queer Marxism in Two Chinas*, 48–58.
8 Dai Jinhua is a well-known feminist Marxist theorist who teaches Cultural Studies at Beijing University. See Dai, *After the Post-Cold War*.

Appendix
Works by Cui Zi'en

Bibliography

BOOKS

1988

The Tragedy of Youth: A Human Topic in World Literature. 《青春的悲劇：世界文學中的一個人類主題》 Beijing: Heping chubanshe.

1989

On the Fiction of Li Yu. 《李漁小說論稿》 Beijing: Zhongguo shehui chubanshe.

1993

Desire, Drugs, and Roses: Traveling in World Cinema. 《欲念、毒品和玫瑰：世界電影羈旅》 Beijing: Huaxia.

The World of Artists. 《藝術家的宇宙》 Beijing: Sanlian shudian.

1997

Peachy Lips. 《桃色嘴唇》 Hong Kong: Huasheng shudian.

1998

I Love Shidabo. 《我愛史大勃》 Beijing: Huaxia chubanshe.

Bed of Roses. 《玫瑰床榻》 Guangzhou: Huacheng chubanshe.

Enter the Clowns. 《丑角登場》 Guangzhou: Huacheng chubanshe.

Fairytales of Triangle City. 《三角城的童話》 Hong Kong: Huasheng shudian.

2003

First Audience. 《第一觀眾》 Beijing: Xiandai chubanshe.

Pseudo-Science Fiction Stories. 《偽科幻故事》 Zhuhai: Zhuhai chubanshe.

Ace of Hearts Blowing His Horn. 《紅桃 A 吹響號角》 Zhuhai: Zhuhai chubanshe.
Peachy Lips. 《桃色嘴唇》 Zhuhai: Zhuhai chubanshe.
Uncle's Elegant Life. 《舅舅的人間煙火》 Zhuhai: Zhuhai chubanshe.

2004
Long Live the Artists. 《藝術家萬歲》 Guangxi: Guangxi Normal University Press.

2005
Memories of Light and Shadow. 《光影記憶》 Beijing: Sanlian shudian.

2007
The Whereabout of Crimson. 《胭脂的下落》 Kunming: Yunnan renmin chubanshe.

2012
Big Dipper. 《北斗有七星》 Guangzhou: Huacheng chubanshe.

PLAYS

1991
"Broken Myths and the Young Protagonist Yet to Make His Appearance." 〈破碎的神話和未出場的少年主人公〉 *Film and Literature* (June).

1992
"Train, Train, Hurry Up." 〈火車火車你快開〉 *Film and Literature* (Feb.).

1994
"Passage of Time." 〈歲月〉 *Television, Film, and Literature* (June).

1995
"First Love." 〈關於初戀〉 *Television, Film, and Literature* (May).

1998
"Naked Politics." 〈裸體政治〉 *Tendency* (Oct.).

2000
"Long Games." 〈長長的遊戲〉 *Film and Literature* (Jan.).

SHORT FICTION

1995
"Imprisoned Expectations and Magnesium." 〈受到監禁的的預期和鎂〉 *Flower City* (Apr.).

1996

"The Limits of a Thrown Walnut."〈拋核桃的極限〉*Flower City* (Jan.).

1998

"The Twisted Text of Pluto."〈冥王星曲折文本〉*Savanna* (May).
"Midnight on Saturn."〈土星時間零點整〉*Flower City* (June).
"Hatching Dinosaurs."〈孵化小恐龍〉*Writers* (Nov.).

1999

"A Resume of Shame."〈履歷表的恥辱〉*Flower City* (Mar.).
"Book of the Sky Revealed."〈破譯天書〉*Flower City* (Apr.).
"Bacteria-Born Species on Vulcan."〈火神星菌生人〉*Flower City* (Apr.).
"The Grand Prize of Movies in the Solar System."〈太陽系電影大獎〉*Flower City* (Apr.).
"Childhood Companions on the Moon."〈月亮上的童伴〉*Flower City* (Apr.).
"Fluorine as a Point of View."〈氟也許是一種視點〉*Flower City* (Apr.).
"Peachy Lips."〈桃色嘴唇〉*Savanna* (Jan.).
"Orphans of the Japanese Empire."〈日本遺民〉*Youth Literature* (June).
"Sitting in the Coldest Corner of Triangle City in Winter."〈坐在三角城冬季最冷僻的角落裡〉*Savanna* (June).
"I Love Shidaobo."〈我愛史大勃〉*Passage of Time* (May).
"Bailu."〈白露〉*Eastern Culture Weekly* (Dec.).

2000

"Younger Sister's Hair."〈妹妹的頭髮〉*World of Literature* (June).
"A Hole on the Forehead."〈額頭上的洞穴〉*Savanna* (May).
"A Collage of Passes to Ganymede."〈木衛 3 通行證拼貼〉*Beijing Literature* (June).
"On the Bottom of the Ladder to the Stars in Heaven."〈天堂星雲梯最下端〉*Flower City* (May).
"Endangered Species Rule!"〈瀕危動物至上〉*Hibiscus* (Feb.).
"Intergalactic Post Office."〈星際郵局〉*Flower City* (May).
"The Poor with Access to Every Kind of Luxury."〈享有每一種豪華服務的窮人〉*Flower City* (May).
"Everyone Is a King."〈每一個人都是國王〉*Hibiscus* (Feb.).
"Big Brother Goes Somewhere Far Away."〈哥哥去遠方〉*Youth Literature* (Apr.).
"Some Admire Wisdom, Others Do Not."〈有人讚美聰慧，有人則不〉*Mountain Flowers* (Feb.).
"Jesus on Mars."〈火星上的耶穌〉*Flower City* (July).
"Butterflies." *Mountain Flowers* (July).

2001

"The Philosophy of Hanging and Erect Body Parts." 〈蝴蝶〉 *Flower City* (May).
"Big Sister Now, Big Sister Then" 〈懸垂著和高舉著的器官哲學〉 *Hibiscus* (May).

2002

"Uncle's Elegant Life." 〈舅舅的人間煙火〉 *Modern Culture Illustrated News* (Jan.).
"Hasty Escape, Opportunities, and Dreams." 〈倉皇逃遁與良機與夢想〉 *Flower City* (Apr.).
"Who Has Gone to Bed with Me." 〈有誰上過我的床〉 *Kaifang* (Apr.).
"The Whereabouts of Rouge." 〈胭脂的下落〉 *City Illustrated News* (Sept.).
"The Narrator Has a Martian Accent." 〈敘事人有火星口音〉 *Flower City* (Apr.).
"Coloratura Sopranos." 〈花腔女高音〉 *Mountain Flowers* (Nov.).

2017

"Platinum Bible of the Public Toilet." 〈公廁白金寶典〉 *Gay Spot*.

Filmography

1999

Men and Women. 《男男女女》 (writer/actor)

2001

Mass. 《MASS》 (writer/director)
The Positive and Negative Sides of Public Toilet 《公廁正方反方》 (writer/actor)
Enter the Clowns. 《丑角登場》 (writer/actor/director)
The Old Testament. 《舊約》 (writer/director)

2002

Welcome to Destination Shanghai. 《目的地，上海》 (actor)
Keep Cool and Don't Blush. 《臉不變色心不跳》 (writer/director)
The Black and White Milk Cow. 《一隻花奶牛》 (producer)

2003

Feeding Boys, Ayaya. 《哎呀呀，去哺乳》 (writer/director)
Night Scene. 《夜景》 (writer/director)

2004

An Interior View of Death. 《死亡的內景》 (writer/director)
The Narrow Path. 《霧語》 (writer/director)
Pirated Copy. 《蔓延》 (writer/director)
Star Appeal. 《星星相吸惜》 (writer/director)

2005
WC Huhu Ha Hee. 《WC 呼呼哈嘿》 (writer/director)
Withered in a Blooming Season. 《少年花草黃》 (writer/director)
Duan Ju. 《短句》 (writer/director)
Shitou and That Nana. 《石頭和那個娜娜》 (writer/director)
My Fair Son. 《我如花似玉的兒子》 (writer/director)

2006
Empty Town. 《水墨青春》 (writer/director)
Erdong. 《二冬》 (writer/director)
Refrain. 《副歌》 (writer/director)
Only Child: Upward Downward, Forward Backward, Rightward and Leftward. 《獨生子，向上向下向前向後向左向右》 (writer/director)

2007
A Touchstone in the Gilded Age. 《鍍金時代的試金石》 (director)
We Are the . . . of Communism. 《我們是共產主義省略號》 (director)

2008
Queer China, "Comrade China." 《誌同志》 (director)

2009
Meat and Three Veg. 《一葷三素》 (writer/director)

2010
The Wild Strawberries. 《野草莓》 (writer)

2011
Gay + HIV+ = David? 《Gay + HIV+ = 大瑋？》 (director)
Shan Hai Bible. 《山海經》 (writer/director)

2013
Zero Thousand Li under the Clouds and Moon. 《浮雲》 (actor)

Bibliography

Bao, Hongwei. *Queer Comrades: Gay Identity and Tongzhi Activism in Postsocialist China*. Copenhagen: NIAS Press, 2018.

Bao, Hongwei. *Queer Media in China*. New York: Routledge, 2021.

Barlow, Tani E. *The Question of Women in Chinese Feminism*. Durham, NC: Duke University Press, 2004.

Berry, Chris. "The Sacred, the Profane, and the Domestic in Cui Zi'en's Cinema." *positions* 12, no. 1 (2004): 195–201.

Berry, Michael. *Choujiao dengchang: Cui Zi'en de Zhongguo ku'er yingxiang* 丑角登場：崔子恩的酷兒影像 [Enter the clowns: The queer cinema of Cui Zi'en]. Taipei: Niang chuban, 2022.

Cao Xueqin. *The Story of the Stone, or The Dream of the Red Chamber*. New York: Penguin Books, 1973.

Cui Zi'en. "The Communist International of Queer Film." Translated by Petrus Liu. *positions* 18, no. 2 (2010): 417–24.

Cui Zi'en. "Endangered Species Rule!" Translated by Petrus Liu. *positions* 12, no. 1 (2004): 165–79.

Cui Zi'en. *Queer China, "Comrade" China*. Independent Chinese documentary film. China, 2008.

Cui Zi'en. "Uncle's Elegant Life." Translated by Lisa Rofel. *NANG*, no. 7 (2019): 53–58.

Dai Jinhua. *After the Post–Cold War: The Future of Chinese History*. Edited by Lisa Rofel. Durham, NC: Duke University Press, 2018.

Dai Jinhua. *Cinema and Desire: Feminist Marxism and Cultural Politics in the Work of Dai Jinhua*. Edited by Jing Wang and Tani E. Barlow. New York: Verso, 2002.

Dai Jinhua and Meng Yue. *Fuchu lishi dibiao* [Emerging from the horizon of history]. Zhengzhou: Henan renmin chubanshe, 1989.

Derrida, Jacques. *Dissemination*. Chicago: University of Chicago Press, 1981.

de Villiers, Nicholas. *Sexography: Sex Work in Documentary*. Minneapolis: University of Minnesota Press, 2017.

Evans, Harriet. *Women and Sexuality in China: Dominant Discourses of Female Sexuality and Gender since 1949*. London: Blackwell, 1997.

Goethe, Johann Wolfgang von. *The Sorrows of Young Werther*. 1774. Translated by Thomas Carlyle and R. Dillon Boylan. New York: Dover, 2002.

Hershatter, Gail. *Women and China's Revolutions*. Lanham, MD: Rowman and Littlefield, 2019.

Kang, Wenqing. "The Decriminalization and Depathologization of Homosexuality in China." In *China in and beyond the Headlines*, edited by Timothy Weston and Lionel Jensen, 231–48. Plymouth, UK: Rowman and Littlefield, 2012.

Kang, Wenqing. "Male Same-Sex Relations in Socialist China." *PRC History Review* 3, no. 1 (October 2018): 1–36.

Kang, Wenqing. *Obsession: Male Same-Sex Relations in China, 1900–1950*. Hong Kong: Hong Kong University Press, 2009.

Kawabata, Yasunari. *The Dancing Girl of Izu*. Translated by Edward Seidensticker. *Atlantic Monthly*, January 1955.

Leung, Helen Hok-Sze. "Homosexuality and Queer Aesthetics in Chinese Cinema." In *A Companion to Chinese Cinema*, edited by Yingjin Zhang, 518–34. Oxford: Blackwell, 2013.

Li, Xiaojiang. "Economic Reform and the Awakening of Chinese Women's Collective Consciousness." In *Engendering China: Women, Culture and the State*, edited by Christina K. Gilmartin, Gail Hershatter, Lisa Rofel, and Tyrene White, 360–82. Cambridge, MA: Harvard University Press, 1994.

Liu, Lydia H., Rebecca E. Karl, and Dorothy Ko. *The Birth of Chinese Feminism: Essential Texts in Transnational Theory*. New York: Columbia University Press, 2013.

Liu, Petrus. *Queer Marxism in Two Chinas*. Durham, NC: Duke University Press, 2015.

Liu, Petrus. *The Specter of Materialism: Queer Theory and Marxism in the Age of the Beijing Consensus*. Durham, NC: Duke University Press, 2023.

Mishima, Yukio. *The Decay of the Angel*. Translated by Edward Seidensticker. New York: Alfred A. Knopf, 1971.

Moravia, Alberto. *The Woman of Rome*. 1947. Translated by Lydia Holland and Tami Calliope. New York: Farrar, Straus, 1949.

Pickowicz, Paul. "From Yao Wenyuan to Cui Zi'en: Film, History, Memory." *Journal of Chinese Cinema* 1, no. 1 (2007): 41–53.

Robinson, Luke. *Independent Chinese Documentary: From the Studio to the Street*. New York: Palgrave Macmillan, 2013.

Rofel, Lisa. *Desiring China: Experiments in Neoliberalism, Sexuality, and Public Culture*. Durham, NC: Duke University Press, 2007.

Rofel, Lisa. "The Traffic in Money Boys." *positions* 18, no. 2 (2010): 425–58.

Spencer, Norman. "Ten Years of Queer Cinema in China." *positions* 20, no. 1 (2012): 373–83.
Voci, Paola. *China on Video: Smaller-Screen Realities*. New York: Routledge, 2010.
Wang, Qi. "Embodied Visions: Chinese Queer Experimental Documentaries by Shi Tou and Cui Zi'en." *positions* 21, no. 3 (2013): 659–81.
Wang, Qi. "The Ruin Is Always a New Outcome: An Interview with Cui Zi'en." *positions* 12, no. 1 (2004): 181–94.
Yue, Audrey. "Mobile Intimacies in the Queer Sinophone." *Journal of Chinese Cinemas* 6, no. 1 (2012): 95–108.
Zhang, Jie. "Cui Zi'en's Night Scene and China's Visual Queer Discourse." *Modern Chinese Literature and Culture* 24, no. 1 (Spring 2012): 88–111.
Zhong, Xueping. *Masculinity Besieged? Issues of Modernity and Male Subjectivity in Chinese Literature of the Late Twentieth Century*. Durham, NC: Duke University Press, 2000.
Zhou, Yuxing. "Chinese Queer Images on Screen: A Case Study of Cui Zi'en's Film." *Asian Studies Review* 38, no. 1 (2014): 124–40.

Contributors

Cathryn H. Clayton is associate professor and chair of the Department of Asian Studies at the University of Hawai'i at Mānoa. Trained as a cultural anthropologist, she teaches and writes interdisciplinarily about China, Macau, nationalisms, and their discontents. Her first book, *Sovereignty at the Edge: Macau and the Question of Chineseness* (2009), won the Francis L. K. Hsu prize from the Society for East Asian Anthropology. She has published several English translations of Chinese short fiction and nonfiction.

Elisabeth Lund Engebretsen has a PhD in social anthropology from the London School of Economics (2008) and is currently professor of gender research at the University of Stavanger, Norway. Engebretsen is the author of *Queer Women in Urban China: An Ethnography* (2014) and editor of *Queer/Tongzhi China: New Perspectives on Research, Activism and Media Cultures* with William F. Schroeder and Hongwei Bao (2015). A coedited anthology on feminist activism in post-2010s China with Jinyan Zeng is forthcoming.

Yizhou Guo got her PhD in feminist studies from University of California, Santa Cruz. Her research was about the intersection of postsocialist affects and radical queer political imaginary in China. She currently works as a human-centered user experience designer, converging the power of empathy with technology.

Derek Hird is senior lecturer in Chinese studies at Lancaster University, UK. His research interests focus on Chinese middle-class masculinities, Chinese male beauty cultures, happiness and health in Chinese populations, and critical pedagogies for modern languages. He is coeditor of the Transnational Asian Masculinities book series and has published widely on Chinese masculinities. His book-length publications include the coauthored *Men and Masculinities in Contemporary China* (2013) and the coedited volumes *Chinese Discourses on Happiness* and *The Cosmopolitan Dream: Transnational Chinese Masculinities in a Global Age* (both 2018).

Wenqing Kang is associate professor of history and gender and women's studies at Cleveland State University. He is the author of *Obsession: Male Same-Sex Relations in China, 1900–1950* (2009).

Petrus Liu is associate professor of Chinese and comparative literature and of women's, gender, and sexuality at Boston University. His most recent book is *The Specter of Materialism: Queer Theory and Marxism in the Age of the Beijing Consensus* (2023), also published by Duke University Press.

Fran Martin is professor of cultural studies at the University of Melbourne. She has researched extensively on Chinese sexual minority cultures and has published her translations of contemporary queer short stories from Taiwan in *Angelwings* (2003). Her research monographs in this area include *Situating Sexualities: Queer Narratives in Taiwanese Fiction, Film and Public Culture* (2003) and *Backward Glances: Contemporary Chinese Cultures and the Female Homoerotic Imaginary* (Duke University Press, 2010). Her most recent book is *Dreams of Flight: The Lives of Chinese Women Students in the West* (Duke University Press, 2022).

Casey James Miller is an assistant professor of anthropology at Muhlenberg College in Pennsylvania. His research on queer anthropology, the anthropology of gender and sexuality, and contemporary Chinese culture and society has been supported by fellowships and awards from the Fulbright Program, the National Institutes of Health, and the National Science Foundation. His first book, *Inside the Circle: Queer Culture and Activism in Northwest China*, is forthcoming.

Lisa Rofel is professor emerita and research professor in the anthropology department at University of California, Santa Cruz. Her most recent publications, all with Duke University Press, include (as coauthor with Sylvia Yanagisako) *Fabricating Transnational Capitalism: A Collaborative Ethnography of Italian-Chinese Global Fashion* (2019); (as editor) *After the Post–Cold War: The Future of Chinese History Essays* by Dai Jinhua (2018); and (as coeditor with Carlos Rojas) *New World Orderings: China and the Global South* (2023).

William F. Schroeder is an independent scholar and writer whose research has focused on queer affect and kinship studies in the PRC. He holds a PhD in sociocultural anthropology from the University of Virginia.

Place of First Publication

"Uncle's Elegant Life" (舅舅的人间烟火), *Modern Culture Illustrated News* (現代文明畫報), January 2002; and in *Collected Works of Cui Zi'en* (崔子恩文学作品集), vol. 2. Zhuhai: Zhuhai chubanshe, 2003.

"Intrigue like Fireworks" (奸情如焰火), in *I Love Shidabo* (我爱史大勃). Beijing: Huaxia chubanshe, 1998.

"Some Admire Wisdom, Others Do Not" (有人赞美聪慧，有人则不), *Mountain Flowers* (山花), February 2000; and in *I Love Shidabo* (我爱史大勃). Beijing: Huaxia chubanshe, 1998.

"Orphans of the Japanese Empire" (日本遗民), *Youth Literature* (青年文學), June 1999; and in *Collected Works of Cui Zi'en* (崔子恩文学作品集), vol. 2. Zhuhai: Zhuhai chubanshe, 2003.

"The Silent Advent of the Age of Sexual Persuasion" (言性时代悄然莅临), in *Fairytales of Triangle City* (三角城的童話). Hong Kong: Huasheng shudian, 1998.

"Men Men Men Women Women Women" (男男男女女女), in *The Whereabout of Crimson* (胭脂的下落). Kunming: Yunnan renmin chubanshe, 2007.

"Men Are Containers" (男人是容器), in *Fairytales of Triangle City* (三角城的童話). Hong Kong: Huasheng shudian, 1998.

"Fire and Wolf Share a Fondness for Male Beauty" (老火和老狼同好男色), in *Fairytales of Triangle City* (三角城的童話). Hong Kong: Huasheng shudian, 1998.

"Teacher Eats Biscuits Thin as Parchment" (老师吃饼薄如纸), in *The Whereabout of Crimson* (胭脂的下落). Kunming: Yunnan renmin chubanshe, 2007.

"Platinum Bible of the Public Toilet" (公厕白金宝典), *Gay Spot* (點GS), 2017.

Place of First Publication